# THE DELVER

## THE VRIX #2

# TIFFANY ROBERTS

# THE DELVER

**She is the dawn after a long, dark night, and he will make her his.**

Urkot has always felt unappealing, undesirable. Unwanted. Scarred by war and lacking the grace and speed of other male vrix, he resigned himself to a life without a mate long ago and thought he was content with that fate.

Everything changed when he met Callie. Beautiful, passionate, fierce, clever Callie. So small, so soft. So human. When she looks at him, he feels worthy. Whole.

She captivates him, and his longing for her has made the stone around his hearts crack and crumble. Yet he dares not hope. What does he have to offer her? He is no hunter, no weaver, no leader. He is a simple delver.

Silently, he's wanted, he's craved, he's yearned.

But as that silence becomes unbearable, and that need overwhelms him, Urkot's world of cold stone and clinging darkness swallows him and Callie. If they are to survive, he must be her rock, her shield, and she must be his guiding light through the shadows. She must be his strength.

With ravenous creatures lurking around every bend and Urkot's desire for Callie burning brighter than the sun, he knows only one thing—every moment with her is precious.

And he will not waste another.

------

*The Spider's Mate Trilogy Spin-off Series. For a better reading experience, we highly suggest reading Ensnared, Enthralled, and Bound, followed by The Weaver.*

*Check the author's website for more detailed content warnings.*

*Thank you for being my rock...*
*And for your patience with my stoneheadedness.*

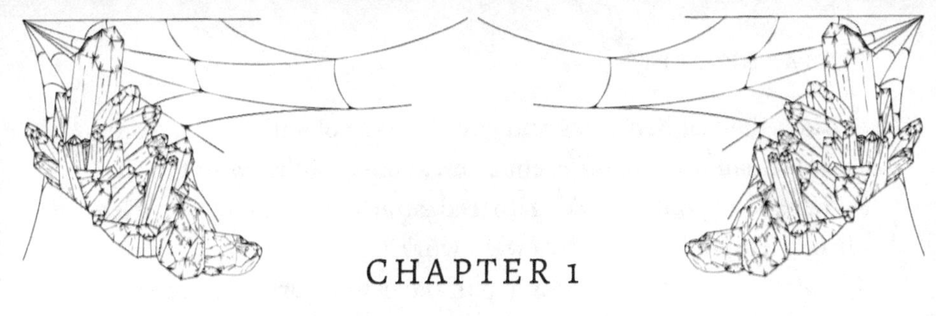

# CHAPTER 1

THE SONG of Urkot's hearts, of his soul, had always been found understone.

It was the clacking of tools against rock, the light scraping of legs over a cave floor, the airy whispers of the ground breathing, and the voices of his companions talking, boasting, and jesting, all layered and bolstered by faint echoes to enwrap him in a familiar cocoon.

He'd known this song from his earliest memories, and it ran through this cave just as surely as it ran through Takarahl, where he'd hatched and had spent most of his life. Long had it meant duty, purpose, family. Long had it provided comfort in its steadiness and dependability.

Urkot paused his tools and glanced around. This chamber was what delvers back in Takarahl called a crystal garden. Countless crystals in formations of varying sizes covered the walls, shedding a gentle blue light that made him recall old tunnels, old faces.

Five thornskulls stood spread out within the chamber, their burly forms stained new colors by the crystals' glow. Like

Urkot, they all had picks and chisels made of yatin horn, stone-headed hammers of different sizes, and bags filled with the silk-wrapped crystals they'd gathered attached to loops on their broad leather belts. All five were working.

Zotahl and Tahlken, both a bit older than Urkot, were experienced delvers who'd been harvesting and expanding this cave for years. Both possessed calm, quiet confidence that Urkot appreciated.

The other three, Enikor, Jezahal, and Dostrahn, were relatively younger—younger than Urkot and his friends had been when they'd gone to claim glory in Zurvashi's war all those years ago. The trio had no shortage of confidence, but their skills were as rough as unpolished stone. Their voices were loudest, most often accompanied by chitters.

Urkot turned his attention forward and resumed his work, carefully freeing a crystal from the surrounding rock. After wrapping it in a scrap of cloth, he placed it in the bag hanging from his belt, adding it to the others he'd harvested.

Normally, the thornskulls did not gather crystals in such large amounts, but these were for the upcoming festivities. Singer's Promise was coming, the day when the vrix of Kaldarak would celebrate the end of the floods and thank the Rootsinger for the bountiful harvests to come in the season of warmth and sunshine. The delvers were enthusiastic about their part to play this year. Urkot was excited right alongside them.

He enjoyed their companionship, enjoyed talking and working with these thornskulls. The understone song they produced was the same as the one he'd always known. It didn't matter that they were thornskulls instead of shadowstalkers, or that this place was several days' travel from Takarahl.

But that song didn't call to Urkot as it once had. It was the same, yes, but everything else had changed.

He had changed.

Urkot was sure of that, even if he couldn't tell exactly how he was different.

"You give few words this day, Three-Arm," said Zotahl from beside Urkot.

With a quiet chitter, Urkot glanced at the yellow thornskull, drawing his upper forearms together in an apologetic gesture. "Forgive me. I am…tangled in my thoughts."

Zotahl clicked his mandible fangs. "Your thoughts give you trouble?"

Using delicate taps with his hammer, Urkot wedged the tip of his chisel behind another crystal, grasping the formation with his lower hand, before pausing. The answer was *yes*, but was this the time, the place, to explore his hazy, confusing feelings?

"They are heavy," Urkot finally said, tapping the chisel deeper behind the crystal. "But it is a weight I can bear."

"Even the lightest burdens grow heavier with time," said Tahlken from his place on the wall behind Urkot. "Carry it no longer than you must."

"This is true beneath sun and sky," Zotahl intoned.

Urkot's gaze flicked upward. The cave's ceiling was run through with fissures no wider than silk threads, with down-ward-pointed stone formations clustered around those cracks. "True beneath dirt and stone as well, I hope."

The two thornskulls chittered and returned to their tasks.

Not very long ago, Urkot wouldn't have believed friendship could be shaped between shadowstalkers and thornskulls, especially not after the bloody war they'd waged against each other. The scars inflicted upon the survivors' spirits were so deep that nothing could have healed them. Thornskulls were enemies, forever enemies—that was what the vrix of Takarahl had long been taught. That was what Queen Zurvashi had told them.

She had lied.

And now Kaldarak, home of the enemies he'd once fought so fervently, was Urkot's home too.

Truly, *everything* had changed.

The crystal in his grasp came loose. He folded silk around it and added it to his bag.

A glint on the cave floor drew his attention down. Tilting his head, he lowered himself and plucked up the tiny object, holding it closer to his eyes to examine it.

With flat planes that formed a rough, not-quite-even cube and no natural luminescence, this crystal was unique within this chamber. While the glowing crystals usually ended in jagged points, making them resemble fangs jutting from the jaws of a fearsome beast, this one was reminiscent of the humans' odd, flat teeth.

*Callie would appreciate it.*

Urkot's mandibles rose in a smile, and a trill vibrated his throat. He opened his bag wider and retrieved a pouch from within to tuck the little cube-shaped stone inside.

His hearts thumped with eagerness; suddenly, he wanted nothing more than to be through with his work so he could hurry back to Kaldarak and give Callie the crystal. He'd given her many stones and crystals over the last several moon cycles, and he never tired of the joy that shone in her smile and her eyes with each such gift.

Would she have a human name for this crystal, as she did for so many of the others he'd given her? Sometimes, she'd talked about the rocks excitedly, using many words he didn't under-stand—and saying the ones he did understand almost too fast for him to follow. Yet her passion was always clear even when her language was not.

And her smile was so warm, so bright, that it never failed to quicken his hearts, to make his heartsthread thrum, to make him wonder...

To make him yearn.

He hadn't allowed himself to do that in a long, long time. Hadn't dared want, hadn't dared hope, because he'd known that he was undesirable. With a shorter, broader, more powerful frame, he was unlike most other shadowstalker males. Even before he'd lost his lower left arm, females had not looked upon him with favor. Especially not while Ketahn and Rekosh were nearby.

He'd never held any resentment over it; it was simply the truth of his existence. He had his friends. What more could he have needed?

Or so he'd told himself.

And then he'd met Callie…

Urkot's life had ever been one of hard, unyielding stone, of deep, devouring darkness, of burdens carried in silence. Callie was so soft, so fragile, so radiant. She belonged in a much different world. She belonged above, where her radiance would rival that of the cresting sun, brightening the world with color.

Yet he'd seen how Ketahn and Ivy matched one another despite their differences, and over the last two moon cycles, he'd seen how happy Rekosh and Ahmya were as a mated pair.

He resumed his work, but he could not put an end to those thoughts.

Was it foolish for Urkot to want the same?

He'd found new family within his tribe and had made unexpected friends amongst the thornskulls. Here in Kaldarak, he'd found peace.

Was it not selfish to long for more? Would not the gods punish such greed?

Urkot and his friends had overcome many hardships, had endured great suffering, to claim the lives they had now. Better to enjoy these blessings than seek more. Better to protect what happiness they'd claimed than risk everything by pursuing needless hunger. His focus, his purpose, was his tribe. Their joy, their safety, their comfort.

And still, just the thought of Callie's smile, of the way she wiggled her backside when she danced, of the curious, mysterious light that sometimes sparked in her eyes when she looked upon him…

Heat skittered beneath his hide, and something pulled taut low, low in his belly, making his stem twitch behind his slit. The sensation was potent enough that it caused his hands to falter. His hammer missed the chisel, clacking against the stone wall.

"Watch as I claim glory," Jezahal called, his voice ringing through the chamber.

Urkot nearly offered thanks to the gods for providing a distraction from his thoughts. That inner heat did not dissipate, that tightness did not ease, but at least there was something else for him to focus upon.

He looked toward the three younger vrix, who had gathered at the far end of the chamber. Jezahal stood closest to the wall, in front of a crystal formation almost as large as his torso.

"Our *daiya* asked for glowstones to make Kaldarak mirror the stars in the night sky. I will give glowstones worthy of being the moons for those stars!" With that declaration, Jezahal put his tools into motion. His hammer and pick set a frantic pace, their falls echoing to make it sound as though eight more vrix were working alongside him.

But the others had halted to watch the Jezahal. A different sort of tightness coiled in Urkot's gut, cold and twisting, as he followed Zotahl and Tahlken closer to the younger trio. He slipped his tools into the loops on his belt, but their familiar weight there offered him no comfort.

"Take care, little broodling. This cavern does not yet have its ribs," warned Zotahl, glancing at the ceiling.

That concern was part of Urkot's unease. The thornskull delvers had only recently expanded the outlying passage enough to enter this cavern, and they hadn't yet installed log supports to brace the ceiling and walls.

"Easy, Jezahal," Urkot said as his gaze settled on the cracks in the stone around the large crystal. "Do as Zotahl says and take care."

Dostrahn chittered. "Three-Arm and old brittle fangs mean to deny the glory you would bring to Kaldarak."

"Better your hands empty and your hide intact." Urkot's eyes traced a crack running down the wall and nearly a segment across the floor before he shifted them up to follow another deeper fissure that led toward the ceiling.

As Jezahal hammered and pried, bits of stone flaked off around the higher crack. "Fear will not stay my hands."

Urkot shook his head. "The roots are too deep. You will not free this glowstone without breaking half the wall."

The upper crack widened. Only by a thread's width, perhaps, so little that it might've been a trick played by the crystals' pale glow, but it was enough to twist Urkot's insides tighter.

"Jezahal," he growled, tracing that crack higher, "you must stop."

"The *daiya* will declare me Jezahal, Bringer of the Moons," the thornskull said excitedly. Burying the tip of his yatin horn pick in the fissure, he wrenched on its handle.

The faintest tremor coursed through the ground beneath Urkot.

So many thoughts could've swept through Urkot's mind in that moment—that he should've been sterner, that he should've shared more hard-won knowledge with the young delvers, that he should've told them that he, Zotahl, and Tahlken could fulfill Nalaki's request without further aid.

But no thoughts came. Instead, he darted forward, past Zotahl and Tahlken.

An immense *crack* split the air in the chamber.

Urkot grabbed Jezahal by the arms and shoved his forelegs hard against the cave floor in the opposite direction, reversing his momentum and dragging the thornskull back.

A chunk of rock nearly as large as Urkot fell from the upper portion of the wall. It crashed down with a deafening sound, accompanied by countless smaller stones. Dust billowed into the air.

Urkot fell to the hard ground, dragging Jezahal down with him. The dust cloud obscured his vision and tickled his throat, setting him to coughing.

"Who is harmed?" Tahlken called between his own coughs.

"We must leave this chamber," Zotahl said.

Grunting, Urkot hauled Jezahal upright and blindly led the thornskull toward the chamber's exit. The young thornskull stumbled at first but soon recovered his balance.

The delvers regrouped in the tunnel outside the crystal garden, where the dust created a light haze. Fortunately, everyone had made it out, and though the younger vrix were dazed, no one had been harmed.

Fire roared in Urkot's chest.

Growling, he stomped a foreleg on the ground and slashed the wall with his claws as he spun to face Jezahal.

"You would risk us all to seek glory?" he demanded.

Jezahal kept his eyes downcast, his posture crumpling. Though he was two handspans taller than Urkot, he seemed terribly small and meek now.

"Every choice you make down here, every act, will affect your companions," Urkot continued, clacking his mandible fangs. "Respect the stone. Protect your fellow delvers."

"I hear your words, Three-Arm," Jezahal rasped.

Dostrahn coughed, the sound echoing along the tunnel before he muted it with a hand.

That fire hadn't yet died within Urkot. Part of him wanted to strike Jezahal in fury, but what would that accomplish? It would've been no more helpful than the memories now clawing their way to the surface of his mind, all demanding his attention, demanding he relive that old pain and grief again.

He refused. Refused all of it.

And besides…hadn't he too chased glory in his younger days? Hadn't he and his friends risked everything for a taste of life as warriors?

"Come," Zotahl said with a gentleness Urkot envied in that moment. "Let us stride to Kaldarak. If our *daiya* requires more glowstone, we will return with the new day."

The others began down the tunnel, leaving Urkot and Jezahal behind. The only light here came from glowstones that thornskull delvers had placed on the walls, leaving it far dimmer than the crystal garden.

Covered in dust that dulled his red hide, Jezahal stood with his head bowed. Gone was the confidence of earlier, gone was the youthful spirit, the hunger.

"I have no wish to see anyone harmed," Urkot said, voice low and gravelly. "Today, we all stride away. You have learned a hard lesson, but it could have been harder still."

"Yes."

"And tomorrow, I will delve beside you again." Urkot closed the distance between himself and Jezahal, cupped the back of the thornskull's head, and leaned their headcrests together.

Jezahal's eyes rounded, and he tensed.

"I will watch for you, and you will watch for me. As sure as stone is hard." Releasing the thornskull, Urkot stepped back.

Jezahal brought his forearms together and bowed deeply. "Forgive me, Urkot. My *shar'thai* dimmed today, but I shall stoke its flame, that it may burn bright enough to guide you through any darkness. Only thanks to you was it not snuffed out."

Urkot tapped a knuckle to his headcrest, and the two made their way down the tunnel.

The thornskull's words had been heartfelt and touching, but there was only one light Urkot longed to look toward in the darkness, only one light he longed to pursue.

Callie's smiling face appeared in his mind's eye.

He could but hope her radiance would keep those insistent memories shrouded in the shadows where they belonged.

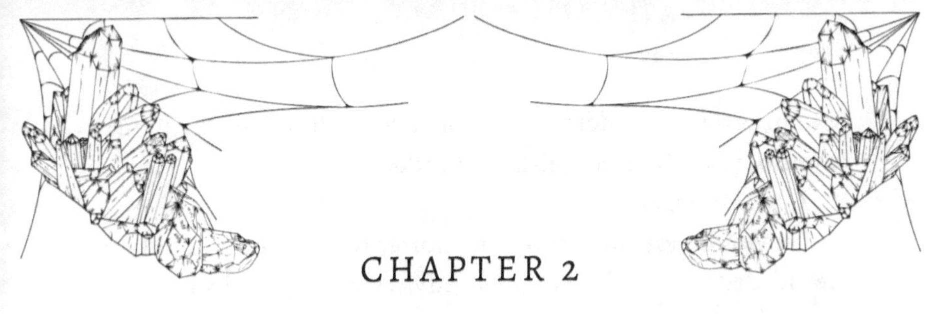

# CHAPTER 2

THE SUN WAS ALREADY BEGINNING to fall when Urkot and Jezahal rejoined Zotahl and the others outside the cave. Deepening shadows dominated the surrounding jungle, and the gaps in the leaves overhead offered glimpses of red-gold clouds against a pink sky that would soon darken to violet.

Though the air was hot, thick, and redolent of plants and decay, Urkot welcomed it into his lungs. Far better than breathing in dust.

Together, Urkot and the thornskulls set out for home, following the base of the rocky hills and cliffs that formed one side of the valley cradling Kaldarak.

Even the falling sun gave better light than the cave's glowing crystals, restoring some color to the thornskulls' dusty hides.

While the elder thornskulls showed no signs of having been affected by the rockfall, the younger trio only gradually shed their uncharacteristic quietness. Their voices became part of the jungle sounds for Urkot—no different than the rustling of leaves, the creaking of wood, or the distant calls of beasts.

And none of those sounds could silence those that existed in his mind. The thunderous roar of rocks falling, raining upon a cave floor; strained, anguished, muffled cries…

*Not here, not now.*

He would not allow those memories to bury him. Could not. He needed to be like stone, steady, reliable, unwavering. His strength would bolster that of the other delvers. No more cracks.

So he strode onward, making himself chitter at his companions' jests, telling himself there wasn't a tortured roar building in his chest that he needed to let out.

Urkot knew the trek to Kaldarak was short, but it felt as though a full eightday had passed by the time they reached the base of the waterfall that flowed from the temple atop the hill high above. Mist cooled the air, and the sound of water crashing into the pool overcame all others—save for those from his past.

Tahlken strode to the edge of the pool, where he unslung his bag and set it, along with his belt and tools, on a rock. "Come. Let us wash away the dust and our worries."

The other thornskulls joined him, shedding their belongings at the water's edge.

Urkot hung back. His hearts were thumping, and his chest felt constricted. He looked upon these thornskulls, his friends, and all he could see were five vrix who'd nearly been lost on his watch.

"Do you fear you will sink, Three-Arm?" Zotahl asked, glancing over his shoulder as he stepped into the water.

The others chittered good-naturedly. Urkot forced out a chitter of his own, hoping it did not sound as strained as it felt. "Stone has a better chance of floating than I do. But…the cool water does not help my old hurts."

A dull ache pulsed on his left side as though in response to the lie, and for one brief, cruel moment, he felt the arm that had been taken from him seven years ago.

He barely resisted the urge to cover the scar with a hand.

Though they voiced their disappointment, the thornskulls did not argue. Urkot was grateful for that much. He needed quiet, needed solitude, needed time. Time to slow his hearts, to steady his breaths, and to again bury his memories deeper than Takarahl's darkest, longest forgotten tunnel.

Alone, he strode to the grand stairway that was Kaldarak's entrance, offered a greeting to the pair of thornskulls standing vigil at its base, and ascended the winding steps up into the trees. Reaching the platform at the top did nothing to calm him; he had many such platforms and several bridges to cross before he could claim solitude.

As he hurried toward his den, he greeted the thornskulls he passed as kindly as he could. Each such exchange, however short, heightened the pressure inside him, making every breath harder, every heartbeat louder.

His stride faltered when he saw a few of his tribemates ahead—Ketahn, carrying his broodling, Akalahn, accompanied by Rekosh, Will, and Diego. Rekosh's red markings stood out starkly against his black hide, more so than the purple of Ketahn's. The two vrix were like brothers to Urkot, sharing a bond so strong that not even the gods could have broken it. Will and Diego were a mated pair, humans from another world beyond the stars, just like Callie, but they had also become family.

Perhaps Urkot could turn around before they saw him and go another way…

Guilt sliced through his hearts, making his muscles tense, yet he could not suppress the urge to flee. Were anyone to have called him a coward right then and there, he couldn't have disagreed.

Ketahn spied Urkot and lifted a hand in greeting. Akalahn raised all four of his chubby little arms in an exaggerated imitation of his sire, bouncing in Ketahn's hold.

Urkot's mandibles rose in a smile. A bit of that pressure lifted with them.

But as Urkot neared his friends, Ketahn and Rekosh's mandibles sagged, and the two humans frowned, the dark strips of fur above their eyes—their eyebrows—drawing closer together.

"Are you all right?" Ketahn asked in English. "Did something happen?"

For all the jokes about Urkot's head being full of rocks or his hide being more stone than flesh, Urkot felt as though Ketahn saw through him as easily as he would've the waters of a shallow stream.

"I am fine," Urkot replied. He did not care for the taste of such lies upon his tongue, but this burden…it was his alone to bear.

"You're covered in dust," Diego said, brown eyes raking over Urkot from the tips of his legs to the peak of his headcrest.

"*Covered*," Will echoed. "I almost didn't recognize you. You're almost as white as Garahk."

"You okay?"

Spreading his arms, Urkot glanced down at himself. Most of his black hide was hidden beneath a veil of pale dust that must've made him look more like a spirit than a vrix of hide and bone. He chittered. "Delving is dirty work."

Rekosh folded his arms across his chest, drumming the fingers of one hand on his upper arm. "This is much more than usual."

Akalahn wriggled in his sire's arms, and Ketahn sank down, placing the broodling on the platform boards.

"Urkot…" Ketahn intoned as he rose.

"Stone fell, but none were harmed. Only dust." Urkot patted his abdomen, sending up a tiny white cloud.

Will leaned back, waving a hand to disrupt the dust as it

neared him. "Breathing that stuff in can't be good for you. Not for humans, anyway."

"Doubt it's good for vrix either," said Diego with a frown. "You ever have problems with your breathing, Urkot?"

"No," Urkot replied. The strain in his chest now was different, wasn't it?

Both Ketahn and Rekosh were studying him closely. He knew that just as water could wear down stone over time, his friends' weighty gazes would wear down his resolve.

Urkot dropped his eyes to Akalahn, and again his troubles briefly receded. With a blend of vrix and human features, the broodling was unlike anyone or anything else in the world—or any other world, since the humans claimed there were uncountable worlds hidden amongst the stars in the night sky.

Little Akalahn moved on six wobbly legs, walking around and beneath his sire with all four purple eyes wide and bright.

Ketahn also glanced down, and his gaze softened. When the broodling wandered toward the platform's edge, Ketahn extended a foreleg, hooked it around the broodling's middle, and gently guided him back.

Akalahn chittered in delight, smiling not only with a lift of his little mandibles, but by curving his mouth, which was more flexible than that of a full-blooded vrix.

"Ivy says it is too soon for him to walk and climb," Ketahn said.

Diego chuckled. "Normally, it would be. He's only two months old. A human baby wouldn't even start crawling for another five months, much less walking and climbing."

"Perhaps it is because your kind only has two legs?" Urkot asked. "More easy to walk with more legs."

"Might be on to something there," said Will.

Urkot couldn't be sure what the human meant. The only thing he was on was the platform, and there was no question about that. Why *might*?

Akalahn latched on to one of Ketahn's legs and climbed a handspan off the platform. Chittering, Ketahn lifted that leg, plucked the broodling off, and set the little one down atop his hindquarters. Akalahn settled against Ketahn's back, tiny legs spread to the sides.

Adorable as the broodling was, Urkot couldn't shake the sense that something was…off. He tilted his head and looked from Rekosh to Ketahn and back again. "Where are your mates? I have not seen either of you without them since Rekosh claimed Ahmya."

"She is visiting with Lacey. *Girl time*, they said," Rekosh replied.

"I sent my Ivy with Ahmya, so she may relax." Ketahn reached back with a lower arm to rub his broodling's black and gold hair. "She tells me her heart leaps into her throat every time she sees Akalahn climb. She does not know why I am not worried when we awake to find him hanging from the ceiling."

In all the years Urkot had known him, Ketahn had never shown interest in taking a mate, had never spoken of siring broodlings. And Urkot had never imagined it. Ketahn always strode along his own path, straight into the unknown and right on through it.

He had come to this—a mate, a broodling—in his own way, and it suited him so well that Urkot couldn't help but hope for himself.

Rekosh extended a foreleg, bumping a leg joint against the bag on Urkot's belt. "More stones? I wonder what—or is it who—they are for?"

Urkot withdrew with a grunt. "Glowstones for Singer's Promise."

"None for Callie?"

*There is one for Callie.*

*The most unique in the bag.*

Using his lower hand, Urkot adjusted the bag's lay. Hopefully that little cubed crystal hadn't been damaged when the rock fell.

What if it had been Urkot's tribe down there with him instead of the thornskulls? What if one of his friends, one of his family, had been harmed? Visions of that horror attempted to take shape in his mind. Only his grip on the bag kept his hand from trembling.

"You are sure you are well?" Rekosh asked in vrix. The playful gleam that danced in his eyes whenever he traded friendly barbs had vanished.

"Yes," Urkot replied in the same language. "I am tired."

Rekosh hummed, the sound at once thoughtful and unsure.

Akalahn chirruped, leaning toward the side of Ketahn's hindquarters.

"We're heading back to the lounge," Will said in English as he held a finger out for the youngling to grasp. "Cole's been slow roasting some meat for half the day, so everyone's going to eat together. You should come, Urkot."

Ketahn chittered. "I am sure your gut growls with hunger."

Urkot knew he should've been hungry. After a long day of harvesting crystals, there should've been a vast, gnawing hollowness inside him. But all he felt was that crushing dread, twisting tighter in his stomach with every beat of his hearts. It left no room for hunger.

And the thought of sharing a meal with his tribe, of having to look into their eyes and continue pretending he was fine while he felt like *this*, was more than he could bear.

They'd all been through enough. They didn't need to bear the weight of his burden too.

"I must clean," he said, scrubbing his hands together before using his lower hand to pat the bag. "And then...*dathar othar.* What are the human words?"

"Tend them," Ketahn said.

"Yes, tend them."

"Hiding away now, just like Telok?" Rekosh asked with a chitter.

"Telok says he does not hide. He hunts."

"Telok may say whatever he wants, it does not change the truth."

Urkot grunted. "What would he hide from? Telok has small fear."

Releasing Will's finger, Akalahn climbed up Ketahn's back, grabbing shoulders and hair to haul his little body up. He seemed determined to perch atop his sire's head until Ketahn reached up, snatched the broodling down, and cradled him in his arms. Akalahn trilled, swatting at the loose strands of hair now dangling over his sire's shoulders.

As though none of that had happened, Ketahn said, "It is not *what* he is hiding from, but who."

Will laughed. "I don't get what's going on with those two. He's fine around the rest of us."

Diego shook his head. "I can *spekyulate*, but…it's on him to figure it out. Just hope he realizes how it makes her feel."

"Telok is often blind for one who sees so much." Rekosh turned his palms skyward and shrugged, another gesture learned from the humans.

"We are all blind sometimes," said Ketahn.

Those words were far heavier than they should've been, but Urkot couldn't understand why, couldn't grasp at the threads in his mind.

It didn't help that Rekosh was staring at him with that piercing gaze.

"Go on and get cleaned up," Diego said, breaking Urkot free of that stare. "If you feel up for it when you're done, we'll probably be around a while. And knowing Cole, there'll be plenty of food left over."

Urkot nodded, raised a hand, and tapped his knuckle to his headcrest in a show of respect. Diego mimicked the gesture.

Rekosh hung back as the others continued onward, tilting his head as he regarded Urkot. Urkot's hearts quickened. Somehow, his friend knew, and he would make Urkot share everything, would make him dig out the memories…

In vrix, Rekosh asked, "You are going to the temple?"

Mandibles twitching, Urkot narrowed his eyes. That question wasn't at all what he'd expected, which only made him more wary. "Yes…"

The piercing gleam in Rekosh's red eyes was replaced by a mirthful glint as he chittered.

Mandibles sagging, Urkot stared at his friend. "Have a few too many threads been severed in your head, weaver? What is amusing?"

Rekosh nudged Urkot's foreleg with his own. "Nothing, delver. Enjoy the pools."

As Rekosh strode past, Urkot turned to watch him. On any other day, he would've pressed Rekosh to speak plainly. They would've gone back and forth, like they were wrestling over the same length of rope, with the weaver delighting in every moment of it until finally revealing the source of his amusement. All in jest, of course.

But this was not any other day.

Grateful the encounter was over—and flooded with fresh guilt over that gratitude—Urkot hurried to his den.

Kaldarak was fast falling under the jungle's night song as the sun fell and deep, dark blues and purples spread across the sky. Flamekeepers with torches moved about the platforms, igniting bowls of spinewood sap to fight the growing darkness with blue-green flames. With their daily tasks done, many thornskulls were outside their dens, conversing and sharing meals. Soft notes played on string instruments drifted on the air, weaving through the other sounds like wandering ghosts.

Blue crystal light illuminated Urkot's den when he entered. He didn't pause to look around, didn't think; he removed his bag and belt of tools, setting them aside, retrieved a jar of vine-root oil, a comb carved of bone, a handful of cleanleaf, and a large cloth, and strode back out again.

With each step he took toward the temple, he felt the urge to move faster, to match the pace of his racing hearts. Though such haste would only draw unwanted attention, resisting that urge grew more difficult by the moment.

The temple was a huge, imposing shadow on the rocky hill overlooking Kaldarak. Eight towering figures stood atop it—the gods, their forms made mysterious and eerie by the encroaching darkness. The temple's features were indistinct but for the glow of spinewood sap fires leading across the rope bridge and at the temple's entrance.

The night's first stars sparkled overhead as Urkot crossed the bridge. The sound of conversation and music faded behind him, slowly overtaken by the noise of the waterfall flowing out of the temple.

For that moment, he was utterly alone. No one near, no voices, no faces, no eyes upon him.

Was this how it felt to journey through the emptiness between the stars, or to be buried in a cave-in, cocooned by nothingness?

It was peaceful. Sorrowful. And...empty.

Releasing a heavy breath through his nose holes, Urkot forced himself onward.

Inside the temple, the tiered pools were fed by hot springs, making them soothingly warm. Once Urkot was in the water, his worries would melt away, his aches would fade, and the dust would be washed from his hide. His body would relax, and his mind would follow.

When he reached the temple's entrance, he stopped and signed in reverence to the Eight, raising his arms and crossing his forearms at their middles in front of his chest. He felt his missing lower left arm again as he made the gesture, much more clearly than before. He felt its muscles stretch and flex beneath his hide as it moved into position, felt it touching his right arm.

But his lower left arm was gone. It had been claimed by the mire and had rotted away, like the bodies of so many shadowstalkers and thornskulls during the war. Forever lost.

His gesture to pay respect to the gods was, as it had been for the last seven years, incomplete. He could only hope that they did not see it as disrespect, that they could sense his intent, or...or that perhaps they could see the spirit of his missing arm.

If it still haunted him, surely the gods were also aware of it?

The sensation of that limb having been restored vanished, leaving behind an intense tingling on his hide. He covered the rough scar on his side with his lower right hand, pressing his palm over it, but the sensation was slow to fade.

Urkot bowed his head. "Flamebearer, thank you for your guiding light. Delver, thank you for sparing us, even in our carelessness, and seeing us home safely from the darkness."

Straightening, he lowered his arms and entered the temple.

The air within was thick, warm, and damp. Several spinewood sap flames provided light, casting slow-dancing shadows on the decorated stonework. Whatever his thoughts on the skill of thornskull stoneshapers compared to their shadowstalker counterparts, he could not deny the care and expertise that had built this place.

As he entered the main chamber, where the stone shaped by vrix met the natural walls of a cavern, he could not help but think of Takarahl again. Yet for as often as he thought about it, he did not miss it. Nor did he miss his siblings who yet dwelled there—ten brothers and four sisters who he'd worked alongside for most of his life but had never truly known. Not like he knew the family he'd made. Not like he knew his tribe. There'd been respect amidst his blood kin, and fondness, but what he felt for them wasn't like the bond he shared with his chosen family.

Steam rose from the pools, filling the air, and the sound of water flowing down the tiers to eventually feed the waterfall was perfect for quieting thoughts. The light of the fires reflected upon the pools' surfaces, granting them an alluring glow.

Only as he approached the lowest pool did he notice movement within it. A figure stood beneath the water spilling from a higher level, back turned toward him. A human figure, with bare brown skin.

Urkot's hearts sped anew, hammering inside his chest.

*Callie.*

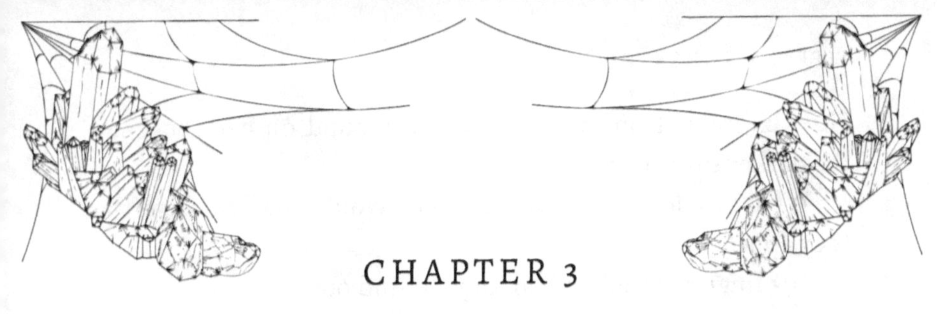

# CHAPTER 3

Urkot had seen the male humans without their coverings. Several moon cycles ago, when he and his tribe had first arrived in Kaldarak, he'd even glimpsed Ivy naked in this very place. She had shed what the humans called *modesty* long before they'd come here.

But of Callie, he'd seen only hints of the body hidden beneath her clothing, teasing him with her curves and softness. He'd never seen her utterly bare.

Until now.

The blue-green firelight reflected on the waterdrops clinging to her supple brown skin and her long, curly, dark brown hair, making her look like she was clad in stars. She shifted, turning slightly toward him, and tipped her head back. More droplets sparkled on the lashes of her closed eyes.

Urkot remained as still as stone. He was afraid to move, afraid to breathe, afraid that so much as blinking would make her disappear. All he could do was stare at the beautiful sight before him.

With a soft sigh, Callie raised her arms and smoothed her palms over her hair, rinsing the fizzy cleanleaf from the strands.

His gaze caught on the large, plump mound on her chest and the darker tip at its peak.

What would her breasts feel like? Would they be as soft as they appeared?

His fingers flexed with an urge to find out.

All his life, he'd worked with unyielding stone, yet now he longed for nothing more than to feel the give of Callie's flesh beneath his fingers, to feel her soft skin against his hard, tough hide, to feel her warmth seep into him.

His gaze dipped to follow the flow of shimmering water down her body, stopping on the curve of her hindquarters. Her *ass*, as the humans called it.

It should've simply been another strange human body part to him, a curiosity at best. But he'd been fascinated by Callie's ass ever since she'd performed her victory dance after defeating him in stonetoss a lifetime ago at the Pit. Long before he'd been able to understand any of her words.

Even if what she'd said had been meaningless to him then, the way she'd moved her body, her hips, had entranced him.

Now her ass was exposed to him, allowing him to see how lush and soft she was all over.

And there was something else revealed to Urkot now—a marking on the right side of her hindquarters, just above the lapping water.

His eyes narrowed.

There were human letters on her skin, between two symbols called hearts.

Callie moved again, swaying her hips as she continued rinsing her hair, but Urkot could not take his eyes off that marking. Vrix females did not have natural markings, and seeing one on Callie's skin rekindled that desirous stirring in his belly. The sensation warmed, spreading down to his stem, which pulsed behind his slit.

Every part of her begged for his touch. He knew his hands

would fit perfectly around her waist and over the curves of her hips, knew her breasts would fill his eager palms.

Urkot clenched his shaking hands against the surge of longing. His cock swelled, pushing on the inside of his slit.

Threatening to extrude.

Eyes flaring, he drew his claspers tight against his hide to keep his stem confined.

Callie turned, facing him, and his eyes fell upon the slit between her thighs, where darker folds of flesh were exposed from within.

His longing intensified eightfold, and he pressed his claspers around his slit hard enough to feel their tips digging into his hide. A tremor wracked his body.

This was desire, need, unlike anything he'd ever experienced. It was instinct, yes, but it was so much more. It was *her*. His Callie. He'd never wanted, had never *craved*, anyone like he did her.

And it wasn't simply a need to touch her.

He needed to rut her. To take her body in his hands, bind her in his silk, and thrust his stem into her slit.

To claim her as his.

Callie's sharp gasp broke through his lustful haze. Urkot's gaze shot up to meet her wide, brown eyes, which were made all the darker by the cavern's shadows.

"Shit!" She quickly banded her arms across her chest and ducked into the pool until her breasts were submerged.

An uncomfortable sensation skittered beneath Urkot's hide. Shaking his head, he stepped forward only to halt. He lifted his arms, pressed his forearms together, and struggled to find the right words in English.

"Calm, female." His deep voice rumbled from his chest, resonating within the room.

She narrowed her eyes and eased toward him, keeping her body beneath the water. "Urkot?"

He nodded. "Sorry. I did not mean to scare you."

Callie chuckled. "You just startled me. I didn't expect anyone to come here this late."

Urkot chittered, lowering his arms. "That is why I come. For quiet."

"Oh. I'm almost done. I can hurry so you can have the place to yourself."

His insides sank at the thought of her rushing away. Solitude in this place had been a welcome idea only moments ago, but now it was more than he could bear. "Stay. Please."

"It's not a big deal. I've been in here for a while now, and I'm probably all *proonee* anyway."

"But who will help if I sink like stone when I go in?"

Her laughter was like music, flowing straight into his hearts and making them feel full.

Callie's lips stretched into a wide grin, revealing her blunt white teeth. The expression made tiny, adorable indentations appear on her cheeks—dimples. "The pools are only a few feet at their deepest. Even if you sat down, most of your body would still be above the water."

She moved to the edge of the pool, her grin taking on a teasing slant as she gazed up at him. "I think you want me to stay because you like me."

Without meaning to, he moved closer to her, drawn by something he could not see, smell, touch, or hear—a tether made of silk so fine it was invisible, running from his heart-sthread to hers. And he felt its pull down in the deepest parts of his soul.

His mandibles lifted. "I most like you."

"Ha! I knew I was your favorite."

"You must not tell the rest. They will be...*jelly*?"

She shook her head with a chuckle. "It's so strange hearing that word come from you. But no way am I keeping this secret. I'm going to rub it in Cole's face." Her smile faded as she held his gaze. "For real though, are you sure you want me to stay? I know what it's like to want to be alone. I won't take offense."

"Stay, Callie." He placed a hand on the stone lip at the pool's edge, as close as he could bring himself to touching her. "It is everything else I want to be alone from."

Her features softened, and she nodded. Water dripped from her hand as she lifted it and gestured up and down at him. "Why are you all…white?"

"Rock fell in the cave and made big dust."

Callie's lips parted with a gasp. "Oh God, are you okay?"

Urkot nodded and tapped his chest with a fist. "Only dirty."

"And the others? No one was hurt?"

"No one was hurt, thank the Delver." He barely suppressed a shudder as thoughts of what could've happened swirled in the back of his mind.

"Good." She studied him for a moment, her gaze seeming to pierce right to the turmoil hidden inside him, before she moved back from the pool's edge. "Come on, big guy. Get in the water."

He could not express how grateful he was that she hadn't questioned him further. She clearly knew something was amiss, knew that he was burdened, but she was simply…making space for him.

And he couldn't deny that the way she called him *big guy* sparked a little more of that heat low in his belly…though he liked it even better when she said his name.

After placing his belongings beside hers on the pool's rim, he stepped into the water. He strode to the small waterfall, which he used to rinse the dust from his hair and hide. The water's heat eased his muscles and soothed his aches.

Urkot stood there for some time, letting the water flow over him. With Callie's quiet presence nearby, he felt a little more grounded, a little more himself, with each moment.

Everyone was fine. Everything was fine. There was no reason for alarm; the worst had not occurred.

Finally, he stepped back, lifting his upper hands to wipe the water from his face. Droplets sprayed from around his nostrils as he exhaled. While the water would never wash away the permanent stone dust staining his fingers and tips of his legs, it felt good to have the rest of his hide mostly free of the stuff.

When he inhaled, the warm, humid air was fragrant with the crisp smell of cleanleaf.

He turned back toward Callie. She stood facing away from him, running her hands over her arms and body to scrub her skin with fizzing cleanleaf. Her thick hair was already becoming curlier as it dried. He longed to run his hands through it, to feel those curls coil around his fingers.

His gaze dipped, following the graceful line of her spine down past her hips, until settling on her ass again. He couldn't help but study that small marking. The humans had shown him some of their letters, but unlike Rekosh, Urkot had not studied them nearly enough to understand them.

"What does that mean?" he asked.

Callie set the used husks of cleanleaf on the edge of the pool before peering at him over her shoulder. "What does what mean?"

Urkot pointed at her backside. "The mark."

She blinked, brow furrowing. "Mark?" Her confused gaze followed his gesture. Then her eyebrows shot up. "Oh! Ohhhhh..."

With a chuckle, she cocked a hip and pointed at the mark on her ass. "You mean this? I completely forgot I even had it." Covering her breasts with her left arm, Callie twisted toward him and arched a brow. "Urkot, were you staring at my ass?"

He tilted his head to the side. "Yes."

Her jaw dropped as she stared at him. Then she laughed. "Wow. Okay. You're blunt."

"No, I am Urkot." He raised his mandibles in a smile.

There was a playful smile on her lips when she replied, "Yes, you made sure I knew that."

Urkot knew exactly what she was talking about. During their trek across the swamp while fleeing from Takarahl and Zurvashi, an insect had landed on Callie's hair. After he'd plucked it off her, she had thanked him, calling him *big guy*. But he'd wanted to hear his name from her lips. Had *needed* to hear it.

He recalled the give of her skin beneath his fingers as he'd held her jaw, recalled the way her soft lips had moved as they'd shaped his name. He recalled the shift inside him, the thrumming along his heartsthread, the still-fresh desire that had blossomed in that moment.

"Your mark," Urkot pressed.

"You're so bossy," she said, lifting her hip to allow him a better look at her ass. The blue-green light bouncing off the water highlighted her wet skin. "It's called a *tattoo*. It's not something we're born with, like your markings. These are done with needles and ink to permanently mark our skin. I got this one when I turned eighteen. It was...a secret act of *reebellyun* against my parents. Not that they ever found out I got it."

"*Reebellyun?*" Urkot carefully repeated.

"Means to go against something. Like you *reebelld* against Zurvashi."

A low hum sounded in his chest. "You made war on your parents?"

"Okay, so maybe that wasn't the best comparison. It was more that I was defiant. My parents were against me and my siblings getting tattoos. They always wanted us looking our best because our appearances reflected on them. So, the moment I turned eighteen, I got a tattoo where they'd never see it because *I* wanted it."

Urkot understood little of the world the humans had come from, and most of what he'd learned from Callie and the others had only left him with more questions. Shadowstalkers some-times adorned themselves with silk, gold, leather, and beads—much more often during Zurvashi's reign—but had never intentionally left permanent marks on their hides.

"Humans choose to mark themselves this way? Why?"

"There are many reasons. Some people get tattoos because they're cultural or spiritual. Others get them as a form of self-expression or just because they like something. It's art."

He ran his eyes over the marking again. Despite his curiosity, it was difficult to prevent his gaze from wandering to admire her ass in its entirety. "What does your tattoo mean?"

Callie let out a small laugh. "Um… Keep in mind I was young when I had this done and I wanted something on the naughty side. Kind of like a dirty little secret."

"Tell me."

"It…says *spank me*."

"Explain."

"Oh my God," she groaned, letting her head fall back. "I can't believe I'm going to do this."

When Urkot was about to ask what she meant, Callie lifted her head and shifted her body, showing him her profile while keeping an arm banded across her breasts. She met his gaze. There was shyness in her eyes now.

"I, uh, think it's easier to just show you," she said.

Then she slapped her hand down on her ass.

The impact produced a sharp *crack*. Her flesh gave beneath the blow, shaking visibly. Urkot could only stare and hold his hands at his sides, keeping his fists tight, unable to move.

Gods, he wanted to take her ass in his hands and feel it yield to his palms.

It took longer than it should have for him to produce any words. "You…*want* to be hit?"

She thrust a finger at him, and their gazes locked. "Don't *keenk* shame me."

Urkot's mandibles fell. "I…what? I do not know *keenk*."

Chuckling, Callie shook her head. "You're killing me here, big guy." She ran her fingers through her hair. "A *keenk* is something someone finds sexually arousing."

That meant…

His eyes widened, and his cock stirred anew behind his slit. "Ah…"

She turned her face away, seeming to look everywhere but at him. "Spanking in this way isn't really a hit that hurts. I mean, it can hurt, but it can feel good when done right."

Her eyes again met his. "Really, *really* good."

There was something in her gaze that Urkot could not name, something that called to him. Was he interpreting her words, her expression, incorrectly, or…or was she looking at him like she wanted to explore this *kink* with him?

No, it couldn't be that. Why would she want that? Why would she want his big, rough, clumsy hands on her soft skin?

But even the tiniest possibility of her wanting it, of her wanting him…that was enough to amplify his longing, his desire, and make it hotter than the water in which he stood.

"I will…remember," he rasped. How could his tongue feel so dry when the air was so wet?

Callie cleared her throat. "Well, I've given you enough of a show for tonight. Now…" She twirled her finger in the air.

Urkot blinked. "Now?"

She laughed. "Turn around, Urkot, so I can finish up."

"Ah, yes. Modesty." He turned away from her and strode to the edge of the pool, where he'd left his things. He would not allow himself to look back, no matter how tempted he was to do so. The glimpse he'd had earlier had to be enough.

He collected the cleanleaf and, forcing himself not to glance in Callie's direction, walked to the spot where she'd been standing when he'd first arrived. Urkot leaned his head back and let the falling water cascade over him. When he straightened, he crushed some cleanleaf and used it to scrub his hair.

All the while, he heard the quiet sounds of Callie moving in the water, washing herself.

He would not look. But in his mind's eye, he saw her hands move over her body, caressing her skin, kneading her breasts. His palms tingled with the craving to grasp her. To slap her ass like she had, to feel that flesh give beneath his touch. He longed to witness her reaction—to see just how arousing a spanking would be for her.

And though he did not act upon them, those thoughts had consequences. The heat in his blood surged, pulsing through his entire body, and his stem ached, pressing forward. He pinched his claspers around his slit, but he could not trust them to keep him from extruding. This was too much.

Uncertain of what else to do, he lowered himself, ensuring that his slit was hidden beneath the water's surface. But the new warmth around it did not ease his desires.

Steady and unmoving as stone. That was what he needed to be, for his sake and for Callie's. But it was difficult. So, so difficult. Even if he managed to keep himself outwardly composed, there was so much happening within him, a storm building, raging.

Clenching his jaw, he leaned back into the falling water to rinse his hair. He closed his eyes, plunging himself into darkness as the water overwhelmed his hearing. But Callie still shone in that darkness. She was too bright to be snuffed out.

Tension coursed through him. Even the times he'd been stricken by the mating scents of female vrix had been easier to resist than this. Did she have any idea how wholly she was tempting him, how greatly she was testing his self-control?

Urkot released a heavy breath through his nostrils and inhaled slowly, focusing on the feel of his chest expanding as he filled his lungs. The odor of the water battled the crisp, sweet fragrance of the cleanleaf, but there was a hint of something else in the air, something familiar, something he could never have ignored.

Callie's scent.

It was at once delicate and earthy, with a hint of morning dew and a sweetness that was all the more alluring in its subtlety. He'd breathed in her scent many, many times before, but this time was different. This was the first time he'd smelled her while his desire was roaring, while his control was tattered. And it was nearly enough to convince him to cut the last threads of his restraint and give in to instinct and need.

After taking several slow breaths, holding each until his chest burned, he finally leaned forward. The echoing sounds of water flowing in the large chamber returned to him.

Keeping his back toward Callie, he opened his eyes and scrubbed his body. Fortunately, the feel of his own rough hands on his hide did not stoke his inner flames, but he took no risks. He worked as quickly as he could, lifting his lower body from the water only long enough to clean himself before sinking back down to keep his slit and claspers hidden.

"Can I..." He lifted a hand and twirled his finger like Callie had earlier.

She chuckled. "You can turn around, Urkot."

He did so to find Callie sitting on the edge of the pool with her legs folded up and crossed. She'd wrapped herself in white cloth, concealing much of her flesh from view. As much as he craved another look at her body, he thanked the Eight she was covered, because even the tiniest glimpse would've severed his control.

She smiled at him and dipped her fingers into the open jar of vineroot oil beside her before running them through her curls. "Feel better?"

*Better* didn't seem like the right word. He certainly felt... strongly, felt different, but did he feel better? Not while this desire consumed him. Yet he did not have the words to express his true feelings to her, and he did not know how she would've taken them if he had.

"Yes," was all he could bring himself to say.

Callie swept her gaze around the chamber. "I think I've grown *uhdikted* to this place."

Urkot strode toward her, water quietly sloshing around his legs. "*Uhdikted*? I do not know that word."

"Sorry. It means that you like something. A lot. So much that it becomes a habit that you can't break. An...obsession."

Was he becoming addicted to *her*?

He stepped over the pool's edge and plucked up his own cloth to dry his hide. "Why are you addicted to this place?"

She gathered more oil on her fingers and slowly combed them through her hair, working out the tangles. "Because it's like...like nourishment for the soul in a way I never understood before.

"Everything was always go, go, go since I was a little girl. As a kid, my siblings and I were always moved from one place to another depending on my parents' house flipping projects during the summer. If it was during the school season, we stayed with our grandmother so we didn't miss any classes. We never really had a stable place where we could just *be*.

"We finally settled down when our parents became *reeltorz* when I was a teenager, but because they worked in the luxury market, they had certain expectations of me. During their social events, I had to be polite, I had to smile, I had to be an *exempluhree* child to help them look good. And under no circumstance was I to cause any trouble in school."

Urkot dabbed his face with the cloth and lowered himself onto the ground beside her.

Covering the jar with the lid, Callie picked up her comb and ran it through her hair as she spoke. "I had to perform at school because my parents expected the best grades, so all my off time was spent studying and doing homework and whatever other extra *kurrikyular* activities would make my college applications look good.

"I had to aim for the top of the class in college because companies were going to look at that when I started my career. And then I was immediately swept up with the Homeworld Initiative for training. It was just...nonstop.

"And growing up in Manhattan? It's so fucking loud. There's constant noise coming from all over. The cars, the honking, the sirens, the trains, the people. It's everywhere." She looked at him, lips downturned in a small frown. "Sorry. I just kind of went off on my life, and you probably didn't understand one word of it."

"I knew two words, maybe three," he said with a gentle chitter.

Callie chuckled, the crease in her brow relaxing. "That's about how I feel sometimes when Rekosh gets going in vrix."

Urkot raised his mandibles. "I know Rekosh's words, but I do not listen. I listen to you." He extended a foreleg and brushed it along hers. "I hear the feeling in your words, even if I do not know them."

His fine hairs picked up her scent, and he had to fight to hold back a low, appreciative growl as his desire flared again. The smell of cleanleaf clinging to Callie's skin couldn't mask her natural fragrance.

Before he could pull his leg away, she settled a hand atop it and smiled at him. "Thank you, Urkot."

Warmth pooled in his belly at her touch. Delicately, he covered her hand with his own and lifted it, turning it so her palm was up. Her hand was so different from his. So much smaller, with five slender fingers rather than four thicker ones. Blunt nails instead of black claws. Smooth skin instead of callused hide.

He hooked his thumb over her palm and brushed it along one of the lines there, marveling at the feel of her.

For all their differences, their hands were remarkably alike in form and function. Just as humans and vrix were alike in the way they thought, the way they felt, the way they communicated.

In the things for which they yearned…

Urkot slid his hand over hers, palm to palm, and his hearts leapt when Callie laced her fingers with his. His gaze darted up to find her watching him with a soft smile.

"As for what all that has to do with why I love this place…" Keeping their fingers locked, Callie looked around the cavern. "When we first came to Kaldarak and Garahk led us in here, all my troubles just melted away the instant I got in the water. Every day since that bitch queen has been gone, I've felt this sort of…peace. No expectations, no pressure. I don't have to perform anymore. I can just be…me. And everyone accepts that, accepts me, just as I am.

"But as much as I love hanging out with everyone, sometimes I just need quiet. And this place is the perfect kind of quiet when no one is around."

"I know that need." He gently squeezed her hand. "That is why I am here."

Callie returned her attention to him. "I'm sure it gets really loud in the tunnels."

His eyes fell shut as the sound of falling rock echoed in his mind. "Yes. Sometimes big loud."

She brushed her thumb back and forth over his. Urkot wondered if she sensed his turmoil, if that touch was her way of soothing him.

Her very presence was a light in the darkness, guiding him back to safety, to surety, to *her*. But Callie's touch was so much more. It flooded him with warmth, as thrilling as it was comforting, and hatched a thousand new desires in his mind.

He would have been content to sit here, holding her hand, until long after Takarahl and Kaldarak were lost to time.

"You know," Callie said, "I never wanted to get into chemistry. That was something my parents pressured me into."

Urkot opened his eyes to see her staring down at their entwined hands. He spoke slowly to ensure he found the right words. "Most vrix learn crafts from parents. That is why I am a delver, Rekosh a weaver, Telok a hunter. But some choose different. You are here now. A new world, a new life, yes? What will you choose?"

She chuckled. "I mean, my degrees are basically worthless now, and it's not like I have to earn an income anymore. But… for the longest time, I wanted to be a *geeoluhjist*—that's a scientist who studies the earth. I always loved rocks and minerals, and I had a huge collection of crystals and gemstones as a kid, so it seemed natural."

Callie grinned at him. "Which is why I've loved all the little gifts you've given me."

He cursed himself for having left his pouch in his den. This would've been the perfect moment to give her the crystal he'd found today, and that would've been the perfect gesture to finally put the lingering tightness in his chest to rest.

Chittering, Urkot ran the back of a finger down her cheek, tracing the line of her jaw, until it reached her chin. He grasped it, tipped her face higher, and leaned close. "I will find more pretty stones for my pretty female."

Callie's eyes rounded, and her skin warmed.

It was only then that Urkot realized what he'd said.

*My pretty female.*

He'd laid claim upon her.

His own eyes widened. Those words had come out so naturally, without a thought, and they felt right. Felt true.

Callie didn't rebuke or deny him, didn't withdraw or shudder in disgust. Instead, something in her gaze shifted, softening as her eyes flicked between his. Reaching up, she gently curled her fingers around his wrist and smiled. "I would love them, Urkot. And…maybe I could join you in the caves sometime to explore."

Terrible cold swept through him, tensing all his muscles at once.

Even under the best circumstances, he would've deemed it too dangerous, but with today's events fresh in his mind, he was horrified at the thought of Callie going down there. Right now, all he could think about was her being harmed.

All he could think about was her being killed.

Words clawed up his throat and lodged in it as he released her and withdrew his hands much more quickly than he intended to. He would not allow thoughts of her in the cave to take over his mind. He'd crumble, his every thread coming undone, were his mind to continue along that path.

No. He would keep her away, above ground, where it was safer. He had lost too many vrix he cared about to the dangers understone. He could not expose her to those same dangers. He could no longer bear the thought of a world without her.

Twisting to grab his jar of vineroot oil from the edge of the pool, he opened the lid and began rubbing the oil on his chest and abdomen. He forced himself to focus on the quick, rough motions of his hands, on the feel of his callused palms and fingers scraping his hide.

"Urkot? Are you okay?"

"It is not safe," he said, nearly in a growl.

Callie sighed, and Urkot glanced at her in time to see her roll her eyes. It was…unsettling when humans did that.

"This whole planet isn't safe," she said. "I could take one step out into the jungle and get eaten by a carnivorous *plant*."

"No."

"Urkot, come on. Don't—"

"No."

Callie huffed. "I agree with Rekosh. You are stoneheaded."

Urkot's hands stilled, and his mandibles twitched.

So what if he was stoneheaded? If it kept the ones he cared about safe, he would accept it gladly.

He resumed coating his hide in the oil, trying his best not to look at the tempting female beside him. But even if he wasn't looking at her, he was always aware of her, always aware of the unseen tether that ceaselessly drew him toward her. From the edge of his vision, he saw her rise to her feet.

Grunting, he bent his arms backward to spread oil on his back. As always, his bulky arms and broad shoulders made it impossible to reach most of his back, forcing him to strain and stretch.

"Here, let me do it," Callie said as she took the jar from him. "It's okay to ask for help sometimes."

Without awaiting his reply, she moved behind him, threw one leg over his hindquarters, and straddled him. He blinked, momentarily stunned. Gathering his long, damp hair, she draped it over the front of his shoulder. And then her soft hands were upon his hide, rubbing the oil in, fingers working firmly over his taut muscles.

Now, his entire body stilled. He hadn't expected this, never could've expected it. Tingles spread across his hide as she massaged the oil into his back, the fine hairs on his legs rose, and pressure built deep within his chest and core.

Urkot grasped his forelegs with all three hands, squeezing them as though it could dull the sensations she was causing. It wasn't merely her hands; it was her weight on his hindquarters, the warm, bare skin of her legs pressed against him, and her soft ass atop him, covered by only a thin layer of cloth. Her scent permeated him from her calves brushing his leg hairs.

Never in all his years had anyone offered to do this for him. Never in all his years had anyone touched him this way.

For it to be Callie…

His eyes fell shut, and a shuddering breath escaped him.

Her hands started at his upper shoulders and worked down his back. A shiver coursed through him when she reached the base of his spine. His stem twitched against his slit, and his claspers drew in tight against it.

*By their eightfold eyes. Shaper, unmake me!*

She lifted her hands. Relief followed. Urkot drew in a deep inhalation, willing his body to calm, attempting to retake control. Callie was doing him a kindness. He would not answer it by being swept into a mating frenzy.

Her slick, oil coated hand returned to his body, over the raised scar where his lower left arm had once been.

Urkot's hearts stopped. When they resumed beating, they pounded so fast and hard that they would surely burst from his chest.

This was more than mere kindness, more than the warm touch of a friend. Her gentle hands bore unspoken care and quiet familiarity. That she would tend to him this way, even to this part of his body...

His cock throbbed, his slit bulging with the pressure it exerted, and Urkot groaned low and deep.

"Feel good?" Callie asked, caressing and kneading his hide.

He could only hum in appreciation. That was fortunate, as the only adequate words that came to mind were human ones he'd heard from Cole many times—*fuck yes.*

"Good." Her voice was huskier than he'd ever heard it, and it came from much closer, her warm breath brushing the back of his neck. She withdrew her hands. "All done."

It took a moment for him to make sense of her words as his body mourned the loss of her touch. He craved her hands on his hide, yearned to draw her closer and place his hands on *her.*

Slinging her leg back over his hindquarters, she slid down to stand between his bent legs.

Urkot snapped his eyes open and turned his head toward her.

With a wide grin, Callie stepped in front of him and held out the jar. He accepted it absently, unable but to stare at her.

"Have a good night, big guy," she said with a playful tap on his chin.

After gathering her belongings, she walked out of the chamber.

Urkot's eyes remaining on the empty entryway through which she'd left the temple.

Fire roiled inside him, along with a deep, gnawing hunger that no food could ever satisfy. Something had changed within Urkot. Something had awoken within him. And he was beginning to understand that it would not be lulled back to slumber.

His hide pulsed and tingled. He could almost feel Callie's weight upon him, her hands moving over his back, her warmth. Almost... And that only made the desire he felt for her vaster than the Tangle and hotter than any flame.

Perhaps seeing two of his friends claim human mates had compelled Urkot to reflect upon what he was missing. The happiness Ketahn, Ivy, Rekosh, and Ahmya had found flooded Urkot's hearts with joy, but there was a part of him which that joy could not reach. An empty space that could not be filled.

A loneliness his friends could not cure.

To think that Callie could fill it, that she would choose to do so, seemed foolish. Yet he could not deny that both his body and his hearts reacted to her in ways he could not ignore.

It seemed this long day was destined to become a longer night.

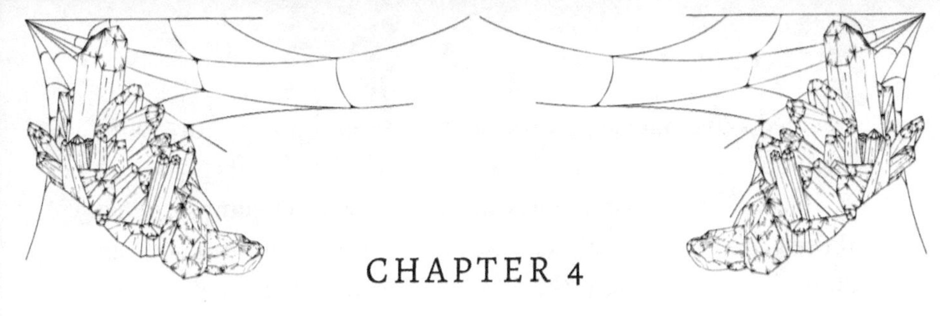

# CHAPTER 4

"Ta da!" Callie held up her first completed grass basket of the morning. "Look upon this masterpiece. It's perfection."

The morning sunlight highlighted the basket's green leaves, setting them aglow as she turned it from side to side.

Lacey, who was weaving her own basket as she sat beside Callie, chuckled. "Remarkable improvement from the first one you ever made."

"That"—Callie leveled a finger at her—"shall not be discussed. It never existed."

"Whatever you say." Lacey coughed into her fist as she said, "It was terrible."

"I heard that!"

"What was terrible?" Will asked as he approached, carrying a large wooden platter bearing an array of fruits and vegetables, eldernuts, and smoked fish. He wore woven, knee-length shorts, gifted to him by Rekosh, their white fabric complementing his dark brown skin.

Lacey and Callie also wore Rekosh's creations. Lacey's was a yellow, sleeveless dress, which was striking against her pale, freckled skin, and Callie's was a green tank top and shorts with laces on the outer thighs.

Though some of them still had their HWI jumpsuits, all those garments were either worn from heavy usage or had been altered to better suit the climate. Rekosh had made it his mission to weave clothing for all the humans. It was a challenge he delighted in. Of course, he saved the best outfits for Ahmya, and she was the only one who wore clothing made with his silk.

"Breakfast, finally." Callie set her basket aside and reached out to Will with grabby hands. "Gimme, gimme! I'm starving."

He stopped next to the spread blanket Callie and Lacey were sitting upon and teasingly swung the platter away, his brown eyes narrowing. "Ah-ah. Not until you guys fill me in. The terrible thing?"

"Nothing," Callie said quickly.

Lacey chuckled. "I was just reminding Callie of her first attempt at basket weaving."

Will snickered. "Yeah, that was pretty bad."

"Woooow," Callie said. "At least I *tried*, unlike you."

"Hey! Only because I burned my fingers trying to get extra supplies for us."

"Which is why you get a pass. Now both of you stop mocking my first basket—may it rest in pieces—and give me food."

Laughing, Will bent and set the platter down in front of them before sitting atop the blanket. "Bon appétit."

"You're a saint."

Callie plucked up a yellow riverberry and tossed it into her mouth. The moment she bit down, the sweet yet sour juice burst on her tongue. She hummed appreciatively. It was delicious, similar to a grape both in flavor and texture, and was easily one of her favorite alien fruits. Thankfully, they grew in abundance along the nearby river, allowing her to forage them as often as she pleased.

Eating another berry, she drew in a deep breath and swept her gaze to the side, across the suspended rope bridge that connected the humans' treehouse platforms to the rest of the village.

There was activity all around Kaldarak as its residents prepared for Singer's Promise. Thornskull vrix with hides of earthy reds and oranges, yellows, browns, and greens mingled with each other, working in harmony as broodlings played or helped their parents. The white male thornskulls stood out the most from the rest, though they were far rarer.

Callie spotted Garahk, one of those white thornskulls, just as he drew his mate Nalaki's headcrest down to his own. Their five broodlings were gathered around their legs.

She smiled at the open affection the leaders of Kaldarak showed one another.

When she'd first met Garahk, he'd been terrifying. The huge, powerfully built vrix had been covered in mud, with wicked spikes on his shoulders and headcrest. But despite his intimidating exterior, he was a compassionate, thoughtful leader, a male of honor with a gentle nature.

As Will and Lacey chatted, their voices seeming far off, Callie searched the platforms, but she didn't spot any of the black shadowstalker vrix.

*Looking for a particular combination of black and blue, Callie?*

She smiled.

*Perhaps.*

The morning breeze, carrying the fresh scent of mist, flowed over her skin. Callie turned her head toward the ancient temple. Sunlight shimmered on the waterfall, breaking into a blooming rainbow on the mist that hung in the air.

Her skin warmed at the memory of what had happened in that temple last night. She'd bathed in those pools after sunset many times, and never once had anyone walked in on her. The vrix seemed to visit the temple most often in the morning. Callie had come to see it as her perfect escape, her little sanctuary, where she could let her guard down for a short while.

Out of everyone in Kaldarak, it had been Urkot who'd walked in on her as she stood naked within the hot springs. Urkot, who had been her friend, who had gifted her precious, pretty stones because he knew she loved them.

It should've shattered her sense of security, but oddly, it hadn't. She'd always known there was a chance of someone walking in on her. It wasn't as though the pools were private, and they certainly didn't belong to her. But that it had been Urkot? That had sent a rush of exhilaration through her.

How long had he stood there? How long had he been... watching her?

Warmth sparked low in her belly. She liked the thought of him watching her bathe.

Callie ran her fingertips down her cheek. She could almost feel the ghost of Urkot's finger trailing over her face, could almost feel his rough, possessive touch as he grasped her chin, forcing her to keep her eyes on him.

Had he truly called her *his* pretty female?

*What is happening to me?*

She was horny, simple as that, and she'd just experienced one of the most erotic moments of her life with a spider man. She'd sat astride his hindquarters, had felt the warmth of his body radiating between her thighs. She had rubbed oil into his hide, had explored his broad back with her hands, learning every plane of his defined muscles, marveling at the strength he'd built over years of labor in the tunnels. Fuck, he even had dimples on his lower back. Now that was sexy as hell.

And God, was he big...

A sharp snap broke through Callie's thoughts, dashing away images of nighttime bathing and memories of sensual touches. She jerked back to the present, eyes widening.

"Hello!" Lacey snapped her fingers again beside Callie. "Earth to Callie!"

"We're not on Earth," Will said with amusement.

"You know what I mean."

Callie looked between the two of them with a furrowed brow. "What?"

Lacey chuckled. "We asked what has you biting your lip with that far-off look in your eyes."

Callie's skin flushed as she reached forward, picking up a piece of smoked fish. "Nothing."

Lacey smirked, one red brow arching. "Uh-huh."

"That definitely wasn't the expression of someone thinking about *nothing*," Will said before tossing a nut in his mouth.

Callie stuffed the fish into her mouth, grabbed another large, fanned leaf, curled it into a circle, and picked up her knife to cut notches in the stem. "Like I said, it's nothing. I was just enjoying the riverberries."

"Callie," Lacey said, holding out a length of silk string, "We've all had riverberries, and I've never once seen anyone make the face you just did while eating them."

"Maybe I just *really* like riverberries." Callie took the offered string and tied it around the stem, hooking it in the notches she'd made.

"Okay, okay. Keep your secrets." Lacey picked up a wedge of moonblossom fruit and leaned back, propping herself up on one hand as she ate.

Callie tied one more string around the stem before she began weaving the fronds.

There weren't any secrets to spill. Urkot had come upon her while she was bathing; what was the big deal? It wasn't like nudity was taboo here. The vrix didn't care one way or another since they didn't really wear clothing. Urkot had probably been staring at her in curiosity because their species were so different, and she was reading too much into it.

*I will find more pretty stones for my pretty female.*

Or maybe there had been more to his gaze...

"You guys don't usually drag your asses out of bed this early," Cole said as he jogged down the stairs from the above platform, where Callie and Lacey lived. Ahmya's home, tucked between both of theirs, was vacant since she and Rekosh had been given a larger den next to Ketahn and Ivy's.

Will glanced up from the basket he'd started. "Good morning to you too, Cole."

"Not everyone wakes up at the ass crack of dawn," Callie said.

"We're amazed if *you* wake up before noon." Cole laughed as he hopped off the last step, his boots making a loud thump that vibrated the wooden planks. He was wearing dark green shorts that were laced low on his hips and a matching vest that showed off his muscled arms and skin that had been bronzed by hours spent in the sun. A bow was hooked over one of his shoulders, and a quiver of arrows hung from his hand. Apart from his modern-day boots, he looked like a ranger from a fantasy novel, ready to lead his companions into the depths of a monster infested forest.

"I mean, he is right," Lacey said with a smirk.

"Hey!" Callie threw one of the long, broken leaves at the red-haired woman. "I'm up when I need to be."

Lacey caught the leaf with a laugh and extended it to tickle Callie's arm. "Not always. It can take some coaxing."

Callie chuckled and scooted out of Lacey's reach, batting at the leaf. "Okay! Okay! So I'm not a morning person. Sue me."

"I'll get my lawyer right on that."

"Going hunting, Cole?" Will asked.

"Yep." Cole laid his bow and quiver on the floor, then swung his backpack off to set it beside them. He plopped himself down between Callie and Will and snatched up a couple slices of fish.

"Joining Telok with the hunting party. Nalaki wants plenty of meat for tomorrow night."

Lacey wrinkled her nose with a huff as she worked the long, thin leaves, weaving them into a tight, layered pattern. "And here we are on basket duty. Why do you get to do the exciting stuff?"

"Because Telok likes me." Cole tossed the fish in his mouth and chewed as he grinned at her.

"Ouch," Callie said with a wince.

Lacey glared at Cole. "Asshole."

No one knew why Telok and Lacey were so at odds with one another. The black and green vrix had been protective of Lacey as they'd trekked through the jungle in their mad dash to escape Zurvashi, but once they'd reached the safety of Kaldarak and put down roots, Telok had withdrawn from her. While he was amicable with the others, he was impatient and surly with Lacey. It was as though he'd built a wall around himself and had given everyone but Lacey a key to the gate.

And Lacey was taking it pretty hard. She tried to hide her hurt with cross words or by laughing it off, but Callie saw through her bluff. Telok's behavior cut her pretty deep.

As Lacey stewed and worked, Callie gathered a small handful of eldernuts and slipped one past her lips. The taste reminded her of a walnut. It was strange how so much of this world was alien and different, yet such similarities were everywhere.

Cole glanced around. "Where's Diego?"

Will's lips stretched into a wide, shy smile as he rubbed the back of his head. "He's sleeping. We, uh, got in a pretty good morning workout."

"Just say it!" Cole said with a laugh. "You guys fucked."

Pressing her lips together, Callie smacked the bare part of his thigh.

Cole flinched and covered the spot she'd hit. "Ow!"

"Leave him alone," she said.

"I'm just joking. There's nothing to be embarrassed about."

"You don't have to be so crass."

"Yeah," Lacey chimed in. "Maybe they made love. You know, all romantic like."

"I'm right here," Will said.

Cole chuckled. "So which was it then, Will? Rough and sweaty, or slow and sensual with all the pretty words and shit like that?"

"How about," Diego said as he stepped out of his nearby den, letting the curtain fall behind him, "it's none of your damn business."

He made his way toward them, his dark brown eyes on Will. When he sat down next to him, he cupped a hand behind Will's head and pulled him into a deep kiss. Will's eyes widened before drifting shut as he kissed his partner back.

"Ow ow!" Lacey hooted as Callie grinned.

Diego broke the kiss, wrapped an arm around Will's shoulders, keeping the man close, and plucked up a riverberry. He grinned at Cole as he held the riverberry to Will's lips. "It was both."

"Damn. I'm jealous," Callie said.

Lacey propped her elbow on her knee and rested her chin on her hand. "Right?"

"Hey!" Cole flung his arms out wide. "I'm right here."

"We know," said both Callie and Lacey at once.

Cole huffed and proceeded to eat.

Diego looked at Will, who smiled and pecked a kiss on Diego's lips before wrapping an arm around his back.

Seeing this intimacy, this closeness, this…love, made Callie all the more aware of what she was missing. Of course she had the companionship of her friends, but that wasn't the same. Ahmya and Ivy were doted upon by their vrix mates, and Will and Diego lived happy, carefree lives here without judgement. They were thriving, flourishing.

What Callie wouldn't have given to have someone to look at her with the same adoration that shone in Diego's eyes when he looked at Will. To have someone to sweep her off her feet and kiss her hard enough to steal her breath, to have someone to hold her close through the night.

To make love to her.

*I'm just so fucking lonely.*

*Maybe I should proposition Cole...*

No strings. Just a fuck—just scratching an itch. She could have an orgasm or two to hold her over for a while and see if that rid her of this irksome loneliness. She was sure he'd be down for it.

But the thought of having sex with Cole didn't arouse or excite her. It left her feeling cold.

He was her friend, and she valued him as a friend, even loved him as a friend. But she didn't want him in a sexual way.

A memory played in her mind—Urkot standing in the hot springs beneath falling water, with his long black hair, streaked with threads of blue and white, unbound, and rivulets streaming down his back. As she'd watched him last night, she'd stared at his broad shoulders, transfixed by the play of muscle in his thick arms as he'd run his clawed fingers through his hair. And when he'd turned to face her, his glowing blue eyes had been brilliant in the chamber's dim light.

He'd been a monster fucker's wet dream.

She'd yearned to comb her fingers across the shorn hair on the sides of his head, following it up to the long, silky strands on top, yearned to run her hands over the hard planes of his chest, yearned to...

Yearned to know what his cock looked like, to see it. To... feel it inside her.

*What the hell, Callie? Where'd that thought come from? What happened to not wanting to fuck a spider?*

Face growing warmer by the second, Callie furrowed her brow and bent over her basket, letting her long curls fall forward on either side of her face.

*Maybe I had a change of heart after seeing how loved Ivy and Ahmya are by their mates?*

Why shouldn't she consider Urkot? They'd slowly grown closer over the last several months. He was kind and thoughtful, and he made her laugh. And as far as physical appeal, well...

Callie didn't know when her perception had changed so drastically. How could she have gone from seeing human men as sexy to looking at a spiderlike alien and thinking the same? Spiders had always been repellent, terrifying things despite their small sizes, and she'd always been grossed out by bugs.

And yet she was seriously considering an intimate relationship with a vrix.

People on Earth would have thought she was depraved. Hell, she'd questioned Ivy's sanity in the beginning. *Sex with a spider? Gross!*

But then Callie had come to know the vrix. While they looked different, they were the same as humans on the inside. They were people, with thoughts and emotions, with hopes and dreams, with friends and family. And as illogical as it should have been, humans could procreate with them. Akalahn was proof of that.

She wasn't religious, but wasn't that some kind of divine sign that humans and vrix were meant to be together?

*It's science, Callie. It was humans playing God and using us as test subjects.*

But that didn't mean anyone at the Homeworld Initiative had ever anticipated contact with an intelligent alien species, or that they'd meant for the serums they'd injected into the colonists to allow the human body to adapt to procreation with nonhuman beings. Ivy had conceived a viable hybrid vrix child, carried it to term, and given birth to something so strange and so, so beautiful…

It was an outcome no one could've predicted.

It was an outcome that shouldn't have been possible.

Humans and vrix were two different species. They should not have been compatible.

Yet they were.

With every passing day, it was harder for Callie to deny her growing attraction to Urkot. She couldn't stop her eyes from straying toward him and raking over his body, couldn't help the way her own body reacted in his presence, couldn't prevent the warmth that bloomed in her core when she noticed him watching her with keen interest. Every time he touched her, her skin tingled like it was charged with electricity.

And she wanted to experience more of that sensation. She wanted to feel it all over. She wanted…

More of him.

"You must go," came a deep, raspy voice, breaking Callie from her reverie.

She blinked down at her work. With her head up in the clouds as she fantasized about a certain sapphire-eyed vrix, the leaves had come loose, completely undoing the tight weave she'd started. This didn't resemble a basket in the slightest; it was just a frond with bent leaves now.

*Ugh.*

She lifted her head to see Telok standing on the platform, in front of the bridge, with all four arms crossed over his chest and his bright green eyes narrowed at Cole.

"He's eating," Lacey said, glancing at Telok before waving him off and returning her focus to her basket. "So shoo. Begone with you."

Telok's mandibles twitched, and his posture stiffened. His gaze flicked to Lacey. The hard, mask-like faces of the vrix couldn't really change expressions, but Callie swore something passed over his for an instant, somehow heated and dark, frustrated, crestfallen, and hungry.

But it came and went so quickly that she couldn't be sure if she'd only imagined it.

"Yeah," Cole replied, tossing a chunk of goldcrest mushroom into his mouth. "What she said."

With a growl, Telok strode toward Cole, who was about to eat another piece of goldcrest. Cole's hand paused in the air as the two stared at each other.

Slowly, the vrix bent down and extended an arm. With an unceremonious, comically soft *thwap*, he slapped the mushroom out of Cole's hand. "No eat. Hunt."

Cole scowled and pointed at his chest. "Me human." He pointed at the platter of food next. "Need food."

"Me vrix." Telok thumped his own chest with a fist. "Already eat. Have work to do. Go hunt now."

"Don't be an asshole."

"Do not be late."

"Dick," Cole muttered before shoving a handful of riverberries in his mouth. He stuffed another fistful of nuts into the pocket of his shorts as he rose.

"Takes one to know one," Lacey said without looking up from her work.

Both Diego and Will chuckled.

Telok turned his narrowed gaze on Lacey. "I am not limp, dangling, wrinkly skin."

"Hey!" Cole exclaimed.

Callie laughed. "Well, your English vocabulary is definitely expanding."

"Callie, could you please pass me some moonblossom fruit?" the redhead asked, holding out an upturned palm.

Drawing her lips inward, Callie bit down on them and tried to curb her amusement as she picked up the fruit and put it on

Lacey's waiting hand. Not once did Lacey acknowledge Telok as she curled her fingers around it, brought it to her lips, and calmly took a bite, her tongue sweeping out to catch the red juice at the corner of her mouth.

With those intense green eyes locked on Lacey, Telok snarled. He shifted toward her, mandibles spreading, but seemed to be halted by some invisible force. Lacey continued to ignore him, chewing her food completely unbothered.

"Come," Telok snapped at Cole with a clack of his fangs before stalking away in the direction from which he'd come.

"Cranky fucker," Cole grumbled as he picked up his pack and slung it over his shoulders. He pointed at Lacey. "I blame you."

Lacey's head snapped up, and she gaped at him. "Me?"

He gathered his bow and arrows. "Yes, you."

"You're the one that called him an asshole and a dick! I just agreed with you. So don't go blaming his shitty attitude on me."

Cole drew in a deep breath, opened his mouth as though to argue, then let out a grunt.

Callie snickered. "She's got you there."

"Damnit."

"Better run along," Diego said with a grin.

"Go kiss and make up," Will said.

Cole flipped them off, turned, and followed Telok across the bridge, keeping his middle finger prominently displayed the entire time.

Callie and the others laughed. They ate, chatted, and worked as the sun crept higher, and Callie couldn't help but reflect on her time here in Kaldarak.

The last few months had been…odd. Not bad, but odd. Since Ahmya had moved out of her den to share a place with Rekosh, and Ivy had been busy as a new mother, it felt like their little tribe had fractured.

She knew that wasn't the case. They all remained close, and

saw each other all the time, but things had changed. Their small, tight-knit community was slowly integrating into the larger community of Kaldarak. They were making friends with the thornskulls, finding their places amongst them. That was a good thing.

Except…Callie didn't feel like she was finding her place. In some ways, she was more lost than ever. She'd spent most of her life working hard in school to earn her degrees, preparing to build a career. She'd joined the Homeworld Initiative to put her knowledge to use.

Callie had been recruited to be part of a team of scientists tasked with terraforming Xolea and ensuring the prosperity of the colony. She would've been working to ensure the safety and security of their food and water supply, while also analyzing native vegetation and chemical compounds.

But all the equipment she would've used was lost with the *Somnium's* cargo hold. Maybe it was somewhere on this planet, crashed and forgotten for decades. Maybe it was still floating somewhere in the vast expanses of space. Hell, there was even a slim chance that it had reached its intended destination—minus a few compartments full of would-be colonists.

She and her friends knew only that the ship had been hit by something, and that their section had broken off and fallen here. And if Ketahn hadn't found it and accidentally awoken Ivy… Well, Callie and the other survivors would've died when the wreckage inevitably lost power in a couple years.

*And we never would've known.*

They'd been put into stasis, expecting to awaken on Xolea. But they would've simply slept for eternity.

She was grateful to be alive, and she always would be, despite the hardships they'd endured and those that would undoubtedly come. Yet she found herself staring at a new problem, one that felt insurmountable.

Where did she fit in this new world? What was expected of her here?

The vrix knew what foods were safe to eat, and with a few exceptions, most of those foods were safe for human consumption. The water was safe to drink, the air safe to breathe. And one of the few pieces of technology they'd salvaged from the wreckage was a portable device that could scan food, analyze its components, and determine whether it was dangerous. It did Callie's job for her—a job that wasn't even necessary most of the time.

"Callie, you okay?" Diego asked.

She turned her head toward him. Diego and Will were looking at her with concern in their expressions. It was only then that she realized that she'd been sitting there, staring off into the jungle, with a finished basket sitting on her lap.

When had she completed it? How long had she been spacing out?

"Yeah," she said, offering them a smile. "I'm good. Just a lot on my mind lately, I guess."

"Anything you want to talk about?"

"Nah, it's nothing. I'm fine. Really. But thanks, doc."

Will frowned. "Well, if you ever do need to talk, we're here."

"All of us," Lacey added.

Callie's eyes stung with the threat of tears. She let out a laugh as she wiped moisture from her eyes. "Damnit, stop. All this love is gonna make me cry."

"Don't you dare! I have no intention of crying, but if you do, I'll be bawling like a baby."

Diego chuckled. "Just make sure you keep hydrated."

"You would say that," Callie said with a smirk. She stacked the finished basket with the others that were piling up. "I'm actually gonna take a break. I'll be back in a bit."

"We'll be here." Will gestured to the pile of fronds. "Still got lots of work to do."

Callie pushed herself to her feet. "Make sure to finish the baskets before I get back then."

Lacey smacked Callie's calf with a leaf. "Trying to get out of work."

"Damn right!"

Callie made her escape as her friends laughed behind her. Her bare feet padded across the warm platform as she made her way to the stairway that led up to the second level.

Thankfully, her den stood nearest to the stairs, and the moment she brushed aside the silk hanging in the doorway and stepped inside, comfortable quiet greeted her. Callie closed her eyes and let out a long, slow exhalation. She could still hear muffled, faraway voices as the others talked below.

Diego had been a nurse on Earth, and he'd naturally fallen into the role of doctor in their group. He'd even been learning more about the vrix in order to help them with their ailments as best he could.

Will, who'd been an information technology tech, had fortunately found his place working alongside Diego as a healer. There weren't exactly many computers on this planet.

Lacey had run her own business on Earth, selling homemade soaps, shampoos, oils, teas, honey, and baked goods. Her knowledge was being used now to supply the humans with those little necessities and comforts.

Cole had been a construction worker, and his skills had been invaluable in building the human dens here in Kaldarak. His woodworking projects were beloved by human and vrix alike. And his experience from hunting and camping for most of his life left him in an excellent position to provide for their community.

Ahmya, who'd been a florist in her former life, had also found purpose here. The garden she'd established at her new den was already providing the humans with some vegetables, herbs, and ingredients for Lacey's teas. On top of that, she was apprenticing under Rekosh, learning to sew and make clothing for the other humans.

And Ivy... Callie couldn't put into words her admiration for that woman. Ivy had been introduced to the vrix, to this world, alone. She'd had to learn an alien language and how to survive in this jungle in real time. She'd nearly died many times, including once when she'd eaten a food that was safe for vrix but had made her terribly ill. Everything she'd eaten had been trial and error. A risk. She hadn't even had the luxury of the few items the humans had salvaged from the ship—fire starters, extra clothing, rations, boots, lanterns, a food scanner, metal knives.

Ivy had said she was no one on Earth. She'd been lost, homeless, trapped, desperate. Here, she'd become a survivor. A leader. An inspiration. And now she was a mother too. She had a purpose.

*I don't.*

Callie helped everywhere she could. She helped Lacey make her soaps, helped with the cooking, helped Diego and Will whenever they needed an extra hand. She'd helped Cole a couple times, though she usually felt like she was in his way despite how grateful he always was for the assistance. She'd tended Ahmya's plants with her before Ahmya had changed dens.

A well of emotions expanded within Callie's chest, constricting her lungs, and once more, she felt like she was on the verge of tears.

In her old life, she'd never really had anyone there for her. Instead, she'd had those goals, those expectations, and they'd kept her grounded. They'd given her direction. It was easy to know which way to go when the path had been laid out in advance.

But here...here, she was adrift on the open ocean without a sail, without oars. The goals she'd been chasing when she boarded the *Somnium* were meaningless now, and the expectations had vanished. For the first time in memory, she just had to…be. And though that seemed like it should've been laughably simple, she wasn't even sure how to start. The growing anxiety crawling under her skin insisted that she should've been working toward something.

She was flailing. Floundering. What would give her meaning here? What would fill the chasm left by the absence of those goals, by the loss of that lofty mission?

*You've got to be the only person on this whole planet who's crumbling because you don't have enough pressure on you, Callie.*

To her frustration, that thought only sharpened the sting in her eyes.

*I'm not going to cry. I'm* not *going to cry.*

She opened her eyes and blinked rapidly, letting out one calming breath after another. She swept her gaze around her home—the thick pallet on the floor that was her bed, the earthy tones of the sheer silk decorating the walls, the vase of fresh flowers on the table beneath the window, the clothes hanging neatly on their pegs, and the chest of tools on the floor near the doorway.

Her chest felt even tighter. Because ultimately, despite containing all her possessions, this room was empty. Cold. Lonely.

How she wished there was someone here to just…*hold* her. To comfort her, to ground her when she felt like she was losing herself. To look at her and see her, to tell her she was Callie… and that Callie was all she needed to be.

Her eyes settled upon the oval limestone bowl sitting atop the nightstand. A shaky smile curved her lips. She walked to the bowl, knelt on the floor, and peered inside. To anyone else, it was just a bowl full of rocks. Nothing special. But to Callie, each one of these stones was a precious gift.

From Urkot.

She ran her fingers over them. There were so many colors, ranging from neutral, earthy browns and grays to vibrant splashes of red, green, blue and purple. Some possessed stripes, some had swirls, some bore glimmering flecks of minerals. And mixed in were chunks of crystal both rough and smooth, some of which glowed at night.

Urkot had given each one of these to her simply because they were pretty and he knew she would like them. It was thoughtful and so incredibly sweet. And as far as she knew, he only did this for her.

Once more, her mind turned to the prospect of taking him as her mate.

She knew vrix tended to be forward when it came to matters of mating. They weren't shy about declaring themselves and their desires. Yet while Urkot had made some indications, such as the possessive way he often touched Callie, or how he looked at her like he wanted to devour her, he'd never said anything. He'd never laid claim upon her.

But Callie *knew* he was interested. Alien or no, there was no mistaking it.

So what was holding Urkot back?

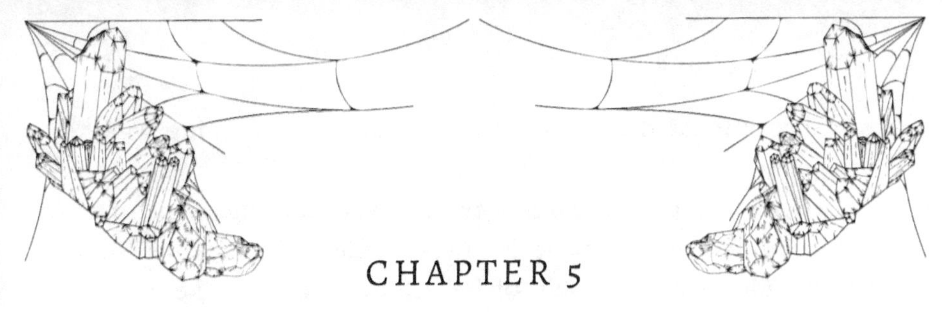

# CHAPTER 5

CALLIE SMOOTHED her hands down her body and over her silky dress. It was sleeveless, with thin, double straps that wrapped around the back of her neck, a tight-cinched waist, and a flaring skirt hanging midway down her thighs. The beautiful cornflower blue material was ruffled at the hem, and it fluttered and caressed her legs with her every movement. She cupped her breasts, which were hugged by the snug bodice. The neckline, dipping in a low V, showed off a generous amount of cleavage.

"Wow," Callie said breathlessly. "Who needs to spend thousands of dollars on a designer dress when you have Rekosh."

"And who cares that it's silk from a spider's ass," Lacey said, admiring her own green dress. Hers was also a halter top, but the skirt was straight, with a long slit down each thigh.

"Well, yours aren't made with *his* butt silk. Only I get to wear that," Ahmya laughed. "I helped sketch out the ideas for the designs, but he's literally the master weaver."

Ivy chuckled. "I'll be sure not to tell Ketahn you said that." She brushed her fingers over the embroidered flower patterns on the gorgeous, sheer red dress Ahmya wore. "But I agree."

Lacey pressed her fingers to her mouth, eyes going wide. "Ohhhh."

Callie swept her gaze over Ivy, who was the only one wearing something made by Ketahn. Her white, opalescent dress glittered in the light of Rekosh's den, almost like it was threaded with silver. Glowing blue crystals were embroidered along the waist, flowing up the bodice and the single shoulder strap.

"I don't know," Callie said. "Looks like Ketahn is still a contender for the title."

"Their competitiveness is never ending," Ahmya said.

Lacey grinned and gestured at her dress. "Yeah, but we're benefiting from it."

Callie laughed. "Damn right, we are."

"Oh!" Ahmya stepped away, moving to a nearby table. "I have one more thing for you guys."

She returned carrying an armful of flower crowns. She reached up and settled one atop Lacey's head, followed by Ivy's, Callie's, and then her own. Each wreath was made with unique flowers laced with silk ribbons that matched their dresses.

"Oh my gosh, did you make these?" Ivy asked, running her fingers along the white ribbons dangling over her shoulder.

Ahmya clasped her hands at her middle and smiled, her cheeks flushing. "I did."

"They're beautiful." Lacey reached up to adjust her crown and smiled in return. "Thank you."

Callie pulled Ahmya into a tight hug. "You're so damn sweet. I love you to pieces."

Ahmya chuckled, voice muffled from her face being squished against Callie's arm. "Love you all too."

"Alright ladies…" Lacey walked to the door and held aside the silk curtain. "Shall we join the festivities?"

Together, they left Rekosh and Ahmya's den, slipping on the pretty shoes he'd made for them. In the time since the women had gathered to prepare for the celebration, the sun had set, and the real party had begun below Kaldarak's platforms. The air had cooled, caressing Callie's skin soothingly, and she could feel the beat of drums pounding an infectious rhythm down on the ground.

Kaldarak itself had been transformed by nightfall. The work Urkot and the other delvers had done was on full display, with hundreds upon hundreds of glowing blue crystals dotting the wooden platforms and rope bridges.

"It's gorgeous," Ivy said.

"It is," Callie breathed. "It's like a real-life fairy village."

"Now just picture the vrix flitting around with fairy wings," Lacey said.

Ahmya laughed and gave the woman a gentle shove. "Stop!"

"What? I think they'd look pretty badass with wings."

As they trotted down the large, spiraling stairway leading to the ground, the music grew louder. The drums were accompanied by the twang of string instruments and the clacking of wood, blending together in a joyous, upbeat song. Callie had heard music being played in the village, but this was the first time she'd heard anything this lively from the vrix.

A huge bonfire burned in a meadow, away from the trees, surrounded by a ring of stones. The fire set everything alight in orange, and where that light failed, the blue glow of crystals held back the shadows.

A large, wooden effigy stood nearby—a female vrix with her arms raised, her body covered in flowers, vines, and bits of colorful silk. Her hair was a cascade of grass and leaves dotted with little buds and blooms. The Rootsinger, who the vrix believed had provided all the jungle's plant life.

There were baskets and baskets filled with fruit and vegetables, the bounty that the vrix had harvested to celebrate the end of the flood season. Raw meat had been laid out on huge leaves, but there was a hint of the savory scent of cooking meat on the air. It touched Callie that the thornskulls had thought of the humans.

Thornskulls of all colors were chatting, dancing, and playing games, all of them swept up in good cheer. Callie spotted Diego and Will dancing together and laughing with the thornskulls. This was just another way that vrix and humans were similar—both species loved a good party.

The women stepped off the stairway and made their way through the crowd.

"*Akean*," Callie said to every thornskull who greeted her, offering them warm smiles.

Vrix parted, opening a path as a tall, broad, reddish-brown thornskull draped in white silk and flowers approached. The female spread her four arms wide and raised her mandibles.

"Ah, you are here, humans!" Nalaki said, her deep voice full of warmth.

Lacey threw her arms to the sides and spun in place. "Suitably fancy, I hope."

Nalaki lowered her arms and dipped her head. "Beautiful. Rekosh is blessed by the Weaver." Her gaze fell upon Ahmya. "Many females favor him, but his heartsflame burns only for you."

A soft smile spread across Ahmya's lips as she pressed a hand to her chest. "As mine burns only for him."

Callie tipped her head back. The crystals adorning the village were as numerous and luminous as the stars in the sky. She smiled and swept her gaze around, taking in the beauty of those little lights. She couldn't help but think of the distance she and her companions had crossed to get here. All those stars, all those planets, all those possibilities…

And yet they'd ended up here, with the vrix. Even if she didn't know what her purpose was here, this was where she was meant to be. She knew it deep in her heart.

"This is amazing, Nalaki," Callie said, fighting back a surge of emotion as she looked at the queen.

The daiya pressed her palms together. "We celebrate the work we have all done to welcome the season of promise and plenty. You are part of that. You are ours, we are yours."

"We are happy to be part of this tribe," Ivy said. "Where is Garahk?"

Nalaki chittered and swept out an arm, pointing past the throng of vrix. "My heartsflame is there, as is yours."

Callie's eyes followed Nalaki's gesture to a chaotic scene. A large group of vrix, adults and children alike, were playing a frenetic game at the center of the clearing. They all carried sticks shaped into flat, paddle-like ends, not unlike cricket bats, and were using those sticks to hit a leather ball into the air, seemingly trying to keep said ball off the ground.

Garahk was easy to spot thanks to his snow-white hide, but the two shadow stalkers also playing stood out just as starkly—Ketahn and Rekosh, their respective purple and red markings uniquely glowing amongst the earthier tones of the thornskulls.

She also spied a smaller figure amongst the vrix. Cole. Despite his stature and what the vrix considered a lack of limbs, the human seemed to be holding his own in their game, deftly maneuvering between—and sometimes beneath—the larger players.

The ball soared through the air. Cole vaulted up onto Garahk's hindquarters, stood tall, and gave the ball a mighty smack with his stick.

Callie's eyes widened as the ball hurtled through a vertical wooden hoop set atop a tall pole.

Half the players cheered as Cole threw his arms up in triumph, hooting and hollering enthusiastically.

As the players shifted on the field, assuming different positions, Callie's gaze wandered over the crowd watching the game and locked on a very familiar vrix on the sidelines.

A shadowstalker with blue markings unlike anything in Kaldarak.

Urkot.

He wasn't focused on the game at all, no. His attention was upon the broodlings who were swarming him—all five of Garahk and Nalaki's brood, along with Akalahn. The little ones were climbing all over him, latched onto his legs, hindquarters, and back, chittering as he attempted to pluck them off with playful ineptitude.

"I'm, uh…gonna go say hi to Urkot," Callie muttered as her feet, all on their own, moved her toward him.

She watched as he spun about, reaching for the little ones on his back with exaggerated clumsiness, and an odd warmth spread in her chest. Just as she neared him, the broodlings converged, climbing over his shoulders to cling to his chest. With a dramatic flair, Urkot fell backward, banding his arms around the little ones to keep them in place. He landed on his back, legs sticking straight up in the air before curling inward.

It was easily the most spidery thing she'd seen from him, but damn if it wasn't endearing.

The broodlings swarmed over him happily, as triumphant as Cole had been moments before.

From what Callie had seen of the vrix, they weren't just a closeknit community—they were like a huge extended family. She'd always heard that it took a village to raise a child, but most people, at least in the United States, didn't have the means to make it a reality. Whether it was a matter of time, of money, or of feeling increasingly isolated from one's neighbors despite the ever-increasing population, she'd never seen that old saying put into practice before now.

She rubbed at her chest. She loved her parents and brothers, but this closeness was something she'd never experienced as a child. Her brothers had been much closer to each other than to her and had spent most of their time glued to video games. And her parents…

Callie knew her parents loved their children, that they'd worked hard to provide a good life for Callie and her siblings. But they'd never…let go. They'd never allowed themselves to be silly, to be carefree, to roll around on the ground as their kids dogpiled them.

Not like Urkot.

*God, he'd make a good father.*

Eyes widening, Callie halted.

*Why the hell did I just think that?*

Because it was true. Urkot was protective, kind, considerate, and as gentle as he was strong. He loved his friends like siblings and had wholly accepted the humans as part of his family. And seeing him now, playing with the broodlings…

*He would make a fucking amazing father.*

Callie had never thought about having kids. At least, she had never thought about having them soon. She'd always been focused on her career. Being a mother had been a possibility for the murky, far-off future, once she'd established herself. When she'd joined the HWI and committed to the one-way journey to Xolea, she'd known it would've been expected of her eventually, though it never would've taken priority over her mission. She'd been a chemist foremost. A vital specialist, crucial for the success of the colony.

But now, watching Urkot playfully growl at the broodlings and them growl and chitter back, she felt as though her ovaries were about to explode.

*One step at a time, Callie. You're not even mates!*

*Yet. We're not mates yet.*

Because she had her sights set on a target, and she was going to take her shot.

As though he'd heard her thoughts, Urkot's bright blue eyes flicked toward her. They flared.

Callie smiled wide and closed the distance between them, stopping beside him. "The mighty Urkot has been defeated."

His mandibles rose in a vrix smile. "They will make fine warriors."

With one chubby little fist, Akalahn took hold of Urkot's mandible, staring at it like it was the most amazing thing he'd ever seen.

Urkot's eyes softened as he gazed at the child. "Or weavers, potters, delvers…whatever they choose, they will be most good."

*Well, that's it. My ovaries just exploded. I'm a goner.*

Mindful of the broodlings crawling atop him, Urkot rolled onto his side, positioned his thick legs beneath him, and pushed himself upright. While he was considered short by male vrix standards, his powerful frame towered over Callie. She couldn't stop her gaze from roaming over him as he plucked a broodling off his chest to set upon the ground.

*Stop staring, Callie. He's going to notice.*

Blinking, she shook off her stupor and met his gaze as he straightened. She gestured toward the rowdy game going on nearby. "Why aren't you playing?"

"Too tired."

Callie laughed. "So you chose to wrestle with a bunch of kids instead? From what I've heard, taking care of one baby is exhausting enough, but six?"

Chittering, Urkot lifted an arm. Honuhn, Garahk and Nalaki's son whose hide was as white as his father's, dangled from the limb.

"Different tired," Urkot said. "More good tired."

Callie smiled at the broodling. "Considering all the work you and the other delvers did to make this place a starlit wonderland, you deserve a break."

Urkot tipped his head back to look up at the crystals glowing above. "You like it?"

Moving a little closer to him, she peered up. "It's beautiful. Makes me want to do the same thing in my den, so I can feel like I'm looking at the stars every time I go to sleep."

"All you need, Callie, I will give," he rumbled, his voice barely audible over the music and shouting from the game.

She lowered her gaze to find him staring at her. There was a glint in his eyes, but it was no reflection; it was an inner light, a fire, heated and heavy, that said far more than his words. It was a vow.

When he told her he would give all she needed, he wasn't talking about crystals alone. He was promising much, much more.

Warmth flooded her and pooled low in her belly.

A swell of voices rose over the music, drawing Callie's attention to the game. Many of the vrix, including Garahk, were holding their sticks high in the air.

Cole thrust his arms straight up, raising his stick in both hands. "Victory!"

The broodlings holding onto Urkot dropped to the ground and scurried to their fathers as the game dispersed. Mandibles raised, Ketahn swept his son up and greeted Ivy with a dip of his head, pressing his headcrest to hers. Callie's heart squeezed seeing the tenderness and love they shared.

Cole leaned his stick on the rack with the others and jogged toward Callie and Urkot, grinning. His bare chest and arms glistened with sweat.

"That was a fucking blast," he said.

Callie chuckled. "You looked like you enjoyed yourself. You rocked it out there."

"I can hold my own, doesn't matter how big they are." He ran a hand through his damp hair as he smirked at Urkot. "You'll have to join next time. I've got wins against Rekosh and Ketahn now. You and Telok are next on my list."

"I must say no," Urkot replied.

"Too scared?"

"No, I am protective of my tribe. Your pride would take a wound too big for you to survive."

Cole laughed. "Ouch, man. When you strike, you strike deep." He looked back to Callie and swept his gaze over her. "Damn, you look hot in that dress."

"Aw, thank you." Grinning, she grasped the sides of her skirt and spun in place, letting the silk flare. "Probably the prettiest dress I've ever owned."

He waggled his eyebrows and leaned close. "Do I get a victory kiss?"

Callie pressed her fingers to his chest and gave him a push. "Even if you weren't all sweaty, it'd be a no."

Growling, Urkot gnashed his mandibles, making his fangs clack as he inserted himself between Callie and Cole. "Come, human. I will give kiss."

Cole chuckled and took a step back. "Nah. I'm gonna pass on that."

"You want a kiss for victory, or kiss from her?" Urkot pressed, advancing the same distance Cole had retreated. There was tension in him that hadn't been present a moment ago, making the muscles of his broad back taut.

"It was a joke, Urkot," Callie said softly, placing a hand atop his hindquarters.

He let out a heavy breath, and she watched him gradually ease.

"Just a joke, man. Besides, I'm not into spiders." Cole lifted his hands to his face to mimic mandibles. "These just don't do it for me."

The remaining tension bled from Urkot, and his mandibles fell. "You think I am ugly?"

Callie scoffed. "Cole! How could you?"

"Woah, woah!" He threw his hands up. "I never said that."

Urkot looked at Callie, bowing his head. "He does not like me."

She didn't miss the mirthful glimmer in his bright blue eyes.

Cole lightly patted Urkot's shoulder. "I'm sure you're a fine specimen…for a vrix."

"Callie, do humans have other words for much big sad?" Urkot asked.

"Jesus," Cole said as he ran a palm over his face. "Look, it's not you, it's me, okay?"

Callie propped her hands on her hips. "Really, Cole? You're going to use that line? Like that makes it better after the damage you've done to this poor vrix?"

He retreated, walking backward as he thrust a thumb over his shoulder. "I'm just gonna…go get a drink."

Cole turned and hurried away, disappearing into the sea of vrix.

"Coward!" she called after him with a laugh. Turning back to Urkot, she softened her smile. "I think you are very handsome."

Urkot trilled and stood a little taller and straighter. He eased closer and leaned into her, his rich, earthy scent flooding her senses. Its warm, spicy notes, reminding her of brandy, were intoxicating. That scent settled over her mind in a fog, obscuring her thoughts.

He caught a strand of her long hair on his finger and lifted it from her shoulder. "The dress does not make you beautiful, Callie. You are beautiful."

Callie's breath hitched. His interaction with Cole had been playful and teasing. This was completely different—it was evident in the intent in his eyes as they held her gaze, in the steadiness of his deep voice, and in the care with which he pronounced each word in a language he'd learned just to communicate with Callie and her friends.

He wasn't simply being nice. He meant what he'd said, and she felt it.

The heat that had suffused her core earlier came rushing back, making it clench.

"Thank you," she said softly, unable to look away from his glowing eyes.

Urkot's chest swelled as he drew in a deep breath. A rumbling sound, not unlike a purr, emitted from him, and he shifted a foreleg, brushing it along her calf. Her skin tingled at the delightful contrast between his rough hide and his soft, fine hairs.

"Callie, your scent..." He grunted, and a tremor coursed through his body.

Her cheeks burned.

*Ah, yes. Vrix and their super senses of smell. And this one is smelling just how much he's turning you on.*

What was there to do other than own it?

"Mmhmm." She placed a palm on his warm chest and leaned close. "It's because I *like* you, Urkot."

Releasing her hair, Urkot flinched back, legs scuttling over the ground as his eyes flared. He stared at her, silently, and blinked, cocking his head in an oddly birdlike fashion.

He was too stunned to speak.

Callie chuckled, lowering her hand. "I guess you weren't expecting that?"

His mouth opened, closed, and opened again, but no words emerged. Finally, he shook his head.

She crossed her arms over her chest with a smile. His reaction was adorable.

Bending forward slightly and raising her chin, she asked in a sweet voice, "Do you like me, Urkot?"

Determination and certainty sharpened the light in his eyes. "Yes."

It would always amaze Callie how such a small, simple word could be so profound, how it could bear immense meaning and weight far beyond what should've been possible.

"Oh," she said softly. This time it was her turn to be caught off guard. She'd hoped, but she hadn't expected such an admission to come so readily, so honestly. So unwaveringly.

Urkot stepped forward again, eliminating the space he'd opened between them. He reached for the small pouch hanging from the leather belt around his waist. Untying the knot, he slipped his hand inside. "I have a gift for you."

He produced a small, folded silk cloth, resting it on his palm. With another hand, he carefully unfolded the cloth to reveal what was inside. A cubed chunk of white, clear stone. Calcite. Cut and polished with care.

"Oh Urkot..." Callie picked up the stone and studied it. Glimmers of light from the crystals above and the nearby bonfire shone on the calcite's surface, making it seem like it had its own glow. He'd gifted her many, many stones, but this was her favorite so far.

She closed her fingers around the calcite and drew it to her chest. "It's beautiful." Rising on her toes, she pressed her lips to the side of his face. "Thank you."

Urkot's body stiffened until she began to pull away. His hand darted up, catching her jaw and halting her, keeping her face angled up. Voice low, gravelly, and commanding, he said, "Do that again."

Callie grinned. "As you say."

She moved to kiss his cheek once more, but before her lips made contact, Urkot turned his face toward her, causing her mouth to press to the hard crease of his.

A gasp of surprise escaped Callie. His grip on her tightened as a shudder coursed through him. He released a breath, which flowed over her lips.

"Oh, you sneaky vrix, you," she whispered with a chuckle. She flicked her tongue out against his mouth, teasingly tracing the crease, then swiftly pulled out of his grasp, taking several steps back.

Urkot's breaths came harsh and fast through his nose holes, and his body was tense as he lowered his hand. Callie didn't miss that his claspers shifted, one crossing over the other to press down on his slit. She knew exactly why he was doing it, and it sent a rush of arousal through her, pouring heat into her core and making her nipples harden.

That arousal only intensified when his blue tongue slipped out and trailed slowly, deliberately, across his mouth as though he were savoring her taste.

*Oh, fuck me.*

What would it feel like to have that long, thick tongue stroking her pussy? Pushing inside her?

Would his cock be that same shade of blue?

*Whoa now, Callie. You know you want him, but that doesn't mean now. Slow down, girl.*

But God was it hard to take it slow when it had been *so* long. Especially knowing how sexually satisfied Ivy and Ahmya had been, and how desperately Callie's body was yearning for touch.

A distraction. That was all she needed. Something to get her mind off thrusting tongues and blue cocks.

*Stop it!*

The beat of the drums pounded through her, urging her to move to its rhythm, to surrender to instinct—but not *that* instinct. Not sex, but something achingly close. Something just as primal. Something she could lose herself in just as thoroughly.

Callie reached out, took hold of Urkot's upper right hand, and gave it a tug. "Dance with me, Urkot."

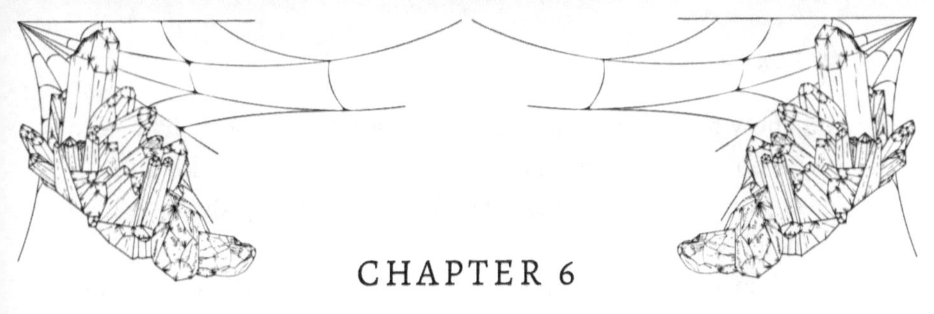

# CHAPTER 6

As though Callie's sweet, seductive scent weren't enough to overwhelm Urkot, as though her words hadn't pierced his hearts to resonate along his heartsthread in a ceaseless thrum, now she'd taken his hand. Her small, soft hand had closed around his big, rough one, and she was leading him to dance.

Urkot had never danced. He'd never been chosen by a female.

But Callie was choosing him now.

He offered no resistance as she drew him into the crowd of thornskulls. For the first time in his life, his body felt light, agile, as though he were floating like a cloud. He was led not just by her hand, but by the invisible silk thread that bound them. A thread that was bringing them closer and closer.

He couldn't have resisted if he'd wanted to.

Callie glanced at him over her shoulder, and their gazes locked. Her warm brown eyes held such depth, such emotion, such tantalizing heat. If he stared into them long enough, he would find peace and happiness. He would find everything he'd ever craved.

Though he did not understand human mating rituals, this

somehow felt like one. It was not the solidifying of their bond, it was not the declaration of a claim, but it was something intimate. Something important. He felt it in the way she held his hand, felt it in his hearts.

When she stopped and turned to face him, the rest of the celebration ceased to exist. The rest of the world ceased to exist. There was only Urkot and Callie.

She released his hand. He fought back the instinct to reach for her, to grab her and draw her close.

Keeping her eyes locked with his, she began to move.

Urkot had seen her dance before, but this...this was different. Her body swayed from side to side, arms rising slowly, hands delving into her hair. Every part of her moved in time with the drums, so perfectly that it seemed as though she were dictating their beat.

It was slow, sensual, beckoning, drawing his attention to her every curve, accentuating the unique way her body could move, making his stem stir behind his slit and his hands itch to be on her skin.

This was a mating dance. It had to be.

And she might as well have ensnared him with a rope and drawn him in.

He stepped to her and trailed his fingers across the silk on her belly as he circled behind her. Callie didn't shy away from his touch, and her eyes didn't leave his until he was at her back.

Urkot encircled her with all three of his arms, drawing her against him. A shudder wracked him as she pressed closer. He could feel her heat through the silk, could feel the softness of her dark brown hair on his hide, and her scent... It overpowered everything around them. Earthy and sweet, but now it was enriched by the headiness of her desire.

Desire...for him.

Unbidden, Urkot's claspers stroked her hips.

Her arms draped around his neck as she danced against him,

and his body swayed along with her, complementing her motions. He lost himself in the rhythm, in the fluid movements, in her feel and her smell and her nearness. Lost himself in her.

Each brush of her ass against his sensitive slit sent a torturous pulse of pleasure to his core. Only his stony resolve held back his surging desire and denied his instinct to claim the female in his arms, but every bit of delicious friction between their bodies was like the strike of a pick, chipping away at a crumbling rock.

When he claimed Callie, it would not be before the eyes of others. He would not share any part of her. She was his alone.

Callie turned her head and tipped her face up, meeting his gaze. Those dark, dark eyes glittered with reflected light from the crystals. Her lips curved as she cupped his jaw, her fingers on either side of his mandible. "Urkot…"

"Callie!" a chorus of human female voices called.

Both Urkot and Callie's faces turned toward the voices. Lacey, Ahmya, and Ivy hurried toward them, with Rekosh and Ketahn trailing behind.

Callie dropped her hand and stepped away from Urkot. "Hey!"

The females gathered around Callie, taking her hand and tugging her farther from Urkot.

Urkot stood rigidly in place. He gritted his teeth and fought back the urge to snarl at the females for daring to take Callie from him, his hearts pounding more thunderously than the drums.

"Come dance with us," Ahmya said.

"We need some more girl time," Ivy said. "And Ketahn's not much of a dancer."

"I dance," Ketahn said, narrowing his eyes.

"You're too stiff."

"Rekosh is a really good dancer," Ahmya said.

Rekosh chittered and leaned down to nuzzle her hair. "I am,

but you females go. Enjoy yourselves." His crimson eyes shifted to Urkot, gleaming with a knowing light. "We will have some… male time."

Ivy released Callie and walked up to Ketahn. She wrapped her hand around the back of his neck and pulled him down, pressing her mouth firmly to his as she grinned. Very quietly, she said, "We'll perform the mating dance later."

Ketahn trilled, brushing his foreleg along hers before she withdrew to join the other human females.

As the group led Callie away, Lacey stepped up to her, peeking at Urkot. "Did I seriously see you kiss Urkot earlier?"

The hide around Urkot's mouth tingled with the memory of Callie's lips, so soft and warm. Callie glanced back at him, smiling a sultry little smile, but she was already too far away for him to make out her reply to her companion.

Had Rekosh and Ketahn not moved directly in front of him, Urkot would've given chase. Even now, some part of him demanded he shove his friends aside and go after Callie. She was his. How could he let her go? How could he let her be taken from him?

He needed to be as stone, unmoving, steady, controlled. Everything he felt was too new and intense, and he could not let it seize him. He could not surrender to this…this…

Frenzy.

That was the word. This was the onset of a mating frenzy. He'd resisted the pheromones of female vrix, had gone through his whole life without feeling even a shred of such desire. Callie had unraveled him in a single, all too brief dance.

And in the aftermath of that dance, his entire body throbbed and ached, and his hide thrummed with the ghost of her touch —of her rubbing against him, of her hair brushing his chest, of her arms around his neck.

What would it feel like to have her slit close around his

stem, to have his shaft buried in her soft body? What would it feel like when she came undone around him?

He had no experience with mating. He knew only what little he'd heard. Yet the strength of what he felt for Callie, the depth of it, only made his yearning for her all the stronger.

His claspers cinched tighter around his slit, intensifying the ache behind it, and he dragged a hand down his face. He needed to turn his mind away from such matters. But there seemed to be room only for her in his head.

*Is that so bad a thing?*

Rekosh chittered. The sound broke Urkot from his thoughts, calling his attention to his friend.

"Powerful, is it not?" the red-marked vrix asked.

"What do you mean, weaver?" Urkot scraped a foreleg over the ground in an attempt to force the lingering tension out of his limbs.

"That desire, Urkot."

Urkot glanced at Ketahn for aid, but Ketahn simply folded his arms across his chest, a hint of an amused glint visible in his eyes. Little Akalahn, who had been so vigorously playing not long before, was sound asleep in a basket strapped to Ketahn's back despite all the noise.

Huffing, Urkot shook his head. The heat inside him had taken on a different feeling, skittering under his hide. "Speak plainly, Rekosh."

The tall, spindly weaver leaned close to Urkot—far closer than was necessary—and whispered hoarsely. "You long for Callie. Long to claim her and rut her."

With a grunt, Urkot planted a hand on Rekosh's chest and shoved him away.

Rekosh chittered as he stumbled back a few steps.

"It does not take eight eyes to see you have wanted Callie for a long time," Ketahn said, his mandibles ticking upward. "You alone did not accept it."

"Why would I not accept my own desire?" Urkot asked as that insidious heat strengthened. He felt as transparent as the crystal he'd gifted Callie, as though his friends were staring right into him to see his thumping hearts and everything they contained.

"Because you feared she would not want you in return," Rekosh replied in a gentle tone.

Those words coiled in Urkot's chest, squeezing everything, constricting his breathing. His hands curled into fists.

Rekosh brushed a foreleg against Urkot's. "I do not mean to anger you, my friend."

The weaver's familiar scent filled Urkot's senses. They'd known one another for many, many years, had grown into adulthood together and faced horrors and hardships as brothers. After the war, Urkot and Rekosh had spent more time with one another than any of their group—with Ahnset having been busy as a Fang, Telok often away hunting, and Ketahn having moved his den to the Tangle to escape Takarahl.

As much as they teased one another, they'd never sought to inflict hurt. Not once in all those years.

"I know." Urkot forced his fingers to loosen and his limbs to relax. "This need... The frenzy was clouding my mind. It..."

"We know how it feels," Ketahn said solemnly.

"All too well," Rekosh agreed.

Urkot inhaled slowly, shoving off the weight of their conversation, before looking between his two friends. "We are missing someone. Is Telok about?"

Chittering again, Rekosh glanced around. "If he is, he is using all his skills to remain out of sight."

Carefully, Ketahn adjusted the lay of one of the basket straps across his chest. How a bit of movement could've jarred the broodling when all this sound had not was a mystery. "He does not care for such gatherings. Never has."

Urkot huffed and stomped a foreleg. "We should drag him

here regardless. He helped hunt for this food, and he is part of our tribe, part of Kaldarak. He is our family. Why should he not be here?"

Rekosh let out a thoughtful hum. "He will join when he is ready."

"He should not hide himself away."

"None of us should." Ketahn was staring directly at Urkot, gaze heavy but nonjudgmental.

Mandibles twitching, Urkot looked past Ketahn toward the human females, who were dancing not twenty segments away.

His eyes naturally fell upon Callie. There was something different about the way she danced now. It was carefree, joyous, reflecting the wide, radiant smile on her face and the laughter in her sparkling eyes. Her movements weren't sensual and seductive, but playful. And they were no less mesmerizing.

He could not help but look upon her with wonder. Her smooth brown skin, her curly hair, her soft lips and rounded curves. Her spirit, burning ever bright. Her mind, so quick, so knowledgeable. She was unlike anyone, and he wanted her for his own.

*And she wants me.*

Unbidden, a trill escaped him.

"You would have thrown a hundred barbs at me had you caught me staring at Ahmya like that a few moon cycles ago," Rekosh said.

"Seems this is your opportunity," Urkot replied, not looking away from Callie.

"My opportunity or yours, stoneskull?"

Urkot blinked, finally breaking his gaze away from Callie to look at Rekosh, and cocked his head.

"You are not unworthy, Urkot," Ketahn said, bumping a leg against Urkot's. "You deserve happiness as much as any of us."

"You have simply been too hard-headed to see it," Rekosh added.

"Perhaps you are right." Urkot chittered to himself, swinging his attention back to Callie. "Just like you to pierce my hide, needlelegs."

"So you will finally stop pretending you do not want her? It has grown rather exhausting."

"I want her. All of her, now and for the rest of my days." Urkot drew himself taller as a new sensation filled his chest—a new certainty. "I will claim her as my mate. As my everything."

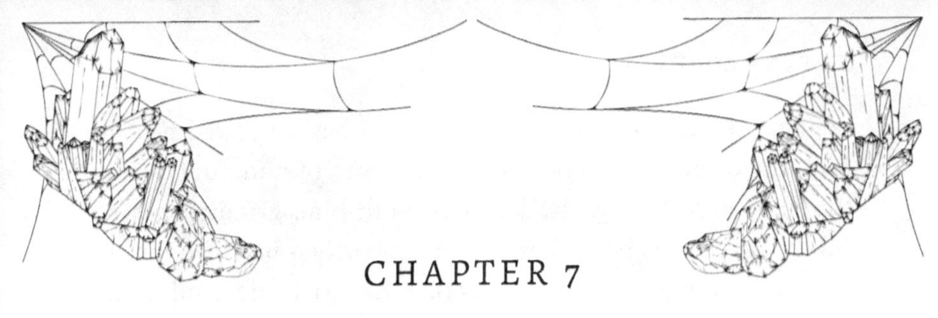

# CHAPTER 7

EXCITEMENT BUBBLED within Callie as she followed Ahgratar into the wide cave mouth, her pack bouncing against her back. The atmosphere change was instantaneous. The sounds from the jungle dulled, and the sunlight faded with each step, allowing darkness to close in all around. Only the glowing crystals on the walls and the one in the orange thornskull's raised hand lit the way. Every few yards, crude lumber supports braced the walls and ceiling, reminiscent of the ribs of some huge beast.

She clutched the handle of the basket she was carrying. Anxiousness fluttered alongside excitement in her belly.

The moment she'd overheard Ahgratar announce he was bringing food to the delvers, Callie had pounced on the opportunity, offering to help carry the food.

Urkot was down here.

It wasn't simply a chance to explore a cave, but to see him, to spend time with him. To witness Urkot in his element.

Callie tucked her hair behind her ear as she peered around the thornskull and looked down the eerily dark tunnel ahead.

She didn't understand her nervousness at the prospect of

seeing Urkot. Only three days ago, she'd bathed naked next to him, had even spanked her own ass in front of him. And during the festival yesterday, she'd danced with him, grinding not so subtly against his body. His desire for her had been evident in the hard bulge behind his slit against her backside. And Callie had taken pleasure in it.

She had kissed him, had told him she liked him. She'd been anything but shy.

So why this timidity now?

Maybe it was because she was looking at Urkot in a different light. He wasn't just her friend. He was…more. And *more* was new, thrilling, unknown. Even a little frightening.

What she was experiencing was the kind of giddiness someone felt around a crush. And God, she hadn't felt anything like this since high school. But this felt like…*more*.

The ground sloped downward, and Callie touched the rocky wall for support, thankful for the treads of her boots despite how worn they'd become. While the floor was mostly flat and clear of hazards, she didn't want to risk a slip.

The jungle sounds were long gone, replaced by the scrapes and taps of her escort's legs on the cave floor and the gentle crunch of tiny stones under her feet. Gone were the scents of vegetation and flowers and hot humid air, overtaken by the earthy smell of stone. The air was cooler in here, the sensation pronounced by her blue crop top and skirt, which barely covered her ass.

Even when she wasn't touching them, she could feel the walls around her. It felt like they were pressing steadily inward, shrinking the space between them. Some primal part of her brain recognized this place as a trap—she was stuck down here with nowhere to run, no room to move, to breathe, to—

*Take it easy, Callie. You're fine.*

Callie drew in a deep, calming breath. Urkot was down here

somewhere. He did this every day, and he'd lived underground in Takarahl for most of his life. Everything was all right.

When the ground finally leveled out, another sound, faint but distinct, echoed through the tunnel from somewhere ahead. The steady clacking of tools against stone.

"Almost, hoo-man," Ahgratar said in English.

*Oh, thank God.*

"Great!" Callie replied with a smile.

As exhilarating as it was to finally be inside a real cave, it was also terrifying. She'd spent most of her life in the city, which had often felt claustrophobic, but at least she'd been able to look up and see that sliver of sky whenever she'd wanted. She couldn't do that here.

And that wasn't even taking into account the dangers beyond slips and falls, like cave-ins, deadly gas buildups, getting stuck in tight passages, flash floods…

*And I wanted to do this for a living?*

She probably wouldn't have survived her first day.

Right now, it was Urkot that drove her onward.

Ahead, she glimpsed a spot where the blue glow was more concentrated. It seemed like a trick of her eyes at first, but as they neared it, she realized it was an opening into a chamber off the main tunnel. That was where Ahgratar turned.

He entered the chamber first, and Callie followed close behind. The thornskull called a greeting to the vrix within and declared that he'd come with food. But Callie barely heard their enthusiastic responses. Eyes wide, she could only focus on the chamber itself.

She understood then how thoroughly the vrix had shaped the tunnel they'd followed to get here. These walls were crude, uneven, natural. And they were covered in countless crystals growing in clusters and formations, bathing the space in brilliant blue luminescence.

This was like standing inside one of those geode lamps. Her

brain insisted it couldn't be real; places like this only existed in fantasy stories. And yet here she was.

The delvers had been gathered near the far end of the chamber, though most had ceased their work to come meet Callie and Ahgratar. She smiled and greeted them in their tongue as she and her companion pulled back the cloths over their baskets and offered food.

But even as the eager thornskulls took seasoned meat from her basket, her eyes drifted back to the pair who were still working—a large, yellow male thornskull and Urkot, whose blue markings had taken on a new radiance in this light. The two were hammering a rough-hewn log into place as a support, securing the above crossbeam against the ceiling in the process.

She found herself admiring the way Urkot's muscles flexed and stretched as he worked. It wasn't merely the power in them, it was the control. Amongst the shadowstalkers in their tribe, Urkot had always seemed the least agile, the least graceful, but she realized now how precise and deliberate his movements were, like each was carefully calculated.

"Zotahl, Three-Arm, come before the food is gone," Ahgratar said, his booming voice carrying over the others' chatter.

Zotahl gestured sharply with one hand in acknowledgement. Neither he nor Urkot looked away from their work until they'd adjusted the log a little more. Seemingly satisfied with its positioning, they turned toward Ahgratar.

Urkot's eyes flicked to Callie and opened so wide it was almost comical.

Grinning, she raised her hand and wiggled her fingers in a wave. "Hi."

His eyes narrowed to furious slits, and he stormed across the chamber. Before Callie could back away, he caught her arms with all three of his hands, his grip tight. The basket slipped from her grasp and fell to the floor.

"Why are you here?" he growled,

Callie gasped as she stared at him in shock. "Ahgratar was coming, so I—"

Urkot's head snapped toward Ahgratar, and in vrix almost too fast and angry for Callie to understand, demanded, "You brought her here? Damn your eyes, why?"

All the thornskulls were staring at him now, their eyes flared. One had paused his hand partway to his mouth with a piece of meat dangling from his fingers.

Ahgratar held up a palm to Urkot. "She gave aid, Three-Arm. There is no harm."

"She should not be down here! It is not safe." Urkot swung his gaze back to Callie and shifted back to English. "I said do not come."

Callie quirked a brow. "No, you said *no*. You never told me not to come, specifically..."

"It is not safe. *No* is simple, yes?" He released her arm with one hand and dragged his palm down his face with a frustrated groan, leaving a steak of white on his hide. "You knew my words. Knew my meaning."

"But that doesn't mean I'm going to obey."

"In this you obey!" Urkot snarled.

Callie flinched, stunned at the ferocity in his voice and his tightening grip on her arms, which she was sure would leave bruises. Fire sparked in her chest, quickly burning away her startlement. She glared at him. "Don't yell at me, Urkot."

He opened his mouth, paused, then snapped it shut with an audible *clack*. His hand returned to her arm, and he guided her away from the others, toward the back of the chamber. Once there, with his large body blocking her view of the thornskulls, he tilted his head forward and closed his eyes. His shoulders rose and his chest expanded as he took in a deep inhalation.

"I did not yell," he said finally, calmly.

"You got all snarly with me. That's the same thing."

And it had surprised her. Urkot had never raised his voice to her before, especially not in anger. This…this wasn't like him.

She frowned as she studied him in the crystals' glow. He was tense, and she felt faint tremors coursing through his arms.

This wasn't rage. This was…fear.

For her.

There was something he was hiding, something that pained him deeply, and her presence here had triggered it.

Her indignation disappeared as swiftly as it had come.

"I'm okay, Urkot. Everything is okay," Callie said in a soft voice. Leaning forward, she touched her forehead to his head-crest. "I…just wanted to see you."

He released a heavy breath through his nostrils. "You can see me in Kaldarak."

Callie chuckled softly. "I wanted to see you now and bring you food."

"Ah, Callie… Hard-headed female," he said gently.

She smiled and pressed her head a little more firmly to his, nudging it as she settled her hands on his chest. "Takes one hard head to know one."

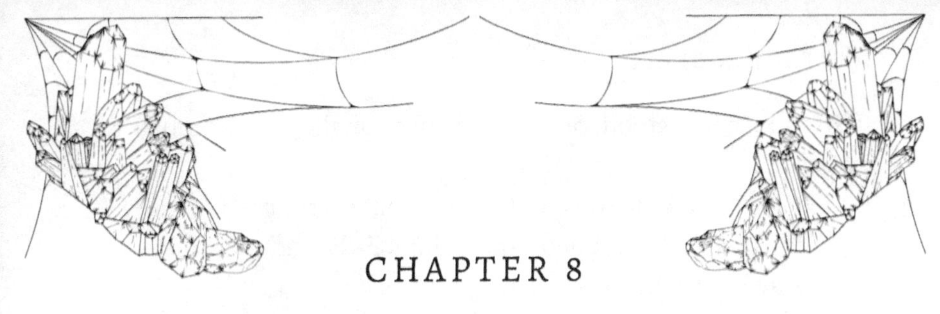

# CHAPTER 8

Urkot chittered. He couldn't argue with her, not any more than he could deny how right it felt to have Callie so close to him, headcrest to forehead.

For vrix, this was amongst the greatest displays of trust. Such closeness, with mandibles within easy striking distance, was reserved only for the most meaningful relationships. And she had initiated this. Despite her small, fragile body, despite his size and strength, she had been the one to enter this vulnerable, intimate position.

*I...just wanted to see you.*

For someone to have made the journey here just for him—to see him, to feed him—and for that someone to be Callie… How would he ever be able to express what that made him feel? How would he ever explain how light and energetic his spirit felt, how full?

Even if he didn't have the words, he could no longer remain silent. He could no longer hold it all inside. He would not waste these opportunities.

He took a deep breath, steadying himself. "Callie, I—"

A faint tremor coursed through the ground beneath his legs.

His fine hairs stood on end. Insides tangling into knots, he hissed.

Callie's brow furrowed. "Urkot? What's wrong?"

"Must go," he replied, snatching Callie off her feet and drawing her against his chest.

As he spun toward the chamber's entrance, the reverberating sound of cracking rock rent the air, louder and more unsettling than a thousand bones snapping at once.

The cave floor buckled.

Urkot's stomach lurched, and he stumbled despite having all six legs on the ground.

He heard the thornskulls shouting, and he glimpsed them scrambling to right themselves. The tremor became a deep rumbling, and the knots within Urkot pulled taut, sinking low.

*No! Delver, please! Not here, not now.*

*Not her!*

The ground crumbled beneath him. His hearts halted, caught in the cold, crushing grip of terror.

*Callie.*

Cupping a hand behind her head and squeezing his eyes shut, he curled his body protectively around her. They clung to one another as the ground swallowed them.

All was chaos and pain and deafening noise. Rocks battered and scraped Urkot's tumbling body from all sides. Dust choked him and burned his throat and lungs. The rockfall swept them down, down, down, on a river of roiling, unforgiving stone.

Through that eternity, which spanned impossibly few heartbeats, he remained most aware of Callie. He felt her body, her grip, her nails biting into his hide, felt her reacting to every jolt. He felt her screaming against his chest, even if he could not hear her.

Only his racing hearts overcame the din.

He came to a hard stop atop a bed of jagged rocks with Callie beneath him. More stone rained onto Urkot, and he strained with one arm to keep as much of his weight off her small, soft body as he could even as more stones piled atop his back, increasing his burden. His upper right arm trembled, his muscles ached, and he growled in fury, in despair, in determination.

And then there was stillness, accompanied by a silence so deep that a high, piercing tone filled his hearing.

His eyes snapped open. Dust hung thick in the air, made more difficult to see through due to the faint glow of the crystals spread throughout the surrounding rubble. As that dust settled atop him, it seemed as heavy as the stones crushing him.

Tremors wracked his body, and his ragged breaths tore through his throat. Ghostly pleas for aid and cries of agony rose within his mind, accompanied by a tang of blood that cut through the dust; he did not know if the scent was real or remembered, but it did not matter. Those calls…

His hearts quickened, and the tremors intensified. He squeezed his eyes shut once more.

But there was no safety in the dark, no silence, no solace. Just that crushing weight, that smell, those desperate cries, and helplessness.

"Urkot?"

His softly spoken name came from far away as the cries and the piercing sound, growing louder and louder, rang in his head.

"Urkot?" someone repeated, louder this time, breaking through the cacophony in his mind as frantic hands moved over his chest, shoulders, neck, and face, until finally they cradled his jaw and angled his head down. "Urkot! Say something! Please!"

He forced his eyes open. Callie was beneath him, her skin and hair covered in white dust. Her eyes, those large, beautiful brown eyes, were pools of concern and fear as they gazed up at him.

She was alive.

They were alive.

"Callie," Urkot rasped. He clutched her tighter, unwilling, unable, to let her go. Afraid to let her go. Afraid that what he was seeing wasn't real, that he had failed and she was lying lifeless in his arms.

"Oh, thank God," she breathed in a rush. "Are you okay? Are you hurt?"

"I..." Urkot's chest was tight, making each breath a struggle, and countless new pains throbbed all over his body. The voices had retreated, but that weight continued bearing down on him, both within him and atop him. "I am okay. Are you—"

Callie coughed, her body jerking. When she drew in rasping breaths, he felt the strain in her chest, felt the tension in her muscles. She was trapped, caught between him and the harder, uneven stone beneath.

He was crushing her.

"I think I'm okay," she said once the coughing subsided, voice strained. She wiggled her feet, but they didn't budge from where they were pinned. "My...my legs hurt, but I don't think anything is broken. Are you okay?"

"We must move, Callie. Not safe." Bracing a hand on the rubble, he pushed his torso up. But when he attempted to move his legs, they met considerable resistance—the rock piled atop them was trapping them in place, and he would not easily free himself.

A few smaller rocks came free, tumbling down the pile with a series of *clacks* that echoed in the darkness.

Urkot's hearts thundered as those voices threatened to swell again. He clenched his jaw and fought them back. He was here, now, with Callie. Keeping her safe was all that mattered.

He released her with his other upper arm, planting it on the rock below like the first, and tightened his hold on Callie with his lower arm. "Hold me. Tight."

She wrapped her arms around his neck without hesitation.

"Do not let go."

"I won't."

Urkot drew in a deep breath, ignoring the burning in his lungs. With a snarl, he dragged himself forward, pushing with his arms and legs. The weight of the stone atop him continued its resistance.

*I will not let this be our end. I will not let Callie share the fate of so many others I have lost.*

Gritting his teeth, he called upon all his strength. His body trembled with the exertion, but he did not relent, even as more rocks came free and fell around him. He felt rough stone scraping his hide, felt everything atop him shift as his hindquarters and legs began to come free.

With a great heave, he thrust himself forward, tearing the lower half of his body free. Callie cried out beneath him. The pain and fear in that sound chilled him to his core, but he could not tend to her yet. He curled around her again, caging her with his arms and legs as he tumbled down the rubble. Stone fell behind them with a great clamor, a second rockfall triggered by his escape.

When he felt the solid cave floor beneath him, he scrambled away, cradling her against his chest. The sound was thunderous. Callie clung to Urkot, arms around his neck and face buried against him.

Her warm, heavy breath against his hide was a source of comfort; so long as she breathed, he had not yet failed.

Urkot pressed his shoulder to the wall. Keeping his back to the rockfall, he shielded her body with his until the sound of falling stones finally ceased, leaving only his and Callie's ragged breaths to break the silence.

"Is it safe?" she asked.

He lifted his head and glanced over his shoulder. Though fresh dust had risen, it wasn't as thick as before, and it was the only thing moving behind them. "For now."

Carefully, he stood up, setting Callie on her feet before him. Aches and pains radiated through him from the tips of his legs to the point of his headcrest, but he gave them none of his attention. Instead, he stepped back, placing his hands on Callie's shoulders as he looked her over.

She was covered in pale dust, which made it easier to spot the places where blood welled from her broken skin. He turned her. Her pack had protected her back and shoulders from the rocks, but her thighs and calves...

Her cry echoed in his mind.

Urkot growled as he lowered himself to the ground, hands dropping to her hips to keep her still. The skin on the backs of her legs had been too delicate to withstand the harsh, jagged stone where they'd been pinned.

"Callie..."

Twisting her torso, Callie looked down at him and settled a hand atop his. "I'm okay, Urkot. They're just scrapes. They'll heal. It... It could have been much worse."

Urkot let his head fall forward, pressing it to her lower back as he closed his eyes and clutched her hips.

It could have been much, much worse. His Callie could have been taken from him. But she was here, alive. He could feel her softness beneath his palms, could feel her heat, her touch.

A tremor wracked him as he breathed in her scent.

"I am sorry," he whispered in vrix.

"Hey now," she said gently, turning in his hold.

Before he could raise his head, she cupped his jaw. He opened his eyes and gazed up at her.

"Don't do that. We're okay." She brushed her thumbs along the sides of his face and smiled. "We're alive, and that's what matters. We'll figure the rest out."

He flexed his fingers upon her hips, tempted to draw her closer. Instead, he nuzzled her palm, relishing her touch and her scent. But it was too dangerous to remain here, and the others...

*The others.*

Urkot jerked up. Callie lowered her hands and took a step back, giving him space as he turned to look at the aftermath of the rockfall.

They'd dropped into another tunnel, and the rubble was piled to the ceiling, allowing not even a glimpse into the chamber they'd come from. Dully glowing blue crystals were scattered amidst the debris, shedding soft light.

The walls of the crystal garden must've collapsed as well. Gods, but it didn't seem possible that he and Callie had survived relatively unscathed.

*Thank the Protector for shielding us.*

"Zotahl?" Urkot called, stepping toward the rubble. "Tahlken, Enikor?"

His voice echoed off the walls, becoming a hollow mockery of itself.

Callie slowly approached the rockfall. Her sharp gasp rang through the chamber. She climbed atop a larger boulder, but Urkot thrust his foreleg out, stopping her from going any further.

She whipped her face toward him, pointing at the rubble. "There, Urkot! I see one of them!"

He followed her gesture with his gaze, and his hearts stuttered. An unmoving, dust-coated yellow arm jutted from the stones near the ceiling of the tunnel.

Zotahl.

*No. No...*

Urkot had witnessed such stillness before. He was all too familiar with it, but that made it no easier to accept, no easier to bear. He struggled to draw adequate air into his lungs. Crackling heat coursed beneath his hide, and his head felt suddenly light, making the tunnel sway and rotate around him.

Callie pushed against his leg, breaking past it and climbing up the rocks. A few came loose, tumbling down, snapping Urkot out of his daze.

"Callie, no!" He strode forward and banded an arm around her waist, lifting her off her feet and pulling her back against his chest.

She wriggled, trying to get free. "We have to help them!"

"Callie—"

"Put me down!" Callie demanded as she tried to pry his arm from her around her middle.

Wrapping his other arms around her to combat her struggles, Urkot carried Callie away from the rocks.

"Urkot, I can help! We can't just leave them in there!" Clenching his arm, Callie turned her tear-filled eyes up to his. "Why aren't you helping them?"

A pang of guilt struck his chest, piercing him as surely as any spear could have. His stride faltered. Urkot sank down onto his bent forelegs, keeping Callie clutched against him. He lowered his head, resting his headcrest against the back of her hair as shivers coursed through him.

"Flamebearer, guard their *shar'thai*, that they may join the spirits of their ancestors," he said softly in vrix. "May the flames of their spirits burn as brightly in death as they did in life."

He meant each of those words with all his hearts, but they felt hollow, felt useless. Felt pointless. What comfort could he provide for those who were already gone? Why would they want anything from him when he'd been unable to protect them in life?

"No," Callie breathed, shaking her head. A sob escaped her. "No, no, no, no. T-They can't be dead. They're *not* dead. We just...we just need to help them, Urkot. We can dig them out. Please."

"If we dig, more stone will fall...and we will join the others."

"No!" she cried. "He's r-right there. We can see him. If we, if we…"

Her shallow breathing, already rapid, quickened and grew more strained. He could feel her heart racing in her chest in an alarming flutter.

Urkot turned Callie to face him. Tears flowed from her eyes, having already carved paths through the dust on her cheeks, and she was trembling. His chest ached; he could not bear to see her this way. She didn't deserve to experience this pain, this terror.

"Callie…"

Hiccupping, she turned her head as though to look back toward Zotahl. Urkot stopped her by taking her face between his hands and guiding it to his.

"Look at me, female," he rumbled, voice steady despite his tumultuous emotions.

Her glistening eyes met his. The fear and helplessness in their brown depths were crushing.

Leaning down, he touched his head to hers, keeping their gazes locked. "Breathe, Callie. Breathe with me."

He took in a slow, deep breath, letting his chest swell with it despite all the pressure inside. Though it took her a moment with her hiccupping, she did as he instructed. They exhaled together with the same slowness, pushing through the shakiness of their breath. As they breathed in and out, they continued staring into each other's eyes, and he kept his hands on her face, unwilling to let her go.

They existed with each other, for each other, sharing breath, sharing life. It was all they had in that moment, and it had to be enough.

Callie closed her eyes and leaned her head a little more firmly against his as she placed her hands on his chest. She whispered, "I'm okay."

Urkot crooned and brushed his claws through her curls. "Good, female."

"I'm sorry for what I said, Urkot. I didn't mean it. I...I know you would have helped if—"

"Shh. I know, Callie. I know. It is okay."

She released another shuddering exhalation before raising her head and turning back toward the rockfall. Her glistening eyes shone in the dim blue light. "Are we trapped here?"

Reluctantly, he stood up again and set Callie on her feet. He strode to the edge of the rubble and gazed over it once more. There was no sign of the chamber above, and no way to tell how much stone was caught in the opening, awaiting an opportunity to fall.

He hummed, low and deep. Something felt wrong here. He'd seen cave-ins before, when tunnel walls and ceilings weren't properly reinforced, but this had been different. This lower tunnel had weakened the floor of the above chamber, but the shape of this corridor wasn't natural.

Bending, he plucked a glowing crystal shard from the rubble and stepped to the wall.

His eyes narrowed as he brushed his fingers over the stone. The grooves and chips it bore were unmistakable.

This tunnel had either been expanded or carved out by hand.

His attention caught on another set of marks on the wall. These were different. Four thinner, shallower lines, running parallel to each other, with the bottom one shorter than the rest. They hadn't been left by any tools.

Unease spread through Urkot.

Raising a hand, he set his fingers over the marks. His claws lined up perfectly with the grooves. Slowly, he traced the lines with his fingers.

They were claw marks...left by a vrix.

His fine hairs stood on end as his foreboding grew. It was at that moment that he felt it—the faintest breeze through those hairs, a barely-perceptible flow of air along the tunnel, leading deeper.

He looked down the tunnel. The crystal glow continued for only a few more segments, leaving gaping darkness ahead. But that darkness was connected to the surface somewhere.

"We cannot go back," he said, finally returning his attention to Callie. "But we are not trapped."

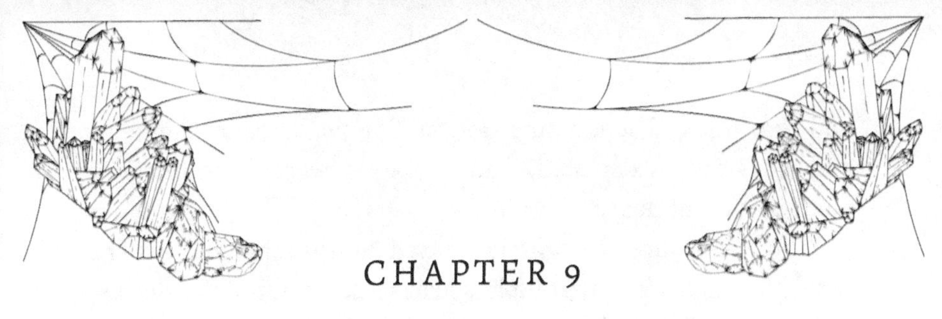

# CHAPTER 9

CALLIE TRAILED behind Urkot with her thumbs hooked under the straps of her backpack and her eyes downcast to watch her footing. Thankfully, her solar lantern, held aloft in one of Urkot's upper hands, cast a bright white light along the passageway, making it much easier to avoid tripping or rolling an ankle. She could only hope it would last long enough for them to find a way out of this place.

This tunnel was nothing like the one she'd followed Ahgratar into. The floor was uneven and covered in rocks, and the walls fluctuated erratically between wide and narrow, and were slanted at such steep angles in spots that Urkot had to duck low to get through.

Besides the sounds of their steps, it was ominously quiet. That silence was oppressive. Any other sound, such as the occasional clatter of a rock, was like booming thunder, putting her more on edge. She was sure the roof would collapse on them at any moment.

Callie squeezed the straps as she glanced past Urkot, deeper into the dark, winding tunnel. Who could say how far they'd have to walk? They could have miles and miles of travel ahead, and that was a discouraging notion. She was already mentally and physically exhausted, and her eyes were tired from a combination of dust and crying.

Too often, her thoughts returned to the chamber where they'd fallen, back to that lifeless arm sticking out of the debris. Too often, her thoughts returned to the other delvers.

Were they trapped elsewhere?

Had any of them made it out, or...

Were they all dead?

Callie didn't want to contemplate that. She had to believe some of the thornskulls had survived, that they'd escaped the crystal chamber, that they'd reached safety. She couldn't... couldn't...

She couldn't come to terms with the horrific reality that they'd likely all been crushed to death.

And she and Urkot could've shared that fate. Had he not acted so quickly, had he not grabbed her and safeguarded her with his own body...

They'd been impossibly lucky to have survived with nothing more than sore muscles, bruises, and minor cuts and scrapes.

She looked at the vrix in front of her.

Whatever she felt must've been inconsequential compared to what Urkot was enduring. He'd been the one the rocks had fallen upon. He'd been her shield, her shelter from the storm, protecting her while his body was battered. And he'd lost his companions.

Her chest tightened, squeezing her heart, and she wiped her eyes as she fought back tears.

*Fuck, I've never cried this much.*

Everything was going to be okay. They had a goal, they had each other, and they would get through this. Callie had to stay strong, had to believe they'd make it out of here safely. She refused to wallow in despair.

Her brow ceased as she studied Urkot. In the lantern's harsh light, the pale dust covering his body made his old scars stand out in relief. Would any of the little wounds he'd suffered today add to those scars? Would his body, already marked by a lifetime of conflict and struggle, bear new marks after this?

It was comforting that his gait was normal, though he moved with purposeful caution. Not so comforting was the tension in his posture. It was in the set of his arms, the tightness in his shoulders and their slight hunch, in the way his head swiveled while he scanned the tunnel ahead. And the light was strong enough to highlight the fine hairs on his legs; they'd been standing all this time.

Callie and Urkot had been through danger, had been through crises. Urkot had often been the one to cut the tension with a bit of humor, to lift everyone's spirits by being a solid, dependable, positive presence. This silence wasn't like him.

He was on alert. For more cave-ins, or something else?

Tilting her head, she frowned. "What's wrong, Urkot? I mean"—she waved a hand—"besides the obvious."

Urkot halted, shoulders rising with a deep breath. Callie stopped beside him.

Mandibles twitching, he huffed and gazed down at her. "In Takarahl, there are stories told to all delvers. Old stories. They tell of vrix deep understone, with pale hides and unending hunger."

"Okay, that sounds…sinister. What do you mean by unending hunger?"

"The stories tell that they will eat anything they can find. Anyone they find."

"Wait, wait, wait. Are you talking about cannibalism? That there are vrix that *eat* each other?"

"Yes. They are called spiritstriders."

Callie gaped at him. "Oh, that's so fucked up."

"A big time ago, spiritstriders made war on shadowstalkers. They took many shadowstalkers alive, to sacrifice to gods buried in the deep...and to devour them. But shadowstalker strength was too much for them. They fled into the darkest tunnels, and my kind closed those tunnels to keep the spiritstriders from returning.

"But when I was a broodling, we were told to take care because spiritstriders would await in the tunnels, taking lone delvers and dragging them into the darkness below."

"That's horrifying to tell a child," Callie said, aghast. Being scared of monsters under the bed was one thing, but human parents usually went out of their way to diminish such fears. To have a parent say that there were ravenous creatures lurking in the darkness, waiting to steal you away and eat you...

How had Urkot lived with such fear?

"Delving is danger," he replied, his words thick and raw with sorrow. "Better to be aware and afraid than to not know. I have never seen a spiritstrider...yet vrix would sometimes vanish in the tunnels. Perhaps they were just lost... I do not know. But most were never seen again."

Rubbing her bare arms as though it could rid her of the deep, sudden chill in her bones, she glanced down the tunnel into the darkness the light didn't reach. "But that's just a creepy ass story, right? There aren't really spiritstriders down here."

When he didn't answer right away, she looked back at him. "Urkot? They're not really down here, right?"

But he'd turned to stare in the direction from which they'd come, mandibles again twitching. "Where the rocks fell... There were marks on the walls. Claw marks in stone." Urkot again met her gaze. "I do not think we are alone here."

Callie's eyes widened, and words burst from her before she could stop them. "The fuck you say?"

Her voice reverberated along the tunnel, echoing back at her.

Urkot banded an arm around her middle and covered her

mouth with his hand as he looked, wide-eyed, toward the darkness.

Silence returned.

Barely above a whisper, he said, "We must keep our words soft, Callie."

She stared up at him as that deep-seated cold spread through her body.

He kept his attention on the tunnel. "I do not know if the marks were made by vrix or by beast. But if there are spirit-striders in these tunnels, they may have heard the rockfall. They may come. We must be away."

"Are we going to die?" she asked against his palm.

He turned his face toward her, and those bright blue eyes locked with hers. "No," he said vehemently. "I will protect you."

Urkot stroked her hair with his hand and caressed her cheek with a thumb. "*Nothing* will harm you, female."

They continued onward silently, Callie with a fresh batch of anxiety, following the uneven tunnel as its downward slope brought them deeper and deeper into the earth. Urkot kept her close, helping her over some of the looser stones and larger boulders. Though he didn't speak, his presence alone was calming.

There were crevices in the walls, too low and narrow for Urkot to fit through, but that didn't stop Callie's imagination from running wild. She expected to see glowing red eyes staring back at her from those shadowy openings, or clawed hands reaching out to grab her and drag her into the abyss.

*Stop it, Callie. That's not helping. You're just freaking yourself out.*

A new sound broke the silence. It was faint at first, but constant, and grew in volume as they walked. Soon, she was able to identify it—the burbling of running water.

She was glad to have something to counteract that stifling silence besides their echoing steps.

When they reached a section where the ceiling hung low, Urkot stopped and held a hand up to her. "Stay. I will see."

Callie grabbed the wrist of his lower right arm. "I don't want you to go alone."

His eyes softened as he looked at her hand. Gently, he pried it from his wrist and gave her the lantern. "I will be much fast, Callie."

"*Please* be careful."

He reached into the pouch on his belt and took out a chunk of glowing blue crystal. Brushing his knuckles over her cheek, he offered her a vrix smile. "I am most careful."

That touch, combined with his smile—no matter how different it was from a human's—made her heart flutter.

And then his warm fingers were gone from her skin, leaving her feeling cold as he turned away, dropped low, and crawled beneath the ceiling. She clutched the lantern to her chest, keeping her eyes on him until he was out of sight. Over the sound of the water, she heard the crunch and scrape of his hide against the stone and loose pebbles. Those sounds disappeared too soon.

Callie bit down hard on her bottom lip as she waited, looking once more down the tunnel behind her.

The lantern's glow was a blessing and a curse, warding away the dark but making everything beyond its light impossibly, impenetrably black. She felt like she was in the last pocket of existence in a vast void, surrounded by nothingness.

"Callie, come," Urkot called.

She knelt on the rough stone and peered under the low ceiling. He was crouched on the far side, dimly lit by the crystal in his hand, the blue markings on his limbs glowing in its light.

"Okay," she breathed. "I got this."

She removed her backpack and set it before her, opening it up. She switched off the lantern and flattened it into a compact disc. Her heart leapt at the darkness that enveloped her. With shaky hands, she slipped the lantern into her bag and closed it up.

Ducking down, she looked toward Urkot. The crystal's blue glow was stronger now that it wasn't overpowered by bright white light.

"I'm coming." On hands and knees, she crawled forward, pushing her bag along before her. She did her best to ignore the bite of the stone against her palms and legs.

"Good, female," he said. "Come."

God, this was *not* the context in which she wanted to hear those words in his deep, rumbling voice. She would've preferred hearing them while he was above her, thrusting his big, thick co—

*Not the time, Callie!*

*Why not? It's a good distraction from the possibility of this ceiling collapsing on me, and from the claustrophobia, and the danger of being eaten by a vicious cave vrix.*

*Bring on all the kinky spider sex!*

"Now you are a delver too," Urkot said as she neared, derailing those spicy thoughts.

She chuckled. "I'm not gonna make a habit of it."

When she pushed her bag close enough for him to reach, he dragged it toward him. Then his hand was there, waiting for her. Callie crawled the remaining distance, and once her head was clear of the ceiling, she placed her hand in his, allowing Urkot to help her to her feet.

She'd emerged in another tunnel, perpendicular to the one she'd just exited. A fast-running stream lay before her, its waters flowing downslope to her left. Its surface shimmered with reflected light from Urkot's crystal. The air was damper here, carrying that clean, freshwater smell.

"We can rest here and wash," Urkot said, gesturing to the water. "I will check your hurts."

Callie nodded, grateful for the respite. She was eager to get the gritty dust off her skin, certain that it would chafe her inner thighs were she to walk much farther.

She removed her boots and studied the stream. The water was clear, and she could see the pebbles at the bottom, but the faint reflections of the walls and ceiling made it difficult to judge the depth. "Is it deep?"

Urkot grunted, extended a foreleg, and dipped it into the stream. When it stopped, the water hadn't even reached his first leg joint. "No."

"Great. And, uh…there's nothing in there that's going take a bite out of me? Nothing venomous?"

Fuck. She hadn't even considered all the unsettling creepy crawlies that'd be skittering around this place. Thankfully, they hadn't come across any.

Yet.

"In small water like this, only small fish." To demonstrate, he lifted his upper hands, holding his palms only a couple inches apart. "It is safe.

"If any fish nibble on my toes, you can't blame me for screaming," she warned as she stepped into the stream. The water rushing past below her knees was colder than expected, making her skin break out in goosebumps. She wiggled her toes; the pebbles on the streambed were thankfully smooth.

Bending down, she splashed her legs, biting back a hiss even though she took care with the abrasions behind her thighs. Despite the flares of pain, the cool water was a balm to the wounds. In front of her, Urkot set the crystal on the ground and stepped into the stream to clean the dust from his hide.

She washed her arms and scrubbed her face. Short of dunking herself under the water—which she wasn't about to do —there was nothing to be done about her hair and clothing besides a brisk shake and a pat down.

Once they'd both washed off most of the dust, Urkot

approached Callie. Without a word, he braced his hands on her hips and lifted her out of the water.

Callie gasped.

He set her on her feet at the water's edge and turned her away from him. It wasn't even a moment before his palms were on the outsides of her thighs, raising the back of her skirt.

"Urkot!" she squeaked in surprise, looking at him over her shoulder. "What are you doing?"

"Tending you."

Why did those words sound so fucking sexy?

*Because he can tend to me any way he wants.*

"Oh." She faced forward. "Okay, um…tend away."

He curled his big, rough hands around the fronts of her thighs, fingers hooking over the sensitive flesh of her inner thighs, and spread her legs farther apart. Her heart fluttered in response, and heat kindled low in her belly.

It wasn't just the position of his hands, no. It was their strength, their surety.

The shadows on the cave floor shifted as he moved the crystal. He leaned closer, and she felt his hot breath on the backs of her legs, the sensation pronounced by the cold water clinging to her skin.

His upper hands shifted to her outer thighs and slowly slid down. So, so slowly. Their touch was startlingly light, which made it all the more delicious. She'd never experienced such sweet friction.

When he hummed unhappily, she swore the sound vibrated into her, threatening to coalesce in her core. One of his thumbs brushed the back of her thigh, just beneath a scrape, and the tip of his claw grazed her.

Callie barely suppressed a shudder as that inner heat flared.

His hands continued their downward trek with remarkable steadiness.

How? How could he be so calm and in control when this

simple touch was building pressure in her core, pooling desire in her belly, and setting her every nerve alight?

It had to be a result of...of adrenaline, right? After their near-death experience, she was simply feeling everything at a heightened level. This was just a natural biochemical response to what they'd been through.

His hands glided lower, and his thumbs skimmed the backs of her knees. A thrill coursed through her. She caught her bottom lip between her teeth and grasped the front of her skirt in both hands, clutching the fabric.

God, she wanted his hands all over her body. Wanted him to touch her *everywhere.*

Did he even realize what he was doing to her?

*If you don't calm down, Callie, he's gonna start smelling exactly what you're thinking pretty damn soon.*

She heard him move behind her, but she didn't dare turn to look. Instead, she focused on the stone ahead, slightly visible in the dull blue light. A few minutes ago, she'd been desperate to think about anything but cannibalistic ghost vrix prowling these primordial caves, but what other thoughts could possibly distract her from the things Urkot was making her feel now?

"I am sorry," he rumbled, curling his fingers around her ankles and squeezing gently, comfortingly. "I tried to shield you when we fell."

He brushed the callused pad of a thumb up her Achilles tendon, and she nearly whimpered at the tenderness of the gesture. But it was his words, filled with pain and guilt, that cut through the desire he'd roused in her.

"You have nothing to be sorry about, Urkot," she said, finally turning her head to look down at him. "You risked yourself to save me. My skin will heal. What matters is that we are both alive."

Even if his hard, masklike face couldn't change, his blue eyes shone with all the emotion his voice had expressed. But there was something beneath all that, something unwavering and unbreakable. A solid stone core that became more apparent as he spoke.

"We will leave this place, Callie. Alive and together. We will feel the touch of the sun again. I weave my words into a bond, stronger than any thread."

Callie's chest constricted at the conviction of his vow, and she told herself once more that she would not cry. Instead, she smiled. "Stronger than Rekosh's?"

Urkot chittered low and deep, his mandibles rising. "He spins words of silk. I carve them in stone. Mine will always be stronger."

She chuckled, glad that she was able to lift his spirit, at least a little. She caressed his face. "We will leave this place. Together. I carve these words next to yours."

Holding her gaze, he nuzzled her hand, tenderly scraping his rough mouth against her skin. It tickled her palm and reignited the warmth in her belly.

The soft sound he made was very close to a content purr. That a small moment like this could mean so much and be so soothing, despite everything they'd been through, was a wonder to Callie, and she would hold onto it forever.

Urkot released one of Callie's legs to cover her hand with his. He pressed her palm more firmly to his face before guiding it down. A nudge on her shoulder had her facing forward again.

"See? Bossy," she said with a chuckle.

"Not bossy. Urkot," he grumbled, not without a hint of humor.

Callie couldn't help the grin that spread across her face. She loved it when he was bossy.

She felt him moving behind her, but she didn't know what he was doing until his fingers touched one of her larger abrasions, covering it with a familiar substance—the sticky silk the vrix used to seal wounds.

Though the pain caused by that touch was brief, she flinched. Urkot crooned, his deep hum creating a lovely melody with a powerful resonance. It was surprisingly pleasant.

While she wouldn't have believed it months ago, that sticky silk put her at ease. Perhaps it was only in her head, but that didn't matter. Better to have the wounds securely covered than exposed to all the dirt and germs and who-knew-what down here.

With continued care and consideration, he treated her other larger scrapes with more silk, crooning that same soft tune whenever she reacted to the pain.

She couldn't help but imagine a very human scene—little Urkot, sniffling and upset, running to his mother with scraped legs, and her crooning to him just like this as she covered his wounds with silk.

Would he do the same for his children?

She recalled the way Urkot had played with the broodlings during the festival and knew she already had the answer.

When he finished applying the sticky silk, he stepped back and crouched, scooping up handfuls of water and pouring them into his mouth. As he drank, she grabbed her boots and pulled them on. She straightened to find him holding a handful of water up to her.

"Drink, female," he ordered.

She smirked. "And you say you're not bossy."

Chittering, he moved his offering closer.

Callie cupped the underside of his hand, leaned forward, and drank. The water felt wonderful on her tongue and down her throat. She hadn't realized how parched she was until that moment. He offered her another drink, and she accepted it gratefully.

When she was done, she wiped the water trickling down her chin with the back of her hand as Urkot grabbed her pack.

"We must be away," he said, swinging the bag around behind

her and helping the straps over her arms. He turned his hindquarters toward her and held out a hand. "Come, Callie. Ride me."

"You know I'm capable of walking just fine, right?"

"Save your strength."

"You need to save your strength too, Urkot."

"I am strong. Always."

"Hard-headed male," she muttered as she took his hand and carefully threw her leg over his hindquarters. He was the one that had taken the brunt of the cave-in.

Urkot chittered. "Takes one hard head to know one."

Wiggling her bottom, she adjusted herself until she was straddling him, legs on either side of his waist. She pressed herself close to his back and wrapped her arms around his broad chest.

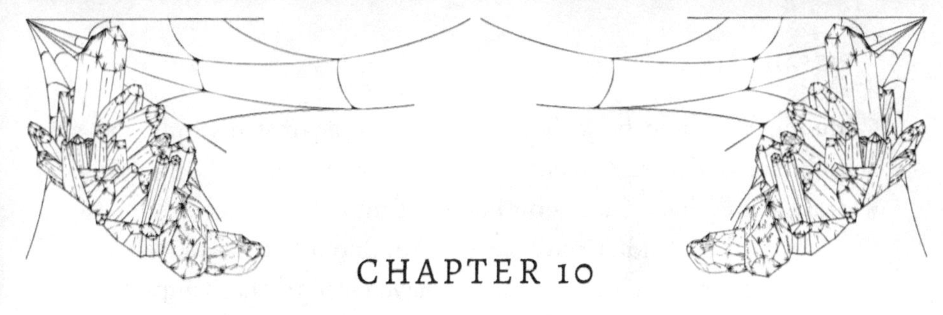

# CHAPTER 10

WATER SLOSHED around Urkot's legs as he strode along the stream. The aches wracking his body had deepened, making his muscles stiff, but he ignored them as best he could. Better some soreness than broken bones.

The thornskull delvers flashed through his mind—their faces, their colorful hides, their voices and chitters. Swallowing fresh guilt, he forced the memories away. What had happened could not be changed. What was lost could not be reclaimed. Guilt would not bring back the thornskulls, and neither would it carry Urkot and Callie to safety.

Callie stroked her thumb over his abdomen, calling his attention to her arms, which were wrapped around his torso. He curled his lower arm over them, holding them snugly in place.

She was here with him now, holding him, and she was as much the reason he was still moving as his own toughness or the grace of the gods. He needed to protect her. Needed to save her.

Yet her presence left him conflicted.

She was a comfort to him. Her warmth and weight upon his

hindquarters and back, her gentle breath against his hide, her hold, so tender and needful; all of it calmed him. Callie had dragged him back from looming panic more than once.

But she shouldn't have been here. Shouldn't have been in this dangerous situation, shouldn't have faced the hardships, the horrors, that she'd experienced today. Right now, she should've been safe in Kaldarak with the rest of their tribe.

The stream flowed along a gradual downslope. He was not happy about journeying deeper understone, but the airflow, subtle though it was, led in this direction.

Somewhere far, far ahead, there was an opening to the surface.

*Please, Gods, let it be one we can use.*

*And let the path to it be clear.*

The Eight would tire of his prayers before this ordeal was through…and he would surely tire of making them. He'd always honored the Eight, especially the Delver, who watched over all vrix who plunged into the unknown, be it in the depths of the ground or the jungle.

"So, are you going to say I told you so?" Callie asked, her voice scarcely loud enough to hear over the sound of water.

Urkot tilted his head. "What did you tell me?"

Callie chuckled. "I mean, are you going to tell me that you were right. That I should have listened to you and stayed out of the cave. You said it was dangerous and well…here we are."

He never wanted Callie to be in danger, never wanted her to suffer, and he would've preferred it had she avoided all of this by heeding his warning.

And yet…some part of him was glad she was here. Was glad he did not have to endure this alone. He wasn't sure if he could do this without Callie, lost in this darkness without her light.

"I was right," he said slowly, making sure he chose the correct words, "but you were right too. Danger is everywhere.

We cannot hide from it all. And it is better that we are here together than here alone."

He gave her arm a squeeze. He enjoyed the feel of her skin, enjoyed how soft and pliant it was.

She eased closer, pressing her chest firmly against his back. "Speaking of hiding... In case there are spiritstriders down here, couldn't we have done that while waiting for the others to try and dig us out? I thought when you're lost, you're supposed to just sit tight and await rescue."

"No one will know we are missing until next suncrest. And even if they come most fast, it will take days to clear the stones without delvers, if they are able to at all. Perhaps eightdays, if the rockfall went beyond the crystal garden."

"Oh. And the food was—"

He heard her mouth snap shut, cutting off whatever words she might've said, but he understood where her thoughts had gone. The food she and Ahgratar had brought was buried beneath the rubble. Lost, along with their thornskull companions. He and Callie had nothing except themselves, whatever she carried in her pack, and the few tools on his belt.

"We must go on," he said, instilling the firm words with as much gentleness as he could. Because he knew, in the end, the gods wouldn't do anything for them. Urkot and Callie had to keep moving forward, had to search, had to fight, had to survive, through their own strength and willpower.

The only thing that would get them out of this place was each other.

Eventually, the sound of the stream changed, becoming layered with an echoey hissing. Urkot discovered why when they reached the end of the tunnel.

There, the water flowed over a cliff, pouring into a deep crevasse.

Bracing his hands against the wall, he peered over the edge. Darkness shrouded the bottom.

Callie made a distressed sound and tightened her grip on him. "Um, the plan is to not go down there, right?"

"Right," he agreed, easing back.

A faint air current flowed from somewhere above, caressing his hide and the hairs on his legs. He raised the crystal in his hand, scanning the walls of the pit.

"So what's the plan now?" Callie asked. "Do we need to go back and follow the stream the other way?"

His gaze halted on an opening across the gap, several segments higher than their current position. He dragged his eyes up to the ceiling, which was another couple segments higher. Its stone was fraught with crevices and irregularities that would make for ample grips. It would be a long, slow climb across, but they had no other choice.

"We go on," he said.

"You said we're not going in the pit."

"We will not. We go up and across."

"Wait, what? What do you mean *across*?"

Urkot pointed up at the opening on the other side. "There."

Callie rose and leaned over his shoulder, her curls tickling his hide as she squinted to see. Urkot held the crystal higher. He often forgot that humans had poor vision in dim light.

"Oh fuck," she rasped. "You want us to go up there? Like, across this gaping pit?"

"Yes."

"But there's no path! And it's too far to jump, even for a vrix."

"Not jump. Climb." Urkot backed away from the edge and stepped onto the solid cave floor.

"Climb? Urkot, I can't climb that. There's nothing to even climb."

The fear and uncertainty in her voice was like a thorny vine constricting his hearts, squeezing and piercing deeper with each word. Reaching an arm back, he offered her a hand. She took it; he felt her arm trembling before he helped her down from his hindquarters.

Once she was on her feet, he turned to face her, placing his hands on her shoulders. She met his gaze with wide eyes.

"You will not climb, Callie," he said.

Her eyes flicked toward the chasm.

He hooked a finger under her chin to draw her attention back to him. "Hold me. That is all you must do."

"Won't you be holding me?" Her voice was uncharacteristically small.

Urkot lifted his mandibles and chittered. "Not enough arms."

She scowled at him. "That's not funny, Urkot. This is...it's..."

"It will be fine," he said, withdrawing his upper arms from her to hold up both thumbs in a gesture he'd learned from Cole. "Two fines, see?"

That earned the ghost of a smile from her, barely more than a twitch of her lips—but it was something.

Collecting a wad of sticky silk, he attached it to his glowing crystal before pressing that crystal to his headcrest. He tipped his head toward Callie. "Say good?"

He felt the crystal slowly tipping forward, stretching the silk.

She laughed, shaking her head. "Goofball." She held out her palm. "Give me some sticky string."

Chittering, he produced a small strand and handed it to her, ducking lower so she could secure it around his head, fastening the crystal in place.

Callie lowered her arms. "That should hold."

"Thank you." He straightened and began drawing silk from his spinnerets, passing it to his hands in a thick strand. "My silk will hold you, and you will hold me. We have climbed together many times, yes?"

She nodded. Her pink tongue slipped out briefly to wet her

lips, and it took everything in him not to fixate on the gesture. Everything about her fascinated him, called to him, but her mouth, her tongue...those were especially alluring.

He wrapped the rope around his waist and tied it tight before reaching around Callie's waist to do the same. He gave it an extra, playful tug, drawing her closer and disrupting her balance. She chuckled as she fell into him, her palms slapping his chest.

"We are bound, female," Urkot rumbled. He settled his upper hands on her hips and lifted her up against his body, cradling her ass with his lower hand to keep her steady. "Now wrap yourself around me."

Cheeks darkening, Callie stared into his eyes as she wound her arms around his neck and her legs around his midsection. He felt her thigh muscles tense as she drew herself closer.

Urkot's breath caught.

Heat—delicious, tantalizing heat—caressed his abdomen where her bare slit pressed to him.

His fingers flexed, digging into her giving flesh as a shudder coursed through his body. He became even more aware of her warmth around him, of her sweet, delicate scent, of her soft, smooth skin. His claspers stretched upward, curling around her thighs.

He never could've guessed how right it would feel to have her in this position, how tempting it would be, how thrilling. Nor could he have known how difficult it would make everything. How would he safely climb when all he could focus on was the press of her slit, the feel of her body? How was he meant to think when her scent filled his mind in a fog?

"You promise you won't drop me?" Though Callie's breath was delightfully warm on the hide of his neck, her words brought him clarity.

He held her tighter. "Never."

Rather than succumb to the temptation to remain like this, just the two of them, Urkot returned to the cliff's edge.

His hearts thumped. The danger of this undertaking was not lost on him, nor were the likely consequences of failure. Callie's safety, her life, was his responsibility. Nothing else was as precious, even if the universe was eightfold larger than the impossible vastness the humans had described.

Urkot glanced down. Not even his eyes, after years of working in near complete darkness, could penetrate the blackness below. It was alarmingly easy to imagine spiritstriders lurking down there. Visions of pale vrix swarming up from below, hissing and growling as they scaled the chasm walls, danced on the edges of his mind.

A shudder threatened to course through him, and he gritted his teeth to hold it back. Callie had been unsettled enough by his talk of spiritstriders; she did not need to see the truth of his unease.

He turned his back to the pit, ignoring the way it made his fine hairs rise, and released Callie.

She gasped and squeezed him tighter. Fortunately, even without the support of his arms, she remained snugly in place, aided by his claspers.

"I have you," Urkot rumbled.

"I know," she murmured against his neck.

After drawing another strand from his spinnerets, he reached up and attached it to the roof of the tunnel with sticky silk. He was overly thorough, using more than was likely necessary, but he refused to take chances when Callie's life was in danger.

Keeping the strand unbroken, he shifted toward the side of the tunnel. The crystal tied to his headcrest cast its soft glow upon the bare stone, leaving erratic shadows on its craggy surface.

Urkot ran his hands over the stone, seeking adequate handholds. As soon as he found some, he drew in a deep breath and pulled himself up. His muscles strained. The punishment they'd endured in the rockfall was too recent, and the brief stop to wash in the stream hadn't afforded him any rest.

He willed the discomfort away. There was only one way to go, and it certainly wasn't down.

Urkot planted four of his legs into crevices on the wall and climbed higher. With his rear legs, he pulled out more silk and carefully passed it to his lower arm, attaching it to another point on the wall.

Callie trembled against him, her body tense. She kept readjusting her fingers, digging her nails a little deeper into his hide whenever she did so, as though fearing she'd lose her grip.

Her will to survive was strong, and he feared they would need as much of that strength as they could muster to make it home.

"Good," he rumbled as he neared the ceiling. "Much good, Callie."

"It's fine," she replied spiritedly. "I'm fine. Not scared at all."

Urkot knew that wasn't true, and it only made him admire her more.

Fastening the strand to the ceiling, he hooked his forelegs around it, braced his middle legs against the wall, and used his upper hands to grasp the stone overhead. Slowly, he pulled himself outward, tipping his body horizontally.

"Still fine," Callie breathed, somehow tensing further as her weight settled atop his torso.

The urge to wrap an arm around her was almost overwhelming. Resisting it certainly didn't help the strain in Urkot's body.

He forced himself to breathe slow and steady, holding himself in place as he pulled more silk with his hind legs and passed the slack to his lower hand. Had he not been battered and bruised in the rockfall, he wouldn't have felt the exertion quite so soon or as thoroughly.

Urkot attached the rope to the ceiling again, a little farther from the wall. He hooked the previous section with his middle legs and carefully moved his forelegs to the next, drawing himself along the ceiling and away from the wall with his hands. His body was now fully suspended, his weight held by the rope.

Callie shifted her head to glance over his shoulder. She immediately buried her face against his neck. He could barely make out her hasty, muffled words.

"Oh God, why did I do that?"

He didn't have to look to know what she'd seen. Yawning darkness beneath them, like a huge, shadowy beast waiting with gaping jaws for its prey to make a mistake—or tire out—and fall right in.

"Nothing to see," he said, voice tight as he drew more silk to attach to the next point and create a new section of rope.

"Not funny," Callie replied.

Chittering, Urkot moved his forelegs forward on the rope, again pulling his torso along. His abdomen burned, the muscles working harder than ever to keep his body straight and level. It almost made the strain in his hands, arms, and legs seem mild.

He tilted his head back to look toward the opening, and his insides twisted. It seemed so far away.

Urkot proceeded, carefully lengthening the rope to support himself, crossing the ceiling one segment at a time. Soon enough, his breaths grew harsher, heavier, and his aches grew deeper and more insistent.

Scalding pulses radiated through his chest and shoulders, his belly and back, his arms and legs. Tremors coursed through his limbs.

"We're okay," Callie whispered. "You got this, big guy."

He felt her heart fluttering against his chest, felt her rapid breathing, felt her trembling and her desperate grip. Felt Callie…and her fear.

Yet despite her fear, he did not doubt her belief and trust in him. And that made a difference. A true, significant difference.

He had given his word that he would protect her, and he would not break that vow. He'd cross a thousand such chasms the same exact way, never stopping, if that was what it took to keep her safe. He would always find the strength to push onward for her…

Because more and more, it was clear that Callie was the greatest source of his strength.

Just a few more segments. That was all he had to cross. A few more segments, and this ordeal would be through. Then they could slow down.

Ignoring the pain and discomfort, Urkot kept moving, repeating the same pattern until, finally, he reached the far wall.

He produced more rope, passing it up to his hands and attaching it to the cavern roof with an overabundance of sticky silk. Once it was secure and he'd given it a few good tugs to test its hold, he wound some of the rope around his hands.

"Hold tight, Callie."

Her arms and legs squeezed him. "I am."

Urkot slipped his middle legs free of the rope, and his body bowed.

The new diagonal slant made Callie slide down his torso. She sucked in a sharp breath and clung to him, but she hadn't moved even a handspan before her thighs hit the upper segments of his forelegs, halting her.

Once again, her core was so close to his slit, and after that friction, that tantalizing slide of her body against his, he—

By their eightfold eyes, even now? Even in this place, with all that had happened, and despite his pain and exhaustion, he could not deny the thrill of having her pressed against him so intimately. Without meaning to, without trying to, she could rouse such heat in his blood, could stir his stem.

"Sorry." Callie's face warmed against his hide.

No matter how tempted he was to discover how it would feel if she used those soft, full lips to trail kisses over his neck and chest, he did not allow his thoughts to stride that path.

And he could not allow himself and Callie to remain in this position indefinitely.

"Are we—" Her mouth snapped shut and her arms squeezed his neck as he tightened his claspers around her thighs and dropped his forelegs from the strand above.

"Still have you." The increased strain on his arms was instant as they took all his weight.

He and Callie dangled there. No more than a single moment passed, as fleeting as a beat of his hearts, but it came with the sense that the two of them were floating in nothingness. No stone to grasp, nothing above or below or to any side except air thick with darkness.

That should've been unsettling, even frightening, but with Callie holding him, with her being the only solid thing he could feel…it was almost soothing.

Slowly, he lowered himself along the hanging strand, using all three hands to ensure he maintained a firm grip. He extended his hind legs into the opening. As soon as they touched the floor of the passage, he reached out to grasp the tunnel wall with his lower hand and pulled himself inside.

Stumbling away from the cliff's edge, he braced his right arms on the wall and sagged against it. He felt like the weight of all the surrounding stone was collapsing upon him.

"Urkot." Callie drew herself more upright, one hand clutching his hair as she embraced him and pressed her cheek to his. "Let's fucking *never* do that again."

Chittering, he wrapped his left arm around her and breathed in her scent gratefully.

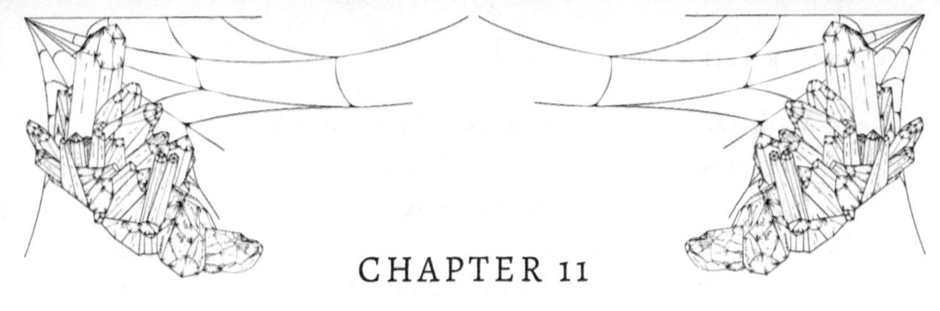

THOUGH CALLIE HADN'T BEEN the one to climb across a ceiling over a bottomless pit, her legs were unsteady as she released Urkot and planted her feet on solid ground. Heights had never bothered her much in the past. Hell, she lived in a tree house a couple hundred feet off the ground, and she walked across swaying rope bridges on the daily in Kaldarak.

But hanging over a dark chasm with nothing more than sticky rope holding you up was a whole new level of terrifying. She trusted Urkot, and knew he was unimaginably strong, but she'd felt the strain in his body. She'd felt the trembling in his limbs and the roughness in his breathing as he'd pushed his endurance to its limits and beyond.

That his body hadn't given out before reaching the other side was nothing short of a miracle.

With fingers stiff from clutching onto Urkot, she untied the silk rope binding them together and let it fall to the ground. Shrugging off her pack, she opened it and withdrew the waterskin.

"Drink," she said, holding it out to him. "I won't take no for an answer."

With a gentle chitter, he accepted the waterskin. "Bossy."

"Damn right I'm being bossy right now. Drink."

There was a gleam in his sapphire eyes before he tipped his head back and poured water into his mouth. After swallowing, he let out an appreciative sigh and offered the waterskin back to her. "Thank you."

Callie closed it and returned it to her pack. As tempted as she was to drink, they needed to conserve their supply for now. There was no way to know when—or if—they'd find a safe water source to replenish it.

When she looked back at Urkot, she couldn't stop a chuckle from escaping her. The crystal was still stuck to his headcrest, lighting up his face quite dramatically. She swung her backpack onto her shoulders, stepped close, and reached up to remove the silk from around the crystal, carefully prying the stone free.

"You know," she said, staring down at the clump of sticky silk as she rolled it between her fingers, "back on Earth, I freaked out anytime I came in contact with spider webs."

Urkot lifted a hand and peeled the remaining silk off his headcrest. "Because it meant there was a spider close?"

"Well, that too. But it was just a…gross feeling. Now I don't find it gross at all." She looked up at him and smiled. "Even if it comes from your butt."

He huffed. "It does not come from my butt."

"Whatever you say," Callie laughed as she flicked the small wad of silk away. "Why did this silk come off so easily, but the stuff you used on the rock held our weight without coming loose?"

"Not the same sticky." He shook his hand. The silk clung to his finger, refusing to come off until he finally wiped it away on the cave wall. "We can make it as needed. Thin or thick, much sticky or small sticky."

"Wow. Your spider butt *is* pretty amazing."

Crossing his arms over his chest, Urkot turned, giving her

his back, and twisted to look down at his hindquarters, which he wiggled. "You want to spank it, do you not?"

A laugh escaped from Callie. "You're serious?"

He tilted his chin down, his bright blue eyes boring into her in a way that promised wicked delights. "Give me a good spank, female."

*Holy fuck.*

This was a side of Urkot she'd never witnessed. It was unexpected and had caught her completely off-guard, but at the same time, it was arousing and exciting as hell.

"Well," she said, settling her hand upon his warm hindquarters, "I suppose you do deserve a reward for getting us across."

Callie slowly ran her palm down his hide, curling her fingers to lightly scrape him with her nails. She felt a shiver course through him, and somehow, the blue of his eyes darkened.

Drawing her hand back, she gave that sexy spider butt a firm smack.

His hindquarters twitched, and a low sound emanated from his chest, half growl, half purr. It made her pussy clench and spread heat through her core.

"I...take it you liked it?" she asked.

Because she had sure as hell liked his reaction.

He faced forward and lifted his lower right hand, beckoning her with a curl of his fingers. "Come. We must stride."

Callie blinked.

*Huh?*

Urkot started walking along the tunnel.

"Wait, what?" she asked, hurrying to catch up to his side. "I spank you and all you give me is *We must stride?*"

"Yes."

She frowned, all arousal and good humor washing away with her rising concern. He'd been nearly crushed by rocks during the cave-in, had carried her hundreds and hundreds of feet along the stream, and had hauled both of them across a chasm. She'd felt the strain in his body and could see the weariness in his eyes. Bone-deep exhaustion weighed upon her, and all she'd done was hold on to him. She couldn't imagine how sore and tired he was.

After that climb, she'd expected him to take a break. Now, she worried he was going to push himself too far.

Callie caught his arm, giving it a gentle tug, which brought him to a halt and drew his attention to her. "Urkot, you should rest."

"Soon." Urkot covered Callie's hand with his own. How could it be so big and rough, so callused, and yet so comforting and gentle? "We must go a little more. Will rest in a small time."

"Promise?"

He nodded and touched his leg to hers. "Yes, Callie."

They continued onward at a slow pace, constantly scanning their surroundings for potential hazards. She couldn't tell if he'd altered his speed for her sake or his own. Either way, she was grateful for it. He'd taken another crystal out of his pouch so she could keep the first. She'd offered to take out her lantern for more light, but Urkot had shaken his head and told her to save it until they truly needed it. For now, the crystals were the safer option, as their blue light was not out of place in these caves and would draw far less attention from any creatures lurking in the dark.

Callie requested a brief stop so she could relieve herself. She'd excelled at mountain-womaning it in the jungle, so why not tick off another checkbox by peeing in a cave? But the novelty didn't make the experience any more pleasant. She found a spot out of Urkot's view, but there was no hiding the sound.

Her face was aflame when she finished and rejoined him. Thankfully, he made no comment, and they walked on.

For the most part, the winding tunnel was spacious, and the

floor seemed to have been worn smooth by a no longer present water source. But there were spots where Urkot had to squeeze his broad shoulders and large hindquarters through narrow gaps, and a few points where they had to climb a little higher, only for the tunnel to slope back down. The temperature was noticeably lower than that of the crystal chamber. Callie wondered how far beneath the surface they'd gone.

"Do you still have family in Takarahl?" she asked, needing to break the eerie, stifling silence.

"Yes," he replied, his voice low, soft. "I was hatched in my mother's fourth brood. Many brothers and sisters in Takarahl."

"Fourth brood? How many broods did your mother have?"

"Six."

Callie gaped at him. "*Six?*"

Urkot nodded with a chitter and held up two hands, three fingers raised on each and thumbs folded. "That is this many, yes?"

Snapping her mouth shut, Callie nodded.

He lowered his hands, though his mandibles rose in a smile. "The way you said it made me think I gave the wrong word."

"Sorry. That's just… That seems like a lot."

His chitter was a little fuller this time, but he seemed to pull it back before it could get too loud. "Much broodlings."

During her time in Kaldarak, Callie had learned a lot about the vrix. They laid eggs, of course, and did so in batches they called broods. A single egg was a rare thing from what she'd been told. More common was three, four, or sometimes five eggs, though Rekosh had once said he'd heard of a female who'd laid eight eggs in a single brood.

That had been considered a fortuitous occurrence, given that the vrix held eight as a sacred number.

Urkot looked at her as they walked. "Do you have siblings?"

"I have two older brothers, Shaun and Xavier."

After she spoke, she came to a painful realization.

Her brothers were no longer alive. They were not going about their lives on Earth while she was here. They'd died long ago, while she'd been asleep on the *Somnium*.

And she'd always known that was going to be the case. She'd joined the Homeworld Initiative with full understanding that the journey to Xolea would take sixty years, that her parents would have passed by the time she arrived, that there'd been a good chance her siblings would've also been gone and their children would've had families of their own.

Being told that before boarding the ship was one thing, but it had only been words then. Not reality. It didn't matter that one hundred and sixty-eight years had passed instead of sixty; the result was the same. Everyone she'd known on Earth was gone.

Rubbing her arm, Callie lowered her eyes to watch her footing, trying not to let her emotions get the better of her. "My parents didn't want a big family. I...was what people would call an accident."

"An accident?"

"An unwanted pregnancy."

Urkot came to a sudden halt and turned toward her, his eyes narrowed. "They did not want you?"

Callie also came to a stop, nearly colliding with him. She chuckled and gave his chest a pat. "It's okay. I was wanted after they found out. They were busy with work, and two kids were already a handful, so my dad had a vasectomy a couple years after Xavier was born. Well, it apparently failed because"—she spread her arms to either side—"here I am!"

Once again, he touched his foreleg to hers, brushing it soothingly up the side of her leg from calf to mid-thigh. The sensation of his rough hide against her skin sent a thrill through her.

He reached out and twined a finger around one of her curls,

studying it. "I do not know *vah-secto-mee*, but I am glad it failed." His eyes met hers. "Much, much glad."

Urkot released her hair and turned, continuing along the passageway.

It took a moment for Callie to collect herself before she followed him. The light of the crystals in their hands pushed back the darkness ahead.

"Tell me of your brothers," he said.

Was he seriously acting like nothing happened after that oh-so-casual intimate touch?

Callie was fast coming to the conclusion that Urkot was a big tease, and that it was very much on purpose.

"Shaun and Xavier were only two years apart in age and were closer to one another. There were six years between me and Xavier, and I felt like the little sister who was always underfoot and in the way. A nuisance. What boy wants his little sister following him around, especially when they're out with their friends? They still cared about me and were very protective even though we didn't do much together.

"But we grew further apart as we got older. Shaun went to college, then got married, moved to Connecticut, and had kids, and Xavier joined the Marines and was deployed overseas. I spent my whole time in high school prepping for college to make sure my applications would look immaculate, and then I dove right into college myself. We all just kind of…lost touch."

Which had made her choice to join the Initiative both easy and painful—easy because it felt like she had nothing keeping her tied to Earth, painful because of the relationships that could have been.

Callie released a slow exhalation and ran her fingers through her hair, sweeping it back. "What about you? Are you close to any of your siblings?"

She recalled how he'd been with the vrix children during the festival. He'd been so natural with them. Coming from such a big family, he'd likely spent a lot of time with his siblings, had probably even helped care for and protect his younger brothers and sisters. It was common in large families on Earth for older children to take on a lot of responsibilities when it came to their siblings.

He hummed thoughtfully. "I was, when we were young."

"But not anymore?"

"I trust them, care about them. But we have not been close in much years. In Takarahl, there are much delvers. We live understone, and delvers must dig new dens, new chambers, new tunnels. There is always work, and it is always dangerous. Some die. More are broken. So, delvers have much broods to make sure there are always more to work, to dig, to shape.

"Once I was old enough to work, I was no longer a broodling to them. I was a delver. And I had to do my work well, had to follow all rules, or others would be hurt. I had to be just a delver with my family." He turned his head to look at her, and there was something in his eyes that Callie hadn't seen before, a blend of sadness and…and yearning.

A yearning for family, for closeness and familiarity?

She knew that feeling well, with her own family having not been close. But it was heartbreaking to learn that, despite having such a large family, he hadn't felt the love he'd deserved. That he and his siblings had likely been born not due to want, but duty. Due to a need to keep the ranks full.

"Only with Ketahn and the others, I am free of the weight," he continued. "Only with them I am just…Urkot. Not delver or warrior. Urkot."

Callie's heart ached for him. "Is that why you didn't stay in Takarahl?"

He stopped again, turning and holding up the crystal in his lower hand. It lit up an alcove on the side of the tunnel that extended behind the wall, forming a small chamber.

"My tribe, my family, is in Kaldarak." Facing her, Urkot

closed what little distance lay between them. He caught her jaw in his upper hands, cradling it, and ducked his head close until he was all she saw. His eyes held hers. "You are in Kaldarak, Callie."

Her eyes widened, and her breath caught.

He'd stayed in Kaldarak not only for his friends, but for her? Had he…had he been waiting for her all this time? Waiting for her to show interest in him, to see his interest in her, to recognize that he wanted more than friendship?

Had she been so oblivious?

All too soon, Urkot withdrew from her and turned back toward the alcove. Callie found herself taking a step toward him, reaching for him, almost begging him to come back. But the words lodged in her throat, and her arm fell.

Raising his crystal higher, Urkot leaned into the nook and examined it. Then he beckoned her with curled fingers. "Come. We rest here."

"Oh, finally," she sighed in relief, moving to his side to look into the alcove. It was the size of a walk-in closet, wide enough for the two of them to fit inside without much room to spare.

She removed her backpack and once more rubbed her arms to ward off the chill in the air.

Urkot stepped inside, turned, and sat down, folding his forelegs in front of him. He took her bag, placed it beside him, then leaned forward, circling Callie's hips with his hands. She let out a little squeak as he lifted her and drew her inside, settling her down on his lap.

He plucked the crystal from her hand and curled his lower arm around her waist, drawing her into the shelter of his body. "Rest, female."

Callie didn't hold back her low groan as she melted against him. Her muscles were sore, her body ached, and her skin was chilled, but Urkot radiated heat, chasing away the cold. So she shamelessly pressed herself against him, drawing her knees up and laying her head on his chest.

"You're soooo waaaaarm," she moaned.

He crooned, the sound vibrating into her as he shifted behind her. She felt him adjust the pouch around his waist, and then the light of the crystals went out.

Callie tensed as she was plunged into darkness.

Then both of Urkot's upper arms were around her, his claws gently combing through her curls. "Calm. Shadows cannot hurt us, and I have you."

Her anxiety faded with his words, and she relaxed against him. She was in Urkot's arms. She was safe.

Callie focused on the feel of him, on his claws stroking her hair, his hearts beating against her ear, the heat of his body. His warm, brandy and musk scent enveloped her, and she breathed it in deeply as her eyelids fluttered closed. Exhaustion weighed upon her, and sleep tugged at her consciousness.

She rubbed her cheek against his chest, cuddling deeper into the security of his embrace.

"You're Urkot to me too," Callie whispered.

She drifted into slumber, but not before she felt his arms tighten around her.

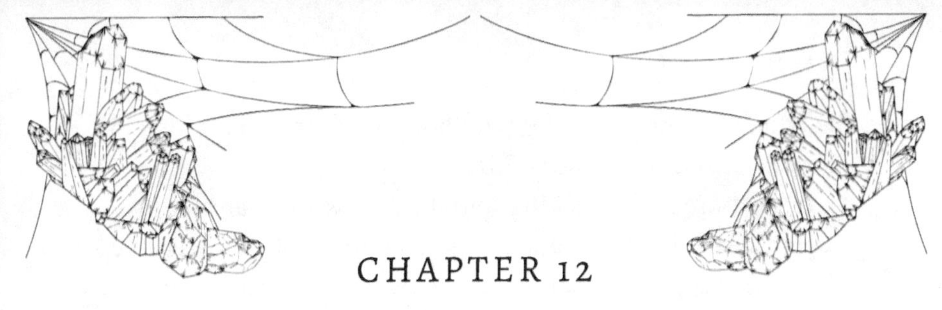

# CHAPTER 12

CALLIE HAD NEVER BEEN a light sleeper. Waking up and getting out of bed had always been a struggle, a test of willpower.

But she'd heard something, something that had pierced her subconscious and woken her ass up *fast*. And going from dead asleep to wide awake was alarming and unsettling enough even without the terror of that unidentified sound.

She opened her eyes; the darkness remained just as complete and impenetrable as it had been behind her eyelids. Still, her gaze shifted restlessly back and forth, as though that could somehow sweep away the dark. She could almost feel the shadows pressing in on her, so thick it made her skin crawl and her eyeballs itch.

Every part of her, including her heart, froze when she heard the sound again.

Clicking. Alien, undulating clicking, echoing along the tunnel.

Before she could even consider whether she should've spoken, her lips parted, and a question tumbled out. "Wha—"

A large, callused hand clamped over Callie's mouth,

silencing her. She grasped it with both hands in a panic, digging her nails into firm, leathery skin.

In the tunnel, the clicking sound ended with an abrupt hiss.

Her heart hammered against her ribs, not slowing even when she recognized that the hand covering her mouth and the warm, solid body behind her belonged to Urkot. She could feel his tension and strain. His muscles were coiled like compressed springs, and there was a faint trembling in his chest as he held his breath.

The clicking came again, a little lower, a little deeper, a little closer. And oh God, she knew what it was even if she didn't know what had produced it.

Echolocation.

Something scraped the stone in the tunnel. To Callie, it very much sounded like an appendage dragging over the cave floor. In the silence of this dark tunnel, the sound was deafening.

With agonizing slowness, Urkot rose from the alcove floor, drawing Callie up with him. He seemed afraid to draw breath; she absolutely was too afraid to do so, despite the burning in her lungs. Her grip on his hand contributed as much to her body remaining upright as her legs did.

Her back was pressed even more snugly against his chest now, and she could feel his hearts thumping as fast and heavy as hers. Any creature that could use echolocation surely would've been able to hear their pounding heartbeats, right? Callie's pulse had to be the loudest thing down here, rivaled only by Urkot's.

Another scrape came from mere feet away. It was a sound she'd heard from Urkot—claws against stone.

That clicking repeated just outside the alcove. How could it possibly sound so…hungry?

Callie's knees felt suddenly weak, and dread seeped into her veins, turning her blood cold.

The monster in the dark huffed. She felt its breath flow

across her face. It sniffed the air raggedly, and Callie squeezed her eyes shut, turning her face away.

That thing was right in front of her, right fucking there, and she couldn't see it, couldn't identify the source of this bone-chilling horror. Never in all her life, not even during her time on this untamed alien world, had she ever felt so scared and helpless.

The creature made that clicking once more. From this close, Callie could feel the sound's faint vibrations against her skin.

*It knows. It knows we're here.*

As though in response to her thought, the clicks descended into a deep, rumbling growl.

Shoving Callie aside, Urkot surged forward. She caught herself against the cold stone wall, but her trembling legs gave out, dropping her hard onto her knees. She barely felt the jolt. Fire blazed in her lungs as she finally sucked in a gasping breath.

Just outside the alcove, snarls and growls filled the tunnel, joined by the noises of an unseen struggle—the dull *thwacks* of blows landing, the scraping of limbs scrabbling over the cave floor, the clacking and gnashing of fangs and teeth.

And even looking right toward those sounds with rounded eyes, Callie couldn't see a damn thing. She couldn't tell what Urkot was fighting, couldn't tell if he was okay, if he needed help.

*Someone please wake me from this nightmare.*

But this was no nightmare. It was very, very real. And Callie couldn't cower here in the dark while Urkot battled for survival. She wouldn't.

Crawling, she blindly and frantically felt around the floor of the alcove. Her bag had to be somewhere close.

Something thudded down behind her. Callie started, jumping against the wall. The monster snarled, and then that unseen creature was dragged back, raking the floor.

With her racing heart lodged in her throat, she quickened her search. Her fingers bumped and brushed over loose stones before finally finding the cured yatin hide bag.

Grabbing hold of the bag, she hauled it toward herself, rising on her knees as she fumbled to open it. In this darkness, her hands felt clumsier than ever. Had she really tied this thing so tight?

There was a squelching sound, accompanied by an agonized growl. She couldn't tell if it had come from Urkot or the monster.

*Oh God, Urkot. Please be okay.*

Liquid splattered on the floor somewhere behind her.

Deep inside, she was icy cold, trapped in terror's unrelenting grasp. But scorching heat thrummed just beneath the surface of her skin. The stark contrast made her feel like she was about to explode.

*Hold it together, Callie. Hold it—*

The knot finally came undone.

"Yes!" She tore open the bag and plunged her hand inside.

Her heart stuttered when another sound, a pained grunt, rose from the fray. That one had undoubtedly been Urkot. Even if she had no idea what to do, she had to do *something*.

Callie's hand found the collapsed solar lantern in her bag. She snatched it out and snapped the lantern open, twisting toward those violent, frightening sounds.

She turned the lantern on.

Callie slitted her eyes against the intense light, which seemed brighter than a thousand suns after so long in total darkness. The creature shrieked and thrashed wildly, drawing a growl from Urkot.

"Oh fuck," Callie breathed as her eyes adjusted to the light.

Mere feet away, Urkot was grappling with the monster—a pale vrix of similar height to him but slighter of build. There was blood, a lot of blood, but between their struggles and the deep, restless shadows created by the lantern, it was impossible to tell who the blood belonged to.

The monster's eyes were shut tight.

She knew only one thing—every second she delayed was another during which Urkot could get hurt.

Gritting her teeth, Callie dropped the lantern, grabbed a football-sized rock from the floor, and shoved herself to her feet.

The pale vrix's mandibles wildly lashed out at Urkot, the pincers at their ends snapping only inches from his face and neck. The two were a tangle of limbs and claws.

Clutching the rock between both hands, Callie charged into the chaos before reason could convince her of how bad an idea it was. She hefted her crude weapon high overhead and swung it down with all her might onto one of the pale vrix's hind leg joints.

She felt a crunch, subtle but unmistakable, as the impact jolted up her arms, knocking the rock from her grasp. The vrix's leg buckled.

Snarling in rage and pain, the pale vrix spun and launched itself at her.

Callie staggered back with a cry.

Illuminated by the lantern, the vrix's features were emblazoned into her memory. A headcrest that curved backward like the dome of a skull. Mouth fangs exposed in a skeletal grin. Lank, dark hair hanging around neck and shoulders. And mandibles ending not in fangs, but wicked pincers with jagged teeth on the insides.

Its gaze was locked on Callie, blazing with fury and hunger.

Urkot's hands clamped around the sides of the vrix's head, halting its lunge abruptly. Its arms and forelegs darted toward Callie, and she retreated until she bumped into the alcove's rear wall. Those clawlike mandibles snapped on empty air.

Urkot dragged the other vrix backward, forcing its upper

body to tip back precariously. Its upper arms reached for him now. With a guttural growl, Urkot wrenched the pale vrix's head to the side.

Bone cracked. The sound was not unlike that of a large branch breaking away from a tree trunk. The pale vrix's body fell limp, held up only by Urkot's hold on its head—which was now facing almost completely backward.

He released his hold, letting the pale vrix collapse in a heap. His shoulders rose and fell with his harsh breaths. Dark crimson glistened on his hide, contrasting the vibrant blue of his markings.

Urkot's gaze met Callie's as he stepped over the corpse to move closer to her. His eyes gleamed with lingering fury, pain, and profound, sincere concern. "Are you okay?"

Hearing his voice break the silence after all the horrible sounds that had dominated the dark was a balm to her soul. An end to the nightmare she'd awoken to.

She flung herself against him, wrapping her arms around his middle in a fierce hug. He didn't hesitate to embrace her.

"You're okay," she said, body trembling, jaw quivering. "You're okay."

Urkot was as solid as the stone around them, but much, much warmer, much more welcoming.

"Calm, female," Urkot rumbled. "We are safe."

Safe. They were safe. They hadn't been torn to shreds, hadn't been killed, hadn't been…eaten.

*Don't think about that!*

Callie closed her eyes and focused on the pounding of Urkot's hearts within his chest. They soothed her, grounded her, and were proof that they were alive. Another danger overcome, together.

She curled her fingers into his back as she tightened her embrace.

*Why can't I stop shaking?*

Urkot stroked his claws through her hair. "Breathe. Calm."

Nothing about this situation was right, nothing was okay, except for Urkot. As long as she had him, she was truly safe.

They held each other as their hearts gradually slowed, as their breathing calmed, as her trembling finally ceased.

But when she inhaled deeply, drawing in his scent, she became aware of something else.

The smell of blood.

Callie jerked away from him, clutching his upper forearms as she scanned his chest and arms. "Are you hurt? There's blood. Oh fuck, there's so much blood."

Urkot glanced down at himself. Some of that blood was definitely his; she could see the scratches and cuts.

He grunted. "I am fine."

"But there's scrat—"

Urkot caught her chin in a firm grip and forced her eyes up to his. "I am fine, Callie. I will heal in small time."

She released a shaky breath and slid her fingers up and down his forearms, unsure if she was trying to soothe him or herself. "Okay. Okay."

His thumb stroked her cheek. "You are okay?"

She nodded. "I'm fine."

"Good." His mandibles ticked up. "Brave female. You protected me."

Warmth flooded her cheeks at his praise. "I tried."

He lifted his other upper hand and brushed the backs of his claws down her cheek. "And that is most brave, yes? To try even when you fear. And you did not just try, Callie. You *did*."

With a trill, Urkot lowered his face toward hers. "You must like me."

Callie chuckled as the warmth inside her burned hotter. "I do."

*Very much.*

"Good," he purred. "My head is hard, but I do not want to test it against your rock."

"Ugh." She gave his chest a shove. "Not funny."

He chittered as he straightened.

The corners of her lips twitched before curling into a smile. "Okay, so maybe it is. But I still don't like the thought of you hurt."

"Ah, Callie…" He moved closer and cupped her face between his big, strong hands. "I will take all hurts to shield you."

Callie's eyes widened as her belly fluttered.

All the men she'd been with in the past had been shallow. They'd focused on themselves, on their wants, their pleasure. After having her heart broken by her first boyfriend, who she'd given her virginity to, and dating men in college who'd only been interested in what they could get from her, Callie had lost interest in relationships. Maybe she'd even lost faith in the whole concept.

There'd been no commitment, no…partnership. No consideration.

Just by themselves, the words Urkot had spoken were more meaningful than anything those other guys had ever said to her. But when paired with the fact that he'd acted those words out every day she'd known him, for months, without ever asking for anything in return?

*I really have been oblivious.*

The vrix in front of her *wanted* her. Not because of what she could give him, but for who she was.

*And I want him.*

Before she could react or come up with a response, he lowered his hands and stepped aside, sinking down to collect her bag. And any words she might have said died on her tongue as she beheld the body of the pale vrix on the ground in front of her.

Callie picked up her lantern and approached the vrix.

Though it was clearly dead, she gave one of its legs a kick to be sure. When it didn't move, she stepped closer and crouched, holding the lantern toward it.

The brief, nightmarish glimpse she'd had when it attacked her had been real.

Its hide was a pale, sickly white, and its body was emaciated, with long, gangly limbs that were smeared with dirt and blood. In places, she could see bones outlined through its hide—especially around its chest, where its hide clung to its ribs. Wickedly long, sharp claws tipped its fingers like blades. But it was its face that was the most terrifying of all.

Shadowstalkers and thornskulls didn't have lips like humans; their hard mouths hid their fangs while closed. But this vrix's teeth were on full display like those of a bare skull, long, thin, and pointed. Its eight beady black eyes were open and lifeless, with three sets atop each other, and the final smaller pair offset to the outsides of the middle row.

Callie stared at its clawed mandibles and shuddered. They reminded her of the mouthparts of a camel spider.

This was a creature made for rending flesh.

"Is…is this a…"

"Spiritstrider," Urkot said from behind her.

She covered her mouth with a hand as she stared wide-eyed at the horrifying vrix. "Oh fuck, fuck, fuck."

The stories Urkot had told her were true. The fears he had shared with her were real.

Standing, Callie spun to face him. "Will more come? If there's one, there must be others close by, right?"

"I do not know." He held up her bag. "But we must go. With the sounds and blood-scent, *something* will come soon."

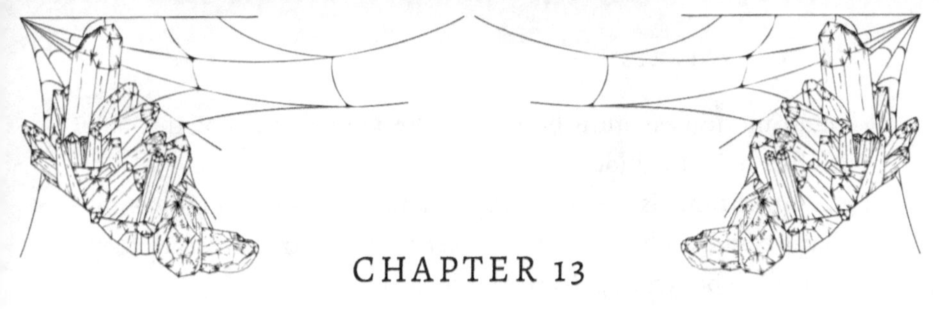

# CHAPTER 13

TIME ALWAYS LOST MEANING UNDERSTONE. Living in Takarahl, Urkot had rarely seen the sky, and he'd never really known whether it was day or night in the world above when he'd slept in his den. When he'd worked in the tunnels, there'd been no sunlight to mark time's passage.

They'd simply worked until the next group of delvers arrived to take over.

Taking up a den in Kaldarak had changed all that. He was aware of every suncrest, every sunfall, knew when it was cloudy, when it was raining. He could tell what time of day it was by the shadows. He'd come to relish the feel of warm sunshine on his hide and fresh air in his lungs.

He could not blame Ketahn for having left Takarahl to dwell in the Tangle all those years ago.

Being in these tunnels now, he'd lost all sense of time again. The darkness, the stale air, the damp stone, it was all as disorienting as it was familiar. They'd walked for what felt like a very long while, following the subtle airflow. At times, he had to stop where the tunnel split, extend his forelegs to either side, and

149

stand motionless until he sensed the faintest current through his fine hairs to guide him.

These tunnels seemed endless, and there was no indication that he and Callie were any closer to a way out. Instead, they seemed to be striding deeper understone.

Urkot turned his head to look at Callie, who walked beside him with a crystal in hand.

His mandibles rose, his chest warmed, and his heartsthread thrummed. No matter how dark these passages were, she shone bright. A flame in the shadows, intense and pure, instilling him with strength and hope. She was beautiful and radiant.

She was his suncrest.

Callie tipped her face up and met his gaze. Her soft smile made his hearts thunder.

He rubbed at his chest and faced forward.

He didn't know how long they'd rested before the spirit-strider had found them. Callie had slept in his arms, he knew that, but what sleep he'd claimed had been broken and brief. He could not completely lower his guard while they were down here. Could not risk being asleep when the next danger arose, not while they had neither shelter nor protection.

Weariness had carved itself into his bones. His body pulsed with deep, throbbing aches, and his hide was tender in many places where it had been bruised while also feeling tight and itchy in others, where his cuts and scrapes were healing.

They would need to find shelter soon, would need real rest, because the longer they went without it, the duller his senses would grow and the slower his reactions would get. He would become too weak to protect her.

"Is it just me, or is it colder?" Callie asked, breaking the silence.

"It is colder."

His gaze flicked toward something far ahead in the tunnel,

well beyond the glow of their crystals. He halted, putting out his lower hand to stop Callie beside him, and tilted his head.

"What is it?" she whispered.

Urkot tucked his crystal in his palm and curled his fingers around it, snuffing out its light, before covering Callie's crystal with his lower hand. As the darkness swallowed them, what he was staring at became clearer—it was another source of that soft blue light.

"You see?" he asked softly.

She stepped forward and squinted. "Is there light ahead?"

"Yes. We stride with care. Stay close."

Uncovering the crystals, he proceeded forward, positioning himself slightly in front of Callie. The light ahead was likely the result of a natural occurrence, but who was to say whether the spiritstriders also gathered crystals to use as light sources?

*I could be leading Callie right to their den.*

But as they neared the light, it wasn't the unsettling clicking of spiritstriders he heard—it was the gentle sound of flowing water, accompanied by a hint of its fresh, crisp scent.

Finally, they reached the source of the light. Crystals grew from veins in the walls and ceiling, in tiny clusters that became larger as Urkot and Callie drew closer to the opening at the end of the tunnel. These were soon joined by another source of light—glowworms. The small creatures wriggled on the ceiling and hung from glowing strands of silk, forcing Urkot to duck to avoid them. Their glow was the same blue as that of the crystals.

"Oh gross," Callie said. "Are those *worms?*"

Urkot glanced back to find her hunched down as she walked, with her hands over her head and her nose scrunched. He couldn't help but recall how she'd reacted when a bug had landed on her hair in the swamp several moon cycles ago.

That had been the first time he'd stroked her hair. That had been when he'd forced her to say his name, to acknowledge him. To see him.

Something warmed inside him at the memory.

He chittered, as much in amusement as to push aside the stirrings deep within himself. "They cannot hurt you, Callie. But they are…sticky."

"Blech. I'll take your sticky, but I'm not touching those things. They're all squirmy and…ugh!" She shuddered.

"They taste good."

She gagged.

Urkot chittered again; he'd known what her reaction would be. The humans had been offered grubs to eat before they'd left their crashed ship behind, and only three had been brave enough to try them—Will, Lacey, and Cole. None had seemed to enjoy the experience.

Apparently, that satisfying *pop* of biting down on a grub was not quite so satisfying to humans, and neither was the flavor. Or the texture. Or the wriggling.

Not any part of it, really.

He extended an arm, holding his hand over her head to shelter her. "Do not worry, female. I will shield you. If any touch you, they will become a snack."

Callie gagged again.

Urkot's mandibles rose as he looked upon the female beside him. She was such an endearing creature.

*Mine. She will be mine.*

Finally, they reached the opening, and all other thoughts fell away from Urkot's mind. He and Callie abruptly stopped, their attention seized by the sight in front of them.

The tunnel opened on a huge cavern. The light of the countless glowstones and glowworms on the walls and ceilings reflected off the water of a clear lake, filling the space with shimmering luminescence. Plants and mushrooms, many of which gave off their own light in pinks, purples, and reds, grew near the water. Faintly glowing fish swam in the lake, their forms obscured by the rippling surface.

But it was the objects rising from the water that drew Urkot's gaze. He tilted his head as he studied them. They were made of stone, covered in algae and moss and worn by untold age, but he knew their shapes—four male vrix, four females.

They were statues of the Eight, partially submerged in this lake deep, deep below ground.

"Wow," Callie softly exclaimed.

Urkot stepped closer to the edge of the rocky drop-off that led down to the water. He crossed his arms in the symbol of the Eight, reminded again of his missing arm.

"What is this place?" she asked.

"A temple. Once."

"How can you tell?"

"That one"—he gestured to the closest statue, a male—"holds a spear. He is the Hunter. The Protector holds her shield, the Broodmother an egg. And that one, the Weaver…"

Callie cocked her head. "That one's not holding anything."

Lifting his upper hands, Urkot spread his fingers in an imitation of the statue. "He held thread between his fingers, but the thread is gone."

"And that one?" She pointed to a male statue at the far end of the pool, which bore a crude pick in one hand and a large, glowing crystal in the other. "Is that the Delver?"

He smiled at her. "Yes."

She hummed, glancing between Urkot and the statue before her eyes settled upon him. She grinned and slowly trailed a finger down his chest and abdomen.

Urkot's mouth parted with a soft, shaky exhalation.

"They should have shaped him like you," she said.

With a trill, he curled his lower hand around her hip and drew her closer. She gasped, hands flying up to settle on his chest, and peered up at him with wide eyes. He wrapped his upper arms around her.

"No," he said, voice falling low. "I was shaped only for you... and you for me, female."

She made a small whimpering noise, keeping her eyes locked with his. Heat suffused her body, burning into him, and her cheeks darkened with it. Her fingers curled against his chest, and he felt the scratch of her blunt claws against his hide. He wanted to feel them dig deeper. Wanted them to mark him, to make her claim on him a true, physical thing.

Callie cleared her throat and patted his chest. "So, uh, where do we go from here?"

The press of his stem against his slit was a clear answer, but not one he could give to her. They needed shelter, needed rest, and he needed to put her safety before his cravings.

Reluctantly, he withdrew from her and faced the lake, searching its edges. There were a few small ledges down at the water's level, but those were too exposed and would leave them vulnerable to any creatures dwelling in the water. They needed height and seclusion. Something that would not only provide protection from unknown beasts, but keep them out of sight from spiritstriders.

Then he spotted it—a higher ledge, which led to a grotto with glowing vegetation hanging on either side of the opening. Reaching it would require a climb, but that made it safer; once Urkot and Callie were up there, they would be out of easy reach.

"There," he said, gesturing toward it. "We will rest there."

Callie followed his gesture with her eyes, which rounded. She looked at him and blinked. "Up there? All the way up there? Meaning, swimming all the way across the water, which has who-knows-what lurking inside, and climbing up?"

Urkot dipped his chin. "Yes."

He collected her glowstone and placed it, along with his

own, in his pouch. There was more than enough light here to safely leave their hands free.

She peeked over the edge at the water below. "Okay… But if I feel something brush against me, I will scream. Just warning you now."

He held up his hand and pinched his forefinger and thumb together. "Small scream, yes?"

Callie faced him with a droll look. "Big scream."

Urkot chittered and thumped a fist against his chest. "This male will protect you from little fish."

"You better hope little fish are all that's in that water."

He certainly hoped so.

Extending a foreleg, he dropped it low to dip into the lake. A chill coursed over his hide and made his fine hairs stand. The water was cold—colder than the stream they'd followed deeper into these caves.

But there was no other way forward.

Turning, Urkot grasped a rock protruding from the tunnel wall and swung himself out over the edge. The tips of his legs struck stone as he steadied himself. He climbed down slowly, until his legs were submerged, then his hindquarters, and finally, his torso. Cold penetrated straight to his bones, making him shudder.

"By the Eight," he rasped.

He released his grip on the wall and kicked his legs, moving back from it before lifting a hand to beckon her. "Come."

She raised an eyebrow. "If that made you shiver and swear, what's it going to do to me?"

"Make you swim fast," he replied, raising his mandibles.

Chuckling, Callie shook her head as she carefully sat on the edge, legs dangling. "I'm not a fast swimmer, but I guess I'll learn."

After drawing in a couple deep breaths, she shoved herself

off. She plunged into the water, disappearing into its dark depths.

Urkot's hearts went still. Panic roiled beneath his hide, its heat quickly overpowering the water's chill.

As he was about to dive after her, Callie emerged with a gasp, swiftly swiping her hair from her face. "Holy fuck, it's freezing!"

His hearts lurched back into motion, beating much too hard and much too fast. *Fuck* was right.

She treaded water, easing closer to him. Her dark eyes were large and luminous as they met his, reflecting the cavern's blue glow, much like they'd looked when he'd come upon her bathing in the temple a few days ago.

"Lead the w-way, big guy," she said, lower lip quivering.

He caught hold of her backpack and drew her closer, guiding her to his back. "Hold on, Callie."

As much as he loved the feel of it when she wrapped her arms around his neck from behind and pressed her body against his, he did not care for the way she was trembling. He'd seen it from the humans before, when the rains came to the Tangle and the temperature dropped. Diego had said that being cold like that could be dangerous for a human to endure for long.

This way, Urkot could get her to their destination as quickly as possible while keeping his body between Callie and anything lurking below.

Urkot swam, doing his best not to think about the lack of anything solid beneath him, forcing himself to ignore the unknown and all the terrors it might've held. The statues, despite being partially submerged, loomed higher and higher as he neared them, coaxing another breathless *Wow* from Callie.

Were she not shivering in frigid water that was home to gods-knew what, Urkot would've liked to stop and examine the monuments up close. He would've studied their construction, would've guessed at the techniques used to shape them, would've tried to puzzle out the shadowy forms he could vaguely see below the water's surface, which hinted at a temple structure that had been swallowed by the lake.

He would've greatly enjoyed working with Callie to piece together an idea of what this cavern must've looked like in a time now forgotten.

But the water was overly cold even to him, and their lives were far more important than his curiosity.

When he reached the cliffside below the grotto, Callie tightened her hold on him and wrapped her legs around his middle without him saying a word. Welcome warmth bloomed in him. He grasped the stone and climbed, pulling them out of the water. Callie's backside settled atop his hindquarters. His body felt heavier than ever, a fresh reminder of the lingering exhaustion in his muscles, but he forced his limbs to keep moving. Rest was only segments away.

Urkot hauled himself up onto the ledge with a grunt and crawled into the grotto's shelter before letting himself collapse on the stone floor. Every muscle in his body burned. Callie didn't release him as she lay upon his back, shivering.

"Y-You okay?" she asked.

He grunted in response, not sure himself if it was a yes or a no.

Her grip on him relaxed, and she extended her leg down. Once her boot was flat on the ground, she climbed off him and stepped away, drawing off her bag and setting it down before removing her boots.

"Jesus," Callie whispered, briskly rubbing her bare arms as water pooled around her. She crouched, opened the bag, and pulled out a rolled-up blanket. It was soaked through. "Fuck."

Urkot narrowed his eyes on her trembling hands as she wrung the blanket out. She stood, giving the cloth a flap to unfurl it, and held it up, examining it with dismay.

He knew it would not warm her. Neither would her dripping clothes, scant as they were.

He pushed himself upright, willing away those aches, and unfastened his belt and the attached pouch. Before setting them down, he took the pair of glowstones back out and placed them on the floor to either side of himself. Then he forced his legs to rise beneath him, extended a foreleg, and hooked it around Callie, drawing her toward him. Gently, he plucked the blanket from her grasp, turned, and used sticky silk to hang it across the grotto's opening. That would help it dry faster and afford them a bit more shelter.

That done, Urkot set his spinnerets to work. He drew out fluffed silk, arranging it on the floor. Each pull was a little more draining, but he did not stop until he'd formed a large nest for himself and his female.

Finally, he turned to Callie again. Her arms were crossed over her chest, hands tucked beneath them, and her shivering was more pronounced. With a growl, he guided her closer as he ran his eyes over her body. The sopping material of her coverings left little to the imagination, clinging to her curves like a second skin. What was the purpose of such garments?

Modesty. Such a ridiculous thing. And yet...he understood the desire to hide aspects of one's body. Understood the shame some of the humans seemed to feel at the thought of being exposed to the gazes of others.

He grasped her arms with his upper hands and drew them apart before seeking the tie on her top with his lower hand. Pulling the string between her breasts that held the material together, he undid the knot. Then he lowered his hand, brushing his knuckles over her belly as he slid his finger beneath the bottom part of the string. He pulled it free.

The material fell away, baring her breasts to him. Her dark brown nipples were taut, the hard buds begging for the touch of his fingers, for the sweep of his tongue, and the supple flesh around them looked so soft, so yielding...

Pressure built behind his slit as his stem stirred, making him clutch in his claspers tight.

Callie released a shaky breath, which made her breasts quiver. "I...t-take it you l-like them?"

Urkot flattened his palm on her belly, battling the urge to move his hand to those enticing mounds, to cup them, to squeeze and knead them, to claim them. "Yes."

She let out a soft laugh. "So b-blunt."

Growling low and deep, he forced his eyes up to hers and released her arms. "Take it off."

"I like it w-when you're b-b-bossy," she said as she slipped her arms out of the holes of her top.

He clenched his jaw and dropped his upper hands to the sides of her skirt, which lay just above the flare of her hips.

Gods, she fit so perfectly in his grasp, like every bit of her was shaped just for him.

Urkot made swift work of the tie at the side of her hip. He caught the garment before it fell, and he clenched the fabric as his eyes locked on her exposed slit. The hunger that only she could inspire raged inside him, setting his blood ablaze.

A red haze shimmered at the edges of his vision, and agony radiated through his core as his hardened stem pushed insistently against his slit. His claspers cinched tight over it in his desperate attempt for control. Urkot's instincts roared for him to take her, take her, take her.

His female stood naked in front of him. It would've been so simple to bind her in silk, spread her thighs, and thrust his cock into her body.

She was his to claim.

"Urkot?"

Callie's soft voice broke through the frenzied haze in his mind, and he tore his gaze away from her slit to look at her without desire clouding his perception. She stood shivering, teeth chattering, with her arms once more crossed over her breasts, hugging herself as water dripped from her hair.

By the Eight, what was he doing? Anger flared within him, and his need to protect Callie drove back the mating frenzy that had been taking root.

His mate needed warmth and comfort, and he was failing her.

Body stiff, Urkot, squeezed his eyes shut and took a deep breath, willing himself to calm. Once he was sure he was in control, he busied himself by taking her garments to the entrance and hanging them near the blanket.

It granted him a few moments of reprieve, the briefest of escapes from temptation.

When Urkot turned back to Callie, she had already climbed into the nest, where she sat with her knees drawn up and her arms wrapped around them. She looked so small. Yet a rush of prideful possessiveness swept through him at seeing her nestled there, surrounded by his silk.

He lowered himself onto the nest beside her, lying on his side, and held up his right arms. "Come, Callie. I will share my warmth."

She hurriedly crawled into the shelter of his arms, stretching out beside him, and Urkot let out a hiss as her chilled skin touched his hide.

"S-Sorry," Callie said.

Without allowing her to even consider withdrawing from him, Urkot wrapped his arms around her and pulled her against him.

Callie moaned, tucking her nose against his shoulder. "God, you're so warm." She snuggled closer until her body was flush against his.

*Fuck.*

That simple human word was the only one that fit the

moment, the only one that could encompass what he felt, what he wanted.

The press of her soft body roused his desire with new ferocity. He could feel her pliant breasts against his chest, could feel her warm breath caressing his hide, could feel her thigh shifting against his slit, teasing at his most sensitive part. Her morning dew scent pervaded his senses, beckoning him to breathe her in, to taste her, to discover if she was as sweet as she smelled.

As her trembling subsided, his hearts quickened, his breaths grew ragged, and his claspers curled around her outer thighs. His hold on her tightened as desire and duty warred inside him. But that desire was fast growing into something else, something stronger, something larger—need.

He needed this female. *His* female.

She sighed and wriggled in his hold, grazing his chest with her hardened nipples.

Urkot shuddered, and his stem extruded from his slit with a force that made him groan.

Callie gasped and went utterly still.

His stem was out. It was out, and it was pressed firmly along her thigh, throbbing against her smooth skin, aching with a primal need. He'd extruded completely, not just in her presence, but against her.

Urkot's cock was as hard as the stone to which he was always compared. And Callie must've felt every damned thread's width of it.

"Urkot..." she said softly, her fingers curling against his chest. "Is that—"

"I am sorry," he said hurriedly, lifting his arms to withdraw from her.

"Don't." Callie caught his side, keeping him from pulling away. "Stay."

He stilled. Moments before, her skin had felt cool and damp. Now her hand was fiery against his hide. His hearts pounded so thunderously that there was no way she didn't feel them against her palm.

"Callie…"

When he didn't move, her grip eased, and she smoothed her palm along his side and down his abdomen, its heat deliciously scalding. Her hand halted right above his slit, fingers teasingly trailing back and forth. He tensed, everything inside him drawing taut, his breath ragged.

"Can I touch you?" she asked.

That crimson haze again stained the edges of his vision. His self-control already dangled by a single frayed thread, and testing it would only result in failure. For her sake, he needed to deny her request, needed to deny himself. He needed to be strong in this, his moment of greatest yearning.

"Let me explore you, Urkot." Callie brushed her lips over the base of his throat.

A kiss.

That simple, gentle gesture was all it took to sever the thread.

This close to Callie, skin to hide…he'd never stood a chance of resisting. Not with her.

And if he were honest with himself, he didn't want to resist.

Urkot lowered his arms, settling his lower hand on her hip and sliding his upper hand along her back and into her hair.

"Touch me," he rasped.

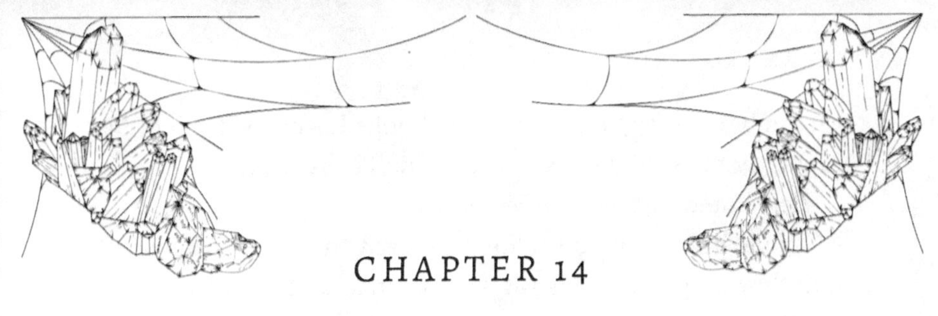

# CHAPTER 14

*Touch me.*

Urkot's words, said in that thick, gravelly voice, echoed through Callie.

She couldn't believe that in a matter of moments she'd gone from freezing, with her body shivering uncontrollably and her teeth chattering, to being wrapped in his arms and feeling as though she was about to burst into flames. Heat pooled in her core, spreading warmth throughout her body, and Urkot's cock, slick and hot against her thigh, felt like a brand.

*Touch him. Touch him. Touch him.*

Callie had been curious about vrix and their anatomy since discovering Ivy had been having sex with one. She'd been weirded out in the beginning because, well, Ketahn resembled a giant freaking spider, but she'd been curious nonetheless.

How did it work? What did vrix cocks look like? What did they feel like?

Now she was about to find out.

She smiled as she continued to tease Urkot's hide with her fingertips. His breath was harsh, his body was rigid, and his grip on her was tight. His claspers, hooked over the flesh of her thighs, twitched higher as though to pull her closer.

He wanted this. He wanted her.

Callie slid her fingers down, toward the base of his shaft, until they dipped into his slit. Unimaginable heat radiated from him there.

Urkot released a puff of air, and his fingers clutched her hair.

"You're wet here," she said, caressing the inside of his slit around his cock. Callie brushed her lips over his throat again as she stroked him from within. "Wet like my pussy."

A tremor coursed through him as his breathing quickened. "What… I… I do not know *pussy*."

Callie grinned. The guttural rumble he put into that word made it even more erotic, like he was already hungry for it even though he didn't know what it was.

Tipping her head back, she shifted her face closer to the side of his to whisper, "My pussy is my slit."

Before he could respond, Callie curled her fingers around the base of his slick shaft, making his breath hitch. Her eyes widened. He was thick. Not that she'd expected anything less, but there was also a knot—a *knot*—just above the base of his cock.

Callie's pussy clenched not in fear but in excitement at the prospect of what that would feel like. To be so full of him, to have his cock lodged so, so fucking deep, locked inside her…

God, she wanted that.

She stroked her fist up, over the knot, taking her time to caress it, before exploring farther up his shaft until she reached the flared head. There, it narrowed to a two-pronged tip with an inch-long slit between.

"Callie," he rasped, his claws biting into her skin as he flexed his fingers on her hip, making tingles spread through her.

"Mmm, I love it when you say my name like that." She teased the opening of his tip with her thumb. "Do you like this?"

His cock twitched. He moved his face to her hair and hissed, "Yes."

That word went straight to her core, and she was all the more aware of the achy hollowness growing inside her.

"Good," Callie said, wrapping her fingers fully around him again. "Because I like touching you."

She stroked her hand down his cock and back up. He quivered at her touch. Slowly, firmly, she continued stroking, up and down, learning the feel of him and loving the sounds he made.

His musky, earthy, intoxicating scent bloomed around her, enveloping her senses, but there was another layer to it she hadn't detected before, one that made her mouth water. Cinnamon and cloves.

*He smells so damn delicious.*

With every pump of her hand, his hold on her strengthened. His breathing grew harsher and more ragged in the quiet of their little haven, and she felt his pulse thrumming against both her hand resting on his chest and her fist around his cock. Every rock of his pelvis, every low grunt, every minute reaction aroused her in turn. The fire burning in him, the heat wrapped in her fingers, grew and grew, and the flames inside her flared to mirror it.

She could feel the slickness of her desire coating her thighs. Her pussy yearned for his touch, to be filled. What it wanted was rock solid in her hand. Not a fantasy, not a toy like she'd often used in her old life, but flesh and blood, thick and hot. Real.

Callie parted her thighs, pushing against his claspers, and felt a whisper of air on her heated flesh as her leg brushed along Urkot's.

His chest swelled with a deep inhalation, and then it

vibrated with a growl so low and bestial that it reverberated straight to Callie's core, making her clit twitch. It was a ravenous sound, so out of character for the controlled, measured vrix she'd come to know, and God was it sexy.

Faster than she could register, he shoved on her hip, rolling Callie onto her back, and surged over her. One instant they were on their sides, and the next he was propped over her, his upper arms braced to either side of her head and his forelegs bent with their joints on the bed of silk. His shoulders heaved with those harsh breaths, and his cock throbbed in her unbroken hold.

Urkot's lower hand gripped her hip a little tighter, pressing those claws more firmly against her flesh. That bit of pain only enticed her more.

She'd thought herself in control? She'd thought she was dictating the pace of this exploration, that he was like putty in her hands? No. He could've seized control any moment he wanted to.

And now he had.

It took everything inside Callie not to squirm beneath him, not to press her thighs together in a vain attempt to alleviate the gnawing ache in her pussy.

His eyes, eight blue flames, met hers. She felt tiny with his body poised over her like this. Felt helpless. And yet she felt absolutely safe at the same time. Catching her bottom lip between her teeth, she held his gaze, silently daring him to continue, to do whatever he wanted.

Urkot's hands clenched the spun silk beneath them. With a snarl, he snapped his pelvis forward. His shaft slid along her hand, forcing her grip over his knot and down to his base.

Callie moved her other hand to his cock and wrapped her fingers around it, one fist over the other. She glanced down. Even in the low light, she could see that it was as blue as his glowing markings.

Bracing his middle and hind legs on the cave floor, he pumped his hips, his slick shaft gliding back and forth through her hands, faster and faster. As he thrust, he lowered his head, drawing in her scent with every panting inhalation, his every exhalation punctuated by a growl or a snarl. Strands of his blue-and-white-threaded black hair fell over his shoulders and around his face. But even as his pace became wild and his claws sank deeper to scrape and gouge at the stone under the silk, his eyes never strayed from hers.

This was Urkot. Barriers down, restraint gone. This was him in his most primal state.

And Callie fucking *loved* it. He was beautiful.

She smiled up at him, keeping her hands double-fisted around his cock as he fucked her palms, coating them with his slick, which she felt dripping onto her belly.

Urkot's pace faltered. His cock expanded, forcing her fingers wider, and quivered within her hold. He opened his mouth, baring his fangs, and dipped his head closer to her before snapping it to the side and biting down on his forearm. Callie gasped, eyes widening, but didn't release her hold on him.

He growled against his arm as his hips bucked, and he shuddered. Hot seed erupted from his cock, spilling onto her stomach and chest. He snarled, biting his arm harder, eyes blazing into Callie's as stream after stream of cum spurted onto her.

And she felt something else, something flittering against her wrist and forearm.

Callie dragged her gaze from his and looked down.

In the blue light of the crystals, she saw three thin white appendages sticking out from the slit at the end of his cock, fluttering in the air.

"Oh…" she whispered.

Heart racing, Callie slid her hand along the head of his shaft toward the tendrils and caressed them. Urkot's body trembled at that gentle touch. Fresh seed shot from his cock as he released his bite on his arm with a rough exhalation.

So they were sensitive. That was good information to tuck away for later.

The tendrils continued to flit against her hand, but she was able to make out their details as one curled around her finger. The feathery parts at their tips resembled a moth's antennae.

She stroked her thumb over one.

Urkot's pelvis bucked, causing his shaft to glide through her fist once more. He caught her wrists with his lower hand and pulled them away.

"No more," he said in a guttural voice.

Callie smiled at him coyly. "Did you…not like it?"

He grunted, baring his fangs. "I liked. Much liked."

His gaze dipped, roving over her slowly, devouring her. It made her more aware of his cum coating her chest and belly, of it dripping down her sides into the nest of spun silk beneath her.

Urkot crooned as he released her wrists and flattened his hand on her stomach. He moved his rough palm over her, through his seed, spreading it and rubbing it in. There was a possessiveness in the way he did it, as though he were marking her. As though he were making his scent, his essence, one with her.

Callie let her arms fall to either side of her head, watching him. There was a heated gleam in his eyes that, combined with his actions, sent a rush of lust through her. That rush only intensified as his hand trailed higher.

When he reached her breasts, he paused with his hand hovering over them. Anticipation stirred within Callie, and her nipples hardened into aching peaks. His mouth parted as he stared at them. Then his large hand fell, clutching one. A low purr rumbled in his chest, and Callie arched into his touch as that sensation flowed into her, lashes lowering. But she didn't close her eyes.

"So soft." Urkot caressed her breast, covering it with his cum. He tilted his head. "Except for this."

He pinched her nipple.

A jolt of pleasure shot straight to her clit, forcing a cry out of her before she could silence it. "Urkot!"

His head dropped, his fingers flexed on her breast, and a strained groan escaped him as he shivered. Another rope of seed spurted from his cock to land on her belly.

Urkot's eyes flicked up and met hers. His breath was ragged, and his body was tense, his hold on her trembling.

Humming, Callie trailed a finger down between her breasts to her belly, swirling it through his warm seed. "I'm finding this incredibly hot."

Urkot followed her finger with those intense eyes. When he spoke, his voice was harsh, full of warning. "Female… You test me. Mating frenzy is close to taking me."

"Oh. Then I guess there's only one solution." Reaching up, she caught a thick strand of his dangling hair and gave it a tug as she smiled. "Fuck me."

Eyes widening, he let out an uncertain trill. "What?"

Letting go of his silky hair, Callie dropped her hand over his atop her breast and clutched it as she smoothed her other hand down her belly. "Let the frenzy take you. Fuck me, Urkot. Rut me. Do whatever you want with me."

She let her thighs fall apart, her knees brushing his legs as she bared her pussy. She trailed her hand lower, over her mons, gathering his cum, until she reached her clit. She moaned as she circled it with her fingertip.

His gaze burned blue in the darkness as it locked on her sex, casting its color upon her.

"I want you," she said in a breathy voice as pleasure spread through her, amplified by the combined slick of his seed and her essence. "I'm not going to deny it any longer, and I'm not going to deny myself. I want your cock inside me."

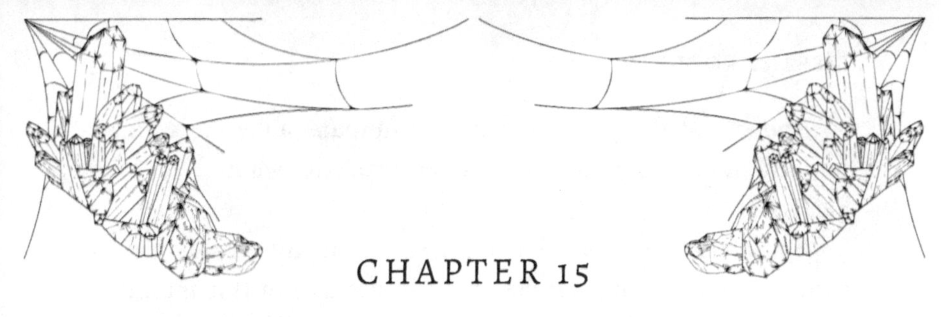

# CHAPTER 15

URKOT SOMEHOW FORCED himself to meet Callie's lustful, half-lidded gaze. She lay beneath him atop the pile of fluffed silk with her curly hair spread around her head and her skin aglow in the blue light, which reflected in her large eyes and granted them their own luminosity. Those full lips were parted, and each of her inhalations pressed her breast, with its beaded nipple, against his palm.

She was beautiful. A point of radiance in the cave's darkness.

The fragrance of her essence, sweeter and more alluring than any nectar, drew his eyes back down to her slit. Her parted thighs hid nothing from him. Her delicate, slender fingers stroked a little nub at the apex of her sex, making her breaths faster and shorter, wringing soft whimpers from her throat, and brightening that gleam in her eyes.

She was pleasuring herself right before him.

And she was staring at him while she did it.

*I want you.*

Callie, who had claimed his affection from the moment he'd seen her without her ever realizing, wanted Urkot. She wanted to mate with him. To rut.

And by all the gods of vrix and humans alike, he wanted nothing more than to fulfill her wish. He wanted to take her, now.

But instinct clawed at his mind, shredding his already frayed control. He could not ignore their differences in this moment. He could not ignore that he was big, powerful, and hard, and she was small and soft. Fragile.

If the mating frenzy overtook him, how could he stop himself from harming her?

"Callie…"

"I need you, Urkot," she moaned as she plunged her finger deep into her sex. Into her *pussy*.

He watched the digit sink into those slick, dark, welcoming folds, and a shiver coursed up his spine. His cock twitched, straining in the air and threatening to spill yet again.

Her body accepted that finger so easily, so readily. Would it accept his stem the same way?

He balled his upper hands into fists, grinding his knuckles against the stone floor through the spun silk.

She was right here, begging for him. Just as desperate as he was.

This couldn't be the time, couldn't be the place, could it? To think that he would claim her here, now, instead of in the nest he intended to make for her in his den…

Yet what had he learned since the cave had collapsed, trapping them down here? Every moment together was precious. Every moment spent denying what they wanted, what they yearned for, was a moment wasted.

If everything could end in an instant, without any warning…why wait any longer? Why deny himself? Why not take what was his? Why not accept this offering with all his hearts and all his desire?

Urkot slid his lower hand down, letting his palm glide over

her skin and grazing her belly with his claws, making her flesh quiver. She arched her back and moaned. That sound thrummed right to his stem, deepening the ache in his pelvis.

He'd been an eightfold-damned fool to think he could've resisted. He'd been a fool to even try.

Lifting his hand from her, Urkot wrapped it around the base of his shaft. He groaned as he squeezed his cock. To his delight, her eyes were fixated on it, and her breaths quickened further.

Urkot shifted his lower body, positioning his legs to brace himself. "You want this?"

Cheeks darkening, she nodded, slid her finger out of her sex, and returned it to that nub, which she stroked lazily. It glistened with her slick.

Unbidden, his tongue slipped out of his mouth and trailed along its seam, yearning for a taste of her. But that was not what he needed now. That was not what either of them needed.

*I want your cock inside me.*

Urkot released a shaky breath and raised his torso upright, moving his upper hands to grasp her hips. He lifted her backside. Callie spread her legs wider, hooking them over his forelegs. The position placed her slit directly before his cock.

"You need this," he growled as his claspers latched around her thighs.

"Yes," she sighed.

Angling his stem, he lined up the tip to the opening of her pussy. His tendrils brushed over her slick flesh. Callie shivered, legs trembling and eyelids fluttering. He flexed his hips forward, pushing the wide head of his cock into her. He could feel it already—that smooth flesh, resistant and yet yielding, eager, hungry. She whimpered.

"Say it, Callie. Say you are mine."

"Fuck me. Please."

She rolled her hips, but he held them firm between his

hands, not allowing her to take his length any deeper even though it pained him to delay that embrace.

"Say it," he demanded.

Panting softly, she clutched the fluffed silk with her free hand while the other continued rubbing her clit with a gradually increasing pace. "Yours. I'm yours. Now fu—"

He pushed forward, keeping her hips locked in place. Her slit parted for his stem, her slick combining with his to allow it in, but it was tight. So tight. Delicious, delirious heat surrounded his cock as he slowly wedged into her, as her body slowly pulled him deeper. The motions of her finger faltered.

"Oh fuck, fuck, fuck," she bit out. "You're so fucking big."

She threw her head back with a groan, her legs tensing. He saw the muscles of her thighs going taut; all his muscles were doing the same as her inner walls closed around him, squeezing more snugly than any fist ever could have, shaping themselves perfectly to him. There was resistance, but only because of how tight she was. How small she was. There was no barrier to keep him from pushing deeper.

His breaths came hot and heavy, tearing out of his throat. His claws pricked her skin as his fingers flexed. He fought back the shudders threatening to overcome him, fought back the red haze gathering in the back of his mind, fought back the instinct to thrust into her with all his strength and rut until he'd spent every thread of his endurance.

This moment was everything. His first time with Callie—his first time mating. He'd never been so close to anyone, so intimate, and he would experience it with a clear mind. He would not allow instinct to ruin this for either of them. He would feel all of this, would thrill in every bit of contact between their bodies.

"Good, female." Urkot slid his thumb along his shaft, spreading his oils and mixing them with hers to continue easing his entry. "You are so hot for me. So wet."

"More," she gasped, setting her finger back into frantic motion. "Need more. God, you feel so good."

He rocked his pelvis and pushed more of his length into her, groaning as her sex constricted around him. The pressure in his stem was immense, impossible, irresistible, and he knew it wouldn't take much for him to burst again. But she needed more, and so did he.

Callie tightened her legs around his and bore down on Urkot's cock, taking him deeper. "Yes! More, please, more. I need all of you."

Feeling those reactions in her body, feeling her pulse through his stem, feeling her heat and the flexing and relaxing of her muscles, it was more than he'd ever imagined. Combined with her words, her moans and shallow breathing, and her heady scent filling the grotto…

"You want more?" He tugged her toward him, stretching her and burying his stem inside her up to the nodules at his base, which seemed too wide for her to take.

"Oh fuck!" she gasped as her back arched again, the motion dragging her sex along his shaft to create torturous friction.

"Gods," he hissed as his tendrils flicked within her sex. He slid a hand around to her back and lifted her torso off the silk and upright. "Perfect. You are perfect. Need more of you, all of you."

The new position allowed her weight to bear down on him. Her slit stretched, but it still could not take in his knot. A shaky breath escaped him.

Callie threw an arm around his neck, met his gaze, and lifted her other hand. "So have more."

He glimpsed her finger glistening with her essence before she moved it to his mouth. His jaw parted, and she slipped her finger in, brushing it over his tongue.

Her salty-sweet flavor danced across his mouth, unlike anything he'd ever tasted. It was pleasure given form, passion given taste, and it was wholly her. Urkot growled. Something low in his belly tightened. His tongue coiled around her finger, greedily sweeping off every drop of essence.

He felt her heartbeat through every point of contact between their bodies, and the thumping of his own hearts grew louder, accompanied by a faint buzzing. Before he understood what was happening, a crimson haze had filled his vision, and heat spiraled through him, flooding his limbs.

Callie withdrew her finger, trailing it down his chin. The smile on her lips was as satisfied as it was needy, both teasing and seductive. He ran his hand up her back and slid it into her hair, holding her gaze.

"Need you," he rasped. "Need to rut you."

She grinned wickedly. "So fuck me, big guy."

He closed his fist on her hair, drawing her head back slightly, and snarled. "*No.* My name. Say my name."

She inhaled sharply, eyes flashing with excitement. Her fingers curled at his back, scraping his hide with her blunt nails. "Urkot. Fuck me, Urkot."

Urkot pressed his mouth to hers, delving his tongue between her lips, and her tongue met it in a sensual, tantalizing dance, following his lead.

"Take me," he growled when he broke the kiss, lifting her by her hips. Her sex slid along his shaft, making him shudder again. Before his stem pulled completely free, he slammed her down atop him again. "All of me!"

He thrust his pelvis up in the same instant, driving himself into her hard, all the way to his base.

Callie cried out, clutching his shoulders and digging her nails in as she threw her head back. Her sex quivered around him, knot and all.

And something within Urkot shattered.

"Mine," he growled between harsh breaths as he pumped into her again and again. The slide and squeeze of her pussy was maddening, and the slap of her flesh against his hide set a frenzied rhythm as he lifted and slammed her down atop his cock. "Mine to claim. Mine to rut. Mine to keep."

She clung to him desperately, her eyes locked with his, her cries matching his pace, her body shaking.

Urkot laid her atop the fluffed silk, keeping firm hold of her hips. Using arms, legs, and claspers, he drove into her, chasing that rapidly growing sensation, chasing the pleasure that would surely tear him asunder.

She writhed beneath Urkot, clawing at the silk, clawing at him, her hair wild around her head. Her breasts bounced and strained at the air, nipples begging for his touch when she arched her back. Each of her movements sent ripples of pleasure through him that built and built toward something greater.

"Urkot," she rasped. "Keep going. Keep going. Don't stop. Oh God, please don't stop."

"You. Are. Mine. Callie," he gritted, each word punctuated by a hard thrust. "My *nyleea*."

"Your mate," she echoed, slapping a hand atop one of his and raking her nails over it hard enough to leave a mark.

Pleasure-pain blasted through him, making him bear his fangs. Dropping onto his upper hands over her, he plunged his cock inside her one final time, burying himself deep. Emberlike lights flashed through his vision as rapture surrounded him, swallowed him, drowned him.

Everything within him seized at once. It was his end; he knew only Callie and his own sensation in that moment, with all the world falling to nothingness. Then his pleasure surged. His stem swelled, and his seed flooded her.

Callie screamed his name, the sound swallowed by his roar. He couldn't see past the crimson cloud, didn't want to; he wanted only to feel.

This time, he could not redirect his instinct. He couldn't stop himself.

His head snapped down, and his teeth clamped on her shoulder. She clutched his head, fingers tangling in his hair, and held him as her sex contracted and convulsed around his stem and her thighs shook. Each flutter of his tendrils strengthened her trembling, making her hips buck against him.

"Urkot!" she cried, voice strained as liquid heat flooded her core. "Oh, fuck, fuck, fuck!"

He could only snarl against her skin.

She would bear his mark. All would know from this moment onward that Callie belonged to Urkot, and Urkot alone. She had chosen. He had conquered. She was his.

*Mine!*

His cock spasmed again, another jet of seed flowing from it. That seed mixed with her essence, hot and slick, filling her and trickling out around the base of his stem. His lower fingers and claspers clutched her, unwilling to let her go, forcing her slit to remain flush with his.

Finally, he loosened his jaw and lifted his head to look down at her. The strange tang of blood lighted upon his tongue.

Callie stared up at him with dark, gleaming eyes, panting. When his tendrils thrummed, she tensed and moaned; the smile curling upon her lips told him that her reaction had nothing to do with pain.

Urkot let out a shaky breath as another wave of pleasure swept through him, heightened by the clenching of her pussy, which squeezed his knot tight. Once it passed, his eyes shifted to her left shoulder, where he'd bitten her. There were multiple bleeding wounds left by his teeth.

His hearts nearly stopped.

How had he allowed himself to be so careless? He'd known, *known*, how tender her human flesh was, how easily she could be broken.

"I am sorry," he rasped. "I did not mean harm, Callie. I—"

She pressed a finger to his mouth. "Shh."

Urkot blinked, staring down at her before brushing his mouth against her finger in a kiss.

Callie stroked her fingers through the shorn hair on the sides of his head and hummed contently. When pleasure rose within him again and another spurt of seed filled her, setting his tendrils to flutter anew, she closed her eyes and squirmed beneath him with a low moan, grinding her pussy against him and taking his knot deeper.

"God, this feels amazing," she said softly, still smiling. "I love your cock and those little fluttering things. I never want this end."

Pride filled his chest. His female enjoyed their mating. The sensations had been thrilling, pleasurable beyond anything he could've imagined, but it was all sweetened immensely by Callie's satisfaction.

"It will not end. Not yet," he said.

Callie opened her eyes to meet his gaze and gently caressed his face. "Good, because you feel so fucking good inside me."

Urkot trilled and nuzzled her neck, breathing her scent deep. "I would keep my stem buried inside you until the Eight take me if I could."

Gathering her close in his arms, Urkot rolled onto his back upon the silk nest, settling within it and curling his legs around his female to provide her with as much body warmth as he could. She lay atop him with her legs spread to either side, her head on his chest, and her damp curls tickling his hide.

In the aftermath of their mating, ripples of pleasure rolled through Urkot, setting his tendrils to quiver inside Callie. He relished every sensation, her every reaction, every soft sound that escaped her.

Gradually, the pulses faded, his tendrils retreated, and his mate's body grew lax. His own body felt heavier with each beat of his hearts, and the aches that had plagued him since the rockfall settled back into place.

But he held on until her breathing deepened and he knew she was asleep. He cherished these fleeting moments most of all—his mate being comfortable enough, trusting enough, to sleep with him like this, with his stem still inside of her.

Then he let exhaustion drag him into darkness.

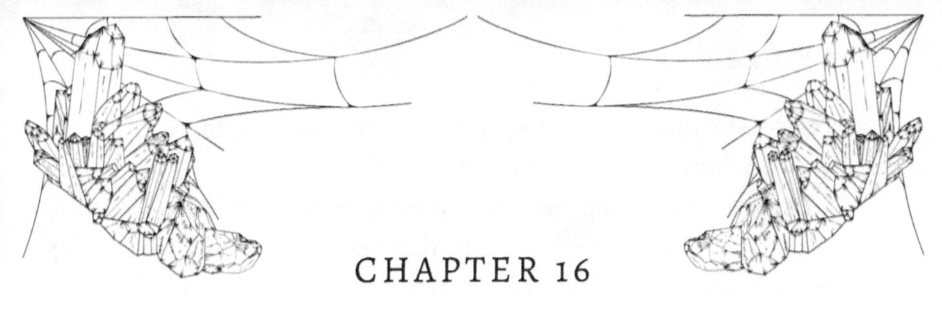

# CHAPTER 16

SHARP, painful cramping and gnawing, nausea-inducing hollowness pulled Callie abruptly from her dreams.

Hunger.

*Rude as hell.*

She squeezed her eyes tighter shut and scrunched her nose, burying her face against Urkot's chest.

Callie didn't want to get up, didn't want to move while she was so cozily cradled in Urkot's arms. She was warm, and this was exactly where she wanted to be.

Yet other discomforts were making themselves known now that she was awake. The insistent fullness of her bladder, the dull aches she'd collected since the cave-in, the faint sting on her shoulder where Urkot had bitten her. Far more pleasant than all that was the soreness between her thighs, where Urkot had so deliciously stretched her.

Callie grinned. She'd never felt so full, had never experienced so much pleasure in her life.

*My spider man used my pussy gooooood.*

Why had she waited so long? She could've been having mind

blowing sex this whole time. It was no wonder Ivy and Ahmya always had such dreamy looks on their faces.

Drawing in a deep breath, she took in both Urkot's scent and the musky scent of sex that clung to them both. Warmth spread across her face; her body was covered in cum.

*I'm thoroughly in need of a wash.*

But that could wait just a little longer. She was content right here, and she didn't want this moment to end just yet.

Turning her head to rest her cheek upon him, she smoothed her palm over his chest and down his side until her fingers met the mangled scar where his lower left arm had once been. Her heart squeezed.

She'd heard the tale of how Urkot had lost his arm when they'd first met Garahk and the thornskulls. Though the thornskulls and shadowstalkers had been enemies when the story had occurred, Garahk had spoken with great respect for Urkot's prowess.

Urkot had been the last shadowstalker standing against a huge, dangerous female warrior who had killed many of his companions before facing him. And Callie knew neither Garahk's story nor Urkot's humbler, more grounded account had done justice to the pain and trauma he'd endured during that encounter.

The female warrior had, with her bare hands and raw, unfathomable strength, torn Urkot's whole arm off. And he, having already suffered a blow to the head that likely should've killed him, had picked up the limb and used it to bludgeon his enemy to death.

When she'd first heard the story, Callie had called it crazy. She regretted those words.

There'd been nothing crazy about what Urkot had done. He'd been placed in a horrible, desperate situation, and he had done everything he could, had pushed beyond all limits, to protect his surviving companions from a terrifying threat. He had faced his own death to help others.

Maybe he didn't see the heroism in that, but it was undeniable. And the price he'd paid...

She couldn't imagine the suffering he'd endured. He'd mentioned himself that he had expected to die in that swamp. Though he'd lived, she didn't doubt that the injury had changed his life forever.

And yet she'd never once heard him complain. She'd never once heard him bemoan his situation. In fact, he'd openly joked about it, teasing the humans by pointing out that three arms was still more than they had.

Urkot was a rock for his dependability, his endurance, his steadiness, his toughness. But he was all that while being so gentle and uplifting. Though his scar undoubtedly carried deep trauma, he'd made it into something more—a symbol of the supportive, caring, selfless person he was.

Lightly, Callie caressed the rough scar.

He tensed beneath her, drawing in a heavy breath, and his arms tightened around her.

"You said you still feel it sometimes," she said softly. "Does that mean you still feel the pain?"

"Sometimes," he rumbled. "But it is...big far away. You know my words?"

Callie pressed her hand atop the large scar, wishing she could soothe it. "I do."

"I know I am not...whole, Callie. That I am less, but—"

"Stop right there," she snapped, lifting her head to glare down at him. "There is *nothing* wrong with you. You're not lesser or incomplete. You're Urkot. You're strong, brave, compassionate, funny, and sexy as all fuck. So don't you dare put yourself down like that, or insult me by—"

Urkot pressed his finger to her mouth, silencing her. "I am sexy?"

Callie huffed and rolled her eyes, but she couldn't help smiling. "Of course you'd lock in on that." Flattening her palms on his chest, she drew herself up his body and pressed a kiss to his hard mouth. "Yes, you are. Even though you're a spider."

He chittered and shifted his upper arms down, palming her ass cheeks with both hands. His eyes dipped to her chest, where her breasts hung heavy upon him. "You are sexy too. *Much* sexy."

Pleasure whispered through her at his touch. His fingers were so, so close to her pussy as he teased her flesh, and the force with which he kneaded her ass ground her clit against his hard abdomen.

She moaned, digging her fingers into his hide as her hips instinctively undulated, her body seeking more of that pleasure. "Urkot…"

Her belly emitted a loud, rolling growl.

Callie and Urkot froze, his hands clutching her ass. His eight bright eyes flicked up to hers.

"Eh, heh heh," she laughed awkwardly. "Terrible timing, but I'm kind of starving."

"Shaper, unmake me," he snarled.

Callie's eyes widened as he grasped her hips, lifted her off him, and rolled, getting his legs beneath him.

"Should have hunted," he muttered as he set her on her feet and pulled away. "Should have found food."

A gush of liquid spilled from her sex, running down her inner thighs and calves. Callie gasped and clutched her legs together, pressing a fist to her pelvis.

*What the fuck?*

Oh, no, no, no. Had she just peed herself?

No, it wasn't pee. That uncomfortable pressure remained in her bladder. This was something else. This was…

His cum.

*Well, what did you expect after all the times he came inside you while you were stuck on his knot?*

She shot a panicked look at Urkot, but he was already moving to the blanket hanging from the ceiling. His blue markings glowed in the crystals' light.

Urkot continued muttering to himself, lapsing into his native language. She was only able to pick out pieces of what he said—something about failing, about not thinking. He yanked down the blanket, head swiveling as though searching the vegetation nearby for something edible.

"Um, Urkot?"

"Damn my eyes."

"Urkot?"

He stepped out of the grotto onto the small ledge and surveyed the cavern, balling his fists with the blanket caught in his upper right hand, muscles flexing beneath his hide.

Sighing, Callie waddled to her bag, cringing as more seed seeped from her. Her feet left wet tracks across the floor.

*There's no stopping it, Callie. Might as well accept it for what it is.*

With a groan, she crouched and grabbed her bag, trying to ignore the liquid splattering beneath her. She rummaged through the bag until she found the large leaf-bound bundles at the bottom, drawing out two.

Her face was aflame when she rose and strode to Urkot, thrusting one of the bundles in front of his face. "Ta-da!"

He started before snapping his gaze to her. Silently, he took the offering, loosened the binding, and peeled back the leaves to reveal thick strips of dried meat inside. His mandibles twitched up and sank. Grasping her wrist, he placed the leaf-wrapped food atop her palm. "You eat."

She held up the other bundle. "I have more. You eat this one."

Urkot shook his head. "This food is for you."

"But there's—"

He caught her chin in a firm grip. "No, Callie. This food is safe for you. But when it is gone because I ate it, what will you have? We cannot cook meat here, and you do not want worms. This must be yours."

"I would eat worms if I had to," she grumbled, inwardly shuddering at the thought.

"If I eat this meat, you will have to eat worms in much small time."

"Ugh, fiiiiine."

He leaned down and pressed his face against her neck, nuzzling it and scraping her skin with his mouth. Callie chuckled, warmth spreading through her at his playfulness. He drew in a deep breath.

"You smell good." A low purr rumbled in his chest, and his tongue ran over the tender bite marks on her shoulder. "If I get too hungry, I will eat you."

"Stop!" Laughing, Callie nudged him away with her elbow. "I probably stink. I'm covered in your cum."

His mandibles rose high, and his eyes narrowed in delight. "Our smell is the most good smell."

"Enjoy it for now, because it'll be getting washed off soon."

"I will cover you in my seed again."

Callie's core clenched at the thought of his cock filling her once more. She wanted to repeat what they'd shared again, and again, and again.

Of course, it would've been a lot nicer to experience it in the safety of Kaldarak rather than being trapped down here.

Stepping closer to him, Callie rose on her toes and kissed the underside of his jaw. "I'll hold you to that. Now go get yourself food."

Just as she was about to step away, he banded an arm around her middle and drew her against him. With her bare breasts squished to his chest, and his lower right hand clutching her ass, he dropped his mouth to hers in a rough kiss.

And Callie parted her lips, sweeping her tongue along the crease of his mouth, coaxing it open and inviting a much deeper, more intimate kiss. For a vrix who had never kissed before, he'd learned fast, letting his tongue twine around and stroke hers.

It ended too swiftly as he released her and stepped back, his legs thumping on the ground. He shook his head, and in a gruff voice, he said, "Eat."

She chuckled as her gaze dropped to see the bulge of his slit, kept shut by the claspers pinching it closed.

He wanted her. Badly.

She'd never known what it felt like to be so wanted until him. Truly, unequivocally wanted. She felt it each time Urkot looked at her, his eyes burning with fierce yearning. It was as though he needed her more than he needed food, water, or air. As though she was the missing piece that made him whole.

*You feel it too, don't you?*

Heart in her throat, Callie watched as Urkot tossed the blanket into the grotto, climbed down the ledge, and entered the water below.

*I do.*

Rushing to the edge, she peered down at him and hurriedly said, "Be careful."

He offered her a vrix smile. "Nothing will keep me from you."

*Ah, fuck. I'm such a goner for this vrix.*

As he dove beneath the water's surface, Callie wandered back into the grotto, setting the dried meat down and digging through her bag until she found a spare piece of still-wet silk. She had other business to take care of before fulfilling her hunger.

Once she'd finished squatting in the back and emptying her bladder, nearly crying at the indignity of it all, she cleaned herself up and returned to her belongings. Strangely enough,

Urkot's cum hadn't crusted on her skin like she would've expected. Instead, it seemed to have acted like a moisturizer.

She snickered as she brushed her fingers over her belly. "Wonder what Lacey would say to that little tidbit."

Callie doubted her friend would be bottling up vrix cum and giving it out as lotion.

*God, I'd love to see Telok's reaction to* that *request.*

Snatching up the leaf bundle Urkot had untied, she drew back the leaves as she settled cross-legged upon the fluffed silk bed. She'd finished an entire strip of meat and had taken a bite out of the second when she heard splashing near the ledge.

She tensed, only now realizing that her knife—the only thing she had to use as a weapon—was buried in her bag, out of reach.

Fortunately, it was a vrix with black hide and blue markings who climbed up onto the ledge a moment later and not one of those freaky ass spiritstriders.

Water ran from Urkot in rivulets, catching and reflecting the cavern's light, as he stood upright. He used his upper hands to wipe excess moisture from his face and chest. A pair of long, pale fish dangled from his lower hand, his fingers hooked in their gaping mouths.

Callie smiled. "Success!"

He held the fish higher. "You want?"

"Not unless you can cook it. They're all yours." She bit down on the dry meat and tore off a chunk, drawing it into her mouth. Her jaw ached as she chewed the tough meat.

Chittering, Urkot eased himself down onto the ground beside her and ate. It felt so normal, so mundane, that for a little while, she almost forgot they were trapped in a seemingly endless cave system.

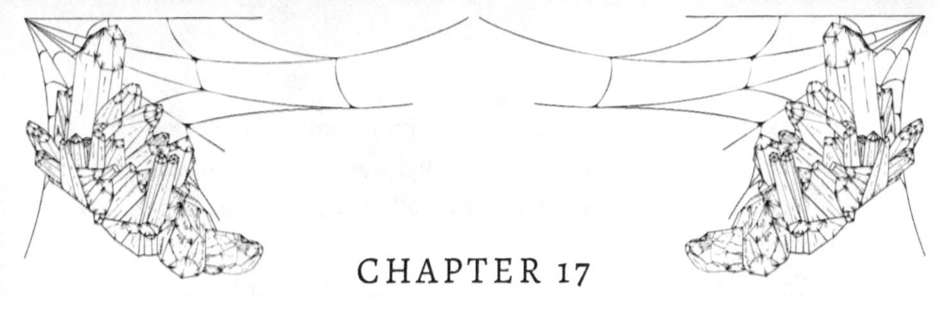

# CHAPTER 17

AFTER EATING and drinking from the waterskin, Urkot and Callie packed her belongings—the blanket, her clothes, and her boots—into her bag. Though he knew they had to press on, to find their way out, to find their way home, he could not deny his reluctance to leave the grotto. It was a special place, just for the two of them.

He would remember what they shared here forever.

Pausing on the ledge, he studied the statues one last time. What hands had crafted them? How many years had their stone faces seen pass, how many generations of vrix had hatched, lived, and died while these monuments to the Eight endured in this dark, peaceful place?

Could Urkot's kind have once lived here?

Callie's gentle touch on his arm drew him back to what mattered—the present. His mate. She peered up at him with a smile, one that revealed those endearing dimples in her cheeks. She'd tied her mass of curls atop her head to keep her hair from getting wet.

"Ready?" she asked.

He raised his mandibles. "Yes."

Urkot stooped so she could climb onto his back, then descended the cliff and entered the water. Callie hissed, her hold on him tightening as curses spilled from her in muttered breaths.

Yes, it was cold, and he would've spared her from it had he been able. But he did enjoy the way it made her press her body more firmly against his.

Urkot held Callie's bag above the surface as he swam across the lake.

*Should have done the same when we first swam to the grotto.*

Fortunately, the only cost of that mistake had been some minor discomfort. The little food she'd been carrying had been wrapped well enough to keep out the moisture. That she had food at all was a point of pride for him. She'd taken the lessons she'd been taught to heart and had brought her bag, packed with necessities, even for what should've been a short trip to the cave.

Another tunnel came into view at the far end of the lake, accessible at the top of a rocky incline. Urkot drew himself out of the water there, and, keeping Callie on his hindquarters, picked a path up to the flatter ground at the tunnel's mouth.

Shivering, she climbed down and accepted her bag, ripping it open and tugging out the blanket, which she used to briskly dry herself.

Urkot stepped away from her to shake excess water from his limbs. He felt the chill too, now that his damp hide was exposed to the cool air—and he felt the air current from the tunnel, faint but unmistakable.

"F-Fuck that water is cold. I d-don't know if I'll ever c-complain about the heat and humidity again," she said.

He chittered. "You will."

Callie snickered. "You know me s-so well."

After taking out her boots and clothing and stuffing the blanket back inside, she closed her pack.

His gaze fixated on her as she dressed. He mourned the loss of her dark nipples as she drew the fabric of her top over her breasts and relaced the front.

Hunger stirred low in his belly, and his fingers flexed. Urkot had not had nearly enough time to explore her body, to appreciate its curves, its softness, to carve its every tiny detail into his memory. Her flesh was so unlike his hide. He could spend eternity caressing it, feeling its gentle give beneath his touch. And right now, he found himself wondering how it would feel under his palms after it had been warmed by the sun.

His gaze dipped to her slit. A shudder rippled through him. Her pussy had wrapped around his cock so tightly, had accepted it so readily, had taken all of him as he'd buried himself deep in the wet heat of her core.

The memory had his stem pulsing and pressing against the inside of his slit. He drew his claspers in to keep his cock from extruding, barely suppressing a groan at the ache caused by his own restraint.

This was no longer the time, and they'd left their sanctuary behind. They were exposed again. Vulnerable.

But by the Eight, he yearned to take her again, danger be damned.

Callie lifted her skirt and wrapped it around her hips, shielding her pussy from his eyes. The urge to grab her, tear off her clothing, and rut her right here swelled within Urkot. In a moment, he could be inside her, could lose himself in her heat again.

Instead, he watched as she tied off the skirt and stepped into her boots.

"Ugh." She scrunched her face, lifting and setting down her feet to produce a soft squelching sound. "You'd think with how advanced HWI was, they would've invented boots that didn't retain water inside."

"It is like when we strode to Kaldarak." Urkot removed a

crystal from his pouch, pushing back the darkness in the tunnel with its blue light.

She slung her bag over her shoulders. "Yeah. Those were some miserable days. At least it's not muddy and raining here."

He placed a hand on the small of her back, guiding her forward as he walked along the tunnel. "I learned much in those days. Learned much of humans. Much of you."

And Urkot would learn much more about her now that she was his.

The sound of their steps, though quiet, echoed on the tunnel walls, broken only by the falling of water droplets to the floor. Moisture glistened on the stone and hung in the air.

Moss appeared on the walls as they traveled, first in little clumps, then in larger and larger patches. Soon, it was accompanied by mushrooms growing from cracks and crevices and leafy plants clinging to the rock. Much of the vegetation gave off its own dim light, which was amplified as glowworms and their strands of glowing silk became more prevalent along the ceiling.

The dampness in the air increased, and Urkot became aware of a faint vibration in the ground. It was nothing like what had preceded the collapse; this was steady, consistent, and did not seem to run deep.

Something scuttled out of the vegetation in front of them, something white and nearly a segment long, with jointed legs all along its thin body. It moved straight toward Callie.

Her screech was loud and sharp as she leapt back and climbed atop Urkot.

"Get it away! Get it away!" she cried, her blunt claws biting into his hindquarters as she draped herself over him, feet raised and kicking. "Ew, ew, ew!"

Chittering, Urkot glanced down at the creature, which wound between his legs. "It is an akreel. They do not harm."

"It's a fucking giant *sentipeed*!"

"No, it is an akreel," Urkot corrected, lifting his left leg foreleg as the creature climbed onto it. "They taste much good."

Callie yelped and scrambled farther away from the insect, clutching Urkot's right arms. "Oh my God, Urkot! Get it away!"

"It will not eat humans." He plucked it off his leg before it could reach his hindquarters, holding it by its neck. Its segmented body curled around his arm and wriggled, legs flailing in the air.

Callie shuddered violently atop him. "God, it's disgusting."

Raising the insect, he examined it. The pincers on its head were snapping, seeking something to latch onto, something to attack. The creatures weren't usually aggressive unless they felt threatened—like this one certainly felt now. Urkot had come across many akreels in his time as a delver, and he and his companions had always treated them as harmless nuisances at worst and filling snacks at best.

Yet unlike vrix hide, human skin was fragile. It was thin and easily broken. As he watched those pincers moving, he knew they would be able to pierce human flesh and inflict pain, even if they were unlikely to do serious damage. It was no wonder humans were unsettled by such creatures.

Urkot looked at Callie, who stared at the creature with her nose wrinkled in disgust.

"Am I not spider?" he asked.

She flicked her gaze to him. "Huh?"

He raised his foreleg and curled it. "Do I not have legs like the akreel?"

"I mean, kind of?"

"Am I disgusting?"

Callie laughed as she slapped his hindquarters. A spank. "No, you're not. Now get rid of it!"

Mandibles rising, Urkot lifted the akreel high, tipped his head back, and opened his mouth.

"Don't you *dare*," Callie warned.

He lowered the insect by a thread's width.

"Urkot!"

Chittering, he closed his mouth, straightened, and tossed the creature into the vegetation on the side of the tunnel. It thrashed for a moment to right itself before scurrying away.

"Is it gone?" she asked.

"It is gone. This male has protected his female."

Callie shifted on his hindquarters until her legs were on either side of his waist, feet dangling. "Well, this male can continue to protect his female by carrying her in case there are more of those things."

She smoothed her hands up his back, and her lips caressed his hide between his shoulders. "You have a sexy back, so I'll just enjoy the view from here."

His fine hairs rose in delight, and he trilled, again forced to draw his claspers in tighter. "Behave, Callie."

Her chuckle was husky as she slipped her hands around him, her fingers teasing his abdomen above his slit. "Urkot, you're just begging for me to do the opposite."

He covered her hands with one of his and growled, pressing her palms firmly against his hide as he strode forward. "It is not safe."

She flicked her tongue over his back, making him shudder. "A little danger is exciting."

He groaned.

*Impossible female.*

She was making it difficult to resist, difficult to stop himself from binding her in silk and punishing her in a way that would pleasure both of them. His core ached from keeping his stem contained, and his instincts roared with the need to rut her. He needed to end this before she pushed too far. Before he lost control.

There was one way to put a stop to her teasing.

His mandibles twitched with humor. "Then I will claim you here, amongst the akreels."

"Ugh!" She drew back and settled her hands on his shoulders. "You sure know how to ruin the moment."

"We will find more moments," he replied, clutching her leg above her knee. "If we do not, we will make them."

She leaned against him and hummed in agreement.

Urkot continued onward, his chest brimming with delightful warmth. He'd always had an easy camaraderie with his friends. They'd jested and teased each other for all their lives, and it had only brought them closer, had only made them more willing to fight for each other, to bleed for each other.

For a long time, he'd thought that was enough, that it was as close as anyone could get to another. Callie had shown him otherwise. She had shown him something he'd never dared to expect for himself.

*You are not unworthy, Urkot.*

Those words from the celebration drifted up from Urkot's memory, carrying all the weight and solemnity with which Ketahn had spoken them. They'd been true all along, but it had taken Callie to prove it to him.

He was worthy. And he'd claimed what he'd wanted all along.

Her.

Gradually, the vibrations grew stronger, and soon the taste of fresh mist danced on the air. And then he heard it—the rush of falling water. It was soft at first, becoming louder with his every step. The mist tickled his fine hairs and dampened his hide.

The tunnel curved sharply before opening into a spacious chamber where a large waterfall flowed from above, filling a wide pool that itself fed a stream. The cavern walls and floor were covered with vegetation, including thick-stemmed flowers with luminous bulbs growing along the banks of the stream. Their white glow rivaled that of the glowworms.

Tiny flying bugs flitted about, some of which would undoubtedly end up caught in the worms' snares.

"This is something straight out of a fantasy book," Callie said with awe. "There's an entire *eekosistum* down here."

"An...*eekosistum*?" Urkot asked, sweeping his gaze around in search of it. She'd made it sound like something large...

"You're already looking at it," she replied with a chuckle. "It just refers to all the life in a certain environment. The living things down here exist in their own little ecosystem...their own little bubble. They've adapted to the conditions to create a sort of community that's entirely unique from the creatures on the surface. Even with these bugs, you have a balance of predators and prey, with the plants as the basis of the food chain."

"So...the Tangle is its own ecosystem?"

"Yep. Same with the swamp. And there can even be smaller ecosystems within a larger one, adapted around points where conditions differ. Like even within the jungle, a different ecosystem might form around, say, a lake, where unique food sources and environmental conditions allow for other creatures to thrive.

"But the balance can be very delicate. The introduction of something new, like a new animal, a new plant, or a new weather pattern, can sometimes disrupt an ecosystem enough to destroy it entirely. We've seen them get altered drastically on Earth, like when humans bring different plants and animals to new areas, or when our activity changes conditions in the environment. And unfortunately, that disruption can eliminate entire species."

He let out a thoughtful hum, studying their surroundings anew. Though human words were often confusing to him, he couldn't deny that he was intrigued by the way Callie saw the world.

He also loved listening to her speak.

"Sorry for rambling," Callie said after a brief silence. "I just find these things fascinating."

"Me too. Thank you for helping me understand."

"Any time, big guy."

Urkot strode to the edge of the pool. Callie carefully withdrew her legs from around his waist, turning as he crouched and held his lower hand out to assist her down. Her boots landed softly on the vegetation below.

"Is the water safe to drink?" she asked.

He drew in a deep breath, flooding his senses with the crisp scent of the mist. "It is."

"Finally." She knelt and bent over, cupping her hands and plunging them into the pool.

Urkot lowered himself beside her, and they drank their fill of the cool, pure water.

When Callie finished, she wiped her mouth with the back of her hand, shouldered off her pack, and took out her waterskin. As she filled it, Urkot stood up and surveyed the chamber.

"Stay," he commanded.

"Yes, sir," she said with amusement.

Tough as it was to step away from Callie, even knowing that she would be within sight the entire time, he strode to the nearby vegetation to collect food. Threadleaf plants, which grew along the walls, had stringy leaves but were bulbous near their bases, and were edible from root to tip. Whiteroots, long, white-stemmed mushrooms that grew in thick patches, had a subtle, earthy taste, but were quite filling. But best of all were the shadowberries, small, plump fruits with dark blue skins that grew in clusters underground near sources of water. Their juice was the perfect balance of sweet and tart.

These were foods that the vrix of Takarahl ate daily. Foods that had seen them through their darkest days, when Zurvashi had denied most of her subjects fresh meat.

He gathered his harvest on his lower arm, keeping it tucked against his abdomen. In *vrix*, he softly said, "Thank you, Rootsinger, for your bounty. May your song endure forever."

Callie had packed the waterskin away by the time Urkot returned to her. He lowered himself to the ground and laid the food out on the vegetation between them, telling her the name of each.

She picked up a bunch of shadowberries by the stem. "I guess it's time for a game of *rushin roolet*."

"A game?" Urkot leaned toward her, unable to mask his eagerness. He'd always enjoyed games, especially when he competed with Callie. "How do we play?"

"It's a game I would play myself. I assume you've eaten all these before?"

Cocking his head, he nodded. "Yes."

"So you know they're safe for you to eat. *Rushin roolet* is a game of chance between life and death." Callie gestured to the food between them. "I don't know which are safe for me to eat, or which could poison me."

Both his mandibles and his shoulders sagged, and something heavy and cold sank in his stomach. "I do not like this game."

Yet he knew she was right. Though humans could eat most of the same foods as vrix, they could not tolerate sweetfang root, a discovery Ketahn had made when Ivy had fallen terribly ill after consuming some. Her sickness had been so severe that Ketahn had feared he would lose her. Who could say what else might harm humans?

Callie chuckled. "Me neither, but without the food analyzer, there's no way to really to know without trying." She pointed at the whiteroots. "Those are mushrooms, so I'm not touching them. Unknown mushrooms are dangerous to fuck around with back on Earth."

Urkot growled low, reaching out to take the shadowberries from her. "You will eat none of it."

She pulled the berries away from him. "We don't know how long we'll be stuck in this place, and the food I have in my pack will only go so far. I can try a little at a time and wait."

"Callie…"

"The injections they gave us should protect me against the worst effects."

"Should," Urkot repeated with a huff. He didn't like that word any more than he liked this game.

"Look, I analyzed that root that made Ivy sick. The toxins it contained really should've killed her. Within a week, she should've been suffering organ failure. Instead, she was sick for a few days and completely fine afterward. Every time Ivy tried a new food, she was taking a risk, paving the way for us before she even knew we were still alive. But that's what life is. That's what survival is."

She looked down at the berries. "Our bodies have changed, *are changing,* to better adapt to this world."

Urkot caught her chin and gently guided her face to his. "And if you get sick? I do not know healing, Callie, and Diego is far."

She curled her fingers around his wrist and smiled. "Had I not brought this up, you wouldn't have known any differently. I wanted you to be aware just in case. Besides, most of the food we've eaten has been completely safe. All things considered, human and vrix diets are shockingly compatible."

He grunted. "I still do not like this."

"I'll take it slow, okay?"

When he grunted, her smile widened, and something warmed inside him. That warmth didn't ease his tension as he released her chin and watched her pluck a berry off the stem and lift it to her lips. He much rather would've had those lips pressed against his hide, against his mouth, instead of a piece of fruit that could cause her harm.

Those alluring lips parted, and she slipped the berry

between them, biting down. She hummed in surprise and appreciation.

His insides felt knotted and tight. It was a strange conflict in him—he trusted her, trusted her knowledge, but that trust did nothing to diminish his worry. And she'd been right. If she hadn't mentioned *rushin roolet* and reminded him of the risk, he wouldn't have thought of it. He would've failed her as a mate because, to him, these were all safe foods that he had eaten countless times without a second thought.

They sat together, the remaining berries in the bunch resting on Callie's lap, and let the waterfall's sound and cool mist envelop them as they waited.

"No tingling, no numbness, no cramping or nausea," Callie said after a time. "And as much as I do have a craving for another one of those berries, I'm going to wait. I'll try the threadleaf later, or else if I do get sick, I won't know which one caused it."

She passed the shadowberries to him. "Eat, Urkot."

Though he knew there was a chance that she'd be affected by the fruit, he couldn't help his relief. He took the berries and returned them to the pile on the ground, instead taking up the mushrooms. If the shadowberries were safe for Callie, and she enjoyed their taste, he'd save them for her.

After he'd eaten, they bundled the remaining food in scraps of silk and packed them in Callie's bag, drank some more water, and continued onward. The glowworms grew scarcer, and the tunnel dimmer, as Urkot and Callie left the waterfall behind.

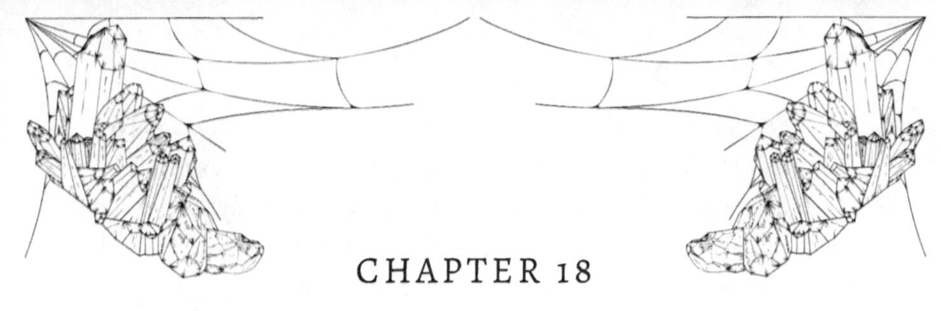

# CHAPTER 18

"A FORK IN THE ROAD," Callie said as they stood in front of two branching tunnels. "Which way does the wind lead you, big guy?"

Urkot grunted, extending his forelegs to the sides. He'd followed the air current thus far, knowing it would take them to some sort of opening to the surface eventually, but he felt it from both branches here.

The tunnel on the left was narrower, with a lower ceiling, and the airflow… The difference was slight, but it was weaker.

"This way," he said, stepping into the right tunnel. Callie walked beside him.

As they proceeded, the passage widened, and a strange, unsettling sense of familiarity teased at Urkot's mind. He paused when they reached an opening on the tunnel wall. Only a moment's examination told him it wasn't a natural occurrence, but a deliberately shaped entryway.

Urkot moved to the doorway and peered inside, holding his crystal up to shed light into the chamber.

"What is it?" Callie whispered.

The chamber's shape, its size, the little alcoves and shelves carved into the stone, it was all familiar to him. Tattered, dirty, threadbare silk cloth dangled from the wall and lay crumpled on the dusty floor in the corner. He doubted even Rekosh would've been able to guess the age of that fabric.

"This was a den," Urkot said.

"Spiritstriders?"

He heard the fear in her voice, and reached out to her, settling a hand upon her lower back. "I do not think so. This is the same as the dens in Takarahl."

"The statues, these dens… Did shadowstalkers live here?"

They backed away from the chamber, and as they continued along the tunnel, Urkot replied, "Perhaps. A big time ago. The first queen, Takari, led our kind to Takarahl from our old home, but the stories do not say where that was."

More dens stood along the tunnel's walls. A few had scraps of silk hanging at the entryways, though the fabric looked like it would crumble to dust if touched.

"I wonder if the thornskulls know this place exists," Callie said. "It's so close to Kaldarak. If there were shadowstalkers here, there must be some history of them. There must be some stories."

"We will ask when we return."

Striding along that tunnel remained odd for him. In some ways, it felt like being back in Takarahl—a Takarahl that had been abandoned and lost to time. It filled him with a sorrow he could not quite explain, balanced only by his deep curiosity.

Had Zurvashi retained power, would this have been Takarahl's fate? Would she have bled the shadowstalkers dry until nothing remained in the city's dark tunnels, not even their spirits?

Faint light spilled into the tunnel from a few of the dens where crystals grew in veins on the walls. Urkot peered into one to find a wall and part of the ceiling collapsed. Glowing crystals were scattered in the rubble, bathing part of the chamber in soft blue light while leaving the rest shrouded in shadow.

That blue seemed cold and harsh here, where it only served to emphasize the chamber's emptiness. All it could truly call attention to was absence—of joy, of life.

Was this what it felt like to be a ghost? Trudging through empty darkness and finding no warmth or solace in the rare patches of light, only more nothingness?

With those heavy, uneasy thoughts churning in his mind as he and Callie neared a bend in the tunnel, Urkot almost didn't notice the light scraping of steps from ahead.

Callie stopped half an instant before him, bringing him to an abrupt halt.

Something growled from around the bend. It was followed by guttural voices and scuffling, scrabbling sounds that echoed along the tunnel, drawing nearer.

Urkot met Callie's gaze. Her eyes were rounded with fear, and he knew her thoughts had leapt to the same place as his— the spiritstrider that had set upon them in the dark.

Hearts pounding, he stuffed his crystal into his pouch, snatched Callie off her feet, and clutched her to his chest as he retreated. She wrapped her arms around his neck and clung to him without question. He gritted his teeth as he moved, his leg muscles straining as he struggled not to make a sound. The spiritstriders, speaking to one another in those harsh voices, continued to get closer.

Urkot entered the first chamber he came upon without hesitation, finding himself in the den with the rockfall.

He hurried deeper inside. Callie curled up in his arms as he sank low in the space between the rubble and the wall, making himself as small as possible and hiding her body in the shadow of his own. His claspers instinctually hooked around her hip to draw her more securely against him. His markings glowed in response to the crystals.

The sounds from the tunnel drew nearer. Two distinct voices, arguing in words he could not understand; clicking echoing along the tunnel and within the chamber; limbs stomping and scraping stone.

All he could do was hope the spiritstriders wouldn't enter this den, and that if they did, their eyesight was poor enough that they would mistake his dark hide for more shadowy rubble and his markings for clusters of crystal.

It was a struggle to keep his strained breathing quiet, and his hearts would not slow no matter how hard he willed them to do so.

The sounds from the tunnel now came from just beyond the entryway.

He held his mate yet tighter.

*Please, let them keep striding...*

There was another harsh exchange between those guttural voices. One word was repeated frequently, sounding very much like *dak*—no in vrix—but Urkot still couldn't make out much else.

A spiritstrider hissed, and the sounds of movement in the tunnel intensified. Figures came into view, indistinct in the scant light that reached the corridor, locked in a struggle that made them seem more like a jumble of mismatched limbs than two individual beings. Urkot could tell only that one of the vrix was larger than the other.

The spiritstriders wrestled, slamming into the tunnel walls and scraping legs and claws over stone. When one struck the doorway with its hindquarters, fine dust and tiny pebbles rained from the top of the opening.

Urkot offered a silent prayer to the Delver.

*No more rockfalls. Please.*

The spiritstriders' struggle swept the pair out of view, farther along the tunnel. Relief sparked in Urkot before he could quash it. The spiritstriders had passed; he and Callie just needed to wait a little while before moving on. The immediate danger was over, and this den was safe.

An agonized snarl from the corridor sent a chill to Urkot's core.

The larger of the two spiritstriders stumbled backward into the chamber. A female—four arms, four legs, no claspers, standing three segments tall. There was a leanness to her frame that was not common in shadowstalker and thornskull females, accentuating the bones beneath her hide in some places and her powerful, sinewy muscles in others.

In the light of the crystals, her pale hide took on a bluish glow of its own.

She clutched a lower arm to her chest. Dark blood flowed from beneath the hand she'd clamped on her forearm. Her clawed mandibles spread wide, and she hissed at the doorway.

The smaller spiritstrider, a male, darted into the chamber, launching himself directly at the female. The speed and suddenness of his attack made Callie flinch and Urkot's leg hairs stand up.

With a roar, the female fell. Before she'd even crashed to the floor, the male, whose glowing hide was crisscrossed with scars, was already winding the silk rope coiled in his hands around her limbs.

Despite her size, the female's struggles seemed only to tangle her further in the silk. Within heartbeats, she was bound by arms, legs, and neck, the male holding the extra rope taut. She growled and snapped the air with her mandible claws, muscles straining as she fought the silk.

Growling, the male pulled on the rope, forcing the female's head back. His slit opened, and his white stem emerged. Using the silk rope to control her and keep her mandibles away, he forcefully mounted the female, latching his claspers around her waist. A low groan escaped him as he thrust hard.

Callie's breath hitched, and she hurriedly but quietly covered her mouth and nose. Urkot stroked her with his fingers, reminding her that he was there as his claspers clutched her.

Tangling his limbs around the female, the male spiritstrider quickened his thrusts, breathing harshly. His claws bit into her hide, producing dark drops of blood that gleamed in the dim light. The female snarled in pain and impotent fury.

"*Kir'ani, kir'ani, kir'ani,*" the male rasped over and over again.

*Mine, mine, mine.*

As the spiritstriders rutted, their grunts and growls echoing off the walls, Callie trembled against Urkot. The savageness and hostility of this mating was so far removed from what he and Callie had shared in the grotto that he couldn't consider it the same act.

Binding, conquering, and claiming were instinctual for vrix, but amongst shadowstalkers and thornskulls, they were urges to be explored with a willing mate. What he was witnessing now...this was the old way. A way that had produced so many cautionary stories, that had left countless males maimed or dead.

This was what Zurvashi had tried to revive in Takarahl through the High Claiming—this battle for dominance, this deadly game of conquerors and conquered. This manner of mating that saw vrix acting like little more than beasts taking whatever they wanted, that encouraged violence and killing so only the strong could produce broodlings.

It was what she'd wanted of Ketahn—for him to prove his strength, his worthiness, by conquering her. To prove he was a mate worthy of a queen...or die trying.

Only a few segments of empty air and formless shadow separated the spiritstriders from Urkot and Callie. He wished he could spare his mate from witnessing this. Wished he could become one with the darkness, like Ketahn and Telok seemed to do, and slip past the spiritstriders, carrying his female to safety.

But he knew he would not get past them without being noticed. Just like he knew he'd be at a severe disadvantage if he chose to fight, even if he were to catch them by surprise while the female was restrained.

He could not fight two spiritstriders while ensuring Callie was shielded from harm.

The only thing he could do was hold his little human, letting her know through his presence that she was not alone, that he was here for her, that he would protect her.

Pace faltering, the male spiritstrider thrust once more, pushing his knot deep within the female, and spasmed with a low growl. "Mine."

He bent forward and bit the female's upper arm. The silk rope he'd held taut slackened.

Snarling, the female spiritstrider tore an arm free. She clamped her hand over the top of the male's head and wrenched it back, making his teeth tear off a chunk of her flesh and exposing his neck.

Before the male could react, the female opened her mouth wide and sank her fangs into his throat. Her mandibles latched onto the surrounding hide.

Callie flinched.

A startled, gurgling cry escaped the male, combining with the sound of liquid spattering the floor.

When the female spiritstrider yanked upward, flesh and muscle shredded and broke, and bone popped. The coil of silk fell from the male's limp hands as his head, attached to his neck only by a few strings of mangled hide and sinew, fell back to dangle between his shoulders. His black eyes stared blankly at Urkot and Callie.

The female shrugged off her bindings and stretched her long limbs, ripping the male's claspers off her body and yanking his stem free of her slit. A gush of glowing seed spilled from her as she dropped the male onto the chamber floor and positioned herself over him. Blood was smeared across her fanged mouth and chin, trickling down her neck and chest, dark against her pale hide.

Already, the smell of that blood saturated the air.

Crouching low, the female stabbed her claws into the male's abdomen and hindquarters, tore them open, and began to eat.

Callie stiffened, her fingers clutching the long strands of Urkot's hair.

Of all the things he had overcome, endured, and survived, of all the bloodshed and death he'd seen, this was the most unsettling. And he could do nothing but remain hunkered down, holding his mate, his senses in a heightened state of awareness so he could react if the female discovered their presence.

Callie drew in a shuddering breath and buried her face against his chest. But hiding her eyes would not stop the sounds. The squelching, the chewing, the bones snapping and cracking, the labored breaths taken around mouthfuls of bloody flesh.

Much as he wanted to, Urkot could not look away. He had to watch the threat. Had to be prepared to fight.

After what seemed an eternity, the female pushed herself up. Her slit opened, and more of the male's seed was expelled from it, falling onto his remains.

She snarled as she ripped away a silk rope still clinging to her leg before slamming the same leg heavily on the corpse before her. Bone crunched under the blow.

The female growled furious, unfamiliar words, bloody mandible claws snapping the air.

Urkot's own mandibles twitched, and his fingers flexed. His hearts beat hard but steady, and his muscles thrummed with readiness. The female would look up. She would see Urkot and Callie. And she would attack.

The female spiritstrider did look up.

But her black eyes did not focus or linger upon Urkot and Callie.

She muttered something in her guttural language and jabbed her leg down into the male's body once more. Striding strode over it, she ducked through the entryway without giving the male another glance. Before she was out of sight, Urkot saw her turn and move in the direction from which she'd come.

He did not ease his hold on Callie as he listened to the female striding away, as he listened to her unsettling clicks echoing along the tunnel. Even when the female's sounds had faded, it was many heartbeats before his tension started to ease.

"She is gone," he rumbled quietly.

Callie shoved away from him and scrambled to her feet, stumbling until she threw out a hand to catch herself against the wall. Her shoulders rose and fell rapidly as she stared at the spiritstrider's mutilated remains lying in the center of a bloody pool. The whites of her beautiful, alien eyes were prominent.

She slapped a hand over her mouth and turned her face away from the corpse as she retched.

Urkot rose and stepped to her, flattening his palm on her back. He whispered, "Easy, Callie."

"*What. The. Fuck*," she rasped. "Urkot, what the fuck was that?"

"She told him no."

"So he *raypd* her?"

"I do not know that word. He claimed her by force, without her want."

"Is that common for vrix? Is it...normal?"

He smoothed his hand up and down her back, soothing himself through that touch as much as he hoped to soothe her. "It was, much years ago. A male would show interest in claiming a female as his mate, and if she denied him, he could prove he was worthy, could prove his strength, by conquering her. By taking her and planting his seed. It is instinct. But even if the male won, the female did not always accept. Males would get hurt. Sometimes get dead."

Callie thrust a finger at the dead spiritstrider. "And then this happens?"

Urkot followed her gesture with his gaze and let out a huff. "This male did not take care in his hunger. And she…had a different hunger."

"I can't say he didn't deserve it, but ugh." She shuddered. "I really, really could've gone my entire life without seeing that."

"I am sorry I could not shield you," he said, turning his eyes back to her. "And when I said I would eat you, it was a joke. I will not eat you, female."

She let out a small laugh. "Not in this way, no."

Blinking, he cocked his head. "There is another way to eat?"

"I am so not explaining that after what we just saw."

He could only stare at her, mandibles twitching as though unable to decide whether they wanted to rise or fall.

Callie ran a hand through her curls, pulling them back as she said, "I can't believe I'm joking about this while there's a mutilated, half-eaten corpse in front of us."

"What are you joking about?"

"I'll explain it later. When we're not…you know. *Here.*"

The way she'd talked about this—whatever it was—had him intensely curious despite the situation. What could she possibly mean by there being another way to eat her? And why had she laughed about it?

"You will," he said firmly.

When Callie nodded with the tiniest smile curling her lips, Urkot forced himself to lower his hand and crept to the doorway. She kept close behind him, giving the body a wide berth.

He peered into the tunnel and checked both directions. There was no sign of the female spiritstrider.

"We will go back and take the other path," he said to her, keeping his voice low. "This one may lead to the spiritstriders' dens."

Callie placed her hand on his arm and gave it a squeeze. "Lead the way, big guy."

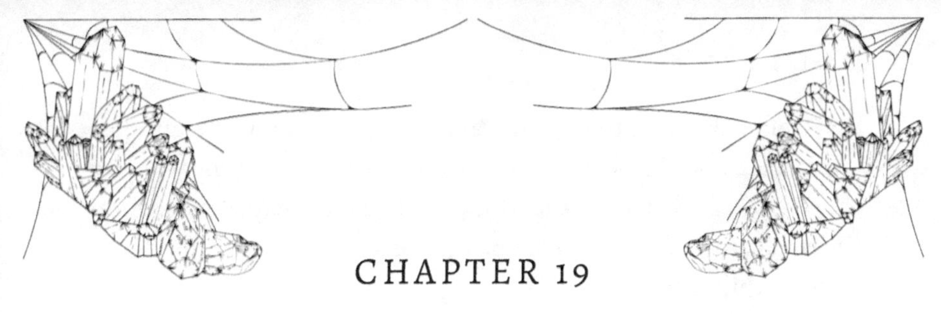

# CHAPTER 19

CALLIE DIDN'T KNOW how much time had passed since they'd entered the smaller tunnel, but it felt endless. It was long, narrow, and winding. There were places where they had to climb up or crawl down, and though she was able to move with of room to spare, some spots were tight enough that Urkot barely managed to squeeze through.

Every time he had to contort his body to navigate some especially narrow or awkward passage, Callie's stomach knotted, and her heart clenched. But despite his broad shoulders, ample hindquarters, and large frame, he maneuvered through it all with a sense of calm and confidence she wished she could emulate.

Because she was feeling it here. *Really* feeling it. Even if she hadn't come close to getting stuck, this tunnel, more than anywhere else they'd been, made her feel trapped because it was so, so dark. The only light came from the crystals she and Urkot held. It felt like the tunnel was closing in around her, like at any moment, the ceiling would buckle and collapse upon them.

It felt like they would be stuck down here forever.

Like they would die here.

Callie clutched the crystal, and its jagged points bit into her skin. Her body ached, her legs were weak, her feet heavy. Her boots shuffled across the floor with every step. Exhaustion grasped at her from the darkness, threatening to drag her down into nothingness.

*We're going to die here.*

*No... No, we're not.*

Sweat beaded on her skin, trickling down her temples, along the back of her neck, and between her breasts. Her skin felt cold and clammy, and her heart was thumping so fast and hard that its every beat echoed in her ears. With each step, her chest grew tighter, constricting her lungs and making it hard to breathe.

*We're going to die. We're going... We're going to...*

*Die.*

*Die.*

*Die.*

Her steps faltered and came to a halt. Trembling, she leaned against the rough stone wall as the shadows thickened around her and crept along the edges of her version.

"No," Callie whispered. "No."

"Callie?"

Urkot's deep voice reached her through the encroaching darkness, full of care and concern.

But she couldn't answer him. Couldn't get any words out through the tightness of her throat. She couldn't...couldn't breathe.

Callie clutched at her chest as she gasped for air, tears spilling from her eyes.

Large hands clasped her face, tipping it up. "Callie! Look at me."

*Urkot.*

Her name, spoken in his voice, so full of fear, broke the

shadows' grasp on her. His sapphire eyes came into focus, glowing bright. A beacon.

"Breathe." He gently combed his claws through her hair. "Good, female. Listen to me. Come back to me, my suncrest."

*My suncrest.*

Callie latched on to that endearment, that voice, that touch. With his coaxing, she took one deep breath after another. Not once did she look away from him. He was her rock, strong, powerful, and steady.

"Good, female," he repeated, brushing his thumbs across her cheek and wiping away her tears.

With his lower hand, he gently pried the crystal from her stiff fingers, then slipped her pack off her shoulders with an upper hand, setting it on the ground.

Softly crooning, Urkot touched his headcrest to her forehead. "We will rest here."

Releasing her, he eased down into a sitting position. He folded his forelegs in front of him, drew her down atop them, and tucked her into the crook of his left arm, allowing her legs to drape across his lap. His lower right hand curled around her knee.

Once she was settled, he opened her bag, took out the waterskin, and uncorked it. "Drink. It will help."

Callie took it with both trembling hands, grateful for his help steadying it as she drank. The water was cool against her hot, parched throat.

Through blurry, tear-filled eyes, Callie watched him close the waterskin and return it to her bag.

And then the dam broke.

A cry burst from her, startling Urkot. It was followed by a series of sobs that she could not contain. Her shoulders shook and her chest convulsed as tears ran down her cheeks.

A distressed buzz emitted from Urkot. He tenderly cradled

her jaw with his upper hand, forcing her to look up at him. "Ah, my suncrest."

Callie clutched at his arm around her waist, trying to rein in her hiccups. "I'm sorry. I-I'm so s-sorry," she said, her eyes flicking between his. "I don't m-mean to be a burden. This isn't like me. I'm j-just so tired and scared, and…and it feels so hopeless. I-I just had this thought that we were going t-to die here and I felt this…panic. And I couldn't let it go. Couldn't stop it."

She drew in a shaky breath. "You're probably feeling the same, but y-you're holding it all in for me. You're strong. And I…I'm just this blubbering mess."

Urkot slid his hand up, wiping away her tears with his thumb as his fingers caressed the side of her face. The low, calming sound of his crooning vibrated into her through his chest, a slow, simple melody she'd heard from him before. That familiarity was another thing for her to grab onto.

She leaned into his touch.

"We fall," he said gently, "and we stand back up. If you cannot stand, I am here, Callie. I will carry you until you can stride again."

His hand slid down to her neck, circling it, his thumb caressing her collarbone. "You are no burden. You are strong, and you always have been. All of us break sometimes. If we do not stop to mend, to heal, we will break again in a small time, like stone being chipped away."

Callie sniffled, and once more let out a deep exhalation, this one much calmer than the last. She did not look away from his brilliant blue eyes, which chased away the darkness.

When his fingers encountered the healing bite marks on her shoulder, he purred, lightly tracing them and sending tingles through her. "I gave you my words, my bond. I will keep you safe, my sweet *nyleea,* my suncrest. I claimed you, you are mine, and nothing will take you from me. Not even the Eight."

His hand moved down her chest, and his palm grazed her

nipple through her top. Callie started and drew in a sharp breath as his touch sent an unexpected rush of pleasure straight to her core.

Urkot quickly lifted his hand, his eyes flaring as his mandibles sagged. "I am s—"

Callie caught his wrist. "No. Please." She drew his hand back to her chest, cupping his fingers around her breast. "Touch me. I...I need to feel you. I need to feel this."

She needed a distraction. Needed to forget that they were trapped, needed to forget that their lives were at risk.

She needed him.

Urkot's fingers flexed, both on her breast and on her knee, and his mandibles rose. He released another low purr. "Ah, Callie..."

And then his hand moved. It wasn't gentle; it was firm, purposeful. He squeezed her breast, kneaded it, and Callie was like clay, yielding to his touch. She arched her back with a sigh.

"So soft," Urkot rumbled.

He lifted his hand. Hooking the string of her top with a claw, he tugged it down, cutting through it. The fabric parted, freeing her breasts.

Urkot touched the tip of that claw to her nipple, making it harden. Callie's breath hitched.

He crooned and circled the nub with his claw. She shivered at its light scrape over her sensitive skin.

"Urkot..." she whispered.

"I love the way your lips shape my name." Closing his fingers over her nipple, he pinched it hard.

Callie gasped, body bucking as her clit twitched. But his arm around her waist kept her in place. Heat pooled low in her belly, and she could feel her slick gathering, could feel it seeping her from pussy.

"And the way your body sings for me, my suncrest." His claspers curled around her thigh.

She clenched his arm as he rolled her nipple between his fingers over and over, creating a maelstrom of pleasure and pain. Her heart raced with the delicious torment he was unleashing upon her.

Urkot drew in a heavy inhalation and released it in a long, low growl. "I smell your desire."

"Yes," she breathed. "I need you to touch me more."

Cradling her breast, caressing it, Urkot slowly ran his lower hand up her thigh.

Her skin prickled in the wake of his touch as it moved closer and closer her to her pussy. Breath rapid with her growing desire, Callie spread her legs, opening herself to him.

His fingers were light on her sex, almost delicate, as though he were afraid to hurt her. He traced her labia in gentle strokes, exploring her, and Callie's channel clenched as shivers of delight swept through her.

She needed that finger inside her.

His finger dipped to her entrance. Urkot groaned as he spread her slick around and pumped the pad of his finger shallowly in and out of her. "Your pussy is so wet. Wet for me."

"It is," Callie moaned, undulating her hips. "It's all for you."

"It is all mine. You are mine." He nuzzled her hair as he circled her entrance. "Give me more."

Whispers of pleasure spiraled through her, but it wasn't enough. She needed more. And God, she was so wet her slick was dripping down her ass. Whatever chill had overcome her before had long since been banished by the fire burning beneath her skin.

When his finger trailed up and grazed her clit, Callie cried out with the shock of ecstasy. "There! Oh fuck, Urkot, touch my clit."

"Clit," Urkot repeated, moving his finger back to it and pressing down. "This?"

Callie dug her nails into his arm and frantically nodded. "Yes."

He circled her clit slowly, reverently, and she moaned, lashes fluttering as her head tipped back and her toes curled. "Keeping going. Please don't stop."

"Ah… So this brings you much pleasure. This tiny bud."

"So, so much. And it feels better when you're touching it."

And it was true. Her fingers couldn't compare to the firm, rough hide of his. Perhaps it was also the connection she and Urkot shared, the bond they'd formed, that made her hypersensitive to every little touch. Because she'd never felt anything close to what she felt with him.

His upper hand fondled her breast, twisting and squeezing and plucking her nipple as his lower hand continued its leisurely ministrations on her clit. Her body hummed. Reaching up, she slipped her fingers into his hair and clutched at it as she spread her thighs wider, reveling in the sensations.

Urkot trilled low. "Your pussy blooms like a flower. And it took my stem so deeply."

Panting, she rocked her hips in time with his strokes as pleasure coiled within her core. She remembered how it felt to have him inside her, stretching her, filling her, which left her core with an empty, yearning ache now.

"I need your cock inside me again," she begged.

His claspers tightened on her thigh, making her aware of the bulge pressing against it.

"Not yet," he said in a gravelly voice. "Not here."

He quickened his strokes on her clit as his tongue trailed over her jaw and traced her mouth. "But I will bury my cock in your body again soon, my *nyleea*. I will feel your heat, feel you squeeze my stem sweetly. And I will fill your pussy with my seed."

"Yes," she rasped, voice growing higher in pitch with her

pleasure. "I want your cum. In me, on me, on my tongue. I want it all."

The growl he released was absolutely bestial and undeniably arousing. "I love having your pleasure in my hands. Love the sounds you make, love you coming unraveled at my touch. Love that you are all mine."

He pinched her clit.

"Urkot!"

Callie shattered. She threw her head back and closed her eyes, body going taut as ecstasy crashed through her.

He released her breast and covered her mouth with his palm, muffling her escalating cries. Pleasure consumed her, taking over her body as she wildly bucked against his fingers. Her sex contracted around nothing, feeling so, so empty.

Urkot touched his headcrest to her forehead and cupped his hand over her pussy. She could feel the prick of his claws against her ass. Breathing heavily against his palm, Callie opened her eyes and met his as her body quivered, riding out the waves of pleasure sweeping through her.

"Ah, my suncrest," he whispered, "how you shine for me."

His fingers stroked her slit slowly, gently, as she came down from her orgasm. Only when her breathing eased and she relaxed in his hold did he stop.

Keeping his eyes locked with hers, he lifted his hand, extended his tongue, and licked his glistening finger with a groan. The way he did it, the way he sounded, made her sex throb anew.

But there was a heaviness weighing down her body, weighing down her consciousness.

Lifting his hand from her face, he rubbed his mouth across hers with a purr as he gathered her closer against his chest. "Sleep, my Callie. I have you."

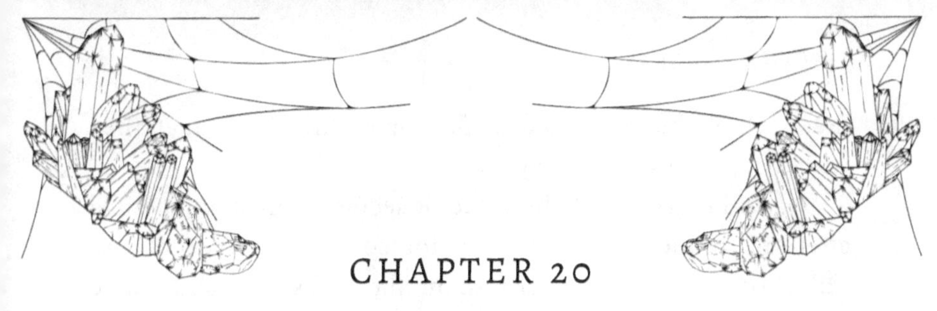

# CHAPTER 20

RESISTING his desire with the scent of Callie's pheromones lingering in his nostrils and the ghost of her essence upon his tongue was torture for Urkot. Before long, his claspers ached with the strain of keeping his throbbing stem behind his slit. He distracted himself by braiding a thin cord of silk for her top to replace the lacing he'd cut.

Though he wanted her to rest, he was relieved when she awoke after only a brief slumber. She drank more water at his insistence—and he at hers—and they resumed their journey. Moving gave him something else to focus on, allowing him to finally set aside that yearning.

Mostly, anyway.

He glanced back to check on her often. Her unease remained clear in her expression, but she kept calm, even through the tightest, most difficult sections of the tunnel. His chest swelled with pride and admiration, which did nothing to ease his passage through those narrow spots.

It felt as though the tunnel would wind endlessly into the deepest, darkest parts of the world, until the shadows were so thick that even the sun would not have been able to penetrate them. Only the continued airflow gave him hope that they would eventually find a way out.

When he first saw light ahead, it seemed unreal, impossible after the tunnel had been dark for so long. Perhaps it was reflections on gem deposits upon the walls? He and Callie covered the glowstones they were using to illuminate their path.

The light down the tunnel persisted.

With newfound energy and caution, Urkot and Callie strode onward. The light grew brighter and clearer with their every step. The tunnel sloped gently upward as it neared an opening, through which that bluish glow spilled.

Sounds carried to Urkot. The burbling of running water, the erratic scrapes and clacks of tools, and hints of harsh voices made indistinct by distance and a mild echo.

His fine hairs rose, and something heavy sank in his belly. He stalked forward, keeping low until he reached the crest of the path and peered over it.

The narrow ledge he now found himself upon overlooked a vast cavern. Glowing crystals, luminescent plants, and glow-worms bathed the space in blue, leaving deep shadows on the ceiling from which pointed rock formations jutted down like jagged, irregular fangs. A winding stream divided the cavern unevenly; for much of its length, the right bank was only a few segments wide, cluttered with plants, rocks, and boulders.

To the stream's left was a wide patch of fairly level ground that led to the cavern wall, which had been shaped into tiers connected by sloping paths and worn climbing spots. Many, many openings were carved along those tiers, some with their own dim lights shining within.

Dens. They were dens. Homes to the spiritstriders who, with their glowing hides, stood everywhere around those tiers. A hundred, at least, perhaps twice that.

"Shaper, unmake me," Urkot rasped. "Fuck."

The vrix were conversing, working, and eating below, sometimes raising their voices and snapping at each other. Occasional clicking echoed through the chamber when spiritstriders navigated the space.

Callie moved up beside Urkot.

He wrapped an arm around her shoulders, covered her mouth, and drew her against his side. She put a hand over his but made no effort to pull it away. Together, they sank lower, nearly flattening themselves atop the ledge.

Urkot surveyed the cavern. The stream continued to the far end, where the walls tapered into a dark crevasse. Several larger openings scattered around had the look of passageways and tunnels. There could've been eighty ways in and out of this place for all Urkot knew—and there was no way to be sure where any of them led.

The airflow was diluted due to the cavern's size, making it difficult to determine its source, but he guessed it was coming from somewhere across the cave. That narrowed the choices down to any of five or six openings.

*Rushin roolet.*

He really, really disliked this game.

Callie gently drew his hand down from her mouth. Voice so soft that he barely heard it, she whispered, "It's…a hive."

*Hive.* That was an apt word. Yet though he did not doubt the spiritstriders would swarm were they to discover his and Callie's presence, they were not mindless insects. They were vrix.

And that made them very, very dangerous.

Callie turned her head toward Urkot and met his gaze. The lighting made her eyes appear much darker than usual, enhancing their usual depth. "What do we do?"

He looked around the cavern again, mandibles falling. His friends would've come up with some clever plan and carried it out with confidence. Despite all he had in common with them, he sometimes felt as though they perceived the world in ways he would never understand. A life of dirt and stone had taught him rigid rules, had taught him responsibility, but things like this…

He'd always relied upon Ketahn's judgment, Rekosh's cunning, and Telok's experience in such matters.

*What do we do?*

The only answer that came to mind was *push forward*. Turning around again would do no good. The other path likely led past the long abandoned shadowstalker dens and right to this place, and he and Callie would have to backtrack a long, long way to find an alternate passage that had any reasonable chance of bringing them to the surface. And though they could forage more food, it would not long sustain them, especially Callie. According to Diego, humans required varied foods to remain healthy.

That was not an option down here, not without Callie taking risks on potentially harmful foods.

Yet continuing through this cavern would be more dangerous than anything they'd done so far. He had no idea if he could outrun all these spiritstriders, but he knew he could not fight them all off.

What would his friends have done?

*That does not matter. They are not here.*

All that mattered was what he would do. He and Callie needed to keep moving, and for a delver, the path forward was often through.

His hearts beat a little faster and heavier as he returned his attention to Callie. He knew that to protect his mate, he would sometimes have to bring her into danger. How could that notion both adhere to and oppose his instincts when it came to her?

"We go through," he whispered.

Callie's eyes rounded, her eyebrows rose, and her lips

parted. She turned slightly onto her side to face him. "That's… Urkot, we can't—"

He quieted her with the press of a finger over her lips. Beckoning Callie with another hand, he retreated from the edge, stood up, and reentered the tunnel. She followed. Once they were several segments from the ledge, he directed her to turn, opened her pack, and took out the damp blanket.

Draping the blanket over their heads, he sank onto the joints of his bent forelegs, pulling her down to kneel before him. The light of a crystal illuminated her face from below, casting odd shadows upon it.

"Is this to dampen our voices?" she asked, words barely audible.

Urkot nodded. He held her gaze and settled his upper hands on her shoulders. "We must go through, Callie."

"Urkot, that's *sooiside*. We can just double back." She gestured in the direction from which they'd first come. "There were a lot of other paths we can try, weren't there?"

But the crease between her brows and the way her features had fallen suggested that she already knew what Urkot did— there was no going back.

"Shit." She closed her eyes and took a slow, deep breath. "Okay. Okay…"

He gently squeezed her shoulders and tipped his headcrest against her forehead.

After a few more breaths, Callie opened her eyes. "You're sure about this? There are a lot of them."

Urkot slid one hand to her neck, thumb trailing along her jaw. "Yes."

"A fuck of a lot of them, Urkot."

His mandibles twitched up, and he barely held back a chitter. "Yes. I fear too. But we will escape."

Callie nodded without pulling back, making her soft skin brush against his hard hide. "Yeah, okay. The spiritstriders…

they seem to have underdeveloped eyes. Poor vision, very sensitive to light. They're using some form of echolocation, so they likely have excellent hearing, and their sense of smell seems comparable to yours. We can assume they're also sensitive to vibrations and airflow like you are. They're adapted to this environment.

"But there's already some ambient sound down there, and I would guess enough scents on the air that they won't notice ours immediately. And it's likely that they won't expect anything to just stroll into their hive, so their guard should be down. If we keep absolutely silent and far enough away…"

He knew Callie well enough to understand that she'd said all that aloud not to inform him, but to collect her own thoughts, to talk herself through her concerns. To convince herself of a course of action.

"They will never know we are here," said Urkot.

"Right. Hopefully. And if they do find us…" Shifting her bag to her front, she reached in an pulled out the collapsed lantern. "This should buy us a few seconds to run if any of them get too close."

She opened his pouch and slipped the lantern inside.

"Good, female." Urkot wrapped his lower arm around her waist and pressed his mouth to hers in a prolonged kiss. She slipped an arm around his neck and leaned into it, holding him tight.

It was a moment of ecstasy, pure and radiant, untainted by the surrounding darkness.

He was fast collecting such moments in his memory, each of which he wished he could lengthen into blissful eternity. But that would only keep him from experiencing all the new moments that awaited in the murky waters of the future.

Urkot took in her scent. It was sweet and potent, carrying the lingering aroma of her essence. Heat suffused his blood, pressure coalesced in his pelvis, and his claspers twitched and reached for her as the desire he thought he'd resisted surged back with a fury.

*Her scent.*

Breaking the kiss, he snatched his claspers back, crossing them over his slit and pressing them down hard enough to create a throbbing ache beneath. In a harsh breath, he said, "By their eightfold eyes."

Callie drew back from him. "What's wrong?"

"Your scent."

"What about it?"

"It is much strong. And…unique."

Her brow creased. "Because I'm human?"

"Yes. But also your pussy."

"My—" Her eyes widened. "Ohhhh."

Then she glared and jabbed his chest with a finger. "You mean this whole time I've been smelling like that, and you didn't say anything?"

Urkot huffed. "It is the best smell. But if a spiritstrider scents you…"

The first spiritstrider they'd encountered had likely picked up Callie's scent and come to investigate the source, hungry and curious.

"Okay, we need to cover up my scent somehow," she whispered, fiddling with the edge of the blanket. "I don't think just a simple wipe down with water is going to accomplish much."

Callie withdrew from the blanket and took a step back, her boots crunching softly on the ground. Urkot tugged the blanket off himself.

She winced, looked down, and paused, her head tilting as her face lit up. "Wait. I have an idea."

Removing the waterskin, Callie dampened a cloth and briskly rubbed her inner thighs and sex. Urkot watched, enrapt, wishing it was his hand cleaning her instead. But he knew he could not trust himself to merely clean her. He knew he would not be able to wipe away her essence and leave it at that.

In a situation like this, mating shouldn't even have been a fleeting thought, yet it remained a driving urge, clawing at his mind incessantly. His want for her was a hunger that could not be sated. And it didn't seem to lessen even at times like this, when it clashed directly with his powerful instinct to protect her.

Callie crouched, returned the items to her pack, then swiped her hands over the ground, gathering a pile of fine dust. She scooped it up and ran it over her arms, turning her brown skin to a shade of gray. It reminded Urkot of the permanent stains on his fingers and the tips of his legs from a lifetime of working stone.

Understanding fell into place suddenly, and he felt like a fool for not realizing what she was doing immediately. It was so simple yet so clever. His mandibles rose. "You are making yourself one with the stone."

As she stood, coating her legs with more dust, she smiled at him. "Hopefully it works."

After she'd covered her skin and patted her clothing and hair, she gathered more dust and approached him. Her palms brushed over the blue markings on his shoulders, dulling their glow. Even the slight abrasion of the dust being rubbed against his hide couldn't diminish the thrill her touch brought him.

"My female is smart," Urkot said, brushing a finger lightly over her arm.

She let out a soft, breathy laugh, and her lips curled up into a smile, making her dimples stand out.

"And she is pretty," he added. "Most pretty."

Callie moved closer and reached up to run her fingers over the markings on his headcrest. "Even covered in dust?"

"No matter your coverings. Always most pretty."

Her smile widened, and she pressed her lips to his mouth in

a gentle kiss. Eyes flicking between his, she said in a quiet voice, "Let's get out of here so my big softie of a male can show his pretty mate just how much he likes her."

"I am not soft, female," he growled, "but I do like you. Much, much like."

And he intended to show her how much. He'd worship her until she sang in pleasure, would taste her as he so deeply desired, would fill her with his seed, would leave no question that she belonged to him now and forever.

Once she'd covered all his markings, he grabbed her bag, intending to stuff the blanket inside. But something within caught his eye. He withdrew her knife, snug in its little sheath.

Urkot put the blanket away and tugged the blade free. Though the weapon was small, he knew it was exceptionally sharp and durable, surpassing anything the vrix could fashion. Turning the handle toward her, he held the knife up to Callie.

She frowned at it.

"If we are discovered…I would not have you without a weapon," he said softly.

"Yeah. Just in case." She accepted the knife, keeping the point angled downward.

Closing her bag, Urkot helped her sling it over her shoulders, then assisted her in climbing onto his hindquarters. She eased into place, wrapping her arms around his chest and her thighs around his middle, with the knife, its blade pointed away from him, tucked in her fist.

He returned to the ledge overlooking the cavern. It followed along the right side of the cave, gradually descending to the floor, and had the look of a deliberately created path, albeit one that hadn't seen use or care in a long, long while.

With Callie secure, he began his descent. Every thread of his attention felt like it was being pulled in a different direction. Not only did he need to watch the spiritstriders, but he had to survey every bit of his path, had to ensure each leg came down in exactly the right place with exactly the right pressure lest the sound of a disturbed pebble or rustling plant draw unwanted attention. The care and control required was a strain on Urkot's entire being, body and mind.

As they neared the bottom, the cavern's distinct scents strengthened. The smell of clean water, cloying plants, and the spiritstriders could not mask the prevalent odors of blood and meat, both fresh and rotting.

The sound of the stream grew louder, and the spiritstrider voices more distinct, but Urkot understood little even with the improving clarity. Their tongue was like a root that had been hacked off its mother tree and had grown into something strange and almost unrecognizable, though the similarities could not be denied upon closer inspection.

When they reached the cavern floor, his chest constricted, and it became a struggle to draw breath. Looking upon the spiritstriders from above had not been nearly so unsettling, despite their numbers. The height of his perch had made him feel separated from the threat and granted him a false sense of safety.

*No retreat.*

Keeping as low to the ground as he could, Urkot crept forward along the stream's right bank. The rasp of leaves against his hide made his hearts leap every time, though he was certain it was a sound he merely felt rather than heard. As much as possible, he kept the larger rocks between himself and the opposite bank, utilizing the cover and scant shadows available to him.

Whenever a spiritstrider made that clicking sound, Urkot's insides churned. A shallow stream and a few segments of open ground was not enough of a barrier.

His whole body ached more with each measured step, but he could not allow weariness to deter him.

A pair of female spiritstriders gave stern words to their

broodlings before striding toward the stream on a path that would bring them directly across the water from Urkot. His fine hairs stood, and his hide felt suddenly taut, as though it were stretched terribly thin over his body. Callie stiffened atop him, pressing herself as flush against him as she could.

*Fuck. Fuck, fuck, fuck.*

*Broodmother, grant us your mercy.*

He hurried to the nearest boulder and hid behind it, bracing an arm against the cool stone.

With his breath caught in his throat, he listened as the females drew nearer, their heavy steps and voices sharpening. Something splashed in the water on the other side of the rock. One female made a throaty, chuffing sound, followed by more splashing.

Urkot held completely still despite the fire pulsing in his tensed muscles. Callie trembled, her face buried against his back, her nails and the knife's handle digging into his chest. He and Callie hadn't been spotted. They were hidden, out of sight.

Weren't they?

The splashing continued. The spiritstriders exchanged a few more words before one began to drink. Her long, deep gulps were so close, so clear, that they made Urkot shudder. His instincts screamed danger, imploring him to either flee this place or fight—to do anything but remain unmoving.

But either choice would make his presence known to the spiritstriders, placing his mate in more danger. No, the safest option was to keep hiding...and hope the spiritstriders didn't catch his and Callie's scents.

Farther away, a broodling cried out in a high wail. One of the females growled. Urkot's fingers twitched, nearly scraping the boulder with his claws.

With a series of angry splashes and stomps, the females stormed away.

Urkot exhaled and drew fresh air into his blazing lungs. His heartbeat pounded throughout his body, fast and loud, making the ends of his limbs feel oddly hot and tingly.

He forced himself forward. This endeavor demanded all his strength, all his control, all his concentration, all of him. Urkot would never understand how Telok and Ketahn moved like this —utterly silent, totally unseen—so effortlessly. But he would endure this again and again, endlessly, if it was necessary to keep Callie safe.

From rock to rock, shadow to shadow, he advanced along the stream. Dread built in his gut every time he lowered a leg; he anticipated a sound that would give him away with each movement. When no such sounds came, he felt no relief. There were too many steps to go before he left this cavern behind.

Yet even as Urkot's tension built, a gentle air current grew more defined. It became his guide, leading toward a tunnel opening ahead, not far from the place where the stream flowed into the crevasse.

Across the water, the spiritstriders continued their lives— they mended tools, divided meat, scraped hides, braided silk cord, talked and played. In so many ways, they were not unlike the vrix Urkot had always known. But he knew there was no peace to be found here, no friendship.

Whether by the gods' blessing, his own efforts, or aimless luck, Urkot made it to the tunnel entrance without drawing attention to himself and Callie. The airflow was unmistakable there. The tunnel was connected to the surface somewhere, beyond any doubt, and that somewhere was closer than ever.

After a final backward glance to ensure they'd remained unseen, Urkot stalked into the tunnel. He followed it cautiously. Soon, the sounds from the cavern faded to nothingness behind him, and the tension that had gripped him since discovering the spiritstriders' hive finally began to ease.

The tunnel wound through a few turns before widening into a chamber where the path curved around the edge of a pool that lapped quietly against the stone. The ceiling sloped down toward the pool, leaving only a hand's width of space between it and the water's surface. A few clusters of crystal on the walls provided dim light.

"We rest a moment," Urkot said quietly.

Sighing heavily, Callie relaxed. She lay there, limp atop him, several heartbeats longer before sliding down from his hindquarters. She stumbled as soon as her feet were on the floor.

Urkot's arm darted out, catching her before she could fall. Alarm flared in his chest.

"I'm okay," she whispered, patting his arm, before he could say anything. "Just forgot how exhausting it can be holding on to you for dear life. Legs are a bit…wobbly."

Keeping his hand on Callie to steady her, Urkot turned his body toward hers and crooned. "Ah, my *nyleea*…"

His legs felt shaky as well, and he doubted his insides would ever come free of the knots they'd been tied into, even after he and Callie were back in Kaldarak.

He lowered his head, brushed his mouth atop her hair, and breathed her in, gladly casting aside the smells of the hive in exchange for hers, which he could detect faintly beneath the dust. She flattened a palm on his chest and leaned into him.

Clicks echoed along the tunnel from somewhere up ahead.

Straightening, Urkot snapped his head in the direction from which the sound had come and listened. More clicking—and voices—growing louder. Drawing closer.

Apparently, the Broodmother's mercy had limits.

He was beginning to understand why some of the humans so often used the word *fuck*; it truly did feel right for so many situations.

That anxious little crease had reformed between Callie's eyebrows when he met her gaze, and fear again glinted in her eyes.

Grasping her free hand, he led her to the water. She hesitated at the edge as he stepped in, glancing down at her boots. A series of growls and snarls from the tunnel made her start. Her shoulders rose with a fortifying breath, and she entered the water. The dust she'd covered herself and Urkot with swirled around them on the surface of the water, slowly dissipating in a lingering cloud.

A shiver coursed through her, and her lips peeled back to reveal her teeth. But she continued deeper into the water regardless. Urkot's jaw clenched tighter with every sound they made as they moved.

A spiritstrider barked something in its harsh language. It was very close now.

Callie tipped her head back to keep her face out of the water, which was soon up to her ears. Urkot pulled her close and curled an arm around her middle. His legs could just touch the bottom as he moved into the shadowy gap beneath the low-hanging ceiling.

The first spiritstrider entered the chamber, followed by three more, all males. Two carried bloodied animal carcasses that were lashed together with silk strand around the legs. Difficult as it was to determine what the creatures were, their fur looked like it belonged to animals from the surface.

Which meant these vrix had exited the cave system recently.

The lead spiritstrider halted near the chamber's center. When a couple of the others spoke, he snapped his mandible claws harshly with a curt word, silencing his companions, before he sniffed the air. His low growl resonated in the chamber.

Urkot eased back, carefully dipping his head lower into the water. Callie did the same. Her body was rigid against him, wracked by shivers that he could feel her fighting to suppress.

The lead spiritstrider strode to the spot where Callie and Urkot had initially stopped. He sniffed repeatedly, snarling after every inhalation, and said something to his companions, who spread out with their mandibles open wide, making their unnerving clicks.

The top of Urkot's headcrest touched the ceiling, and he halted. This wasn't nearly far enough away, especially with the spiritstriders actively searching, scenting the air for what to them must've been two foreign smells. The water would mask Urkot and Callie's scents, at least mostly, but all it would take was the faintest hint...

If it came down to it, Callie could remain in the water while Urkot fought off these vrix. He was outnumbered, but as long as she was out of the spiritstriders' reach, he wouldn't have to hold anything back.

Callie tapped Urkot's back, calling his attention to her. The water lapped around her mouth, and her nostrils flared as she breathed through them. She flicked her eyes to the side and back to him several times, as though attempting to look behind herself.

It took everything in Urkot to stop himself from tilting his head and shifting his mandibles. Lips pressed together and brow creased, she stared at him before again flicking her eyes aside. This time, he followed her gaze with his own, turning his head to look.

Light glimmered underwater behind them, past the point where the ceiling met the pool's surface—beyond the reach of this chamber's meager glow.

Slowly, he backed toward that light, angling his head to keep breathing as the water deepened and the ceiling lowered. Rough stone raked his hair and his headcrest. Much too soon, he reached a point where he could move no farther without submerging himself completely.

Callie pressed the length of a finger against Urkot's hide and slid it straight down. Not a means of comfort, but of communication. A signal. After giving her a gentle squeeze, he released her.

She drew in a deep breath, its sound lost amidst the water lapping the stone and the spiritstriders' grunts and growls, and vanished below the surface.

He felt water being displaced as she swam down, but he forced himself to wait for eight heartbeats so she would have enough room to move. Filling his own lungs with air, he dipped under, and all sound was replaced by the muffled churning of water.

Urkot turned to see Callie. She was a dark form against the glow coming through a circular opening in the rock, legs kicking to propel her forward. Once she was through, he followed. The gap was tight, but his shoulders and torso cleared it. Callie swam toward the rippling surface, through which that blue light was streaming, and he couldn't help but admire the beauty before him—her beauty. With that lighting and the encompassing quiet, the moment was strikingly serene.

His momentum halted abruptly as his legs and hindquarters lodged in the opening. He pressed his hands to the surrounding stone and pushed. Rock scraped his hide, and his muscles trembled with exertion, but he couldn't get enough leverage to free himself, couldn't bring his full strength to bear. Bubbles escaped his mouth and nose as he struggled.

*Fuck.*

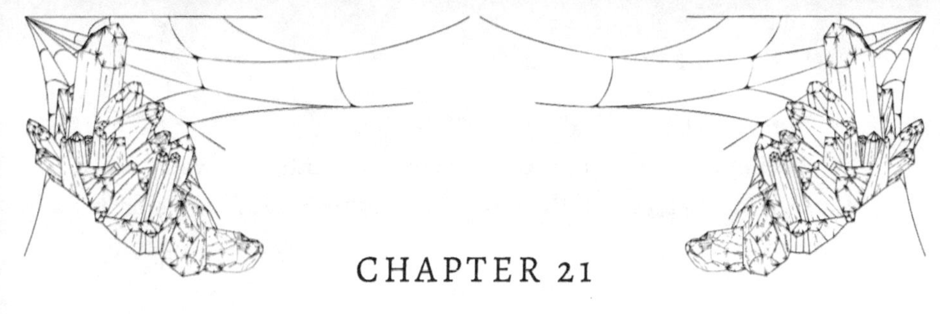

# CHAPTER 21

CALLIE BROKE THE SURFACE SLOWLY, allowing only her head to emerge, and drew in a deep, quiet breath. Taking care to disturb the water as little as possible, she wiped her face and opened her eyes.

There were no spiritstriders in sight.

A flood of relief crashed through her.

Though her heart was still racing from that terrifying trek through the spiritstrider hive, she and Urkot had made it through. But…now what?

The large, circular chamber was brightly lit, with blue crystals of all sizes growing along the walls and the water-covered floor and glowworms crawling on the stone. But there were no openings, no tunnels leading out.

Callie tipped her head back.

No way out except for the wide, round shaft overhead going straight up. That was something. It was a way.

Smiling, she turned to face Urkot. "It's saf—"

Her heart stopped, and her stomach sank like a rock.

Urkot hadn't come up. He wasn't here.

Bubbles broke the surface beside her.

"Oh God, Urkot."

Taking a deep breath, Callie sank back into the water and looked down. Through the blur, she caught sight of him, a dark shadow amidst the blue-tinted stone, struggling at the opening that had led them into this cavern.

Stuck.

*Oh no, no, no, no...*

Callie surfaced, refilled her lungs, and dove back down, propelling herself toward Urkot. More bubbles escaped him, making her panic rise. Was he drowning?

*No! I won't lose him, not now, not ever.*

When she reached him, his bright eyes met hers. There was no mistaking the fear in his gaze. She wasted no time, inspecting the rock around his body, looking for a way to loosen it. Maybe if she used the knife, she could...

No. There wasn't time to chip away at the opening, hoping to fracture the stone just right, and she certainly wasn't going to pry him free with the short blade.

Frantic, she dropped the knife, planted her feet on the stone, wrapped her arms around his waist, and pushed with her legs, using every bit of strength she could. Urkot worked with her, his lower hand on the ground and body wriggling.

He lifted but caught once more.

Bubbles spilled from her lips, and her lungs burned with the need for air.

Urkot fought the stone, wiggling harder. One of his hands caught her arm, and he tried to pry her away, but Callie tightened her grasp. She would not leave him. She refused to leave him.

Heat blazed through her thighs with the exertion. She only poured more strength into her efforts.

*Please! Please, let him get loose! Don't...don't let me lose him.*

Callie was not religious, and she never prayed, but she did

now. She prayed to whoever or whatever was listening, be it God, the Eight, or some other unknowable force.

*Please help him!*

More air escaped her, and darkness encroached on her vision. Internally, she screamed, she cried, she railed as terror gripped her heart.

Just as her body threatened to give out, just as her strength was about to fail, Urkot broke free. Water churned as he grabbed hold of her and kicked off the stone. They shot upward like a rocket.

Breaking the surface, they took in loud breaths that echoed within the chamber. Coughing and gasping for air to fill her needy lungs, Callie clutched Urkot's neck as he swam toward the shallow water. Her entire body trembled.

*I almost lost him. I almost lost him.*

Tears spilled down her cheeks.

When he reached the shallows, Urkot's legs wobbled and gave out. Water splashed around them as his hindquarters dropped. He sat, chest heaving, and banded his other arms around Callie, holding her to him.

"Callie," he rasped, nuzzling her hair. "My mate, my *nyleea*. Are you okay?"

Was she okay? Was *she* okay?

Callie jerked back and caught his face between her hands, meeting his gaze. "Me? What about *you*? You almost fucking drowned, Urkot!"

Narrowing his eyes, he growled and slid his hand into her hair at the back of her head, grasping it. "So did you! You should not risk yourself like that, Callie."

"I got your spider butt out, didn't I?"

"Yes." He pressed his headcrest to her forehead and closed his eyes. A shudder wracked him. "You will not risk yourself again."

"Don't tell me what to do," she said, gentling her voice.

"I am bossy."

"You are. Doesn't mean I have to listen."

Urkot let out a long, low, rumbling growl, but he followed it with two quiet words. "Thank you."

They sat there for a time, simply holding each other and breathing each other in as their hearts calmed. The water rippled around them, lapping against their bodies and the nearby stone, its soothing sounds accompanied by the occasional drip from above.

Despite the cold, despite the fading terror and adrenaline, despite everything, this cavern was tranquil. But Callie recognized that it was only possible because they were both alive, because they were holding each other.

She refused to contemplate what could've happened. Refused to think about what it would do to her if she lost Urkot.

"We must go," Urkot said. "The spiritstriders caught our scents. They know something is in their tunnels, and they will hunt."

"Okay."

Callie adjusted her stiff legs, letting them drop until her boots touched solid stone. She released Urkot and stepped back. Her eyes immediately went to his hindquarters. Once more, something clamped around her heart in a viselike grip. Deep scrapes on his hindquarters and upper legs oozed blood. A small whimper escaped her as she attempted to hold in her tears.

He slowly rose, his body language making every ache and pain he must've felt apparent, and twisted to glance back at his hindquarters. Tentatively, he gave his back half a wiggle. "Too much spider butt?"

Callie looked up at him. His eyes were on her, his mandibles lifted in a smile. A smile for her. To reassure her that he was okay, that his spirit wasn't broken, that it wasn't even cracked.

*I love him.*

*I fucking love this spider man.*

It was a realization that had snuck up on her, that had caught her completely off guard. But it had been there the whole time, hadn't it? The friendship they'd formed had always been deeper than it seemed on the surface. He'd cared for her from the very beginning. He'd constantly gone out of his way to ensure she was safe and comfortable, had always taken the time to make her smile and laugh when she was down, and even though she never appreciated it in the moment, he'd been there when she'd needed a little kick in the ass to get moving—like when he'd dumped water on her face to wake her up during their journey to Kaldarak.

But he'd always been there.

Until he wasn't. Because he'd left for Takarahl with Rekosh and Telok, and he'd been gone a whole month. And though she'd kept company with her friends, she'd always felt like something was missing. Like *someone* was missing.

It'd been him.

*And I almost lost him.*

Callie threw herself against him, hugging him, as more tears slid down her cheeks. But even through those tears, she smiled. "Your spider butt is perfect to me."

Chittering softly, he hooked a finger under her chin and tilted her face toward his. His touch was so light, so delicate, as he slid his hand up to brush the tears from her cheeks. He crooned. "No more leaking eyes. Save your water."

A soft laugh escaped her. "I'll try."

With Callie's assistance, he tended his wounds with sticky silk, and then he helped her get the excess off her fingertips. Seeing him patched up helped calm her a bit more. Vrix healed fast, and they tended to ignore most minor wounds, but all she could think about was the germs and dirt that they were exposed to while traipsing around the jungle.

Of course, all her things were soaked again, but she'd take sopping clothing over death any day.

There was only one way for them to go. Callie had to bite her tongue to keep herself from trying to talk him out of it, from urging him to rest, because she knew he was right. They had to move. She wasn't sure if the spiritstriders would figure out that their quarry had fled underwater, but it would be for the best if she and Urkot weren't here to find out.

So she climbed onto Urkot's hindquarters again, mindful of those freshly covered wounds, and assisted him in binding their bodies together with a silk strand. Rather than simply looping it around their waists, they created something much closer to a makeshift harness.

It reminded Callie of the way skydiving students were strapped to their instructors on their first jumps—a thought she quickly pushed away, because she did *not* want to fill her head with images of people freefalling through the air when Urkot was about to carry her up a vertical shaft.

She clung to him as he climbed. Her muscles screamed whenever they tensed, sore from the strain of trying to free him from the underwater passageway.

*Not going there.*

The sooner she could forget that moment, the better. She never wanted to experience that fear again.

The shaft led straight up. Crystal formations of various sizes grew from its walls, filling it with light, and moisture trickled down the stone. Urkot's muscles flexed and stretched as, foot by foot, he ascended.

As they moved higher, the air warmed, and soon patches of lichen and viny plants were scattered amidst the crystals and stone. Callie didn't look down. She was aware of the chamber below getting farther and farther away, and that would've concerned her had she been with anyone else. But she felt utterly secure with Urkot.

Above them, the light was even brighter, as though wherever this shaft led was absolutely flooded with the blue glow that she was coming to appreciate so much. Of course, her appreciation was likely due to the fondness she'd developed for the color even before getting trapped in this cave system...

When they reached the top, Urkot hauled himself onto solid ground, moved away from the edge of the shaft, and let out a heavy breath. The air was heavier here, warm and humid, a welcome change after the cold that had settled into Callie's bones.

Callie gasped as she peered around, eyes widening.

Of all the wondrous sights she'd seen down here, this cavern made the top of her list. It had a high ceiling covered in stalactites and glowworms so numerous that they resembled the stars in the night sky. Stalagmites rose from below, most of them beneath their inverted counterparts. Lush plants grew in many places, giving off glows of their own, and huge clusters of crystal shone on the walls, again making her feel like she was standing inside a geode. Raised pools of steaming water covered nearly half the cavern floor, from which a few more rock formations rose.

*Hot springs. Fucking hot springs!*

Urkot sliced away the cord binding them together, and Callie hurriedly slid off him, stepping forward to look around in awe.

She approached the nearest wall, one of the few without crystals. Its surface glistened with moisture and was shaped in bulbous, smooth tiers that cascaded down to create something resembling cresting ocean waves that had been flash frozen. "I think this is an active flowstone!"

Urkot moved up beside her, regarding the wall with his head cocked. "Flowstone?"

"Yeah! The water is depositing tiny traces of minerals that

have been building up over eons, forming the stone. That makes it look like…like melting wax."

He extended a hand toward it.

"No!" Callie grabbed his arm and halted it before he could touch the flowstone. "You'll kill it."

Turning his head, he blinked at her. "It is stone, Callie."

"I don't mean literally. The oils in your hand—well, I'm not sure about a vrix hand, but definitely a human hand—will disrupt the flow of water and stop the deposits from building up. So it would basically stop the stone from forming."

Turning his attention back to the stone, Urkot lowered his arm and leaned his face a little closer. "I have seen stone like this. Sometimes, we call it bleeding stone. But I did not know it is still…growing."

She leaned forward to look more closely, bracing her hands on her thighs. "It happens so slowly that you'd have to live for thousands of years to notice any real change."

He hummed thoughtfully.

Together, they stepped back and surveyed the rest of the chamber. There seemed to be only one exit apart from the shaft, a tunnel opening just tall enough for Urkot to fit through if he stooped down. In a show of impressive strength, he shifted a slab-like boulder from nearby and, with much grunting and grumbling, positioned it in front of the opening, effectively covering it.

"We will rest here," he declared, wiping his hands together to brush off the dirt.

Callie glanced back toward the shaft—the very open shaft. "Is it safe?"

"Yes. We will hear if spiritstriders come…but I do not think they will swim."

"Because they can't see well?"

He nodded. "Their clicks will not help them in water."

She didn't have the heart to bring up the many Earth creatures that used echolocation in the sea to great effect. Maybe it wouldn't work the same for the spiritstriders because they hadn't adapted to using it underwater?

Callie set her bag down and strolled toward the nearest steaming pool. "So…you're saying we're safe-safe for now?"

Urkot approached her slowly, head again tilted. "We are."

She bent forward and held her chilled hand over the water. Pleasant heat radiated up from the surface, and it felt so nice, reminding her of just how cold the water below had been.

Callie grinned, hopping in place as she yanked off her boots and tossed them aside. "Good, because I am getting in this water."

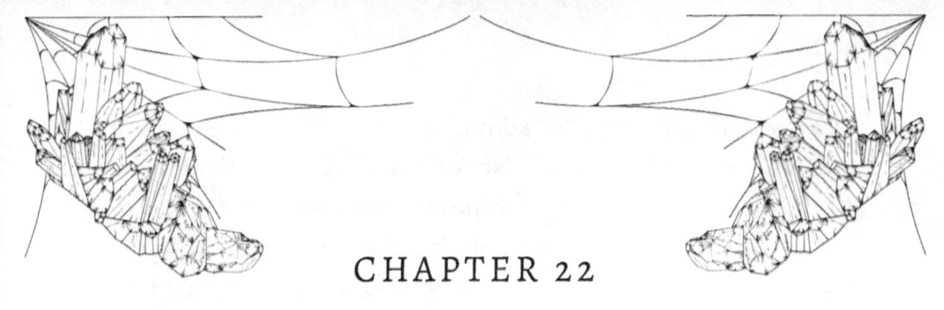

# CHAPTER 22

URKOT RAISED A FORELEG, blocking Callie from advancing. "Wait."

She looked up at him beseechingly, sticking out her bottom lip in what the humans called a *pout*. "But why?"

"It is hot. Maybe too hot."

She turned those longing eyes toward the steaming water, and her shoulders slumped. "I know you're right. But God, it might be worth losing a few layers of skin just to feel warm again."

He narrowed his eyes at her. "No, it would *not*. Bad Callie."

She laughed and gave his shoulder a playful shove. "Not literally, Urkot. I just mean that I really, really want to get in."

His mandibles sagged. He'd seen her shivering, had felt it, and had hated his sense of helplessness in those moments. If they had been on the surface, he could've made a fire to warm her, but understone, he was limited to his body heat and the luck of finding a place like this.

She'd told him how much she loved going to the hot springs in Kaldarak's temple, where she'd enjoyed the warmth and the quiet, where her troubles had melted away. This place was even quieter, even more serene. No vrix around, no animals, only stone carved by the Shaper himself, touched by none besides the gods. He knew it could not eliminate their troubles—only the touch of the sun would do that—but this was a much-needed respite.

Urkot swung his leg in front of him and lowered it toward the pool. Pleasant warmth flowed into its tip when it entered the water.

"Urkot!" Callie jolted forward, grabbing his leg and halting it. "What the fuck? So it's okay for you to risk getting burned but not me?"

He chittered and took her hands, lifting them from his leg. "Yes. My hide is thick. Tough. Yours is soft and thin." Bringing her hands to his mouth, he nuzzled them. "Calm, female. I will not be harmed."

She pursed her lips, grabbed his mandible, and tugged his head down. "Better not be."

Callie pressed her mouth to his before she released him.

"Maybe I will risk more," he said with a purr. "It is worth it for the kisses."

She gave him a droll look, but it cracked when the corner of her lips quirked. "If you want a kiss, all you need to do is ask."

Urkot dropped his mouth over hers, capturing the back of her head with one hand to hold her in place. He relished the softness of her plump lips and her gentle whimper. When he opened his jaws and slipped out his tongue, her lips parted to allow it entry. He swept his tongue inside, curling it around hers, tasting her with a low rumble before he withdrew.

He tipped her head back and stared into her dazed eyes. "Or take."

"Yeah," she said breathlessly. "Or you can do that too."

With a trill, he let her go and shifted his attention back to the pool. He lowered his leg deeper, ensuring that the temperature was safe below the surface. The water reached partway up the second segment of his foreleg before he touched the bottom. Though it was hot, it wasn't scalding; it seemed quite comparable to the water in the temple.

He lifted his leg free and flicked water at her. "It is good, yes?"

Callie laughed, flinching as she raised her hands to ward off his attack. "Jerk. So I take it it's safe?"

Urkot nodded.

She squealed and swiftly yanked at the ties of her top. Once she'd shrugged that off, she shoved down her skirt, and Urkot's gaze was immediately drawn to her rounded ass and that tattoo.

*Spank me*, she said it read.

His fingers twitched. Gods, but he wanted to obey that little command…

Callie swung a leg over the side of the pool and tentatively lowered her foot into the water. She let out a small, pleased hum and stepped in fully.

"Oh, fuck yes," she said as she sank into the water. Reclining, she leaned back against the stone rim of the pool and closed her eyes. "This feels sooo goooood."

Urkot's gaze settled on her breasts, which bobbed gently in the water, their dark brown nipples just peeking over the surface. He clenched his jaw and absently tapped a foreleg on the floor, grinding it into the stone as desire rekindled within him, flooding him with heat entirely separate from that of the hot springs.

How did Rekosh and Ketahn ever accomplish anything while their mates were around? How did either of them resist this overwhelming need to mate, this driving instinct? Urkot wasn't sure how he'd restrained himself as much as he had already.

Because neither his exhaustion nor the constant danger had

dulled his want at all. Every time he looked upon her, every time they touched even slightly for the briefest instant, every time he smelled her or spoke to her, he wanted to mate with her.

At this rate, he would have permanent indentations across his slit from his claspers pressing down so hard to keep his stem contained.

Callie opened her eyes and turned her face toward him with a grin that displayed those adorable dimples. "Are you going to just stand there or are you going to join me?"

*Protector, grant me strength.*

"You know I cannot stay away," Urkot said as pleasantly as he could manage, hoping he did not betray that inner struggle. After removing his belt and pouch and setting them beside Callie's belongings, he stepped into the pool and lowered himself beside her, releasing a trill as the warmth enveloped him. Even with the water covering much of his body, it could not compare to the heat within him.

Despite his raging desire, the water was enjoyable, soothing the many aches in his body.

*Well, all of them but one.*

"Feels good, huh?" she asked.

"It does," he replied, stretching out his forelegs and adjusting the others to allow himself to sink deeper into the water.

Callie sighed and closed her eyes. "I can almost imagine we're back in Kaldarak. Back in the temple."

"We will get back in small time. And then we will stay in the temple as long as you wish, until we are *proonee.*"

She chuckled. "I don't think you get *proonee.*"

"We will still stay as long as you wish."

Another type of warmth spread through his chest as her lips curved into a smile.

Comfortable silence stretched between them, interrupted only by gentle drips from elsewhere in the cavern. And though

Urkot had to remain alert for any sign of approaching spirit-striders, he felt far more relaxed than he had in a long, long while.

"You know," she said, gazing at the ceiling, "it's pretty in here. I mean, if I ignore the fact that all those squiggling glowing things are worms, it's like staring up at the stars. I can almost forget that we're stuck in a cave and pretend we're in some magical hideaway."

He turned his attention upward. All those worms and their glistening threads truly did resemble the starry night sky, and their reflections upon the water's surface made it appear as though he and Callie were lounging in a pool of stars.

"I'm glad I'm here with you, Urkot."

Urkot returned his eyes to Callie to find her looking at him, her expression soft and her gaze gleaming brighter than any star could ever match. He folded his forelegs in the water before him and placed his hands atop them. "I wish I could have shielded you from all this, Callie."

She drew in a deep breath and released it with the words, "I know." Tilting her head, she bent a leg, knee poking out of the water, and ran her hand over it and down her thigh. "But even if you couldn't shield me from it, you are shielding me through it."

Again, his eyes were drawn to her breasts; the disturbance in the water caused by her movement made them bob anew, and he recalled how soft and pliable they were, how perfectly they fit in his hands.

Callie chuckled softly. "I see you staring at them."

He chittered but could not bring himself to look away.

She moved her hands up and cupped the undersides of her breasts, lifting them out of the water and pressing them closer together. "Do you like looking at my body, Urkot? Do you enjoy how soft it is? How soft my breasts are?"

Her hands caressed that supple flesh, doing what Urkot longed to do himself.

His claspers flexed, drawing in hard enough to hurt as his stem swelled inside his slit. He'd never realized just how alluring it would be to see her touching herself this way, but after watching her stroke her clit in the grotto, he wanted more. He wanted to see her pleasuring herself as she stared at him, wanted to see lustful fires ignite in her eyes.

The only answer he could give her was a ragged, "Yes."

"When you came upon me bathing in the temple, how long were you watching me?"

"Not long enough."

Smiling, Callie circled her nipples with her thumbs. They hardened before his eyes, turning into tiny peaks that he craved to flick with his tongue.

"Did you want me then?" she asked. "Did you want to fuck me, Urkot?"

"Yes. I wanted to claim you. To make you mine."

"Mmm...I wanted you too." She squeezed her breasts. "I watched you bathe. Watched the way your markings glowed, the way your muscles moved, and when I was rubbing oil into your hide and felt those muscles under my palms..."

Her hands left her breasts, and she stood. Water cascaded down her body. He battled the urge to run his tongue over her skin and lick up every last drop.

Callie closed the distance between them and flattened her hands on his chest. Lightly, she trailed small kisses along his jaw and neck as one of her hands smoothed down his abdomen and dipped under water.

A tremor coursed through him at her touch. Placing his hands on her hips with his fingers and claws curling into her giving flesh, Urkot released a shuddering breath. His claspers eased their grip.

She traced his slit, stroked it, caressed it, coaxing it open wider. "I wanted to know what your cock would feel like inside me."

"Callie..."

She pushed her fingers into his slit.

His stem burst free, and the tenuous threads that had kept him restrained snapped, severed by the simplest touch from his mate.

With a snarl, Urkot snatched Callie up and into his arms. She squeaked in surprise as he rose from the water and stepped out of the pool. His spinnerets were already working, producing silk rope that he passed from one of his back legs to his lower hand.

"You play, female," he growled. "I cannot."

Callie chuckled as he set her down on her feet atop a carpet of plants. Instinct moved his hands without need for thought, swiftly winding and knotting the silk strand around her torso, framing her soft, soft breasts. He needed to bind her, to conquer her. There would be no escape. She was *his*.

"I thought you liked games," Callie said with a laugh. "Urkot, wait!"

"No. No wait." He slipped a strand between her thighs, where it pressed into her slit, right over her clit. He gave it a firm tug.

Callie jolted with a gasp, her hand slapping against his chest. "Oh, fuck. Urkot!"

"No." He reached for her wrist.

She yanked it back and caught his instead with a laugh. "Urkot, wait. Please!"

He paused, meeting her gaze.

"We're finally in a safe place where it's warm and there's light," she said. "Let's take it slow. I want to explore you."

"Slow?" He hissed as his claspers twitched on either side of his aching, throbbing stem, and his fists squeezed the rope. "I must be inside you, female."

"And you will be, I promise. Because I want that too. But I have something else in mind first." Callie lowered his hand, moving it between her legs, and placed his fingers atop the rope over her slit. Her eyes held his as she ground against his fingers, her lashes lowering. "Don't you want to taste me?"

The memory of her flavor danced teasingly upon his tongue, nearly making him growl, and his stem strained at the empty air in desperation. His need for her was torture, but the temptation of another taste, a real taste, was one he could not deny.

He curled his fingers over her pussy firmly, possessively, drawing a moan from her. "Fuck. Yes. Need it, Callie."

"Good, because I want to taste you too."

Taste him?

Urkot's eyes shifted to Callie's mouth, to those plump, pliable lips. A surge of pressure low in his belly made his leg joints suddenly weak.

She caught one of his mandibles, forcing his eyes back to hers. "Lie on your back."

A war raged within him as he stared at her.

*Take her. Claim her.*

That was his drive, his instinct, his need—to rut her and fill her with his seed. It was the mating frenzy, settling over his mind in a crimson mist, spreading fire through his blood with every beat of his hearts.

But need was not the same as want. He *wanted* this moment with her, wanted to taste her, wanted to revel in pleasure with her. He wanted to fulfill her every desire. And for them both to have what they wanted, he would have to seize those frayed threads of self-control. He'd have to wrestle back his instinct and resist the frenzy.

*Shaper unmake me, I want this.*

Gritting his teeth, he withdrew from her. His hide thrummed, and he felt every thread's width of distance between their bodies as he lay back upon a bed of moss and vines, bending his legs upward. His cock stood erect in the open air, pulsing with need.

Propped on his elbows, he watched Callie approach, her body decorated in his silk and her lips curled in a seductive smile.

She stopped beside him and trailed her fingers over one of his leg joints as her gaze roamed over him. "God, you look so fucking sexy like this."

The passionate sincerity of her words made warmth blossom in his chest. Everything inside him felt tight. It was still so new and strange to be openly, honestly desired. To have someone look at him with such attraction in their eyes, and for that someone to be Callie, made it impossibly more significant.

Holding on to his leg joint, Callie swung her leg over him and sat down upon his chest with her back toward him. Her grip tightened briefly as she sucked in a sharp breath before dropping her hand and wiggling upon him with a whispered, "Oh fuck, that rope."

He chittered deeply, taking delight in the fact that he wasn't the only one struggling with arousal, even if it did nothing to lessen his own discomfort.

Callie smiled at him over her shoulder. "Are you laughing at me?"

"Never," he said as sweetly as he could manage.

"I thought you didn't want to play games, but it seems you do. So I'll play." Slowly, she bent forward. Her palms were hot upon the hide of his belly and her breasts were soft as she lay upon him. She spread her thighs wide, displaying her slit in front of his face. "Do you want my pussy, Urkot?"

At a loss for words, Urkot stared at her backside, hearts thundering. His silk ran down between her ass cheeks and was nestled in the dark folds of her slit. Her essence coated it, glistening in the low light, and its scent flooded his nostrils, stoking the flames at his core. Pure possessiveness ripped through him.

His silk. She was wearing his silk.

Resting his lower palm on her calf and his upper left on her hip, he reached for her with his right hand, grazing the wet silk with the back of a claw.

Callie shivered but drew her backside away just enough to escape his touch. "Ah-ah. You didn't answer me." She smoothed one of her hands farther down his abdomen and teased the top of his slit with her fingers. "Do you want my pussy, Urkot?"

His fingers flexed, pressing his claws into her skin. "Yes."

"Good boy." She dipped her fingers into his slit and stroked the base of his stem. "Do you want to taste it?"

Urkot's head fell back, and his legs raked across plant and stone as she assailed him with pleasure. But he did not look away from her pussy. "More than anything."

She wrapped her hand around his stem, beneath the knot. "Do you want to lick it? To...eat it?"

"Yes." The word came out in a guttural snarl that left his throat raw. When he hooked his finger beneath the silk rope, she didn't pull away. He tugged the rope aside, leaving nothing to conceal her from his ravenous gaze. Those delicate folds, so reminiscent of a flower, sparkled with her essence in the cavern's blue glow.

Settling his hands upon her ass, he used his thumbs to part her slit, spreading it wide. The flesh within her channel was pink, and completely open to him. A growl rolled through his chest.

Callie hummed as she squeezed his shaft. "I take it you like what you see?"

Breath ragged, he said, "Much like."

"Then take what you want. It's yours...and this is mine."

Her mouth closed over the tip of his stem.

Urkot stiffened, eyes flaring. His surprise was swiftly

followed by a blast of pleasure so intense that his entire body quaked.

Callie had his stem in her mouth.

That wasn't something vrix did, not with their rigid mouths and sharp teeth. A male risked his stem being bitten and torn away. Even Callie's blunt teeth could cause harm. But Urkot didn't fear her. He trusted her. And by their eightfold eyes, this was bliss—the heat of her mouth, the suction as she drew him in deeper, the feel of her tongue as it teased his opening and stroked his shaft.

Urkot bared his fangs and clutched Callie's ass, staring at her pussy.

Taste, she had said. Lick. Eat. *Take.*

"Mine," he snarled.

Yanking her closer, Urkot dragged his tongue over her slit from her clit to her ass.

Callie dug her fingers into his belly and moaned around his cock. The vibrations rippled into him, sharpening the waves of pleasure. And her taste? It spread over his tongue like the sweetest nectar, and it only deepened his hunger for more.

He thrust his tongue into her tight entrance.

"Urkot!" Callie gasped.

He swirled and twisted his tongue, pushing deeper, seeking more, more, more. It slid within her so easily, with no barriers to stop it, welcomed by her body. And the feel of her channel clamping around his tongue made him yearn to have his cock inside her, to feel it squeezing his shaft.

Callie wriggled her hips, but he held her firmly, not allowing her to withdraw from him as he plunged his tongue in and out of her pussy.

She moaned and pumped her fist up and down his cock. "Urkot, your tongue…"

And then her mouth was back on him, taking in the head of his stem. She sucked with vigor equal to his as he stroked her from within and coaxed out more of her essence. He needed more, even as it dripped from her and ran down his chin. He needed so much more.

Urkot withdrew his tongue to swallow her essence. Gods, nothing had ever tasted so good. Nothing had ever sparked such a craving in him, such a need. He felt the mating frenzy pushing in from the edges of his mind, felt its claws seeking purchase, heard its demanding roar, but he was not ready to submit.

He would lose himself here—not in the frenzy, but in his mate.

Urkot ran his tongue across the seam of his mouth, licking away her nectar. Each drop was made sweeter by the glide of her mouth around his stem. His pelvis rocked up, and he gritted his teeth against the pleasure threatening to overwhelm him.

His gaze caught on her tattoo.

*Spank Me.*

Callie had told him that it felt good to be spanked, that she enjoyed it. Would it bring her pleasure now?

Drawing back his hand, he brought it down sharply upon her ass cheek, directly over the tattoo.

The *crack* of his palm against her skin was loud, as was Callie's gasp as her head jerked up, releasing his stem from the depths of her mouth. Her body was taut atop him.

Urkot stilled, his hand remaining on her ass. "Did I—"

"Do it again," she said. "Harder."

His eyes widened. There was no mistaking what she'd said, though the words weren't at all what he'd expected. She wanted more. She wanted…harder. That command conflicted with his instinct to protect her from harm. He refused to inflict pain upon his mate himself.

But her voice hadn't conveyed pain; it had conveyed *need.*

His palm kneaded her ass, soothing the flesh he'd struck.

Urkot trusted Callie. Trusted her to tell him what she

desired, to tell him what felt good, to tell him when it hurt or was too much. She trusted him just as much, or else she wouldn't have asked for more.

"Urkot," Callie begged, pushing back against his hand. "Please. Do it—"

He spanked her. Harder.

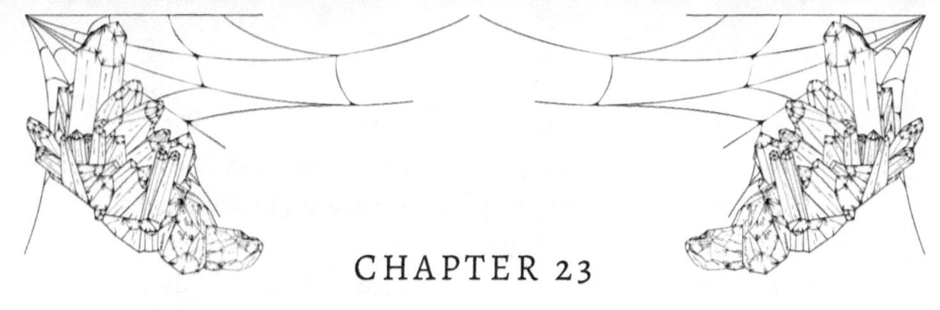

# CHAPTER 23

"Fuck!" Callie cried, her ass tensing as pleasure-pain radiated through her. Her nails curled into Urkot's hide, and she clenched the knotted shaft of his cock as she dropped her head onto his abdomen.

Heat and tingles spread across her skin beneath his large palm She was more aware than ever of how exposed she was. Urkot could do anything he wanted; he could overpower her, use her, fuck her.

And she fucking loved it.

She pressed a kiss to his hide. "Again."

Another sharp, firm crack came, jolting her body and making her ass jiggle. White-hot electric pleasure splintered through her, setting her every nerve alight. Her budded nipples ached as they grazed his hide, her clit throbbed, and her sex clenched, missing the fullness of his tongue, craving the girth of his cock.

Callie lifted her head and looked at his shaft. Thick, blue, and alien, it was slick with the oils his body produced, and it throbbed in her hand. It was beautiful, and it was for her. The scent of cinnamon and cloves was heavy in the air, that spicy taste was potent on her tongue, and she wanted more.

Dipping her head, she licked his slit teasingly, then ran the flat of her tongue up his length.

Urkot hissed, body shivering beneath her, and his cock twitched in her grasp. When she reached the flared head, she took the two-pronged tip back into her mouth. Urkot growled, once more bringing his palm down on her ass.

The shock of sweet agony was followed by the feel of his long, firm tongue dragging over her sex.

*Oh fuck, yes.*

He twirled it around her entrance and dipped it inside, and she moaned around his cock, which earned her both another growl and another spank. She sucked as she bobbed her head, teasing him with her tongue and stroking her fist up and down his shaft and over his knot in time with her movements. It was his taste, his responses, his pleasure that spurred her on. She wanted to see him come undone, to taste his seed on her tongue.

Urkot spanked her again, and again, each strike vibrating straight to her core. The sensations were intense, wicked, and consuming, and she already felt like she was on the verge of coming. She was so aroused that her pussy wept with need, and he was right there to lick it all up.

When his tongue flicked her clit, Callie cried out. "There, Urkot! Lick my clit."

Clutching her ass with his claws pricking her skin, he pulled her closer to his mouth. "Ah, my suncrest."

Warmth flooded her heart at that endearment, and pleasure shot through her like falling stars streaking across the night sky as his tongue vigorously lashed and laved her clit.

"Oh fuck!" she keened, squeezing her eyes shut. "Yes, yes, yes!"

She undulated against his mouth, greedy for more, and he

drew her even closer until he had his jaw around her mons with his jagged teeth teasing her skin. But all she could focus on was his sinful tongue and the blistering sensation scorching through her.

When her orgasm struck, Callie surrendered to it completely.

Her body tensed, her sex contracted, and a gush of liquid heat squirted from her. She cried out silently, having no voice, having no control of her body; it was no longer her own. Wave after wave of powerful ecstasy washed through her with every stroke of his tongue until a ragged, broken sound finally emerged from her throat, a primal cry of overwhelming pleasure.

As tremors wracked her, he withdrew his tongue and clasped two hands around her hips while the third slipped up her abdomen, supporting her chest. Before she knew what was happening through the haze of her climax, Urkot lifted her off him, tearing her away from his cock, and swung his body out from beneath her to set Callie down on her hands and knees.

"Urkot?" Confused, she looked back at him over her shoulder to see him positioning himself behind her. "But you didn't... I didn't—"

He yanked up on her hips, raising her ass toward him. An instant later she felt the head of his cock against her quivering sex.

"Need my seed inside you," he rasped.

Then he snapped his hips forward, burying his length inside her.

Callie gasped at the suddenness of his thick cock filling her. The stretch burned, but it was oh so sweet how that burn bled into pleasure. In this position, he felt immensely larger.

Her pussy clamped around his shaft as he drew it back, allowing her to feel his wide, ridged head along her channel, only for him to plunge deeper, wringing a whimper from her throat. He did it again and again, his thrusts steady, slow, and deep.

"I wanted to taste you," she said breathlessly, pushing back to meet his measured thrusts, which produced surges of pleasure that threatened to make her arms give out. "I wanted your cum on my tongue."

Urkot's fingers flexed, his claws digging into the giving flesh of her hips as a growl rumbled from his chest. "Frenzy is taking me. Need to be inside you. Need my seed inside you." He slammed into her again, harder. "Need to *feel* you on my cock."

Callie curled her fingers into the plant growth beneath her. Her clit pulsed with each thrust, her breasts swayed, and though his cock filled her, there was still an ache inside her that was not satiated. She wanted to be consumed. Needed to be consumed by him.

She needed to again experience that moment of sheer rapture when she and Urkot became one, body and soul, utterly lost within each other.

With a snarl, Urkot drove his cock deep, forcing his knot inside, and held her there, his claspers clamped around her thighs.

Callie whimpered. Fuck, she felt so full of him. She could feel the thickness of his knot, the throbbing of his pulse inside her, could feel his twitching. Even the silk rope wrapped around her body stimulated her skin with every movement.

"Cannot hold it," he grated. His breathing was ragged, his body trembling with tension. "Cannot stop it."

"So don't." Callie dropped onto her forearms, bracing herself, moaning as the position drew even more of him into her body. "Lose yourself. Lose yourself in me. Fuck me, Urkot."

His grip on her strengthened, enhancing the thrilling press of his claws, and a low growl rumbled from his chest. "Shaper, unmake me."

Urkot dropped his upper hands to the ground on either side

of Callie. With his lower hand gripping her hip and his claspers around her thighs, he *rutted*.

He violently pounded into her with a bestial urgency that left Callie breathless. Each thrust felt as though he was trying to get as deep inside her as possible, never going quite deep enough.

Callie clawed at the ground, her body scooting forward with every slam of his hips, but he yanked her back against him each time, unwilling to let her go. Not that she wanted him to. She needed this. Craved this. Every pump struck a chord within her that sent liquid fire roaring through her veins, and every time his knot pushed inside, it left her with the sweetest burn.

Her cries echoed within the cavern, and she turned her face, biting down on her arm to muffle them. Urkot's grunts, growls, hisses, and snarls reverberated, and those carnal sounds of need —his need for her—only excited her more.

Her clit throbbed, her nipples pulsed, and slick dripped her from pussy, running down her inner thighs. Pleasure coiled tight in her core. She felt it building, building, building, a maelstrom threatening to tear her asunder.

Callie lifted her head and reached back, brushing the base of one of his claspers with her fingers.

"*No*," Urkot snarled, pressing an upper hand between her shoulders and shoving her down onto the plant-covered ground. His thrusts gained a new intensity, his cock pounding into her faster, harder, and deeper. "My mate. My *nyleea. Kir'ani. Kir'ani. Kir'ani.*"

*Mine. Mine. Mine.*

"Yes," Callie rasped, body jolting with the savagery of his fucking. "Yours, Urkot. Yours."

Her breath came in shallow pants and sharp whimpers, tension thrummed through her, and the pressure in her core bloomed.

And then rapture cleaved through her, drowning her in

absolute, all-consuming pleasure. Squeezing her eyes shut, Callie screamed into her arm.

Her core contracted, attempting to push Urkot's cock out and draw it in deeper all at once, but his grip on her hip tightened, and the prick of his claws added to the ecstasy that had taken hold of her.

A low hiss tore from Urkot's throat. He did not stop his ruthless thrusts; the wet sound of his cock slamming into her punctuated every burst of pleasure.

Trembling, Callie clutched the vegetation beneath her as her pussy quivered around his shaft. "Urkot."

"Callie," he rasped as he drew back and thrust into her one final time.

She felt his cock expand, felt his knot grow and lodge deep inside her, felt his hot seed flood her. Then came his tendrils, unfurling and fluttering rapidly.

"Oh God," she breathed as a second climax took her. "*Urkot!*"

Spasms rolled through her body, and Urkot snarled, his hand pressing on her back, his body quaking. Stream after stream of his cum filled her, and wave after pulsing wave of pleasure crashed through her with every flutter of those tendrils against her cervix.

Urkot banded an arm around her middle and lifted her, sinking back and drawing her against his chest, pushing his cock impossibly deeper. His head dipped as he embraced her fully, forcing hers to tilt aside. He groaned. "Your body was made for me."

His teeth clamped over the same spot he'd bitten her before.

A blast of pleasure-pain ripped through Callie. She screamed. He covered her mouth with a hand, muffling her cry and the moans that followed it as she orgasmed again.

With each flick of his tendrils and spurt of seed, the tension in Urkot eased, until finally he relaxed his jaw. His tongue swept over her skin, gently licking the marks he'd left. One of his hands, which happened to be atop Callie's breasts, flexed, and his thumb lovingly stroked her nipple.

"Ah, my suncrest," he rumbled, nuzzling her neck and hair. "I wish to remain here, buried inside you. One with you. Forever."

Callie reached up and caressed his jaw as she turned her face toward him, brushing her lips across his hard mouth. "Me too."

They reveled in each other as Urkot descended from his peak, the spasms in his cock gradually growing weaker and more infrequent, the movements of those tendrils becoming lighter and more leisurely. When his knot finally released her, he lifted her from his shaft and cradled her against his chest as he strode back to the steaming pool. She didn't even care that his cum was leaking from her.

He stepped into the water and lay back, settling Callie astride atop him, and wrapped his lower arm around her securely.

Smiling, Callie folded her arms atop his chest, rested her chin upon them, and looked up at him. His hearts pounded beneath her, strong and fast. Her body ached deliciously, her pussy still quivering in the aftermath of their lovemaking. His cock hadn't retreated into his slit, but remained erect, pressed against her backside.

Urkot purred as he cupped handfuls of hot water and poured them over her. She closed her eyes with a sigh, relishing both the heat of the water and that of the vrix holding her. There was a sting on her ass cheek from his spanking, but all she could think was *worth it.*

She felt alive. She felt loved.

During moments like this, she could forget that their lives were in danger, and she hoped she and Urkot would share many more such moments once they found their home.

Because they would get out of here. They had to. Callie

would accept no other outcome. She wanted to live, and she wanted to spend her life with Urkot.

Through all this hardship, through all her fear, Urkot had been her rock. She'd never had a place that truly felt like home, but she had found it in him. He was her safety, her security, her solid foundation. With him, she was exactly where she belonged.

He continued pouring water onto her while his lower hand smoothed over her back, ass, and leg. His touch was gentle and soothing, yet it hinted at the consuming arousal he could flood her with were he to use just a little more pressure or graze her even slightly with his claws.

Urkot's chest swelled with a slow, deep breath. "Callie…"

The weight with which he'd said her name, the rawness that had crept into his voice, had her opening her eyes to meet his gaze.

"I am not a vrix of pretty words. I am no weaver, and cannot gift you silk dresses, and I am not enough of a hunter to bring you the most good meat. I am a delver. A shaper. I cannot give fine things to you, but I can provide for you. I can shield you. And that is what I want… You.

"I have lived so long understone, in the dark. You are my sun. You are my light, you are the warmth on my hide. You are my heartsthread. Even if there are things I cannot give you, I long to spend my life giving you everything I can. Giving you my hearts, my soul…my love."

Tears gathered in Callie's eyes, and her chest constricted with the emotion overflowing within her heart. It was almost hard to breathe. Her heart pounded, and her belly fluttered.

It didn't matter how softly he had spoken, his words had been a claim, as real and solid as the stone around them.

He loved her. Urkot *loved* her.

She laughed softly as she scooted up his chest and cradled his jaw between her palms. "Not a vrix of pretty words, my ass."

Callie pressed her mouth firmly to his.

Urkot banded his arms around her, holding her tight.

When Callie lifted her head, all eight of his glowing eyes, so bright and blue, met hers. They were unwavering as they held her gaze. He was looking at her as though she were his whole world, as though she was all that existed.

She smiled and brushed her thumbs along his jaw. "I thought it was already established that I'm yours."

"You are." He gently tucked her damp curls behind her ear with his claws. "But…"

Callie's brow furrowed. "But?"

His mandibles drooped. "To other vrix, I am different. My shape, my arms. They look upon me, and they…they do not want. They see something less, something unworthy, something not…pretty. Many times, they have made me feel unwanted. Like I do not belong. Like I am not enough."

"Oh, Urkot," she whispered, her heart hurting for him. She pressed her forehead to his headcrest as she continued stroking his jaw. "You are not unworthy, and you sure as hell aren't lesser."

Callie ran a hand down his neck to his shoulder. "These arms are strong. They have carried burdens that would've crushed anyone else, and they have provided shelter in times of need." She moved her hand onto his, which rested upon her thigh. "These hands have shaped stone, creating beautiful works of art, and have fought fiercely to protect the people you love."

She raised her head and slipped her hand down to the large, rough scar on his left side. "This scar is proof of your willingness to sacrifice for others. It is proof of your strength and your tenacity. You fought, and you survived."

He shuddered, and a low buzz sounded in his chest.

"You are more than enough, Urkot. You have always been and always will be. And you are wanted." With a soft smile,

Callie trailed her fingers lightly over the side of his face. "I also find you very pretty."

His mandibles ticked upward, but he huffed. "Just pretty? Am I not sexy?"

Callie chuckled. "You are. Very sexy." She ran her hands over his shoulders and chest as she sat up on him. "Your arms, your body, your cock…"

Lifting her ass, she reached between her thighs to gasp his extruded shaft. Urkot's breath hitched, and his hands caught her hips, fingers and claws digging into her skin. She wiggled herself down his body until she was able to notch the pronged tip of his shaft against her entrance. Slowly, she sank down atop him, moaning as his cock pushed deep inside her. Urkot hissed, his body tensing.

"You are also mine, Urkot." She seated herself until she reached his knot, which spread her wider, and settled her palms over his hands. Her eyes remained locked with his. "And I'm not letting you go, my *luveen*."

A shiver wracked him, moving through her, and he released a shaky breath. "Callie…"

His lower hand squeezed her thigh as his grip on her hips tightened. He lifted her slowly, and Callie's lashes fluttered at the slow drag of his cock inside her, the ridges of its wide head sending shocks of pleasure through her already sensitive channel.

"I will *never* let you go," Urkot growled, yanking her down and forcing his knot deep into her.

Callie threw her head back with a cry and surrendered herself to him.

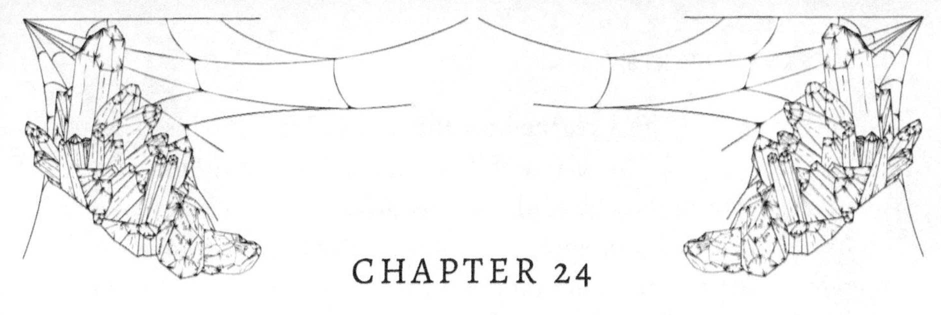

# CHAPTER 24

Urkot lay on his side, facing Callie, atop the nest of fluffed silk he'd made after exiting the pool. His arms were around her, and one of hers was draped over him, lying comfortably over his scar. The warmth of her arm and the softness of her skin was enough to banish the ghosts of any pain he'd ever felt there.

She was breathing slowly and steadily, making those soft growls in her sleep.

*No, growl is not right. They call it snoring.*

And from Callie, it was an endearing sound, one he'd only heard her make when she was in the deepest, most content, most secure of sleeps.

*Callie is mine. Mine. My mate.*

Never had so simple a thought impacted Urkot so profoundly. All his doubts and worries were gone, if only for this moment. There was only joy here, only fullness. There was only that unseen tether linking him to her, binding their hearts together, entwining their heartsthreads.

Urkot breathed her in, filling his lungs with her fragrance. He could always pick it out, even in a place like this, where many other smells vied for dominance.

For so long, he'd yearned for this, for Callie to be his. That she had accepted his claim and made her own upon him was more powerful than he could've imagined. For many eightdays, he'd not allowed himself to hope. It would've been easy to curse himself for failing to act on his feelings, for having wasted so much time, but he would not do so.

He had Callie here and now, and that was enough.

*And I'm not letting you go, my* luveen.

He shuddered as her words repeated in his mind. They'd been a vehement declaration, a passionate vow. And what had come after…

His hide tingled from their mating, and flickers of heat coursed through his blood. The scent of sex lingered in the air, and his scent marked her as surely as his bite on her shoulder had. His gaze fell upon it. The small wounds were covered with sticky silk, but he knew the mark was there and would remain so.

A low purr rumbled in his chest. The urge to rut rose within him. It didn't matter that they'd mated a short time ago, his need for Callie would never be sated. The closeness he shared with her, the intimacy, was something he'd never had with anyone.

Every bit of it was a thrill. The feel of her hot, wet pussy around his cock, of her soft skin pressed to his hard hide, of her hands moving over him, the sound of her voice singing her pleasure, the yearning and love in her eyes as they stared into his…

His slit parted as his aching stem slowly emerged from it.

*I need her.*

With a hum, Urkot rubbed his face against the side of her neck as his lower hand curled around her ass, clutching it.

Callie groaned in her sleep but didn't wake.

"My suncrest." He slipped his tongue out and ran it down her throat.

She tipped her head back, drew in a deep breath, released it slowly, and once more settled.

When he received no other response, Urkot lifted his head and looked down at her. Her eyes remained closed, and her breathing was again slow and even.

He chittered quietly.

Their whole tribe had learned how difficult it could be to wake Callie. He wouldn't have been surprised if she were to sleep through the most violent of storms, with thunder crashing and trees thrashing.

But he needed to have her...and this was his first opportunity to discover how effectively pleasure could rouse his mate from sleep.

Urkot rolled Callie onto her back, extracted his arms from beneath her, and braced himself over her.

"My heartsthread," he crooned before flicking his tongue over the dip at the center of her collarbone.

She did not wake.

Urkot ran his tongue down between her breasts, lazily licking up and down, then over one of her lush mounds, where he circled her dark nipple. It hardened, and a whimper escaped his mate. He moved to her other breast, lavishing her other nipple with the same attention as the first.

Callie moaned, arching her back as her thighs fell open. He loved how responsive her body was to his touch, even in her sleep.

The scent of her arousal bloomed in the air, and he breathed it in. It was sweeter and more potent than any pheromone. He groaned at the throbbing of his cock. Hoping to ease it, he wrapped his lower hand around his shaft, squeezing tight. It did nothing to alleviate the needy ache. The only thing that could provide relief was the heated embrace of Callie's body.

He trailed his tongue lower, down the curved flesh of her breast and over her belly, swirling it in her belly button. Her flesh quivered in response, prompting him to dip his head and nuzzle her stomach.

Had his seed taken root in her? Could it do so, or had Ketahn and Ivy's broodling been a unique blessing bestowed upon them by the gods?

Moving his upper hands to her hips, Urkot lifted his face and looked down at his mate and her flat belly. He wanted his seed to take root, wanted to see her belly round with their broodling. Wanted to place his hand against her smooth skin and feel the tiny life growing not in an egg, but inside his mate.

His cock twitched at the thought, and the ache deepened so much that he had to clamp his jaw tight against it. His gaze dipped to her parted slit. It glistened with her essence, a flower luring him with its nectar.

*Rut her. Fuck her. Fill her with seed.*

A shiver coursed through him, and he tightened his grip on his stem. Yes. He would fill her pussy with his seed again and again to ensure it was planted deep.

*Broodmother, give us a broodling.*

Urkot dropped his face between her thighs. "Awaken, my *nyleea*."

He dragged his tongue up her pussy, groaning at the taste of her.

A low, drawn-out sound answered him—the growling of her stomach.

He replied with a ragged growl of his own, lifting his head to glare at her belly.

Callie chuckled. "I don't think you can scare away my hunger."

His attention shifted to her face. She wore a sultry smile that made her full lips all the more enticing, and her sleepy, half-lidded eyes were dark and gleaming with desire. Damn his eyes, but seeing her that way didn't make it any easier to restrain himself.

*My mate is hungry.*

And that was more important than his want, than his need. She would always come first.

"Cannot scare it, but I can satisfy it." He pushed himself up and turned, meaning to move away and fetch her bag.

Callie sat up and caught him by his stem, her grip tight and firm, causing him to go still and grunt as pleasure blasted through him.

Slipping a hand around the back of Urkot's neck, she coaxed him down with her as she lay back upon the silk, guiding his cock toward her pussy. "I believe there is a hunger we both need satisfied first."

He should've resisted. Should have denied them both this pleasure so he could see to her needs first. Once she was fed, there'd be time...

But he didn't fight her. Didn't even try to resist her guidance. He planted his hands on either side of her head to hold himself over her, and once the tip of his stem was against her sex, he knew there was no going back. There was no staving off his desire any longer.

She wrapped her legs around his waist as she scattered kisses over his neck, jaw, and mouth. "I need you."

"I crave you," Urkot snarled, pushing his cock deep inside her. He squeezed fistfuls of fluffed silk in his hands as Callie's pussy closed around him and embraced him, as it welcomed him into her heat, into the heart of her.

And he never wanted to leave.

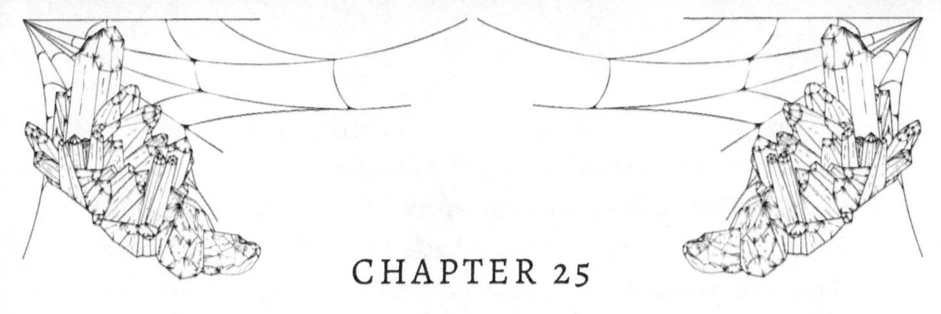

# CHAPTER 25

As Callie finished eating her dried meat and shadowberries, Urkot harvested more food to supplement his own meal. Threadleaf and a bunch of whiteroots wouldn't keep his hunger satisfied for long, but he remained unwilling to eat any of the food Callie had brought along. So there he stood, plucking glowworms off the cave ceiling and gathering them on his cupped hand in a wriggling, luminescent pile.

He wasn't sure what he looked forward to more—basking in the sun's warmth again or biting into a fresh piece of meat.

His eyes dipped to the worms on his hand.

*The meat. Definitely the meat.*

Glowworms were flavorful, and he enjoyed the way they burst when he bit down on them, but they were like the berries and other plants; they wouldn't fill him. They were, at best, a distraction from hunger.

Unless he were to eat half his body weight in worms. Not that his mate was interested in witnessing that...

A thought occurred to him, and he chittered softly and glanced at Callie over his shoulder. She stood, lacing her top as she gazed around the cavern, her eyes sparkling with undiminished wonder and appreciation. Preoccupied.

Throwing his head back, he opened his mouth and dumped the glowworms in. He strode back to Callie as he chewed. When she noticed his approach, she turned toward him and smiled, tying a bow at the top of the lacing.

The string was not fine work by any measure, but it was practical, and it had been made by him. He still could not claim to be a weaver, but his mate was wearing his silk. Urkot couldn't help but feel pride at that.

Some part of him wanted to tear away her clothing even now. Fortunately, that urge was not stronger than his need to move on, to lead his mate to safety.

He swallowed and returned her smile, raising his mandibles and spreading them wide even as he opened his mouth to let the lingering glow from the worms shine through. He'd seen enough of other delvers after eating glowworms to know what it would look like.

Callie's eyes widened. "Is that... Did you just..."

"It is what you call a bright smile," he said, lifting his mandibles higher.

She laughed. "Oh my God. That's funny, but so gross at the same time."

He let his smile fall and his shoulders slump. "I am gross?"

Stepping closer, she tipped her head back, pressed a finger to his chest, and glared at him playfully. "Don't you dare turn my words around. You know you're sexy. The worms are gross." She gave his chest a light pat and moved away. "And I'm not kissing you until you wash your mouth out."

Chittering, he bent down to grab the waterskin from her bag and drank to rinse his mouth.

Callie crouched and picked up something from beside her bag. When Urkot lowered the waterskin, she held a large piece of dried meat out to him.

"Eat it," she commanded.

Urkot shook his head. "No. We must keep that for you."

"Urkot, it's the last piece, and I saved it for you. You're bigger than me, and you need it more than I do."

"I will get more worms."

Callie tilted her head, giving him a droll look. "Those little squirming things are not going to fill you up." She moved the meat closer to him. "Please eat it."

He folded his upper arms across his chest and planted his lower hand on his hip. "I cannot. We do not know how far we must go, or if there is safe food for you on the way."

She stared at him. Slowly, the corners of her mouth curved down, and her bottom lip puckered. "You would decline a gift from your mate?"

Something sank in his belly. "What?"

"I am gifting you food, as your mate, and you are rejecting it." Her lower lip quivered, and she sniffled. "Does that mean… you're rejecting *me*?"

Urkot staggered back a step, arms spreading reflexively. That weight in his gut coiled his insides, and he felt his heart-sthread pulling taut. "What is this? I am not rejecting you. You are mine, Callie. My mate."

"But y-you're rejecting my gift." She turned her face and covered it with her other hand, her curls falling to shield her, and bobbed her shoulders as she let out a series of sobs.

Hurriedly, he took the meat from her hand and shoved it in his mouth. While chewing, he said, "I am eating. See? No more sad, my *nyleea*."

Callie dropped her hands and turned back to him with a wide smile. "Good boy. Ready to go?"

His jaw halted mid-chew as he blinked at her. There was no trace of tears in her eyes, and not a hint of the overwhelming sadness she'd just displayed remained on her face. Urkot swallowed the meat and let out a huff. "Not nice."

Chuckling, Callie looped her arms around his neck and tugged him down. He allowed her to do so; she stopped when their faces were but a breath apart.

"It's called a guilt trip," she said. "And it was for your own good."

She pressed a kiss to his mouth. When she started to pull away, Urkot banded his arms around her and tugged her body against his, latching onto her waist with his claspers.

He growled and leaned his head down, nuzzling her throat, scraping his mouth against the sensitive location between her neck and shoulder where his bite had marked her. She giggled, twining her fingers in his hair as she wriggled against him.

"You will pay for that later, female," he rumbled.

"I look forward to this...punishment."

Her tattooed ass flashed in his mind's eye, and it took all his willpower to resist the urge to make *later* into *now*. With equal struggle, he released her, and they collected their belongings— Callie slinging her bag over her shoulders, Urkot his belt around his waist.

Callie stepped into her boots, which made a squelching sound. She scrunched her nose. "I never thought that dry boots would also rank so high on my list of things I'm looking forward to."

Urkot chittered. "We have many things to look forward to. That is good, yes?"

He moved to the chamber's exit, spread his arms, and grasped the boulder he'd used to block it. His muscles strained as he heaved it aside, using all his strength to ensure it did not fall and produce a sound loud enough to alert every spirit-strider in the world to their presence.

Cooler air flowed in through the opening, sweeping over his hide and fine hairs. The tunnel beyond was lit by the same crystals and plants as this chamber, granting it ample light. He stood there for many heartbeats, listening for any movement from ahead, before waving for Callie to join him. Together, they strode into the tunnel.

It was faint, much too faint to be sure, but he swore there was a hint of the Tangle's scent on the air. Perhaps it was simply his imagination, tainted by hope and desire…

The crystals and plants thinned as Urkot and Callie walked onward, eventually forcing them to take out a pair of glowstones to light their way. Yet that air current remained steady. Its presence diminished the effects the darkness might've otherwise had upon Urkot.

They followed that airflow, and he would've continued past the large offshoot tunnel without a second thought, just like the many other openings they'd passed, if not for him glimpsing rubble from the corner of his eye. He paused and turned toward the opening. The light of his glowstone reached only a few segments into the passage, falling upon loose rocks and something that seemed uneasily familiar.

After glancing back and forth along the tunnel they'd been traversing, Urkot crept into the side passage. As his light advanced, the familiar shape grew clear—a vrix skeleton, its hindquarters and legs buried beneath fallen rocks.

He and Callie stopped and raised their crystals. Before them was a chaotic mass of stones, the aftermath of a rockfall that had sealed this tunnel. Thick dust coated most of it, including the bones, and it looked like it hadn't been disturbed in a long, long while.

"It's a thornskull," Callie said softly.

Urkot dropped his gaze to the skull. The bony spikes on the headcrest were unmistakable.

He curled his suddenly trembling hands into fists. He did not know this thornskull, couldn't have, and yet as he stared at it, he could only see the new friends he had lost. He could only see Zotahl and Tahlken, Enikor and the other young delvers.

He could only see the many vrix who had died in dark

places just like this. All the delvers he'd known, some friends, some family, who had been claimed by the countless dangers found understone. And he could hear the deafening roars of rocks falling, of stone crashing and crushing, swallowing up the screams…

Grief and powerlessness swept over him like the waters of a flood, threatening to drown him. His breaths came ragged and shallow, and his hearts raced, thundering in his chest.

"Hey, hey." Callie moved in front of him and grasped his jaw, cradling it with both hands. "Urkot, look at me."

He pulled his gaze away from the vrix remains and looked into the warm, dark depths of Callie's beautiful eyes.

"It's okay," she said gently, and she drew his head down to press her forehead to his headcrests. "Just breathe."

But he couldn't. There was too much tightness in his chest and throat, too much heat building inside him. He forced his eyes shut and focused on Callie—on her scent, on her touch, on the sound of her voice.

"Breathe for me, my *luveen*. In and out. There you go. Keeping going, just like that. You're here, I'm here. We're still alive, and we're getting out of this place together." She stroked her thumbs along his jaw and pressed a kiss to his mouth. "We have a life to start, to build. The both of us. We'll share a den, have lots of amazing sex, and I mean a lot. And maybe…maybe some babies along the way."

His hearts stilled, and the sounds from his memory went abruptly silent.

*Babies? Broodlings...like Akalahn?*

*She wants to carry my broodlings?*

He searched her eyes. They were filled with sincerity, and sparkled with a hopeful, dreamy light. She'd thought about the same things he had. She'd envisioned the same future he had, a future made together, a life lived together.

She smiled. "You like that idea, huh?" One of her hands slid up into his hair, and she combed her fingers through it. "I watched you at the party, you know, while you were with the broodlings. I saw you playing with them. I won't lie and say it didn't turn me on, because it did. It really, really did. And I… I'd love to see you play with our own kids one day. I know you'd make a wonderful father."

A growl rumbled in his chest as he placed his upper hands on her hips and flattened the lower over her belly. "Yes. I much like that idea."

She chuckled. "Then we need to get out of here so we can get to work on that and have all that hot sex." When she pressed her lips to his mouth again, they lingered, lightly brushing back and forth.

Urkot firmly kissed her in return, closing his eyes and crooning as he drew her closer. His suncrest indeed. She'd chased away the shadows in his hearts so easily, had driven them back to the pits from which they'd crawled.

The tightness in his chest eased, as did his breathing along with it. "I will bring you home, Callie."

"As long as I'm with you, I am home."

His heartsthread thrummed at those words. Such a simple, powerful way to describe what he'd been feeling, to express these complex, deep-running emotions. Callie's presence made him feel at home in a way he never truly had before. And he did the same for her.

When he'd visited Takarahl, there'd been an empty space in his chest, far too vast to have fit inside him. He'd been aware of each moment he spent away from Kaldarak, and those eight-days had felt like the longest of his life.

He hadn't understood the cause of it, not until he'd returned to Kaldarak and had seen Callie again. Not until he'd been blessed by the beauty of her smile and the joy of her laughter.

Only then had that ache been soothed, that hole filled.

The humans had another way to express all those feelings,

one even simpler than Callie's words. Urkot had heard Ivy and Ketahn say it to each other, had heard Rekosh and Ahmya do the same.

Urkot opened his eyes and lifted his head, meeting her gaze. He moved a hand up to her face, cupping her cheek. "I love you, Callie."

He had never spoken truer words. Had never spoken with such confidence, with such vehemence.

Callie's smile was wide and radiant as her eyes glimmered with a sheen of tears. "I love you too."

Urkot released a low, deep trill as he caressed her cheek with the back of a claw. It was hard to look away from her. His beautiful mate, his Callie, his suncrest, his heartsthread.

Yet he pulled his gaze away from her, looking over the rock-fall and down to the skeleton crushed beneath it. Memories raked at his mind, but they did not burst in; Callie's presence and touch held them back.

"I have lost many to the tunnels," he finally said, voice low and raw. "Friends and kin both. I have seen rocks fall atop them, have heard their cries, have watched them die. And every time, I have wondered what I could have done to save them. Have wondered why I walked away when they did not. I know these dangers too well, and yet I go to the tunnels again and again, hoping to spare others from such fates.

"That is why I did not want you to come. I have lost too many in places like this. But to lose you, Callie?" He turned his face to her, and a tremor coursed through him. "I would not survive that."

"Oh Urkot…" She slipped her arms around him, embracing him tightly. "I'm so sorry. I didn't know." Softly, she rubbed her cheek against his chest. "But I'm glad I came to visit you. I'm glad that I'm here with you, that you're not alone here. If I hadn't come, if you hadn't pulled me away from the others… you could have died too."

He'd been so set on moving forward, on not thinking about what had happened and what could've happened, that he'd failed to even consider what she had just said.

Her presence had saved him.

Urkot released a shaky breath and hugged her closer.

*Shaper, shelter us. Protector, shield us. Delver, guide us home.*

The sooner they escaped this place, the sooner they could begin the life for which they both yearned. The sooner he could enjoy his mate without all this danger and worry.

He and Callie withdrew from one another, and despite that need to move on, he found his attention once again shifting toward the thornskull remains. There was something near one of those skeletal hands, something that didn't look like rock or vrix bone.

Head tilted, Urkot sank down and brushed the dust off the object.

Despite being worn and tarnished with age, he knew exactly what he was looking at—a yatin horn that had been fashioned into a pick. The wear at the tip indicated it had seen much use. Only frayed threads remained of the silk that must've fastened it to its wooden handle, of which there was no trace. He did not know how long must've passed for that wood to rot away, but he could feel the weight of countless years pressing down on him.

As far as he knew, thornskulls were not prone to delving very deep, not like shadowstalkers. He could not say for certain if that had always been true. But it didn't seem like this thornskull had been dragged here by spiritstriders—it seemed to have been digging. Delving.

Which meant that the surface had to be near.

More evidence of that had been in the pelts and hides in the spiritstriders' hive and the carcasses the hunting party had been carrying, all belonging to jungle beasts.

Urkot couldn't guess how deep he and Callie had gone, how far they'd traveled, but they *had* to be close to a way out.

Rising, he strode back toward Callie and stroked the backs of his fingers down her cheek. "Come, female. Let us make our way home."

She smiled and nodded. "Let's get the hell out of here."

Side by side, they returned to the main tunnel. Only now did Urkot notice the ample signs that this passage had been widened by vrix hands. How had he missed the marks from picks and chisels on the walls?

The draft strengthened as they continued onward, as did the faint jungle scent it carried. They strode past more openings and ancient, rotted logs that had been placed long ago as supports, led unerringly by the current.

"You're quiet, but I can sense your excitement," Callie said. "These old support beams look like the ones the thornskulls had up where we first entered. We're close to a way out, aren't we?"

With a chitter, he replied, "I think we are."

"Wait, really?"

"Yes."

Callie stomped her feet and clapped with a little squeal, falling slightly behind Urkot. "Thank God, thank the Eight, thank whoever the hell is listening that we're finally going to—"

Her sudden scream cut off her words, piercing Urkot's heart and pouring cold into his blood.

Something scraped over stone, followed by a dull, heavy thump that interrupted Callie's scream. Urkot spun in time to see her on the floor. Her wide, panicked eyes met his.

"Urkot!" she cried, clawing at the ground before she was dragged into the shadows of a side chamber, vanishing from sight.

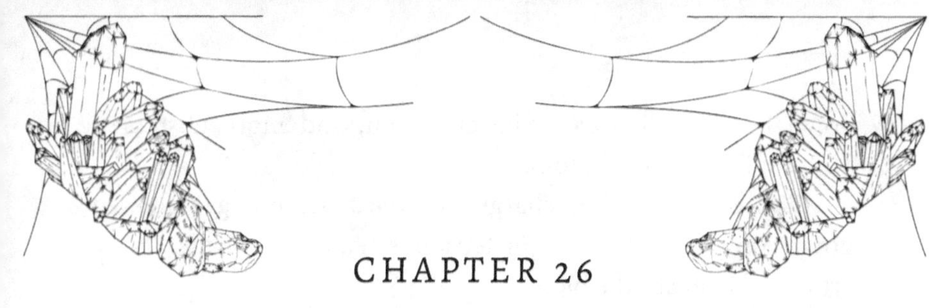

# CHAPTER 26

TERROR THREATENED to overcome Urkot entirely. Countless dark thoughts circled his mind like scavengers waiting out a dying animal, an instant away from swarming and devouring him.

His mate had been taken right before his eyes.

His mate had been taken.

*Nothing will take her from me!*

Raw, potent fury obliterated his fear. He raced after Callie.

The scent of human blood struck him as he reached the opening, and he rushed into the small chamber.

It was lit only by the crystal that had fallen from Callie's hand—and the glow of a male spiritstrider. The pale vrix was so low that he was nearly lying on his belly, with two clawed hands hooked onto Callie's leg, drawing her closer as though he were pulling on a silk rope to drag in a speared beast.

Callie fought, screaming as her fingers raked over the cave floor, seeking purchase. She kicked her free leg desperately. Her boot connected with the snarling male's face. Mandibles snapping at her, the spiritstrider's hand reached higher, raking down her bloodied calf. She cried out, and more glistening blood spilled over the stone.

With a roar, Urkot charged forward, stomping a foreleg down on one of the spiritstrider's extended arms. Bone crunched beneath the blow.

The spiritstrider hissed and snatched its arm back, but kept its other hand on Callie's leg.

"She is mine!" Urkot pushed off with his rear and middle legs, driving the bent joint of his foreleg into the spiritstrider's head.

The force knocked the other vrix away, claws tearing free of Callie's leg. She screamed. The sound twisted Urkot's already taut heartsthread. Clutching her wounded leg, she hurriedly rolled aside.

Urkot dropped his own crystal and leapt onto the spiritstrider. His weight bore down on the vrix, who thrashed and clawed at Urkot, but he felt no pain through his rage as he grabbed the vrix's mandibles at their bases. Those pincers snapped the air impotently.

Growling, Urkot slammed the spiritstrider's head against the floor.

The pale vrix's struggles faltered. Urkot tightened his grip, and using all his strength, brought his foe's head down again and again, feeling the heavy *thumps* of impact jolt up his arms and only pouring more power into every subsequent blow. Even when he heard the spiritstrider's skull crack, he did not stop.

"Will not take my mate."

*Slam.*

"Will not touch."

*Slam.*

"She's mine. Mine. Mine!"

*Slam. Slam. Slam.*

He halted only when a small sound broke through the red haze that had taken hold of him—a whimper from Callie.

"Fuck." Urkot released the unmoving spiritstrider and shoved away from it, turning toward his mate.

She sat, trembling, with her wounded leg stretched before her, both hands clamped around her calf. Blood oozed between and around her fingers. Her breaths were harsh, taken and expelled through clenched teeth.

Urkot scrambled over to her, plucked a glowstone off the floor, and knelt with hands raised and fingers splayed, staring down at her injuries. With all the blood, it was difficult to tell just how many cuts she'd suffered, and their severity was impossible to guess, but they looked grave. His hearts ached seeing the damage that had been inflicted upon her. He knew even the gentlest touch would hurt her more.

But he also knew that a great deal of noise had been made during the struggle—noise that was very much out of the ordinary for these tunnels. Noise that would have traveled far.

He needed to hurry.

Urkot curled his fingers as a heaviness dragged down his insides. "Callie… I must tend you."

Her teary gaze met his. He hated seeing that gleam in her eyes. It was filled with fear, agony, and understanding. Understanding that this ordeal was not yet finished.

Callie gave a shallow nod. "Hurry."

Her nostrils flared as she loosened her hands and pried them away from her calf. Fresh blood flowed from her cuts. Moving as quickly and carefully as he could, Urkot drew out sticky silk and applied it to her wounds.

"Fuck," Callie cried, and her following sounds were cut short as she bit down on her hand. Muscles tense and fingers raking the chamber floor, she squirmed, moaned, and heaved muffled cries that made her shoulders quake. Her every pained reaction, no matter how small, was like a new thorn stabbed into Urkot's hearts.

His fingers were quickly slick with her blood. They'd never felt so clumsy. His large, rough hands were not made for such tasks.

If only Diego had been there to tend her properly.

*Damn my eyes, if only I had protected her from this.*

A sound from the tunnel stilled his hands and his hearts—a series of clicks echoing along the passageway.

His wide eyes met Callie's. Then he hurriedly covered the rest of her wounds with silk, sealing them. It was enough to stop the bleeding for now.

His spinnerets spun a thin rope, which he quickly passed to his hands and began winding around her calf.

More clicks sounded from the tunnel, followed by harsh voices.

*Fuck.*

Rekosh's silken words wouldn't have been any help now, but his deft fingers certainly would've been welcome.

After wrapping the silk snugly around Callie's leg, Urkot tied it in place, hoping the hasty work would hold, and rose, lifting her onto her feet.

Callie hissed and stood with her injured leg bent, keeping weight off it, as he stooped and helped her climb onto his hindquarters. She clung to him with both arms and one leg. Urkot moved immediately to the entryway.

Legs scraped and tapped against stone somewhere not far off. The sound's disjointed rhythm suggested several vrix striding together. He laid his lower arm atop both of Callie's, which were banded around his middle, and stepped into the tunnel.

The air current flowed over his hide and through his fine hairs, carrying that hint of the Tangle's smell.

He cursed when he realized what else it would carry—his

and Callie's scents, straight to the spiritstriders now approaching. And the scent of her blood was most potent of all.

Just as Urkot quickened his pace, one of the spiritstriders let out an unnerving shriek, and frenzied movement echoed along the tunnel.

Hearts thundering, Urkot ran. His legs came down heavily, jostling Callie, who held on tightly. The sounds of pursuing vrix grew louder and clearer.

He offered prayers to all the Eight, asking each for guidance and protection, asking them to see his mate through this alive and well. But in truth, he knew he could rely only upon himself to protect her. There'd be no help down here, not even from the Delver.

Urkot rounded a bend in the tunnel, slapping his hands against the wall to prevent himself from careening into it with his momentum. He pushed himself off it, running harder, faster, his chest constricted and lungs burning.

But the sounds behind him drew nearer and nearer.

The tunnel took another turn, which Urkot stumbled around, before opening into a large cavern.

"Shaper, unmake me," he rasped, skidding to a halt just before he would've plummeted over an abrupt drop off that ended the path.

A few loose pebbles tumbled over the edge and clattered down, drawing his attention along with them. The bottom was barely more than a segment below him, but had he gone over unaware at that speed, it may well have resulted in an injury.

Bones and rocks littered the cave floor, lying amidst a layer of dirt. After the initial drop, the ground sloped upward at an increasingly steep angle, the stone worn in a way indicating frequent traversal.

"Urkot, look," Callie whispered, pointing up over his shoulder.

He swung his gaze in the direction she'd gestured. At the

very top of the slope stood another opening, a cave mouth, through which came a glow unlike any he'd seen since entering the mine with the thornskulls a lifetime ago. It seemed impossible in its brightness, its clarity, its warmth, and yet he knew it was very, very real.

Daylight.

Callie slipped her arm back around him. "We made it."

As though in disagreement, a spiritstrider called out a single, harsh word from the tunnel behind them. *"Taviik'ven!"*

It sounded very much like *tavit'ven*—the vrix command to hunt.

Numerous hisses, clicks, and growls sounded in response.

After everything Urkot and Callie had endured together, after everything they had shared, their journey would not end here, would not end now. Not when sunlight was finally in sight.

"Hold tight," he growled.

He leapt down from the ledge, landing hard on the cave floor. Bones and pebbles scattered. A few of his legs slipped on loose rubble, and he adjusted his weight, throwing his right arms to the side to regain his balance.

Callie squeezed him as he pushed on. Even with six legs, the scree was difficult to cross, constantly shifting beneath him.

The sound of legs scrabbling over stone behind him marked the spiritstriders' entry into the cavern. Their voices rose in a frenzy; they were a pack of predators certain that they had cornered their prey.

Clenching his jaw, Urkot threw himself forward.

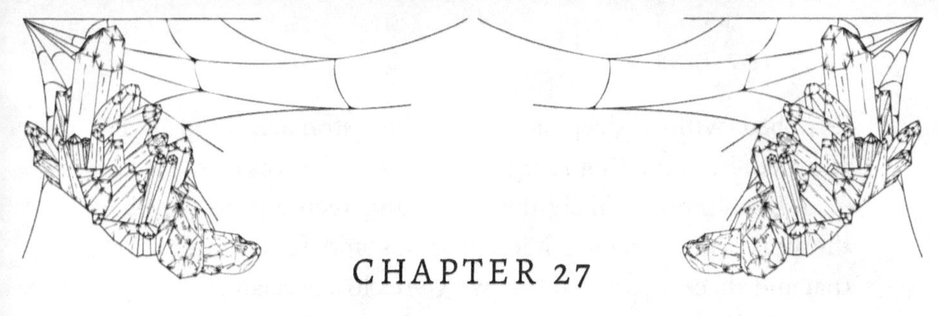

# CHAPTER 27

As Urkot reached the incline, Callie made a grave mistake. She looked backward.

Her heart lodged in her throat, and her fingers dug into the hide of Urkot's abdomen.

Not a single ray of sunshine from above reached this far down, but the diffused light was enough to allow her to see the spiritstriders clearly. She counted six pale monsters rushing down the short drop and gliding over the debris, which had given Urkot so much trouble, like phantoms unimpeded by the corporeal world.

And they were gaining. Fast.

*Fuck, fuck, fuck.*

She faced forward, uncertain of whether she'd thought those words or muttered them under her breath.

Muscles straining, Urkot raced up the slope, leaning forward and using his hands to climb as the path grew steeper.

Behind them, the spiritstriders had finally ceased their terrifying clicking. But it was no comfort to Callie.

Her heart raced, her breath was ragged, her left calf

throbbed with a deep ache, and her stomach flipped and churned. Even holding so tightly to Urkot, she was trembling.

Adrenaline was likely the only thing keeping agony at bay, the only thing keeping her conscious and functioning. Well, that and sheer terror, but the two were closely related.

Callie looked up. They were so close to the freedom they'd sought, so close to escape. Fate wouldn't be so cruel, couldn't be...

And if it was, it could go fuck itself. She and Urkot would make their own damn fate.

Stone scraped beneath Urkot's claws and legs as he scrambled higher, half crawling. The opening was getting closer.

Suddenly, he pitched forward, coming down hard on his arms with a grunt and jolting Callie. She gasped, finding herself practically lying on his back, her pack heavy on her shoulders.

Something had snagged him.

She looked back again.

A spiritstrider held one of Urkot's hind legs, its claws buried in his hide. The pale vrix opened its mouth, spread its pincers wide, and snarled, its beady black eyes looking directly at Callie.

*Oh, God.*

The spiritstrider's companions raced up just behind it, clacking their pincers and growling like ravenous beasts.

Dragging himself onward, Urkot shook and kicked his leg. He dragged the spiritstrider along with him despite its struggles. But Urkot's pace had definitely slowed.

Rocks tumbled down the slope, their clatter echoing through the cavern.

Another spiritstrider vaulted over the first, launching itself at Callie. She cried out and ducked her face against Urkot's back. A heavy weight came down on her bag and yanked back on it. Her shoulders strained as she clutched Urkot's middle, battling that frighteningly powerful pull.

She had to get the bag off. Had to, or she'd be ripped right off her mate to become the spiritstriders' next meal.

Urkot snarled and bucked his hindquarters, but he could not dislodge the unwanted passengers. Callie felt the pull on her bag strengthening. She squeezed her legs around Urkot's waist, gritting her teeth against the fresh, hot wave of agony in her calf. Her grip would not last long.

"My bag, Urkot!"

His lower arm clamped down on her legs, his big hand closing on her left ankle. "Have you, *nyleea*."

That grip was crushing, painful, unbreakable, and she trusted it—trusted him—more than anything else in all the universe.

Callie released her hold on him with one arm. She was immediately jerked backward, her right shoulder on the verge of dislocating from the strain. With a pained cry, she fought her left arm free of the bag's strap. The increased pressure on her right arm broke her hold on Urkot's middle. Her torso tipped backward hard, aided by the steepness of the slope, and her arms flew over her head.

The remaining strap abruptly slipped off as her back slammed atop Urkot's hindquarters, and she found herself in an inverted world, staring downslope at the pursuing spiritstriders.

The vrix that had latched onto her bag growled as it fell away, tumbling over the spiritstrider holding Urkot's leg and knocking it loose. The two rolled down the slope. Only Callie's legs—and Urkot's iron grip on them—kept her in place.

Free of the excess weight, Urkot lurched forward. Several spiritstriders rushed up the slope just behind him as the two that had fallen struggled to right themselves. More were farther down, crawling up with alarming speed.

Callie's eyes widened. There were too many spiritstriders, and they were too fast. Another delay, even a small one, and…

"Callie!" Urkot's grip on her ankle tightened. "Are you hurt?"

"I'm fine," she grated. "Relatively…"

She growled through clenched teeth as she sat up, her abs burning with the extreme exertion.

*Would it kill you to do a few crunches every now and then, Callie?*

As soon as she was high enough, she wrapped her arms around Urkot again, sliding her hands down to his pouch. She reached in and felt around until she found the collapsed lantern. Pulling it out, she switched to a one-armed hold, drew the lantern to her, and snapped it open with a sharp flick of her wrist.

*Please work.* Please, *fucking work…*

She switched the lantern on. She slitted her eyes against the intense white light and twisted, thrusting the lantern toward the vrix chasing them.

Callie saw unsettling spiritstrider faces and gaunt, bony bodies, saw the nearest of them recoil from the sudden light while the others hesitated, hissing and snarling. One turned away with such abruptness that it lost its footing and slid at least ten feet down the slope.

For once, Urkot gained some distance on their pursuers. She faced forward to find the cavern's opening directly ahead, blindingly brilliant compared to the lantern's glow. Urkot darted through it.

Callie closed her eyes against the glare. Her eyelids glowed red, and sunshine, deliciously scalding, baked down on her skin. With her next breath, the jungle's scent filled her lungs—rich, cloying, complex, verdant. Nothing had ever smelled so good.

Nothing apart from her mate, anyway.

"We made it!" she breathed. "We fucking made it!"

They'd reached the surface, had accomplished what had seemed impossible.

But all the warmth and joy flooding Callie was snuffed out by the inhuman, rage-filled screeches of spiritstriders behind her, amplified by the cave's mouth.

She opened her eyes as Urkot spun to face the cave. His lower hand caught her arm and pulled her down from his hindquarters, setting her on her feet.

Pain shot through her leg, and Callie hissed as she stumbled, but his hold on her prevented her from falling. "Urkot, what are—"

He pressed something into her hand, something heavy, and guided her back with a leg.

She staggered backward, fresh pain searing her calf, and stared down at what he'd handed her—his hammer, with its short haft and its worn, blunt stone head.

Callie closed her fingers around the grip and lifted her gaze.

A large, pale form leapt out of the cave. Urkot swung his right arms, slamming them into the spiritstrider while it was in midair and batting it aside. It crashed into the cliffside from which the cave opened and fell to the ground, stunned.

Another pale vrix charged out into the light, and another. Urkot's left arm hooked around one's throat, catching it in a headlock, pinning its mandibles to the sides of its face. The other spiritstrider scrambled over his hindquarters, clawing his hide, huffing the air in search of a scent.

Its head snapped toward Callie. The vrix reached for her, blindly flailing its arms.

Growling, Urkot grabbed the spiritstrider's stringy hair, yanking its head back. Despite restraining two thrashing males, Urkot's legs barely budged. He looked more solid than ever.

Her rock.

The spiritstrider he held by the hair spun toward him. Its sudden change of direction finally disrupted Urkot's balance, and it took advantage by lunging for his throat. Urkot's muscles bulged beneath his hide as he fought to hold the spiritstrider's head back while its mandibles snapped the air mere inches from his face.

"No!" Callie rushed forward without thinking. As she planted her left foot, she felt warm blood trickling down her leg and a deep burn beneath the silk enwrapping it, but she was already committed, swinging the hammer in a downward chop with all her might.

The stone tool struck the spiritstrider's skull with a dull *thud*. The impact made the hammer bounce, breaking her hold on it, and it fell to the ground even as the vrix's legs buckled.

Urkot tugged on the spiritstrider's hair again, forcing its head back. As Callie stumbled and fell back onto her ass, Urkot hammered a fist into the spiritstrider's exposed throat thrice in quick succession. Something crunched on the third blow.

He shoved the limp spiritstrider aside. It collapsed in a heap partly inside the cave mouth. The vrix he held in a headlock was clawing at his arm, making choked sounds. But more movement from the cave meant more spiritstriders about to join the fray.

Callie could only watch, feeling immensely small and helpless, as Urkot punched his foe until the spiritstrider's struggles ceased and its only movements were its involuntary twitches with each heavy blow.

Effortlessly, Urkot hefted the vrix over his head. Powerful muscles flexed in his broad back and shoulders. In that moment, he looked bigger and more fearsome than even the massive yatins—beasts that made elephants seem petite—that had once attacked their tribe.

And despite everything, despite her pain and fear, it was not lost on Callie just how fucking hot he was.

With a bellowing roar that must've made the very stone before him quake, Urkot threw the spiritstrider into the cave.

Callie saw it crash into a pair of its comrades. All three spirit-striders fell down the slope, vanishing from sight.

A voice echoed from within the cave, repeating a set of commanding, indecipherable words. The first spiritstrider to have charged out of the darkness dragged itself onto shaky legs using the cave wall for support.

Keeping her eyes on the spiritstrider, Callie felt around on the ground until her fingers found the fallen hammer. She lifted it into her hands, holding it before herself as though it could somehow ward off her enemy.

Shoulders heaving, Urkot placed himself between the other vrix and Callie, watching as the spiritstrider felt along the wall and clumsily retreated into the cave.

Clicking sounds came from below. Were they…were they retreating?

Urkot stood vigil at the cave mouth for several heartbeats. Blood glistened on his hide from numerous cuts and scratches, including fresh claw gouges across the scar on his left side.

He turned to Callie suddenly, strode to her, and sank down onto bent forelegs. Though he was right in front of her, her eyes fell on the lifeless vrix lying only feet away, the sun beating down on its pale, dirty hide, worried it would spring up at any moment and attack.

"Callie." Urkot caught her chin and, with a delicateness that shouldn't have been possible after the brutality with which he'd fought, tilted her face toward his. "Are you hurt?"

She dropped the hammer and covered his hand with both of hers, shifting his palm to her cheek and pressing her face against it. "No. At least…not any more than I already was."

He glanced down at her leg, and an unhappy buzz escaped him. The white silk he'd wrapped around it was saturated with blood.

"Ah, my sweet suncrest…" Carefully, he gathered her in his

arms, lifting her against his chest as he rose. She hugged his neck.

"We must go," he said.

Pain radiated in her leg, growing with each heartbeat, and she felt blood running into her boot. "Will more of them come?"

Urkot strode forward, leaving the cave behind. "Not while the sun shines."

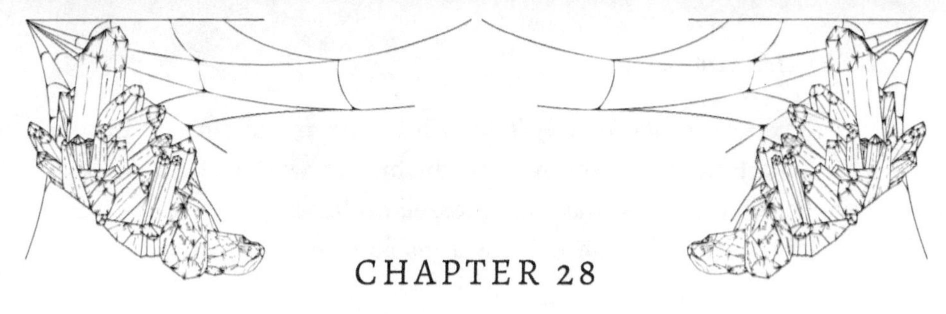

# CHAPTER 28

URKOT'S STRENGTH waned along with the fading sunlight, and by the time the sky had nearly gone dark, he knew he would not be able to continue much farther. Exhaustion, that old, tireless foe, had caught up to him, and he was not foolish enough to believe he could fight it off.

But he could not lose that battle yet, not until he and Callie were as safe as possible. Not until he'd seen to her.

The jungle was only going to be more dangerous once night settled in, and it wasn't only due to the threat of the spirit-striders coming out to hunt. Many of the most dangerous predators prowled the Tangle under cover of darkness—and the scent of Callie's blood would be a potent lure.

Though there was a stubborn part of him willing to push onward until he collapsed, he knew that wasn't helpful for either himself or his mate. He needed to act now...before he became unable to do so.

He'd been moving adjacent to a winding stream for part of the afternoon; he turned toward it now, striding to the water's edge.

"We will stop here." He reached a hand back to Callie.

"Okay," she said quietly, taking his hand and sliding off his hindquarters. When she put weight on her wounded leg, she winced, emitting a cry as she squeezed his hand.

Urkot swept her up into his arms and sat her down on the ground.

He was immediately more aware of the shakiness in his limbs, the raggedness of his breath, and the abrasive dryness in his throat. His body felt far too heavy, as though it was made of stone like Rekosh often joked. Simply remaining upright was a struggle.

*Should not have stopped. Might not be able to move on again...*

Huffing, Urkot lowered himself beside Callie, cupped his hands, and dipped them into the cool stream. Then he tilted his head back and poured water into his open mouth, drinking deeply.

Once he'd drunk his fill, he lifted his water-filled hands toward Callie. "Drink, female."

Her hand trembled as she cupped it beneath his, but she pressed her mouth to the side of his finger and drank.

He brought another handful of water to her lips, then another, until she shook her head.

"No more," she said, nudging his hand away.

Urkot dumped the water into the stream and looked her over. A low buzz resonated in his chest at how ashen her skin appeared. There were deep shadows under her eyes, and tiny drops of sweat clung to her forehead. Scratches and abrasions marred her arms, belly, and legs, her brown hair was a tangled mess, and a few of her nails had been cracked and broken. Yet worst of all was the blood-soaked silk wrapped around her calf.

He should've kept closer to her. Should've noticed the spirit-strider lurking in that dark chamber, should've acted faster.

Despite his weariness, he shifted upon the ground so his body faced her, brought his forearms together, and sank into as deep a bow as he could. "I am sorry, Callie. I failed to shield you from this harm."

Callie caught his jaw and lifted it, forcing him to rise. Her eyes were narrowed in a glare. "Don't you dare apologize. This isn't your fault, Urkot. You got us out of there. You *saved* us."

She leaned forward and pressed her forehead to his head-crest. "And we're going home. Together."

"Together, my *nyleea*." Urkot cradled the back of her head and closed his eyes, breathing her in, feeling her.

But her shivering and the prominent blood scent inter-woven with her fragrance made him pull back. "Your leg."

Callie offered him a weak smile. "Hurts like a son of a bitch."

He released another unhappy buzz. As gently as he could, he slipped off her boot and unwound the silk cord he'd tied around her calf. Callie hissed, gripping her thigh with both hands above her knee.

Once the end of the bloody rope fell away, he tossed it into the stream to be swept away with the current.

"Ah, Callie," Urkot said as he beheld her leg in the final remnants of daylight.

Her calf was swollen, its skin darkened by bruising, with long gouges and punctures from the spiritstrider's claws. Blood oozed from some of the wounds he'd hastily patched. Thank-fully, his sticky silk had staunched most of the bleeding, but the wounds... There were many. Her delicate flesh had offered no resistance to those wicked claws.

He could not imagine how much worse the damage might've been had he been even a moment slower in interven-ing. He refused to.

But there was little he could do for her. She needed Diego, needed the human knowledge and technology he possessed to heal her. All Urkot could do was rebind her wounds and get her back to Kaldarak.

Cupping the back of her foot, he held her leg up and carefully rinsed away the blood. She flinched, and when he used more sticky silk to seal the open wounds, she curled her lips inward and bit down on them. He heard the soft cries she attempted to stifle, felt the strain in her body, and saw the tears in her eyes.

All those reactions created pangs in his chest, each one but a tiny sliver of her pain. He hated that he had to hurt her to aid her. Hated the helplessness he felt. But there was also rage, raw and unsatisfied, toward the vrix who'd harmed his mate.

He produced another silk rope, wrapping it neatly and firmly around her calf to protect her wounds.

When he finished, her body was trembling, she was panting shallowly, and sweat was trickling down her temples. He could still smell blood from her leg, though it was fainter.

Granting her a few moments to recover, he forced himself to rise and searched nearby until he found a plant with broad, potent smelling leaves. He tore a few off and returned to Callie, wrapping them around her calf and tying them into place with strands of silk. It would help mask her blood scent.

After washing the blood from her boot in the water, Urkot carefully slipped it back onto her foot before turning his attention to his own wounds. Though they were many, most were minor and had already stopped bleeding. He packed the rest with silk, grunting softly at the twinges of pain.

This would not be a comfortable night for either himself or his mate.

"Come, my suncrest," he said as he picked Callie up and gently set her on her feet. "We must go high to rest." He lowered himself and held his hand out to her.

Callie chuckled as she accepted his assistance in climbing onto his hindquarters. "Think we'll see Kaldarak from above?"

Urkot drew more silk strand from his spinnerets. "We can look for it."

He passed the rope to Callie, and they bound themselves to

one another, Urkot tying it securely across his abdomen. Then he strode to the base of a large tree and looked up.

Though he'd not spent nearly as long in the Tangle as Ketahn or Telok, Urkot had climbed many, many trees in his time outside Takarahl. But none had seemed quite so large and imposing as this one. He knew it was weariness weighing down his limbs, knew it was exhaustion teasing every side of his mind.

*A little farther, and we can rest.*

Callie slipped her arms around him, and Urkot gently patted them with his lower hand. "Hold tight, female."

"Not letting go."

If he had ever doubted the power of words, those doubts were laid to rest in that moment. Cally's reply burrowed into his heart, flooded his chest with warmth, and lent him strength when so little of his own remained.

"And I will never let you go, my heartsthread," Urkot rumbled.

Sinking his claws into the bark, he climbed.

He found a wide branch midway up the tree and hauled himself onto it. Untying the rope, he helped Callie down with extreme care. After guiding her in front of him, he sank down next to the trunk and sat her upon his folded forelegs. She leaned back against him, and he wound his arms around her, holding her close as his claspers curled around her hips.

He did not like the way her body continued shivering.

Crooning, he rubbed his palm up and down her arms.

"It's strange being so high up again after being underground for so long," Callie said.

Urkot glanced around; the shadows were deep, the sky almost fully dark, but he could see the leaves swaying in the breeze, could smell everything around him, so earthy and alive. "Strange but good. Much good, to be here with you."

"Much good." She rested her head on his shoulder and snuggled closer. For a time, she was quiet, and the sounds of insects and rustling leaves filled the silence as the night deepened around them.

"Do you think they'll find us?" Callie asked.

"Why hunt us? We gave food to them."

"Huh? We didn't give them— Oh. Ugh." She weakly swatted his forearm. "Not funny, Urkot."

He chittered, but his humor was fleeting. He tightened his lower arm around her and nuzzled her hair. "I do not know if they will come, or how far. But I will keep watch."

Over time, her body stopped shivering, and she relaxed. The sounds of the night created a song unique to the Tangle. Below, plants and mushrooms began to glow as the moons rose and the stars sparkled into view through gaps in the canopy.

Urkot turned his gaze skyward, to a large break in the boughs above. So many tiny dots of light, glittering like countless crystals viewed from afar, scattered against splotches of subtle blues, purples, and blacks. It was still strange to him to spend so much time beneath the open sky. When he'd first ventured out of Takarahl to fight the thornskulls in Zurvashi's war, he'd gazed at the stars every night, wondering what they were, wondering if one could reach them somehow.

Knowing that Callie's kind had traveled from those very stars only made them more wondrous to him.

"Do you know which is your world, Callie?"

"Hmm?" she asked sleepily.

"The stars."

She turned her face toward the gap in the boughs, head lolling upon him. "They're different here than they were on Earth. Where I'm from, you could barely see them at night because of all the artificial light. They're prettier here. But my world…it's not up there."

Urkot cocked his head, mandibles twitching. "What do you mean? You are from the stars, yes?"

"I am. But my world is no longer out there. My world is here. With you." She tipped her head back and turned her face toward him, pressing a light kiss to his jaw. "You are my world, Urkot."

He trilled, shifting his head to brush his lips across hers. "Ah, my heartsthread. My world will never be dark as long as you are in it."

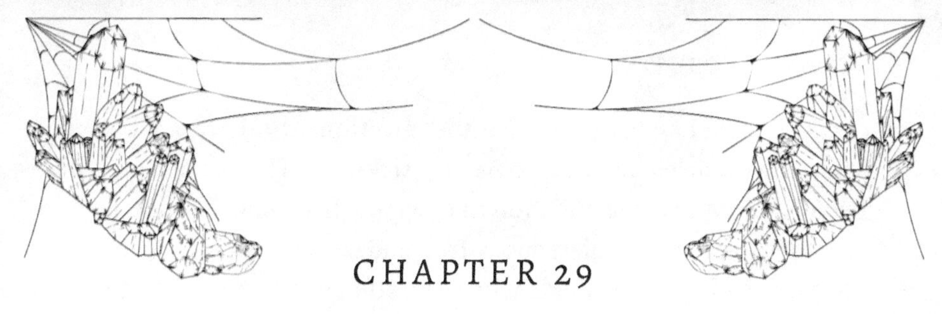

# CHAPTER 29

THOUGH HE KNEW they were nearing Kaldarak, Urkot didn't allow himself any solace. Not until the winding steps that led around the massive trunk of a tree and up into the city were in view. The sight was enough to coax a relieved sigh from Callie and quicken Urkot's stride despite his overwhelming weariness. His sleep had been fitful at best; to his mind, every one of the jungle's sounds might've been a spiritstrider out for vengeance.

But Urkot and Callie were safe now.

Callie, who sat astride his hindquarters with her arms around his midsection, pressed her forehead to his back. "We're home."

He caressed her right leg with his lower hand, giving her knee a squeeze. The heat radiating from her skin was much greater than normal.

She had called it a fever, the result of her body fighting off a sickness that had settled into her wounds. He'd felt the beginnings of that heat in the middle of the night, had felt her shifting against him weakly, restlessly, had felt the cold sweat dampening her skin, and he had heard her soft, pained moans. Her sleep had been as broken as his own.

Callie had assured him that the injections she'd received on Earth would let her overcome the sickness. That didn't alleviate his worry. He did not like seeing his mate ill, and he seethed at his helplessness. He understood exactly what Ketahn had gone through when sweetfang root had sickened Ivy.

Fear.

What if the injections weren't enough? What if her body couldn't overcome this, what if he lost her? The only one who could help, the only one he trusted to help, was Diego, and Urkot needed to get Callie to him fast.

The pair of male thornskulls guarding the stairway spotted Urkot as he strode into the open. Even from a distance, their surprise was apparent, with the yellow one crossing his forearms in the symbol of the Eight.

The other male, green of hide, shouted up to the thornskulls standing guard high above. "Three-Arm has returned!"

It wasn't long before more voices rang out, spreading the message across Kaldarak.

"They sound happy to see you," Callie said.

"Perhaps they have prepared a feast for us?" The emptiness in his gut expanded at his words, begging to be filled.

She patted his stomach. "Think of all the fresh meat you'll get to eat."

Urkot chittered, grateful Callie was well enough to jest with him. But he'd heard the weariness in her voice.

The guards strode toward Urkot and Callie, meeting them several segments away from the lowest step. Urkot knew them both well; he'd hunted with them before.

"By their Eightfold eyes," said Elharat, the yellow thornskull. "We thought your *shar'thai* burned out."

The green thornskull, Okkor, shifted his spear aside as his eyes fell upon Callie. He touched a knuckle to his headcrest and bowed his head. "The *hyu-nan* lives also."

"And the others?" Urkot asked, looking from Elharat to Okkor.

A low, mournful buzz emanated from Okkor. "Ours and yours tried to move the fallen rocks. With all their *shar'thai*, they tried."

"It is true beneath sun and sky," Elharat added solemnly.

"But more rock fell before they found anyone. You are first to return."

"We're it?" Callie asked in English, her voice small and weak.

Turning his head to look at her over his shoulder, Urkot offered a shallow nod.

She frowned, brows pinched. "I knew it wasn't likely, but I'd hoped…hoped at least someone else got out."

"Me too," he rumbled, placing a hand over hers atop his middle.

She was still shivering, and she didn't sound any better than when they'd set out with the first hints of morning light.

Urkot returned his gaze to the thornskulls and said in vrix, "I must take her to Diego for healing."

Each thornskull stepped aside, touching a knuckle to his headcrest, and waved Urkot on. As he strode to the steps, there was a commotion far overhead. He ascended quickly, ignoring the burning in his legs, the haggardness of his breath.

Soon enough, they could rest. Just a little longer, a little further.

Bright rays of sunlight, nearly blinding in their intensity, struck him as he climbed. And after the time he'd spent under-stone, being here with sunshine streaming through breaks in the canopy seemed unreal. All this light, all this life, all this air…

It made his chest constrict, and he shuddered, overwhelmed by a tangle of powerful emotion.

He and Callie had come so close to death, so close to joining the thornskull delvers in that final, endless slumber. But they were alive.

They were home.

And Callie was *his*.

When he reached the platform at the top, thornskulls had already begun gathering on the nearby platforms, and a small crowd was racing across the rope bridge with Rekosh, Telok, and Ketahn in the lead.

An odd sense of lightness swept over Urkot. He stepped forward, feeling as though his legs would float off the wooden planks at any moment and carry him into the sky. Urkot could see the humans behind his shadowstalker brothers, and Nalaki and Garahk, the leaders of Kaldarak, behind them. After making his bond with Callie, he'd thought his hearts couldn't possibly feel fuller.

He'd been wrong.

But the weight of his own body crashed down upon him, eightfold as heavy, as soon as his friends reached the platform. His forelegs gave out under that burden, and he stumbled.

He threw his lower arm back to ensure Callie didn't fall as Rekosh and Ketahn darted forward, catching Urkot's upper arms and steadying him.

With his friends supporting him, he could rest. Could finally rest...

"You have looked better, stoneskull," Rekosh said the merest quaver in his voice.

Urkot chittered weakly. "Still look better than you, needlelegs."

Telok stood before Urkot with eyes narrowed, his mandibles twitching. Tension pulsed from him in withering waves.

"We thought you both dead," Ketahn said, a shiver coursing through him as he squeezed Urkot's arm.

The humans stepped onto the platform—Ivy holding Akalahn, followed by Lacey, Ahmya, Diego, Will, and Cole. Several of them had red, watery eyes, as though they'd been crying.

As though they'd been mourning.

"Callie, Urkot! Oh, my God." Ivy stopped beside Ketahn, holding her broodling with one arm while placing her other hand gently on Urkot's shoulder.

"I knew you guys were alive," Cole said, the words oddly thick.

Ahmya covered her mouth as tears rolled down her cheeks.

"I'm gonna start kicking some asses for scaring the living shit out of us," Lacey said, her glistening, glaring eyes flicking between Urkot and Callie. "You guys can't keep doing this to me."

Behind Urkot, Callie sniffled. "So glad to see all of you."

The sound tugged at Urkot's heartsthread.

"Callie needs aid," Urkot rasped, looking at Diego. "She is—"

"Shit." Diego hurried forward, brow furrowed, with Will close behind. He leaned close to inspect Callie's bound leg.

"Looks worse than it is," Callie said.

Urkot could almost feel the soft, reassuring smile she must've forced onto her lips to counter just how thin her voice sounded.

"Sure, it does," Diego said, sounding not at all convinced. "Will, help me get her down."

"I will carry her to your den." Urkot strode forward.

Or at least he'd meant to. Ketahn and Rekosh's easy hold proved more than he could overcome, and he didn't move a thread's width.

Ketahn flattened a hand on Urkot's chest and patted gently. "You can barely carry yourself, Urkot."

Without a word, Telok strode to Urkot's side. Will and Diego moved out of his way, and he lifted Callie off Urkot's hindquarters, cradling her against his chest. She looked small, sickly, vulnerable.

A flare of possessiveness stiffened Urkot's muscles, and instinctual rage flooded them with heat. Callie was his mate, *his*, and no other male could touch her, could tend to her. Especially not when she seemed so fragile.

But the growl died in his chest, and his body eased. Telok was part of his tribe, his friend, his brother, and Urkot trusted him completely. He also trusted Diego and Will. They were healers—the only ones who could help his mate now.

"Make way," Nalaki shouted as Telok carried Callie to the bridge, followed closely by the two male humans. The thornskull onlookers quickly cleared the bridge and the platform it led to, allowing Telok and the others to pass.

All the humans trailed after them.

"Come, we will follow," Rekosh said before he and Ketahn led Urkot toward the bridge.

Urkot's legs moved now, but he knew he remained upright only because of his friends' continued support...and even with their help, the journey was not easy. Many thornskulls cheered and greeted him as he came into view.

But his attention remained split between keeping his legs moving and searching ahead to see his mate.

Telok was moving much faster than Urkot, allowing only glimpses of Callie's legs or an errant lock of hair.

"You are lighter," Rekosh said with an uncertain buzz.

"I do not feel lighter," Urkot replied, taking another trudging step. "But...I do feel hungry."

Ketahn chittered gently. "We will bring you food."

"Any you desire." Rekosh bumped a foreleg against Urkot's. "As much as you desire."

Urkot shook his head. "Later. When I know she is well."

By the time he reached the platform that held the human dwellings, Diego and Will were already inside their large den with Callie and Telok. The other humans, along with Garahk, Nalaki, and a few thornskulls, had gathered outside. The mood in the air was strange, seemingly at odds with itself—a confusing blend of relief and worry, of happiness and fear.

Not without some effort, Urkot urged Ketahn and Rekosh aside and stood on his own. He longed to go inside with Callie, to hold her hand through whatever she'd have to endure, to smooth back her hair and wipe the sweat from her brow. But he knew he'd only be in the way, especially in his current state.

Telok swept aside the cloth hanging in the den's entryway and stepped out. All eyes fell upon him. His mandibles snapped, making the fangs at their tips clack together, and his hands curled into fists.

"She will be fine." In Telok's rough, raspy voice, those words had an edge of harshness, but that couldn't taint them for Urkot.

His mate would be okay. She *would*.

Exhaling, Urkot tipped his head back. The patches of clear blue midday sky were vibrant against the green of the leaves. The familiar scents of Kaldarak filled his nostrils as he breathed in—plants and wood, drying meat, a hint of burning spinewood sap and waterfall mist. A warm, soothing breeze flowed over his hide.

When he lowered his head, Telok was immediately before him, intensity blazing in those green eyes. Growling, Telok grasped the back of Urkot's head and brought their headcrests together.

"Thought you were gone," the hunter grated. There was no missing the trembling of his limbs.

Urkot threw an arm around his friend. "You are not rid of me yet."

They remained that way for a time, Telok still tense, still bristling, but not ungentle. Once he withdrew, Ketahn and Rekosh made similar gestures, as did the humans. Kaldarak's leaders were the last to approach.

Nalaki settled a big hand on Urkot's shoulder, squeezing it. "Kaldarak is grateful to have two of ours back safely."

"We are glad to be back, *daiya*," Urkot replied.

"I must ask, Urkot…" She lowered her hand, her posture not quite so solid and sure as normal.

His stomach tangled into a knot, and his chest constricted. "We were across the chamber from the others when it collapsed. We found only Zotahl in the rubble, already gone. If you could not find any of the rest from the other side…"

"It is not what I hoped, but it is better to know. Thank you." She bowed her head and made the sign of the Eight. "They have earned their rest."

Garahk stepped up beside his mate, brushing a foreleg against hers. "You must share your words, Three-Arm. Give us your story, so we may know all."

Urkot was tempted to say he was too tired for stories. He wanted nothing more than to go into the den and see his mate, but as he looked at his friends, his family, gathered around him, he knew he could not do so.

They had suffered in his and Callie's absence, and the thorn-skulls had lost beloved kin. They had grieved and known pain. They needed to hear what had happened so they could heal.

And more than that, the threat of the spiritstriders was much too close for him to leave it unspoken any longer. Garahk and Nalaki needed to know so they could act to ensure Kaldarak's safety.

So Urkot shared his words, shared the story. He told them of the collapse, of dragging himself and Callie from the rubble, of discovering Zotahl. Told them about the tunnel they'd found themselves in, and how it appeared to have been carved out by vrix hands, weakening the floor of the crystal garden above. He told them about their trek through the dark, about the spirit-striders that lurked there.

That drew alarmed sounds from the vrix who were listening, though it meant nothing to the humans.

"I knew the whispers were always true," Rekosh said.

"How could you have known that?" demanded Telok.

Ketahn regarded Rekosh with his head cocked. "Those were tales to frighten us as broodlings."

"For ours as well," said Garahk, concern apparent in his voice.

Rekosh displayed his hands, palms up. "Every tale, even the most unlikely, begins with a thread of truth."

Urkot thumped the wood planks beneath him with a leg. "I wish it had been a different thread."

"How many spiritstriders down there, Three-Arm?" Garahk asked, leaning toward Urkot. "Can you say?"

"Many. More than a hundred, I think. They live in a place that may have once been a shadowstalker city."

Ketahn's eyes flared, and Telok's mandibles twitched high, his body tense.

Rekosh eased closer and gently tapped Urkot's foreleg. "I must wring every detail from you after you have rested."

"I am sure you will." Urkot turned his attention to Nalaki and Garahk. "Spiritstriders chased us to the surface when we fled. The sun was too bright for them. They retreated after a fight, but I do not know if they tried to track us after dark."

Nalaki let out a thoughtful hum, eyes troubled. "Do you believe they will see what you did as giving war to their kind?"

"I cannot guess that. Though they speak, I did not know most of their words, and it is not words they wanted to share with us. They gave only fangs, claws, and death. We were prey to them."

"We must keep close watch," Garahk said to Nalaki.

"But we must not give war, not unless they do," she replied evenly. "Kaldarak will not do as the Blooddrinker Queen and make war without cause. If they leave us in peace, we will grant them the same."

Garahk looked at Urkot. "Where did you emerge from understone?"

As best he could, Urkot described how to reach the cave, adding, "I will lead you there, to be sure it is found."

Nalaki snapped her mandible fangs. "You will rest. That is my command as *daiya*."

Urkot tapped a knuckle to his headcrest. "Then I must obey."

"I will gather a party," Garahk declared.

His mate turned toward him, dipped her head, and touched headcrests with him. "Stride with care, my heartsflame."

"Always, my *daiya*."

"Come. I will see you off." She straightened and walked side-by-side with Garahk toward the bridge leading off the platform. Over her shoulder, she said, "Send word of Callie as soon as you know."

Urkot lowered himself onto the platform, allowing his legs to rest. His friends, human and vrix alike, remained nearby him, save for Cole, who headed up to the higher platforms, returning a short while later with a waterskin.

"Drink up, man" the male human said as he thrust the waterskin into Urkot's hand.

Urkot drank gratefully and deeply. The water was a balm to his throat after the grueling journey and so much talking. He wasn't sure how Rekosh, who rarely went a moment without speaking, managed to get by without guzzling water constantly.

When he was done, he handed the waterskin back and thanked Cole. He shifted his legs, finding more comfortable positions for them, and forced his arms to relax, letting out a soft groan as aches and twinges assailed him.

"Let us help you to your den," Ketahn said. "You need rest, Urkot, and we can tend to you there."

Urkot shook his head.

Rekosh huffed. "You need not be stoneheaded now."

Biting back a growl, Urkot let out a slow, heavy breath. "No. I will not leave my mate."

Rekosh chittered. "Finally."

"Finally," Ketahn echoed.

"Wait, what?" Cole said. "When did that happen?"

Ivy rolled her eyes as she allowed Akalahn to climb down to the floor. "You're completely oblivious, Cole."

Lacey crossed her arms and smirked. "Well, damn. Just needed a little danger to turn up the heat and get things moving, huh Urkot? You've been eyeing her ass for months."

Heat suffused Urkot's hide. "Her ass is beautiful, but I have looked at all her parts."

Ivy snickered, and Ahmya chuckled quietly.

"I do not think your words make it better," Rekosh said with a chitter.

Cole moseyed up next to Lacey and wrapped an arm around her shoulders. He grinned down at her. "Guess it's just down to you and me now, Lace."

A low, barely audible growl called Urkot's attention to Telok, who stood nearby with arms folded tight across his chest and the fine hairs on his legs raised, his green glare fixed on Cole.

Lacey stuck her palm into Cole's face and pushed him away. "Not happening. Not on this world or any other, Cole."

"Ouch." Laughing, Cole allowed himself to be shoved, stepping back with his hands raised, palms out. "I mean it's just the two of us left single now. Third wheels, the both of us. What did you think I meant?"

Lacey stared at him. "You know exactly how it came off."

"You're the one with her mind in the gutter. I'm totally innocent." He drew a finger down his chest then across it. "Cross my heart."

"As much as I'd like to see Lacey punch Cole, I have to interrupt," Diego said from the den's entryway.

Everyone turned their heads toward him.

Urkot rose onto his legs, hide tingling. "Callie?"

"She's going to be fine." Diego stepped outside, letting the cloth fall behind him. "I cleaned and bandaged up her wounds. I also applied a salve, so she's not feeling much pain. And her fever's already coming down. That herbal tea Lacey concocted is doing wonders. But it was your first aid that saved her life, Urkot. She lost a lot of blood, and if you hadn't patched up her leg the way you did, she would've bled to death."

Urkot squeezed his eyes shut as his body shuddered. He had come so close to losing her after only just making her his. Her light could have been snuffed out so easily, like a flame blown out by the wind. Now more than ever, he understood just how precious every moment was.

He wouldn't waste any more of them.

"Callie's drowsy," Diego said, "but I'll make sure she gets to her den to rest, and I'll check up on her periodically."

Urkot opened his eyes and stepped closer to Diego. "No. I will take my mate there, and I will stay with her."

"Mate?" Diego's brows rose high. He rubbed the back of his neck with a chuckle. "Damn, guess you two were busy while you were gone. Congratulations."

Urkot trilled low.

"Now it's your turn." Diego lifted the hanging silk aside and gestured Urkot in. "Come inside so I can take a look at your wounds."

Urkot's legs were a little steadier as he strode forward, lent strength by his swelling spirit.

"We'll bring you both food and more water," Ahmya said, taking one of Rekosh's hands.

"Careful not to break your tools on his hide, Diego." Rekosh said, but there was only warmth in his voice. "See you soon, my brother."

When he reached the doorway, Urkot paused and looked back at his friends. At his tribe. They were all so different, and yet they'd come together to forge bonds closer than blood alone could ever create. And no matter the hardships he'd overcome or had yet to face, he would always choose them.

His hearts were full, and his soul thrummed. "Thank you. All of you."

Then he ducked into the den, following the pull of his heartsthread back to his mate's side.

The pungent smell of the plants the humans called herbs struck him first, despite the breeze blowing through the open windows.

Diego walked over to a table where Will was standing, upon which were strips of silk cloth and various tools. "Urkot has some gouges we need to clean and patch up."

Will nodded, rearranging some of the items on the table.

But Urkot's attention shifted entirely to Callie.

She lay in the center of the room, atop a high, raised bed, silk blankets draped over her body from the chest down. A soft, fluffed pillow cradled her head. Her eyes were closed, but the rise and fall of her breathing was not yet deep and steady. He could tell as he neared that some of the color had already returned to her face.

He stopped beside the bed.

Callie stirred and murmured, "Urkot?"

"I am here." Urkot brought a hand to her face and caressed her cheek. Her skin was too warm, but not alarmingly so, and soft as ever.

Her eyelids fluttered open, and her weary eyes glittered at him as she met his gaze. Her lips curled into a smile so pure and genuine that Urkot swore it would make him melt like gold in a forge.

Callie cupped his hand in hers and turned her face, pressing a gentle kiss to his palm. "Missed you, big guy."

He leaned down and nuzzled her forehead, drawing in her scent, filling himself with it. "And I missed you, my suncrest. How do you feel?"

"Shitty. But less shitty than before." She kissed his hand again and took a deep breath before rubbing her cheek against his palm. "Actually, right now…I'm doing pretty good."

Urkot smoothed some of her curly locks out of her face. "You look beautiful."

"Liar."

He chittered. "I cannot lie about that. Never. Every moment I see you, you are more beautiful, Callie."

She looked up at him, a mirthful light dancing in her gaze, and her smile widened. "Rekosh feed you some lines before you came in?"

"No. I have not eaten."

Callie's laughter was the sweetest sound he'd ever heard, even as soft and weak as it was now.

Keeping his eyes locked with hers, he lowered his headcrest to her forehead, cupping her cheeks between his upper hands. "Your beauty will soon be beyond my words, my *nyleea*. Because these are the first of many, many moments to come, and I do not intend to let you out of my sight. Every day, I will look upon you with more wonder than I would the cresting sun or the sparkling stars."

She slipped her fingers into his hair and kissed his mouth. He could feel the slight trembling of her lips as she held them there.

"I love you, my *luveen*," she whispered.

Urkot purred. "And I love you, my heartsthread."

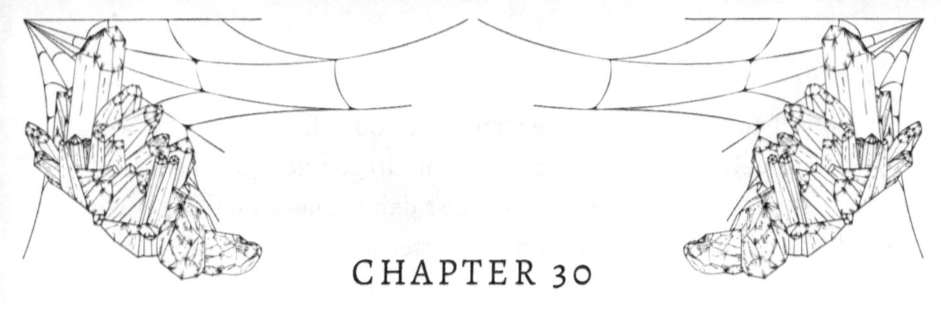

# CHAPTER 30

"The surprise is here?" Callie asked as Urkot lowered her to her feet onto the wooden floorboards. This was the platform where Ivy and Ahmya lived with their mates.

Urkot grazed his mouth over her temple. A kiss. Callie smiled and looked up at him.

"Yes," he said, taking her gently by the shoulders and turning her toward the dens. "But you must not look."

He covered her eyes—along with half her face—with his large hands.

"Not even a teeny, tiny peek?" she asked playfully.

With his lower hand curled around her waist, he slowly guided her forward. "No."

Chuckling, Callie stretched her arms out in front of her as she walked, a slight limp in her gait. Urkot's steps were heavy behind her, sending faint vibrations through the planks, and she could hear the chatter of nearby vrix. The soft sound of far-off music floated lazily in the air.

It was hard to believe that she and Urkot had been trapped beneath the earth only two weeks ago. As excited as Callie had been by the things they'd seen, she wasn't sure she could bring herself to visit a cave again anytime soon. Even Urkot, who'd been a delver all his life, had no desire to go underground again.

When Nalaki had visited Callie's den to check on them a few days ago, he'd told her as much, offering to instead work as a shaper.

Upon impulse, Callie had chimed in and told Nalaki that Urkot was good with his hands. Very, very good.

Nalaki hadn't understood the double entendre, but Urkot had chittered and given Callie a look that was both amused and heated.

That heat hadn't led to anything, though; Urkot hadn't touched her sexually since their return to Kaldarak. Only this surprise of his had delayed her from taking matters into her own hands, like she had their first time together. She understood his restraint, but that didn't stop her craving for him from growing day by day.

She'd spent the first week cooped up in her den recovering from the spiritstrider's attack. She'd never been more thankful to have had those injections from the Homeworld Initiative. Without them, Diego said her best outcome would've likely been losing her leg to the infection that had set in, and the worst case...she would've died.

Urkot didn't like thinking about that. He'd been near inconsolable at the possibility, and he hadn't left her side for more than a few moments at a time during her recovery, despite her fever having subsided by their third day back in Kaldarak. After that, it had been a matter of tending to the wounds on her leg. He hadn't even allowed Diego to touch her, insisting that caring for her was his duty as her mate. He'd treated her as though she was the most delicate thing in the world.

Unfortunately, the injections had no magical healing properties, forcing her to deal with the pain and time it took to heal. Her calf had hurt like a bitch for that first week. That was when Diego had deemed the wounds fit enough to seal using his medical device. Now she was left with faint scars and fading bruises discoloring her skin, and she felt only mild discomfort when she walked. It was a huge improvement.

Callie was tempted to kiss Lacey to thank her for that herbal tea, which helped with the pain. The stuff was heaven sent.

It wasn't until midway through the second week that Urkot had begun leaving her for extended periods of time. He hadn't told her where he'd been going or what he'd been doing, but whenever she'd woken up in the morning or between naps, she would notice some of her belongings were missing. At first, she'd thought she'd simply been mistaken, that her mind was just foggy due to the stress of healing, the grogginess caused by the tea, and the trauma of what she and Urkot had survived.

Yet as more and more empty spots appeared on her shelves, she knew something was up. When her bowl of beloved rocks disappeared, she'd asked Urkot flat out what was going on.

He'd told her that it was a surprise and had been very firm in not revealing anything else despite her repeated attempts to get more information out of him.

Until today. Today, he was finally going to show her what he'd been up to.

She had a pretty good idea, but she wasn't about to spoil anything, neither for herself nor Urkot. His excitement had been infectious.

"You are peeking," Urkot said.

"I am not!" Callie laughed, walking forward, hands still in front of her. Despite his accusation, she was in fact *not* peeking. She was completely at his mercy, and she trusted him explicitly. She was simply grateful he hadn't done this while they were crossing one of the rope bridges. That would've been terrifying, and it would've called for much peeking.

"Are we almost there?" she asked.

A low, contemplative hum resonated from his chest.

"That's not an answer!"

He repeated the sound, exaggerating and prolonging it.

Callie chuckled. "Big meanie."

"My own mate throws barbs at me," he said with a sigh.

Her grin only stretched wider. "You like my barbs. For you, they're practically foreplay."

Urkot chittered. "I much like foreplay, female."

Callie halted abruptly as her hands brushed something soft that gave way to her touch. She recognized the feel—a silk curtain.

"A few more steps," Urkot said.

She carefully swept aside the cloth, her fingers bumping what was likely a doorframe on one side, before continuing forward. Her bare feet came down on something plush and cushioned. She wiggled her toes atop what she was sure was a fur rug.

"Ready?" he asked.

She nodded, a swell of anticipation building in her chest. Urkot lifted his hands away.

Callie opened her eyes and drew in a sharp breath.

The room was open and spacious, nearly three times as large as her den. There were numerous shelves on the walls displaying rocks and crystals of various sizes, many of which she recognized as the gifts he'd given her that she'd collected in her bowl. All were displayed proudly here, each with its own spot, and there was plenty of space for more.

But the most beautiful piece was a clear, multifaceted crystal hanging from the top of a window that faced the morning sun. The crystal fractured the sunlight into dazzling rainbows, which shimmered around the den as it slowly spun in place, filling the atmosphere with magic and wonder.

"Urkot, this...this is beautiful," Callie said in awe as she gazed at all the dancing colors.

He trilled behind her, smoothing his rough palms down her

arms. "This sight will greet us every suncrest. But you will always outshine it."

Warmth flooded her.

With Urkot trailing behind her, Callie stepped farther into the room, following those little dancing rainbows until her eyes caught on the domed ceiling, where dozens of little blue crystals had been embedded. In the daylight, they looked lackluster, but she knew the moment the sun went down, their glow would transform the ceiling.

"Urkot..."

"You said you wanted to look at the stars every time you sleep."

Callie turned her wide eyes toward him. "You remembered that?"

His mandibles rose. "All you need, my heartsthread, I will give."

Tears gathered in her eyes, blurring her vision. She caught his jaw and pulled him down to press her forehead to his headcrest. His hands settled on her hips, holding her close.

Throat tight with all the overwhelming emotion swirling inside her, she said, "All I need, all I want, is you, my *luveen*."

A deep purr rolled through him. "Ah, my *nyleea*."

With a smile, she drew away from him and took in the rest of the room.

All the things she'd noticed were missing from her den were here, along with some things she hadn't realized he'd taken. Her chest of tools was against one wall, beside Urkot's pack, tools, and spears. Her clothes were hanging from nearby pegs, arranged exactly as she'd had them. There was a table in the center of the den with a single chair and a blue vase atop it filled with a bouquet of colorful flowers. A broad worktable stood on the wall to the right, with cloth-wrapped chunks of clay, several large stones, and more tools and atop it. The shelves nearby were full of baskets, pots, and jars that likely held food and other supplies.

And toward the back, near the window with the crystal, was a huge, fluffed silk bed, larger than any bean bag Callie had ever seen. She could only imagine how cozy it was.

This place was a perfect blend of his and hers. A mated pair's den. Their den.

*Our home.*

Tears spilled down her cheeks. Turning, Callie threw her arms around Urkot, burying her face against his hard chest. "I love it so much. Thank you. This is the best gift ever."

He embraced her snugly and nuzzled her hair. "You are the best gift ever, my *nyleea.*"

"Oh, stop!" Callie sniffled as her tears wet his hide. "You're making me cry."

Urkot withdrew and cupped her face, turning it up toward his. His blue eyes brimmed with concern and heartrending tenderness as he wiped her cheeks with his thumbs, mindful of his claws. "Good tears?"

Smiling, she covered his hands with her own and nodded. "Yes. They are good, happy tears."

He crooned and bent down, pressing his mouth to hers, and Callie kissed him in return. She'd never felt this kind of fullness before. Had never felt so much happiness, so much love.

"This is our home," she whispered against his mouth.

"Ours," he echoed in his rumbling voice, carefully combing his claws through her curls.

*Ours.*

God, she loved the sound of that.

Pulling away from him, she turned and padded toward the table. She trailed her fingers over the flat, grainy surface as she glanced over her shoulder at her mate. "This is our table."

Urkot chittered as he strode toward her. He flattened a hand on the tabletop. "Where we will share our meals."

An image appeared in her mind—Callie sitting in the chair with Urkot seated next to her as they ate from a shared platter, the den bathed in the blue glow of the many crystals around the room.

Familiar warmth suffused her. To most people, sitting with a loved one to share a meal and conversation was a mundane thing, often taken for granted. But sitting down together at dinner time had been a rare occurrence for her throughout most of her life. Knowing that she and Urkot could do that not just every day, but every meal if they wanted to, meant more to Callie than she could express.

She walked toward the bed and ran her fingers over the silk blanket covering it. "And this is our bed."

Urkot moved up behind her and trailed a finger down her spine. "Where I will hold you every night as we sleep."

Callie closed her eyes and hummed. "I love the sound of that."

He trilled, his hands framing her hips as his rough mouth brushed over her shoulder, where his teeth had marked her, sending a delightful shiver through her. "As do I."

She skimmed her nose over the side of his face. "Do you know what I love more?"

Turning in his arms, she stepped back and sat on the bed. She smiled coyly at him as she scooted back toward the center. He stood unmoving but for his gaze, which tracked her as keenly as that of a predator who'd spotted his prey.

Leaning back on her elbows, she spread her thighs wide and bunched her skirt in her hands, drawing the hem up to bare her pussy to him. "That this is where you'll be making love to me for the rest of our lives."

With a deep, rolling growl, Urkot stalked forward and slowly knelt atop the bedding. His upper hands grasped her ankles, spreading her legs wider. Callie's breath hitched as the air brushed over her sex, and her core clenched in arousal as his gaze, brightened by a possessive gleam, dipped to her pussy.

"And this is my mate," he said, his eyes flicking up to hers as he lowered his head. He turned his face toward her healing calf and lightly grazed the scars with his mouth. "Who I will love."

Another shiver coursed through her, and she craved more. More of his touch. More of him.

He moved his mouth higher, another graze, another kiss. "Who I will cherish."

When he reached her inner thigh, his tongue slipped out to tease the tender flesh, making her quiver.

Callie moaned, clutching the spun silk beneath her. "Urkot..."

"My mate," he growled once more, his eyes never leaving hers as his tongue lapped her pussy from bottom to top, sweeping over her clit. "Who I will worship."

He plunged his tongue deep inside her. Callie gasped at the surge of pleasure, at the fullness. Whispering his name over and over like a benediction, she thrust her fingers into his silky hair and pulled him closer, undulating her hips to take his wicked, forceful tongue deeper.

And worship her he did.

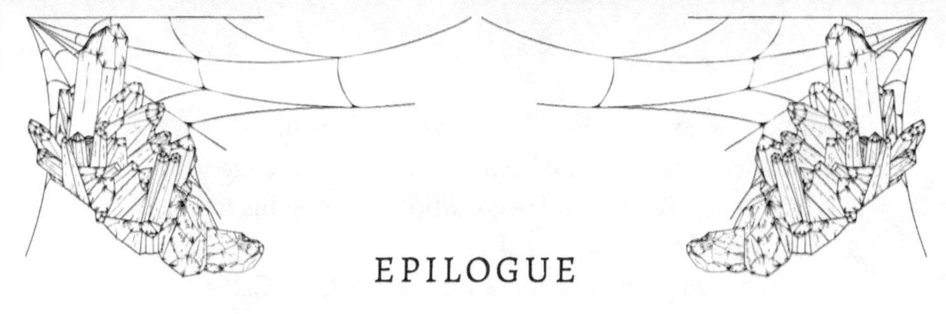

# EPILOGUE

CALLIE LAY on the high table in Diego and Will's clinic, biting her bottom lip and forcing her arms to remain at her sides as Diego's fingers probed her lower belly and pelvis. Nervousness skittered through her.

"When was your last period?" he asked.

"A couple months ago," she said. "After me and Urkot got back from the cave."

"Have your breasts been feeling tender or more sensitive than usual?"

Callie chuckled, recalling how exquisite it felt every time Urkot stroked or licked her nipples. "Oh yeah."

Diego paused, smirking as he shook his head. "Guess I don't need to ask whether you've been sexually active."

"Yeah, that'd be a dumb question. Urkot can't keep his hands off me."

Will, Ahmya, and Ivy, who stood behind Diego, laughed.

"Mmhmm. Same for Rekosh," Ahmya said. "Um, not that I'm complaining."

"Ketahn tried to abstain," Ivy said. "It was easy for him while I was healing from childbirth. But once I started ovulating

331

again… I swear some instinctual switch flipped, and it was just like the first time we mated. And God, that sex was *good*."

Will chuckled. So did Diego, who withdrew his hands from Callie's belly and straightened.

"Well"—Diego held a hand out and helped Callie sit up—"whether the sex is good or not, the results are usually the same. You're pregnant."

Callie smiled wide, placing a hand over her ever-so-slightly rounded belly. "Really?"

After weeks of wondering, hoping, and questioning every odd sensation and every miniscule change in her body, getting confirmation was almost unreal.

Diego nodded. "Without any equipment, I can't say for sure how far along you are, but I'd estimate that your due date is around the same time as Ahmya's, or not long after. Congratulations."

Ahmya squeed and rushed over, throwing her arms around Callie. "We're gonna be mommies!"

Callie hugged her friend back as happiness flowed through her. She looked at Ivy as the woman joined the embrace.

"Our kids are all going to grow up together," Ivy said.

"Can you imagine all the trouble they're going to cause together?" Callie asked.

Ivy groaned as she withdrew. "If they're anything like their fathers, it's going to be a lot."

"Yeah, hearing the stories from Rekosh about when they were young…" Ahmya chuckled as she stepped back.

With a big smile, Will moved beside Diego and slipped an arm around him. "Congrats, guys. But damn, both of you at the same time?"

Callie chuckled. "What did you expect? Sexy times make babies, and these mated males like to fuck."

"Callie!" Ahmya gasped, blushing.

"You know it's true."

Ivy nodded. "Yep."

Callie arched a brow at Ahmya. "You really want to act like we don't hear you every night? And afternoon? And morning? Your den is next to ours!"

"At least I try to be quiet," Ahmya said. "Can't say the same for you."

"That's *trying* to be quiet?"

Ahmya glanced away, but not before Callie saw her lips stretch into a smile. "Okay, so maybe I'm not really trying all that hard."

Ivy crossed her arms with a smirk. "I don't see how you can."

Will cleared his throat.

"Look, buddy," Callie said, pointing a finger toward him, "we were hearing you guys too when we lived upstairs, so don't get on to us."

He brushed a hand over his short-cropped hair, brow furrowing. "You guys can be as loud or as quiet as you want. I'm just, uh, thinking about having to help two women through birth at the same time."

Diego patted Will's shoulder. "Don't worry, Will. You're an experienced veteran now. Besides, all the hard work is on them."

"Anyway." Callie slipped off the table and embraced the two men. "Thank you both. Ahmya and I know we're in good hands."

"So you two seriously haven't been sick?" Ivy asked after Callie backed away from the men. "No horrific cramping? Crippling nausea?"

Ahmya pinched her thumb and finger together. "A little bit."

"Some pain, but no sickness yet," Callie said.

Ivy scrunched her nose. "Ugh. I had the worst pregnancy."

"We know," Callie and Ahmya said together.

"It's still early," Diego said. "You could still experience more as your body continues adapting to the alien DNA."

Callie settled her hands over her belly again and met Ahmya's gaze. She could see the spark of fear in the woman's eyes, the same fear that lurked deep within herself. Not of the baby growing inside them or the changes they might experience, but of the unknown. Childbirth was already a risk, even on Earth, but out here? They had no special equipment to aid them. The tiniest complication could be the difference between life and death.

However, that fear didn't erode her happiness.

*I'm going to be a mom.*

She couldn't wait to tell Urkot. Couldn't wait to see him holding their child, playing with them, teaching them.

"Shall we go find our mates and share the good news?" Callie asked.

Smiling, Ahmya nodded enthusiastically.

"Were they doing their tournament thing today?" Will asked.

"Yeah," Callie replied. "Urkot's been super excited about it, but he says it will all be meaningless unless he gets a rematch with me."

"We'll tag along, then," Diego said. "Always fun to watch."

All five humans exited the clinic. The sun was high in the sky, making the leaves especially vibrant against the patches of blue visible through them. Their shadows danced on Kaldarak's platforms. The air was fresh, sweet, and familiar.

*It's great to be alive.*

Such a simple thought, but it struck Callie profoundly. All the misery and hardship she'd faced to get here had been worth it. Those dark moments only made the good times shine all the brighter, and so much of her light since she woke up on this alien world had come from Urkot.

She chatted with the others as they walked, navigating the city's platforms and bridges with ease and confidence. It still amazed her that this was her life—living up in the trees, calling these big spider people her friends and neighbors. Calling one of them her mate. Her lover.

Her everything.

They found their mates on the central platform with a crowd of thornskulls. The vrix sat around several black circles that had been drawn on the wood floor in charcoal, leaning forward on their hands and bent forelegs, as they took turns tossing small stones into those circles.

Their version of marbles.

It was funny that despite being separated by the vastness of time and space, and being an alien species, the vrix played a game so similar to one that had once been a popular pastime for children on Earth.

She'd never played marbles as a kid, but this version of it held a special place in her heart. She fondly remembered the day when Urkot singled her out and coaxed her to play with him one-on-one. They hadn't understood each other's languages then, but they'd communicated in a different way— through a simple game and friendly competition.

But what had truly connected them was their passion. She hadn't realized it then, but those games were the spark that had ignited something which had smoldered beneath the surface for months after.

And now what they shared was like a blazing bonfire, big and bright and warm.

Cole's blond head stood out amongst the large vrix, as did the black hides of the shadowstalkers who were with him. But it was the vibrant blue-on-black vrix that drew Callie's notice.

Urkot sat next to Rekosh, Ketahn, and Cole at a circle near the outskirts of the gathering. Akalahn was crouched alongside them with his little hindquarters in the air, watching intently as the rocks clacked against each other. Telok was the only one not playing. He stood nearby, arms crossed, gaze roving, looking every bit a grim, vigilant guard.

Callie pointed toward the males. "There they are."

"We're going to grab some food before joining the games," Will said, lacing his fingers with Diego's.

"Have fun!" Ahmya said.

Diego smiled. "Go give your mates the good news."

Callie and her friends made their way through the throng of vrix, whose voices rang out in the air in cheers, shouts, and chitters. Many of the thornskulls hailed the humans as they passed.

When Callie, Ahmya, and Ivy neared the shadowstalkers, the males took notice, and their game halted immediately. Ketahn, Rekosh, and Urkot rose and hurried to their mates, sweeping them up into their arms.

Callie laughed as Urkot hugged her close and rubbed his face right above the bite scar on her shoulder. She held him, twining her fingers in his hair. "Miss me?"

"Always," he rumbled against her neck, the vibrations of his voice rippling through her.

She took in his earthy, intoxicating scent with a soft hum. "I missed you too."

"What the hell?" Cole said. "You can't just stop without calling a timeout!"

"Timeout," Rekosh said.

Cole snorted.

Urkot nuzzled Callie's neck again and took in a deep breath that he released in a growl. His lower hand trailed down her back to her ass, gripping one cheek fully and drawing her closer.

"Urkot!" Callie admonished with a laugh, giving his shoulders a shove.

He nipped her throat with his fangs, sending a thrill through her. "You smell good, female…and I hunger."

"You'll just have to restrain yourself," she whispered. "For now."

Grumbling, Urkot eased his hold on her and lifted his head. Fire burned in his sapphire eyes as he looked down at her. "Fine."

Callie smiled and pressed a kiss to his mouth. "Good boy."

"For now," he purred.

Heat flared in Callie's core, spreading through her in anticipation of what Urkot would do when he was done playing nice.

"So, what's up?" Cole leaned back, propping himself with his hands behind him as he crossed his legs at the ankles. "Where've you guys been?"

"We were visiting Diego and Will," Ahmya said, still cradled in Rekosh's arms. She pointed toward the two men, who were conversing with Garahk near the platters of food. "They said they'll join us soon."

"Cool." Cole glanced around, brow furrowed. "Where's Lacey?"

"She's not here?" Ivy asked with a frown as Ketahn set her down on her feet next to Akalahn, who was reaching for her. She crouched down and opened her arms for the little one, and he clambered into them, nuzzling her chest with a trill. "We thought she was here with you guys."

"We have not seen her," Ketahn said.

"We thought she had accompanied you, Ivy," Rekosh added.

Callie shook her head. "She wasn't with us."

"I will look." Telok moved forward with long, powerful strides that carried him swiftly away from the group.

"So…" Callie pulled her gaze from Telok and looked at her friends. "Should we be worried? The two of them alone together?"

Ahmya drew her lips back with a soft hiss. "Yeah, I don't know."

Cole snickered. "Wanna place bets on who wins their next spat?"

"Lacey," said Ivy. "It's always Lacey."

Rekosh chittered. "It is because they are fighting different battles."

Ketahn cocked his head as he sat, drawing Ivy and their broodling down onto his folded forelegs. "Different battles?"

"Lacey fights Telok. Telok fights himself."

"Ah."

"Yeah, okay," Cole said, rolling his eyes. "Makes perfect sense."

Rekosh's gaze flicked to Callie and Urkot, bearing a knowing gleam. "I am not wrong, Cole, just because you cannot see."

Urkot snorted and shook his head. "I do not know how your spindly legs can hold up so much pride, Rekosh."

Ahmya chuckled and traced a finger down the side of Rekosh's face. "Speaking of pride..." She caught Callie's gaze. "Ready to tell them?"

Callie nodded.

With a long-fingered hand, Rekosh caught Ahmya's chin, turning her face back toward his. "Tell us what, *kir'ani vi'keishi?*"

She beamed at him. "I'm pregnant."

Rekosh froze, staring at Ahmya with flared eyes. "Truly?"

When she nodded, his mandibles ticked upward into a broad vrix smile before he trilled loudly and wrapped her in a tight embrace. Ahmya giggled and hugged him back.

"Ah, my heartsthread," Rekosh crooned.

"Well shit," Cole said, eyes wide. "Congrats on the upcoming lil bugger."

"Cole," Ivy scolded.

"Not bug. Vrix," Ketahn growled.

Cole chuckled and waved a hand. "Yeah, yeah."

Urkot also caught Callie's chin, forcing her attention away from Rekosh and Ahmya to meet his gaze. His eyes were the deepest pools of blue, filled with uncertainty and hope. "You have a secret of your own, my suncrest?"

Callie grinned, took his hand from her chin, and placed it over her belly. "We're also having a broodling. You're going to be a father too."

His trill rivaled Rekosh's, and his voice was gruff when he said, "My *nyleea*." He gathered Callie close and spun her about, his legs thumping the planks beneath him.

Callie laughed, clinging to him as the world twirled around them. "Okay, okay! Stop before I puke!"

He stopped abruptly, drawing his head back with eyes wide. "You are sick? Like Ivy was?"

Urkot and Rekosh looked at each other, mandibles falling as fear shone within their eyes. No words needed to be spoken to convey all that was communicated between them in that single glance.

"No." Urkot shuddered as he clutched Callie close. "I cannot protect you from sick. Cannot shield you from this."

Callie shook her head and cradled his jaw, stroking the base of his mandible with her thumb. "I don't need protection from this, Urkot. I just need you."

"Is it not dangerous and painful?" Rekosh asked Ahmya in a rush. "You are so small. What if something goes wrong, or you are harmed, or you…you—"

Ahmya caught his face between her hands and pressed her forehead to his headcrest. "Shh. It's okay, Rekosh. There will always be aspects of life left to chance, but I'm willing to take the risk to have a family with you. I'm glad to take it."

Another shudder wracked Urkot. "Ah, my heartsthread… I fear for you, but I will not let fear bury my joy. Our joy." He settled his hand back upon Callie's belly, tracing gentle circles with his thumb. "Our broodling."

Callie smiled and covered his hand with her own. "Ours."

"I'll be the first to tell you there are no guarantees," Diego said from nearby, drawing everyone's attention to him and Will, who stood at the edge of the group with a platter of fruit and smoked meat. "But I can promise you that me and Will are going to do everything in our power to make sure both of you, and your babies, get through this safe and healthy."

Rekosh combed his claws through Ahmya's hair, seemingly unwilling to look away from her as one of his hands settled protectively over her belly. "I trust you both with all that is precious to me."

"As do I," Urkot said, leaning his head down to brush his mouth across Callie's forehead.

She closed her eyes and smiled, giving his hand a squeeze. Her heart constricted with overwhelming emotion—with the fear and love she and Urkot shared.

But so long as she was sheltered in his big, solid arms, so long as she had him, fear could never outweigh that love.

"So, who's hungry?" Will asked. "I brought food."

"Starved, man," Cole said.

As their family gathered to share a meal, Callie opened her eyes and met her mate's intense blue gaze. "Well, what do you think? We going to stay here and play, or...do you want to skip right to the victory celebration?"

"I am already the victor," he growled, striding away from the others, "and I hunger for my prize."

# AUTHOR'S NOTE

Thank you so much for reading The Delver! We hope you enjoyed it. Urkot and Callie were so much fun to write, and their interactions, especially with how they joked with one another, were just so natural. There were many scenes where I (Tiffany) was just kicking my feet and grinning to myself while we wrote. Urkot is such a sweetheart and will be telling the best dad jokes.

If you don't already know, yes Telok and Lacey's book, The Hunter, is next and last in our Vrix series. We're thrilled to finally be giving all these beloved vrix from our Spider's Mate Trilogy their happily ever afters. Thank you all for being here on this ride with us, supporting us.

And a special thank you to our sensitivity readers, Diamond, Elwen, and Ruthie. You all helped make sure Callie was represented in the best way!

# ALSO BY TIFFANY ROBERTS

The Delver

The Hunter

## THE CURSED ONES

**His Darkest Craving**

**His Darkest Desire**

## ALIENS AMONG US

**Taken by the Alien Next Door**

**Stalked by the Alien Assassin**

**Claimed by the Alien Bodyguard**

**Saved by the Alien Crime Boss**

## STANDALONE TITLES

**Claimed by an Alien Warrior**

**Dustwalker**

**Escaping Wonderland**

**Yearning For Her**

**The Warlock's Kiss**

**Ice Bound: Short Story**

## ISLE OF THE FORGOTTEN

**Make Me Burn**

**Make Me Hunger**

**Make Me Whole**

**Make Me Yours**

## VALOS OF SONHADRA COLLABORATION

**Tiffany Roberts - Undying**

**Tiffany Roberts - Unleashed**

# ABOUT THE AUTHOR

Tiffany Roberts is the pseudonym for Tiffany and Robert Freund, a husband and wife writing duo. The two have always shared a passion for reading and writing, and it was their dream to combine their mighty powers to create the sorts of books they want to read. They write character driven sci-fi and fantasy romance, creating happily-ever-afters for the alien and unknown.

**Sign up for our Newsletter!**
**Check out our social media sites and more!**
**http://www.authortiffanyroberts.com**